What readers are saying about
the R E D E M P T I O N *series*

"After reading your book I will never read secular fiction again. I literally just finished the first book, and as I'm wiping my tears away with a tissue I write to you. God truly placed this series in your heart; that is very clear."   **—Tammi**

"I have just finished reading your book *Remember*—it was fantastic! You have such a writing gift. . . . God really speaks to me through your work. I am dying to know when the next book is due out."   **—Tricia**

"I just finished reading *Redemption,* and I just had to write and tell you how much I enjoyed the book. I feel as if I know the characters. Thank you for not having Tim and Kari 'live happily ever after.' I was pleasantly surprised to see the book end how real life ends . . . people wanting to serve God and do what He wants, but it isn't always a storybook ending. Thanks again for making the Baxters so real."   **—Debra**

"I cannot put your books down once I start reading them. The tip of your pen is truly anointed. Your books have changed the way I think about my own life . . . and the way I see others. I am learning to see people thru God's eyes. I love your books!"

—Christie

"I love all your books, but the Redemption books are the best. It has brought me closer to the Bible."

—Linda

"Karen's books stir my heart and remind me of what's important in life. She has such a gift. I've read every single one and can't wait for the next!"

—Trisha

"I 100% LOVE your books! You are my FAVORITE author by far. I have laughed and cried in every single book (no exceptions!). Keep 'em comin'!"

—Cassie

"Thank you so much, Karen, for using your God-given gift to write Christian novels. I've read almost all your books and have a hard time putting them down once I've started. I think each book has made me cry! That means they're good.

You have such a gift for wrapping your readers up in the feelings of the characters. I feel like I am right there with them, living their lives. You are truly an inspired author. Not only do I get involved with the characters, but in each book I have gleaned some wonderful spiritual lesson. God has given you a very unique ministry, because I feel that you are more than just an author in your works. Thanks for allowing yourself to be used as His vessel. You have become my favorite author."

—Becky

"I love all of Karen Kingsbury's novels! They make me laugh, cry, and grow stronger! She truly is an amazing author! When you read her books it's like you're sitting with the characters helping them through their pain and rejoicing with them when they're happy! You know you have a good book when you want to read it over and over again. I have felt like that with all of Karen's books!! She is my favorite by far!"

—Megan

"There are not enough words to describe what your books mean to me. God has truly blessed me through your talent and your love for Him. Your books are a balm for a troubled soul. God bless you always and KEEP writing."   —Eugenia

"I love this series! It has really captured my heart, and the characters have become real. *Remember* really got to me because of the characters living through a time we all remember VERY well. Thanks, Karen, and please keep this series coming!"   —Heidi

"Karen, I only started reading Christian fiction a short while ago. The clerk in the store recommended your books above all others. So glad she did! I started reading with *Redemption*, then *Remember*, and can hardly wait for *Return*."   —Barbara

"I am a new fan of yours—in fact, a new fan of fiction in general! I first began reading your books when a coworker recommended the Redemption series to me. I could not put either book down! No emotion was left untouched! The message of God's love that is portrayed throughout the text is so uplifting and encouraging. I work at a local Christian bookstore, and I now recommend your books to ALL of my customers!"   —Elizabeth

"I didn't think you could top *Redemption,* but I was wrong! Those two novels have touched me so deeply, and I can hardly wait to read the other three—I wish they were already in print! Thanks for spreading the word of God—you have a glorious gift." —Diana

"I fell in love with these stories, and I'm recommending them to all my friends; they're wonderful!"   —Tricia

TYNDALE HOUSE PUBLISHERS, INC., Wheaton, Illinois

RETURN

Karen KINGSBURY
with Gary SMALLEY

Published in association with the literary agency of Alive Communications, Inc., 7680 Goddard Street, Suite 200, Colorado Springs, CO 80920.

Designed by Zandrah Maguigad

Edited by Karen Ball

ISBN 0-7394-3901-4

Printed in the United States of America

TO OUR PRECIOUS FAMILIES,

who continue to give us countless reasons

to celebrate God's faithfulness.

AND TO OUR GRACIOUS LORD,

who has, for now,

blessed us with these.

AUTHORS' NOTE

The Redemption series is set mostly in Bloomington, Indiana. Some of the landmarks—Indiana University, for example—are accurately placed in their true settings. Other buildings, parks, and establishments will be nothing more than figments of our imaginations. We hope those of you familiar with Bloomington and the surrounding area will have fun distinguishing between the two.

The New York City settings combine real observation with imaginative re-creation.

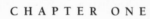

CHAPTER ONE

R EAGAN D ECKER'S HANDS shook as she picked up the telephone and dialed.

The number was so familiar once, back in a time that seemed forever ago, before her world tilted hard off its axis and stayed that way.

She waited, her heart pounding in her throat.

One ring . . .

What will I say? How will they take the news?

Two rings . . .

"Hello?"

"Mrs. Baxter?" Reagan froze.

"Yes?" A slight pause. "Can I help you?"

"Uh . . ." *She doesn't recognize my voice. I must be crazy to call after so long.* "This is Reagan. Reagan Decker."

"Reagan . . . my goodness. It's . . . been a long time, dear."

Luke's mother sounded strange, as though the mention of Reagan's name had cast a shadow over the moment. Reagan considered saying a quick few words and then getting off. But that would never do. This was a call she'd had to make for one reason alone.

She couldn't hide from Luke Baxter forever.

"Mrs. Baxter, I need to talk to Luke, please." Reagan squeezed her eyes shut. A year earlier she'd been quick-witted and outgoing, but not anymore. The spark was gone from her voice. Luke's mother had to notice. She drew a determined breath. "I have something to tell him."

His past had sprouted legs and was chasing him.

That had to be it. Luke had no other way to describe the breathless anxiety marking so much of his time. Sometimes he could almost hear footsteps pounding the ground behind him, and on days like that he would even turn around. As though he might see a person or a being, whatever was after him. But no one was ever there.

The feeling was always accompanied by memories, so Luke finally convinced himself the thing chasing him was nothing more ominous than his past.

A past that colored today and tomorrow and kept him inches ahead of a suffocating fog, a fog in which his new freethinking life was all but impossible.

At first the feeling had hit him every few days, but now it was almost constant. This morning it was worse than ever. Throughout Economics and Political Science and now in Modern History, it made Luke so restless he couldn't concentrate.

The professor was diagramming something on the board, but all Luke could see were images of himself and his family the last time they'd been together before September 11. Little Maddie holding her hands up to him. "Swing me, Uncle Luke, swing me." His parents arm in arm in the background. "How's school, Luke? Have you heard from Reagan?"

With broad strokes, the professor ran his eraser over the board, and the images in Luke's head disappeared. The man turned to the class and started talking, but Luke heard Reagan's

voice instead, the way he'd heard it that awful night when everything changed forever.

"It's okay, Luke; I'll call him back tomorrow . . . it's okay . . ."

But she never had the chance.

Luke squeezed his eyes shut. He was ready to move on, right?
Wasn't that what he'd been telling himself? Then why were these
memories dogging him so? With all the freethinking he'd been
doing, all the clubs and organizations Lori had introduced him to,
he should be consumed with life as it *was*. Not as it had been.

The professor changed his tone. He was saying something
about foreign arms deals, but Luke wasn't paying attention. A
conversation kept playing in his head, the one he'd had with his
mother a few weeks ago.

"You think you have it all figured out, Luke, but the Hound of
Heaven isn't going to let you go this easily."

"The Hound of Heaven?" Luke hadn't even tried to hide his
frustration. His mother knew how he felt about God, so why
couldn't she let it go?

"The Spirit of God, Luke." Her voice held no apologies.
"When someone strays from the Lord, it's usually the Spirit, the
Hound of Heaven, that hunts him down and brings him back."

The Hound of Heaven, indeed.

As if God—if there *was* a God—would care enough about
Luke Baxter to chase him. Luke tapped the eraser of his pencil
on his notepad. No, that wasn't why he felt this way. He narrowed his eyes and focused on the professor. What was the man
babbling about? And why was everyone else taking notes?

A tingling worked its way down his spine, and he shifted in
his desk.

Maybe it was culture shock. After a lifetime of holding to one
set of beliefs, he'd done an about-face, and some kind of fallout
was bound to come. That explained the pounding in his chest,
the breathlessness that sometimes hit him square in the middle
of a college lecture, and the constant stream of memories. Memories that had a vise grip on his mind and soul.

Sure, it was a setback. But no need to tell Lori. She'd only blame it on the mind control his family had held over him for so many years. And he didn't care to discuss mind control with her. He didn't like the way it sounded. For all their shortcomings, all their narrow-minded ways of thinking, his family had *not* performed mind control on him.

Not hardly.

He'd been a willing participant, and though their beliefs were off base, his family loved him back then. They loved him still. That much he was sure of. But he was just as sure that he wanted to move on, to explore a world without absolutes and—what was it Lori called it?—an antiquated morality system? Yes, he was ready to move away from that.

"Mr. Baxter, I expect you to answer me the first time I call on you."

Luke jumped in his seat. Two students sitting near him stifled their snorts of laughter. "Excuse me, sir?"

"I *said*—" the professor's voice dripped sarcasm—"perhaps you could explain the significance of specific arms deals made in the late seventies?"

"Yes, sir." Luke did a desperate search of his mind and came up blank. His fingers trembled and he coughed to buy time. "Sir, I don't have that information at this time."

Another bout of muffled laughter.

"Very well, Mr. Baxter; then may I make a suggestion?" The professor lowered his glasses and peered hard at Luke.

"Yes, sir?" Luke's throat was dry. It was all he could do to keep from running out of the room.

"Either get more sleep or get out of my Modern History class." The man raised his voice. "Is that understood?"

Fire filled Luke's cheeks. "Yes, sir."

When class was over ten minutes later, Luke was one of the first to leave the room. Not only because he didn't want any further discussion with the professor, but because he still needed to run, to keep moving away from whatever was chasing him. His past maybe, or his prior convictions. Perhaps his unfamiliarity with all he'd surrounded himself with.

But definitely not the Hound of Heaven.

☙

Reagan didn't visit Ground Zero often.

She looked out the back window of the taxicab as it rumbled south on Broadway, past boarded-up storefronts and American flags. It was late afternoon and she planned to finish up by dusk. A few more blocks and she'd be there. She narrowed her eyes and found a piece of the skyline far above. *Daddy, if you knew how much we miss you. . . .*

She'd attended two Ground Zero memorial services, and over time she'd come to accept that the pile of rubble and ash that once was the World Trade Center was now her father's resting place. Still, as much as possible, she avoided going there. The roar of construction trucks and the meticulous sifting of debris didn't seem to dim her gut-wrenching pain and emptiness at all.

But today was her father's birthday. And since her mother wasn't feeling up to the task, Reagan was going to Ground Zero alone. They rounded a corner and she could see the crater, the footprint the collapsed towers had left on the floor of New York City. Cleanup efforts were almost finished. Still, as far as they'd come in the recovery, they had weeks before they'd finish. Recovery crews were guessing they'd clear the area in May, some eight months after the terrorist attacks. But for now, a considerable crew still worked on the pile.

The cab was stuck at a light, and Reagan watched. Giant machinery growled, lifting sections of steel beams and crushed cement. Trucks pulled in and out of the area, hauling away one load after another. Her father had known his last moments here. She'd go to the strange memorial, the place where a cross section of steel beams had fallen in the midst of the debris and become a marker for all who passed by.

Since the collapse of the World Trade Center, the cross had been mounted on a platform near the pile of rubble. The place drew Reagan, as it had thousands of other mourners.

Her taxi pulled up as close as possible, and Reagan spotted the makeshift memorial. She paid her fare and stepped out. The cross stood out, circled with tattered teddy bears and bouquets of dying flowers. A few people stood nearby, heads bowed. Not far away was a bench, probably brought in by one of the volunteer groups, maybe left over from a memorial service. It was empty now, and Reagan walked to it and sat down.

She'd met her father here for dinner one evening and used her cell phone to call him from the street.

"Flash your light, Daddy, so I can see where you are." She'd tilted her head back and watched. His office was on West Street, so she knew he was up there somewhere.

"Okay." Her father chuckled and did just that. Three times and then three more times. "Can you see me?"

"Yes!" Reagan stared at the spot. "Now I'll always know where you are."

A nearby dump truck dropped its load with a crash. The ground shook beneath her feet, and the long-ago conversation faded. She still remembered the way her neck felt that day, bent just enough for her to see his office window.

Now she lifted her eyes higher and higher, until her neck felt the way it had that evening. She could see them still, the Twin Towers, even see the spot where her father's office had been. Reagan closed her eyes so the tears wouldn't come. They were inevitable, but she didn't want them now. Not when she had so much to tell her father. So much to tell God.

God . . . amazing you and I are still talking, huh?

The slightest smile lifted her lips. How sad and different life had become. In many ways, she was closer to the Lord than ever before—a strange benefit in the wake of the death and tragedy surrounding her. What a shame Luke hadn't handled it the same way.

Poor Luke.

Reagan heard herself sigh, and she opened her eyes. A bird drifted across the place where the south tower once stood, and a chill made its way down her spine. Every time she opened her eyes she expected them to be here, the Twin Towers standing tall and proud at the center of Lower Manhattan.

She blinked. How could they be gone? Both of them? She squinted as a memory played in her mind: the last time she and Luke had been up there, walking in the clouds, visiting her father in his office. A lifetime ago . . . as though it hadn't really happened at all.

They'd been laughing about something—Luke's dream of working there one day, wasn't that it? Reagan narrowed her eyes a bit more. Yes. They'd been whispering about what type of office he'd have, and how it would be right down the hall from her father's.

"I'll have a water view." Luke grabbed her hand, his chin high, eyes teasing as they stepped into the elevator.

"I'm sure they'll offer you at least that—straight out of college and everything." Reagan poked him in the ribs. "I mean, you're Luke Baxter!"

Reagan blinked the memory away.

Now, instead of soaring towers, she saw only gray clouds. Rain was expected for that afternoon. More rain. After a gentle winter, the spring had been merciless—snow, freezing rain, and icy wind. So many days without sunshine had every New Yorker feeling the gloom.

"Where is he, God?" Her whispered question mingled with the smoky air and got lost in the relentless noise of a parade of dump trucks. "Why can't we find him?"

Unlike some grieving people she'd talked to at church, Reagan didn't need a body to feel closure. A ring, a wallet, a watch—*anything* of her father's would be enough. Instead she had nothing. Just the certainty that on the morning of September 11, 2001,

Tom Decker had been in his office some nine hundred feet in the air. And now he was gone.

Reagan and her mother had talked about it. He could never have survived the collapse. He probably died quickly and without pain, carrying thoughts of his family with him as he passed from this life to the next. But that didn't make it easier—especially when no sign of him had been found.

During the holidays their family, along with hundreds of others, was given a wooden urn from the city, an urn filled with ashes taken from Ground Zero. It might have held her father's remains. But then, it might have held just about anyone's remains. Thousands of people were unaccounted for.

Reagan stared at the cross, and a sense of peace washed over her. "I know, God." She bit her lip. Her voice lacked its former energy and spunk, and in this place it was little more than a whisper. "He's not here. He's with you." Her voice cracked, and again she closed her eyes. "If only I'd . . ."

How could she and Luke have lost control like that? It was a football game, for goodness' sake. She'd been tired from a day of classes and had conked out on the sofa for most of the second half. How did they go from that to lying there kissing? Why didn't either of them have the sense to stop? The questions stockpiled in her heart, but they were nothing compared to the one that still ate at her night and day, seven months after the tragedy.

Why hadn't she taken her father's call?

The ring of the phone was God's perfect alarm, his way of telling her and Luke they'd had enough. Time for Luke to go home, time for her to spend half an hour talking with her daddy. She'd had a choice. Luke almost seemed to want her to answer the phone, as if he were looking for a reason to shake off the passion and head home. But she'd let the machine pick up instead.

It had been the single worst decision of her life.

Reagan opened her eyes and studied the cross once more. In the wake of the collapsed towers on the afternoon of September 11, she took a bus from Bloomington, Indiana, where she'd been attending college, to her parents' home in Upper East Side Manhattan. But how long was it before she went with her mother to church? Before she went weeping to the pastor's wife? Three months? Four?

Guilt had eaten her alive before that encounter. But afterwards, after meeting with the woman for five days straight, Reagan grasped forgiveness and grace as she'd never done before, not even after a lifetime of believing. After that, God was merciful enough to take the broken pieces of her life and patch them into something beautiful again, and she gave her entire effort to the cause. For the longest time, that meant staying away from Luke.

Reagan simply hadn't known what to say to him. He was bound to think less of her, the same way he thought less of his sister Ashley. Reagan had been nauseous and tired and struggling to work through the truth with her mother and brother. What she'd done had been one more blow, one more bit of reality to prove their lives would never be the same.

She had been her father's princess. His one-in-a-million girl. How disappointed he would be if he knew what she'd done.

Tell him, please, God. Tell him I'm sorry for letting him down, but tell him I'm okay now. And tell him how much I miss him . . . please.

A Scripture flashed in her mind, one the pastor had shared with them yesterday: *"Blessed are those who mourn, for they will be comforted."* It was the same verse the pastor's wife had given Reagan when they'd first met together. The message was clearer than the space where the World Trade Center once stood. God understood her pain, and even now he was placing his holy hands on her weary shoulders, comforting her with a peace that passed understanding.

That was the reason she'd survived.

In fact, it was God's peace that finally convinced her to call Luke earlier that week. When Luke's mother answered the phone, Reagan's tears were immediate, choking her, keeping her from speaking.

The moment Mrs. Baxter answered the phone, Reagan recognized something different about the older woman's voice. She seemed . . . upset or nervous about something. Reagan pressed forward. "I . . . I should have called sooner, but . . . well . . ." She uttered a soft, exasperated huff. "I should have called."

Mrs. Baxter was silent for a moment. "I'm sorry about your father."

Luke's mother could have said a dozen things. She could have chided Reagan for not calling sooner, or accused her of hurting Luke. If he told them what happened the night before the terrorist attacks, how they'd been together, the woman could have berated her for that as well. But Elizabeth Baxter was nothing if not kind.

When Reagan realized no verbal beating was coming, she swallowed and grabbed for the next thing to say. "Thank you."

"Are you all right?"

"We're doing better." Reagan's relief spilled into her voice. "How's Luke?"

Again, silence. "He . . . he doesn't live here anymore, Reagan." Mrs. Baxter's voice caught. "He's having a hard time."

Now, as she looked at the remains of the World Trade Center, Reagan's stomach tightened the way it had when Luke's mother first spoke those words. Luke never had a hard time at anything. He laughed and loved and breezed his way through life, from schoolwork to scholarships to his relationship with her. When they were together, the sun rose and set on Luke. Her heart had been so sure they'd stay together forever.

Reagan remembered gulping at that point in the conversation, desperate for some way to respond. "A hard time?"

Mrs. Baxter's tone grew tight, pinched, and Reagan knew the woman was crying. "I'm . . . I'm sorry. This is very difficult."

"You don't have to tell me, Mrs. Baxter. I don't have a right to know. Not after how long I've gone without calling."

"It's okay. I think you should hear it firsthand." She hesitated. "Luke has walked away from . . . well, from everything we taught him. He isn't acting like himself, Reagan. Since he moved out, he rarely talks to us. He won't—" her voice was more in control again—"he won't even come by."

The news had torn across Reagan's heart and knocked her into the nearest chair. It wasn't possible. Luke Baxter? The boy she'd known would rule the business world, the boy with enough charisma to rule the country one day? The Baxter family's golden boy, the baby of the group? How in the world could he walk away from everything that mattered most to him?

Reagan had been afraid to ask, but she couldn't stop herself. "What . . . happened?"

Mrs. Baxter gave a quiet sniff. "He took up with a girl—very opinionated against God and our faith. He . . . he's living with her now."

Reagan had doubled over under the weight of Mrs. Baxter's words. Luke was seeing someone else? *Living* with her? Had the love they'd shared before Reagan returned to New York mattered so little that he'd simply walked into another girl's arms? The only reason she hadn't spoken to him was because she'd been hurt and shocked, unable to think clearly under the burden of losing her father. And she'd been afraid . . . so afraid he wouldn't feel the same about her after what they'd done.

She cleared her throat, but her words sounded like those of a stranger. "I didn't know."

"I'm sorry, Reagan." Mrs. Baxter waited a moment. "Should I have him call you?"

Guilt all but smothered Reagan as the woman waited for an answer. Luke's mother knew nothing of what had happened between Luke and her that Monday night. That much was obvious.

Her answer was quick and certain. "No." She swallowed hard. "That's okay." She struggled to make sense of her jumbled thoughts. "In fact, Mrs. Baxter . . . don't tell him I called. Please." She paused. "Our relationship has been over for a long time. He has a right to go on with his life."

"I think he'd like to know how you're doing."

"It doesn't matter anymore. He's . . . it's over between us." Her heartbeat quickened, and she couldn't draw a full breath. If Luke was living with another girl, he must never know the reason she'd called. "Don't tell him. Promise me?"

Luke's mother hesitated, and when she spoke, her disappointment rang in her voice. "Okay. I won't." Her sigh tugged at Reagan's heart. "But can I ask you a favor?"

"Anything."

"Pray for him." Mrs. Baxter sniffed again. "And one of these days, give him a call."

Reagan pulled herself from the past and sat straighter. She had prayed for Luke all last night, and still she ached at her role in what had happened. Was it her fault? Had Luke walked away from his family, his faith, because she'd refused his calls?

She sighed. The possibility was too awful to worry about right now. Certainly the day would come when she'd have to face it, but not here, not now. She hadn't come to Ground Zero to wrestle tormenting thoughts of Luke.

Once more, she gazed into the gaping hole where the towers once stood, concentrating on how the towers had looked—tall, dominating the skyline. Then she fixed her eyes on the place where she was sure her dad's office had been. "Daddy . . . I'm so sorry this happened to you."

The tears came, not in torrents or even streams, but just enough to sting the corners of her eyes. She blinked and waited until the feeling went away. She'd cried so much after September 11. Entire days had passed when she wondered if she'd ever go an hour without weeping. These days her eyes were usually dry, but the ache in her heart felt pretty much permanent.

She missed her father so much, missed the life they'd had before September 11. "I'm doing the best I can, Daddy." She squinted and blinked back another few tears. "Happy Birthday."

A dump truck rolled past just a few yards away. Reagan never took her eyes from the spot in the sky. "I miss you." She caught kingsbury • smalley

three quick, jerky breaths, and this time she couldn't stop the tears. Her whispered voice was thick. "I . . . I love you, Daddy."

In response, her swollen abdomen tightened, and she rested her open hands across her belly, stroking the place where the baby grew within her. *It's okay, little one. Mommy's all right.*

She was seven months pregnant—no surprise there. But until the test she'd been certain she was carrying a girl. Not so, according to the ultrasound. The baby was a boy. Reagan had already decided on a name.

Her tears stopped. She stood and stretched, wiping her fingers beneath her eyes and taking a final look at the towering metal cross. It was time to go home, time to help her mother with dinner. Besides, she needed her rest. She wanted the very best for her precious baby boy. A boy who would carry the name of both his grandfather . . . and his father.

A boy named Thomas Luke.

CHAPTER TWO

ASHLEY HAD MIXED FEELINGS about the announcement Kari and Ryan were about to make that evening. No doubt they were getting married; the news could hardly be anything else. The Baxter dinner party that night would be filled with laughter and congratulations and remembered moments from when Kari and Ryan first met as kids. The group would eat Chinese food, celebrate with cake, and know in their hearts that two people couldn't possibly be more meant for each other than Kari and Ryan.

For the most part Ashley was thrilled for her older sister. Ryan had loved Kari since she was sixteen, and this . . . this announcement, if that's what it was, had been overdue for years.

But with Landon in New York City, Ashley's happiness couldn't be complete. She gritted her teeth. When would the announcement be hers, and when would life finally take on that happily-ever-after quality that always seemed to elude her? She ran a sponge over the last of the crumbs on the counter and stared out the window at her parents' backyard. She'd spent so much time there as a teenager. The view was simple and striking, and in springtime it held a million shades of green. Maybe she'd set her easel up out back of the old farmhouse for her next piece.

She bit her lip and tilted her head, studying the scene for focal points and contrast. But the backyard images faded.

Why hadn't she noticed Landon years ago? Back before she'd made a mess of her life? The answer came as easily as her next breath. Because she'd been afraid. Afraid Landon was too safe, afraid she wasn't good enough for him. And so she'd gone off to Paris to prove she didn't need him or anyone else. To show them all she could make it as an artist. Instead, she'd come home utterly defeated in all ways but one.

Paris gave her Cole.

Her young son was everything to her now—the music in every song, the poetry that rang in her heart, the inspiration for every one of her recent paintings. He was upstairs making a Lego creation, and any minute he'd bounce down the stairs to show her an alien rocket ship or a super high-powered flying speedboat. He'd inherited her creative bent, no doubt.

Ashley made a few more swipes across the counter, but her hand froze as she heard the back door open.

"Did you get the cake?" Her mother breezed into the kitchen and set a bag of groceries on the counter.

"Got it."

"Perfect." Mom was out of breath as she tossed her keys in the drawer by the kitchen desk and began unpacking. Green beans, canned soup, taco shells. Applesauce. "Go to the store for milk and find a dozen things you need. Always happens." She paused and met Ashley's eyes. "Where's Cole?"

"Upstairs creating."

"And the cake?"

"In the freezer."

"Good." Ashley's mom straightened and sized up the kitchen area. "Thanks for cleaning up." She blew at a wisp of dark hair, peeled off her jacket, and set it on the back of the desk chair. "The whole day was crazy."

"No problem." Ashley wrung out the sponge and stood it up near the kitchen sink. "They're engaged, right? That's the announcement?"

Her mother gave a light shrug of her shoulders as she pulled a pound of butter and a loaf of bread from the grocery sack. "I can't tell."

"Mom." Ashley rolled her eyes and leaned against the counter. "The cake says *Congratulations, Kari and Ryan.* I don't think we're celebrating Kari's new minivan."

"Hey." Her mom raised an eyebrow in her direction. "You weren't supposed to peek."

"So, I'm right." Ashley wrestled the strange feeling in her heart. What was it? Jealousy? Loneliness? Whatever it was, she had to let it go. Kari deserved as much happiness as possible.

Her mother finished putting away the food and folded the brown bag. "They've always been perfect for each other."

"They have." Ashley dried her hands and tried to sound upbeat. "Need anything else?"

"Nope." Her mother took a few steps and glanced at the dining room. "Everything's perfect." She faced Ashley again and her expression softened. "Okay, tell me. What's wrong?"

Ashley headed toward the living room. "Nothing." She shot a smile over her shoulder and then plopped down on the overstuffed sofa. "I couldn't be happier for them."

Her mother followed and took the rocking chair a few feet away. "You still think I can't read your eyes, Ash." She brushed her dark hair back from her face. "When's the last time you talked to Landon?"

"Mother." Ashley gave an exaggerated huff. "This isn't about Landon."

"Okay." She leaned back and set the rocker in motion. "But when?"

Ashley stared out the window. She hated this, hated how her mother could read her. No matter how independent she'd tried to be over the years, she'd never been able to fool her mother.

Ashley crossed her arms and caught her mother's gaze once more. "A few weeks."

Her mother looked like she might say something, but then she seemed to change her mind. In the silence, Ashley sucked in a quick breath and looked out the window again. "He's busy, Mother. It's New York City. If he doesn't focus on his job, he'll wind up like his friend."

"Focus couldn't have saved his friend's life, honey. Nothing could've."

"I know." Ashley bit her lip again and thought for a moment about Landon's friend rushing up the stairs of the south tower of the World Trade Center when the building collapsed that awful Tuesday morning. "You're right. I'm just saying, Landon's busy. Otherwise he'd call more."

Her mother must have sensed that the conversation was over because she stood and took a sharp breath as she looked at her watch. "Everyone will be here in fifteen minutes. I'm going upstairs to check on Cole."

"Okay." Ashley waited until her mom had left the room; then she rested her head on the sofa back and closed her eyes. *God, my attitude's lousy, but Mom's right. Why doesn't Landon call? And how will it ever work out between the two of us with him in New York and me here?*

She pursed her lips and opened her eyes again. What did the pastor say at church last Sunday? God's timing wasn't always our own. Ashley had caught her father's eyes, and the two shared a knowing look. If anyone understood the heartache of waiting, it was her parents.

Luke had been gone for three months.

"He'll be back one day," her dad said when the church service was over. "All in God's timing."

But Ashley noticed his eyes were damp even as he spoke. The situation with Luke weighed on their parents every day. Since September 11, Luke told Ashley he didn't believe in God, didn't expect he ever would again. His relationship with everyone else in the Baxter family was strained if not absent, and her parents bore the brunt of the pain. Yes, her waiting paled in comparison to theirs. But still . . .

Landon needed to make a plan, to let her know when he'd be coming back to Bloomington. That way he could tell her if he planned to marry her somewhere down the road—like once he'd met his obligation to the FDNY. That would make the year go more quickly, wouldn't it?

Dusk had come and gone, and darkness now fell over the April evening. The cold spring weather didn't help Ashley's mood. It only made it hard to get outside and paint. So, rather than be trapped in the house, she was putting in more time at Sunset Hills Adult Care Home. She loved the job, but she was restless, missing something she hadn't quite been able to figure out.

Something—or someone.

Headlights flashed into the driveway, and two cars made their way toward the Baxter house. The party was about to start, and Ashley would do nothing but smile all night. Maybe, after an evening of pretending everything was okay, it actually would be. Even if her happily-ever-after seemed a million years away.

The announcement came the moment they were seated for dinner, just as Elizabeth Baxter thought it would.

All eyes were on Kari and Ryan, and beneath the table Elizabeth squeezed her husband's hand. "This is it," she whispered.

John returned the squeeze and leaned close to her ear. "Finally."

Seconds felt like hours, and the entire room seemed to hold its breath. Kari and Ryan shared a smile. Then Kari shifted a sleeping little Jessica to her other arm and turned to the family. "We were going to wait until dessert, but—"

Groans came from each of the other sisters—Brooke and Erin

and Ashley. "No way, Kari . . ." Ashley jabbed a teasing finger in Kari's direction. "Not after the big buildup."

"Yeah, you're killing us." Erin's eyes shone, and she looped her arm through her husband's.

Elizabeth caught the exchange, and a wave of gratitude washed over her. Though she didn't expect Luke to show up, at least the girls were doing well—Erin and Sam, Brooke and Peter, even Ashley.

"Okay, okay." Kari held up her hands and giggled. She leaned back against Ryan and waited again until the room was silent. "Ryan and I have been talking about things." She glanced up at him. "We've been meeting with Pastor Mark for the past month and—" Her voice broke, and she looked to Ryan for help.

Elizabeth felt the sting of tears in her own eyes as she watched them. Hadn't it been yesterday when they were thirteen and fifteen, a couple of kids meeting each other for the first time at a neighborhood barbecue? And in the years that followed, hadn't they all believed that someday it would come to this? Elizabeth swallowed back the lump in her throat, willing her daughter the strength to do the same.

"I've asked Kari to be my wife." Ryan gave Kari a slight squeeze and the briefest kiss. "And she said yes."

Erin's squeal came first, followed by a chorus of clapping and congratulations.

"I knew it!" Ashley grinned and pushed back her chair, leading the way as everyone—even Cole—got up and surrounded the beaming couple and exchanged hugs and kisses.

"We're getting married September twenty-first!" Kari cast a quick grin at Ryan, and then back at the others. "Isn't that amazing?"

John exhaled and let his shoulders slump forward as he chuckled. "I couldn't have kept the secret another minute."

"Oh, Kari, it'll be a gorgeous wedding!" Brooke put her arms around them. "I'm so happy for you guys."

"And guess where we're having it?" Kari leaned forward, her face wreathed in the undeniable look of a young woman in love.

Erin brought her hands together. "Here?"

"Yes. The ceremony *and* the reception." Kari leaned back. "We want a big white tent where we can eat and celebrate and dance into the night."

"A backyard wedding!" Ashley hooted and high-fived Brooke. "That's perfect."

Elizabeth slipped past the others and took Jessie from Kari. She laid her down on the sofa, covered her with a blanket, then stood next to John, just outside the circle of their children. They'd known about this for weeks, and they were content to let the others give their congratulations first. Elizabeth slid her fingers between John's. "Did you ever think? I mean back when everything looked so awful a few years ago?"

"Actually . . ." John gave a thoughtful tilt of his head. "Yes." The celebration going on a few feet away all but drowned his voice. "There's never been anyone for Kari like Ryan." He sniffed hard. "I can almost feel God smiling down at us."

The congratulations continued, and when they were all seated again they shared sweet-and-sour pork, stir-fried vegetables, almond chicken, and steamed rice. Conversation about the wedding plans continued through dinner and on into dessert.

"So, who's coming?" Ashley was helping Cole with his dessert, cutting it into small pieces. "I mean, are we talking small or most of Bloomington?"

Kari laughed, and she and Ryan took turns explaining that their wedding would be simple, no more than a hundred family members and friends. Though Kari had been married before, Ryan hadn't, and he told the group that he planned to pay for the reception.

"Some of my football friends want to come." Ryan grinned at John. "I think we'll need plenty of table space."

Kari wanted Brooke, Ashley, and Erin—her three sisters—to

be her bridesmaids. "Long silky dresses with cap sleeves!" Kari's eyes lit up. "How does that sound?"

"What about you?" Ashley flashed a teasing look at Ryan. "I'm sure you can't wait to pick out just the right tux. And you need three groomsmen, you know. That's the way it works."

Ryan chuckled and gave Kari a light tap on the head. "Kari's clued me in about all of that."

"He even helped pick the colors."

"Which are?" Erin leaned forward to get a better look at Kari and Ryan.

"Navy blue and silver." Ryan gave a firm nod of his head; then he tossed Kari a doubtful look. "Or was it Essence of Blue and Pewter?"

Laughter rang out around the table. Elizabeth waited until it died down. "Did you decide on the groomsmen?"

"Yes." Ryan grinned at Erin's husband. "Sam, if he'll do it, and Peter and Luke."

A hush fell over the table.

John cleared his throat. "I'm sure that'll be perfect."

Elizabeth stared at her plate. The mention of Luke cast a quiet over a part of her heart, a tight, pinched feeling that choked out all other thoughts and feelings save one: He was gone. Her son, the golden boy whose laughter and promise had graced their home, was gone. No one knew when—or if—he was coming back.

She sniffed and worked the muscles in her throat to keep from giving sadness an edge. John was always so sure everything was going to work out. But what if it didn't? Luke hadn't shown up for this dinner party. What made John so sure he'd come to the wedding? Every week his absence made him feel more distant, less like the boy she'd raised. Less like he was even part of the family.

The conversation did a pinball bounce from the date and wedding party to the type of reception they wanted—formal, with assigned seating and a ballroom floor for dancing. But the details that had occupied so much of Elizabeth's mind the last few weeks were suddenly small and unimportant compared with the fact that Luke hadn't come. Elizabeth smiled and nodded and tried to look interested. But inside, in the hallways of her heart, she was reliving the phone call with Reagan.

How had the girl started the conversation? Hadn't it been something about having some kind of news, something she wanted to tell Luke? But then they'd gotten to the truth about Luke's new lifestyle, and talk had never gotten back to Reagan.

Elizabeth nodded at something Erin said about planning a wedding shower, but she was only half listening. What could Reagan have to tell Luke, and why had she been so adamant about not telling him she'd called? Had she been trying to get ahold of him to tell him she still cared for him, that she wanted to have another chance at a relationship? If so, then it was no wonder the news of his new girlfriend had frightened her off, made her want to never talk to Luke again.

The party wound down, and by eight o'clock Erin, Brooke, and Ashley were finalizing plans to meet with Kari the following week to scan the catalogues for bridesmaid dresses. Kari was the last to leave, and she gave Elizabeth a longer hug than usual. Ryan was buckling Jessie into her car seat in the truck, and John had gone upstairs, so Kari and Elizabeth were alone. For the first time that night, Kari's eyes glistened with tears.

"I can't believe it, Mom . . . I mean, really. After all these years, we're getting married!"

"He's perfect for you." Elizabeth's heart swelled as she cupped the side of Kari's face. "Perfect for Jessie, too."

"I know." Kari wiped at an errant tear. "I think Tim would've been glad that Jessie and I are getting on with life."

"Yes." Elizabeth kissed her daughter's forehead. "Everything's going to work out just right."

Kari hesitated for a second and brought her hand to her mouth. "Sorry. I didn't think I'd be so emotional now." She uttered a sound that was more laugh than cry. "The big announcement's over." For a moment she seemed to steady herself, and her eyes locked on Elizabeth's. "But I wanted to thank you,

Mom. You've . . . you've been amazing through this whole thing. You've always known what to say, what to do." She sniffed. "You're the best mom in the world. I want you to know that."

Elizabeth's throat grew thick. Mirrored in her daughter's eyes were a hundred memories. Kari had shared each of them with her, every incident. She swallowed and the cloud of memories lifted. "It's been a long road, my dear."

"And you've prayed me through every inch of it."

"Yes . . ." She gave Kari a wry smile. "The last few years have given your father and me calloused knees. But not just because of you."

They were silent, both painfully aware of why the Baxter parents had been on their knees lately. Kari gave her a quick kiss on the cheek. "Don't stop praying for him, Mom. Luke's going to be okay. I feel it in my heart."

"So does your dad."

"And Dad's always right." Kari's smile was sadder now, the sparkle in her eyes dimmer. "If Luke calls, tell him we missed him."

When Kari was gone, Elizabeth dragged her feet up the stairs, one slow step at a time. She found John sitting near the fireplace in their room, staring at a photograph. As she came closer, she saw what it was. A framed picture of Luke and John on a hiking trip, taken a few years earlier when Luke was earning his Eagle Scout badge. The photo showed father and son, tired and happy at the end of the trip, their faces smudged as they stood side by side, their arms around each other's necks.

John must have sensed her presence. He stood and returned the picture to the shelf near their bedroom closet. After a beat, he turned to Elizabeth. "He should've been here tonight."

"Yes." She went to rest her hands on his shoulders and soothe her thumbs against his neck. "It's okay to miss him."

He said nothing, merely hung his head.

"You're always saying everything's going to work out and that Luke'll come home in God's timing and that these things happen." Her voice was soft. She knew her words were reaching the private places in his soul. "But you can't fool me, John Baxter. You're worried sick."

John gritted his teeth and lifted his head just enough so that their eyes met. "I . . . I feel like a part of me won't start breathing again until we get him back. The way he used to be."

Elizabeth didn't want to voice the obvious, that sometimes children make a choice to walk away and never return. That truth had hung like a sword over every conversation about Luke since he moved out. Instead she remembered once more her talk with Luke's old girlfriend.

"Reagan called the other day."

John straightened at the news, and his eyes searched hers. "Reagan?"

"Yes. She . . . she said she wanted to talk to Luke. She had something to tell him."

"Did you tell her? About how he's changed?"

Elizabeth nodded. "I had to. It didn't seem fair after all these months to let her think he was the same."

John opened his mouth, but only uttered a tired sigh. He took Elizabeth's hand and led her to the love seat near the fireplace. Two logs blazed just beyond the fireplace screen, and the heat warmed the room. "Are you going to tell Luke?"

"That's just it." Elizabeth stretched out her legs, enjoying how her body felt next to her husband's. Three decades, and she still reveled in the quiet intimacy of being alone with him. "Reagan practically begged me not to tell Luke that she'd called."

"I thought you said she called because she needed to talk to him."

Elizabeth leaned her head on John's shoulder. "That's what she said at the beginning of the call, but by the end—after she knew the truth about Luke—she didn't want me to say a thing about her or the phone call."

"Hmmm." John was quiet. "Makes you wonder what she had

to say." He angled himself so he could see her better. "Are you going to tell him?"

"I don't know." Elizabeth slid to the edge of the sofa and held her hands closer to the fire. She looked at John over her shoulder. "Should I?"

He bit his lip. "Normally, I'd say no. If the girl doesn't want Luke knowing that she called, so be it." He turned and gave a long look at the photo of him and Luke. "But right now I'd do anything to get Luke's attention. Anything at all."

Elizabeth stood and faced her husband. It was the answer she'd hoped he would give, because ever since dinner she'd been desperate for a reason to call Luke. She felt the corners of her mouth lift in a tentative smile. "So, I should tell him?"

John stood and pulled her into a long embrace. When they were finished hugging, he drew back and uttered words strained with emotion. "Please, Elizabeth. Please tell him."

She nodded and checked her watch. It wasn't quite nine o'clock; Luke would be awake. Maybe if she let him know about Reagan's phone call he'd snap to his senses, leave this new girl who'd filled his head with so many lies, come home, and pour his heart out to her and John. He could call Reagan and find out she still loved him, get back on track with his faith and his future, and everything would be the way it had been before September 11, before the World Trade Center collapsed with Reagan's father still inside.

Elizabeth crossed the room and picked up the telephone receiver. It was a good idea, telling Luke about Reagan's call. After all, he'd been different with her, different than he'd been with any other girl. Every other time when Luke had dated a girl, he'd done so more as a way to pass the time. "In like," Elizabeth used to call it. "Luke's in like again."

Not so with Reagan. Something about her had made Luke's eyes sparkle every day of the week, and Elizabeth knew exactly why. Luke hadn't just liked Reagan Decker. He'd loved her.

He probably still did.

That alone was enough to make Elizabeth break the promise she'd made to Reagan. She drew a deep breath. Her hands trembled as she punched in her son's new phone number and waited.

When the phone began to ring, she did something else, the only thing that would ever bring about the miracle their son needed.

She prayed.

CHAPTER THREE

LUKE SPENT AN HOUR standing in front of the apartment window, but he didn't see the lights of Indiana University. He saw a far different sight—the scene probably taking place across Bloomington at his parents' house.

If the thing that had been chasing him was his past, then maybe it was time to let it catch him.

Kari and Ryan were getting married; that had to be it. And though Luke didn't belong with the Baxters anymore, he was happy for Kari. Ryan had been Luke's hero as far back as he could remember. Larger-than-life, high school football star, an athlete who'd earned a full-ride college scholarship and then a spot on the Dallas Cowboys. Ryan survived one of the worst injuries the National Football League had ever seen—all while keeping his faith.

Yes, Ryan Taylor was the best guy Luke had ever known, and until September 11 all he'd wanted was to be just like him. Okay, so he'd never play football in the NFL or even get beyond the intramural sports at IU. But still, he sort of looked like Ryan. Tall and strong, ready to bust up a room with a quick one-liner, blessed with social graces, and devoted to his faith. There were lots of ways he was just like Ryan.

Or at least he used to be.

He worked the muscles in his jaw. Lori was out again; she'd been gone all day to some seminar on self-directed spirituality. She was on a high-protein kick lately—only red meat, eggs, and boneless chicken. Something about getting fuel from the lower evolutionary rungs. The girl had so many approaches to eating he couldn't keep track of them.

Homework helped him pass half the evening, but he'd finished his last bit of reading, and really, he should've gone to the party at his parents' house. He couldn't hide from them forever.

Eventually they'd have to accept that he was different now. They'd have to stop grilling him about his faith and stop asking when he would change back to the Luke Baxter they knew and loved. They could take him like he was or not at all. And if they couldn't, well, what did that say about their supposed faith?

Luke wiped at a spot on the window where his breath had left a circle of steam. Tomorrow he and Lori would attend a campus function for the Freethinkers Alliance. The group intrigued Luke more than the other clubs Lori dragged him to. Even with his new mind-set—the one that wasn't theistic in nature—some of the clubs she belonged to were downright wacky. Anger Diversion Art? One World Optimization? Luke shook his head. Voice of the Trees?

No, he didn't fit into much of Lori's world. But the Freethinkers Alliance—or FTA—now *that* was a group that sparked Luke's imagination. Tomorrow's message was "Removing Bias— Breaking Down the Walls to Freedom." And later that month they'd spend a few weeks on the relativity of truth. Luke could hardly wait for *that* discussion, especially after a lifetime of thinking truth could be found only by walking through the doors of a church or living a life founded on some archaic book of letters.

Luke raked his fingers through his hair and turned from the window. The apartment was meticulously clean. Lori was a stickler for organization. Inanimate objects had a more powerful aura when they were put in their place. At least that was her theory. She had a fit if he left his clothes on the floor, and after a few arguments about the negativity of sleeping next to a pile of day-old clothes, he'd learned to hang them up.

A clock ticked in the background, and Luke sighed. The party would be over by now and he couldn't help but wonder. Had they missed him? talked about him? shared with each other how lost he was now that he wasn't exactly like them? He sank his hands in the pockets of his jeans and headed for the kitchen. A bologna sandwich would help take his mind off his family.

He was halfway to the kitchen when the phone rang.

Only a few possibilities existed anymore, since Luke had lost most of his old friends. And the new ones—usually they were too busy being enlightened to think about something as mundane as calling to shoot the breeze. It was a part of his old life Luke missed, the social part. Playing basketball with his buddies, catching a movie off-campus, hanging out at Art's Attic for a couple games of pool.

Freethinkers didn't spend their time that way; wasn't that what Lori had said? Basketball was a source of unnecessary competition, the kind that eventually led to war; movies were tailor-made for nonthinking middle America and contained political agendas and influential stereotypes that were harmful to free-thinkers. And playing pool at a bar? Uneducated cretins and male chauvinists, that's who found fun in such simple pastimes.

So much for any of his old gang.

The phone rang a third time just as Luke picked it up and punched the On button. "Hello?"

"Luke? Hi . . . it's Mom."

Here we go. . . . He resisted the urge to roll his eyes. "Hello, Mother." He took the phone into the living room and plopped onto the sofa. His father hadn't called in weeks, not since Luke snapped at him to get out of his business. But his mom called no matter what, once every few days at least. So why did she have to sound so strained and frightened, as though he might hang up on her the moment he heard her voice? He cleared his throat. "How was the party?"

"Good. Ryan and Kari announced their engagement." She hesitated. "The wedding will be September twenty-first."

"I figured that was it." Luke closed his eyes and rubbed the bridge of his nose with his free hand. Lori had his mother pegged. From the beginning, she'd said his mother emanated negative vibes. The whole vibe thing didn't sit well with Luke, but it was hard to deny the tension between him and his mother.

"Ryan wants you to be in the wedding party." Her voice trembled. "He wanted me to ask you about it."

Luke squinted toward the window. "I'm not sure. Can I let him know in a week or so?"

His mother paused, and when she spoke again she sounded tired and old. "Kari's your sister, Luke. Why wouldn't you say yes?"

"Because." He let his frustration out in a huff. "Maybe I don't believe in marriage anymore, weddings and all that 'til-death-do-us-part stuff. And maybe I don't want to stand up there dressed in some establishment-driven black tuxedo making a hypocrite of myself." He eased back on his tone. "That's why."

"Well, then . . ." She didn't seem to have an answer for that. "At least think about it. Ryan cares a great deal for you. It would mean a lot for you to be part of the celebration that day."

"Fine." He leaned forward and dug his elbows into his knees. His stomach hurt, but he wasn't sure if it was the "bad vibes" or just the tension of his old life clashing smack against his new one. "I'll let you know."

"Thank you." She paused. "Luke, I have something else to tell you."

A dozen possibilities flashed into Luke's mind. Something had happened to Ashley or Landon . . . Maddie was sick again . . . or his father was passing on an apology. He waited.

"Reagan called the other day. She wanted to talk to you."

At those first two unbelievable words, Luke felt the blood drain from his face, felt his heart beating hard in his throat, sensed the room begin to spin. His mother couldn't possibly have said what he thought he'd heard. Reagan had called? His Reagan? She'd called looking for him? After how long—seven months? The idea was insane.

While his mother was waiting for his reaction, he grabbed a quick couple of breaths. The blood was returning to his face, but in small amounts. "Reagan?" He hated the way he sounded fifteen again, as though all the progress he'd made in the past half a year had disappeared at the mention of her name. "Are you sure it was her?"

"It was her, Luke. She apologized for not calling sooner, and she—"

"Wait." His voice rose a notch. "Start at the beginning. I want to know everything."

"I'm trying. We . . . we didn't talk long."

Something ignited a warning flare in the desert of Luke's soul. "Did you tell her about me? You know, that I was living with Lori?"

His mother's hesitation told Luke everything he needed to know. "What was I supposed to say, Luke? That you were upstairs waiting for her phone call?"

Luke bent at the waist and rested his forearms on his thighs. "Please, Mom. Start at the beginning."

"Okay. She apologized for not calling sooner, and then she asked for you. I told her you didn't live with us anymore, and that a lot of things had changed. She asked what I meant, and I told her."

"Told her what?" Panic joined the other emotions vying for position in Luke's voice. "What exactly did you say?"

His mother drew a slow breath, and when she spoke, her tone was stronger than before. "I told her the truth, Luke. That you've walked away from us and your faith and everything you once believed. That you never even stop by the house anymore, and that you are living with your new girlfriend."

The words hit Luke like so many bullets. "You told her that?"

"Yes."

Luke sat back and tried to assess the damage. Reagan must've been shocked. She might've stopped loving him the night of September 10, but the news would still have been hard for her to hear. "What did she say?"

"I think she was stunned, to tell you the truth. She said she hadn't known. When I asked her if I should tell you she called, she said no." His mother sounded sure of herself now. "In fact, she begged me not to tell you she called."

The room was spinning again. "She . . . she begged you not to tell me?" Why had Reagan called? What if the details about his new lifestyle were such a shock that she ran away again, maybe never to make another attempt to contact him?

"Yes." A sad sigh traveled over the phone line. "I almost didn't tell you. But then . . . when you didn't show up tonight, I thought you should know."

"Know what?" Luke couldn't concentrate, couldn't fathom the idea that Reagan had reached out only to draw back, probably further and more permanently than before.

"The way your new choices are affecting people, Luke. People you used to love."

Luke heard a key in the door and a few seconds later, Lori entered the apartment. Her face was pale, and it looked like she'd been crying. Her shoulders bent forward a bit as she set her books on the table. She rested there for a moment and then joined him in the living room. Luke gave her a little wave, pointed to the phone, and held up a single finger. He covered the speaker with his hand. "Be off in a minute."

She nodded, stretched out on the opposite sofa, and closed her eyes. Whatever the seminar had involved, her aura and vibe level certainly didn't seem stronger. Luke looked away from her and focused on his mother.

"Mom, listen . . ." Luke forced his head to clear. The desperation was gone from his voice, and he felt the room right itself. Why had he reacted so strangely? After all, Reagan had been out of his life for months. Thoughts of her now would lead nowhere. "You did the right thing. She had to know someday."

In the cat-and-mouse game he and his mom seemed to be playing, she was now the mouse again. "So . . . what are you going to do?"

"About what?"

"About Reagan. Don't you think you should call her, Luke? At least make some kind of contact?"

"She didn't want me to know she'd called; isn't that right?"

"Yes, but—"

"Look, Mom, I have to go. Lori's home. Thanks for telling me; you thought that was the right thing to do and I appreciate that." They were out of things to say, and Luke wanted to get away. If Lori was sick, then maybe she needed him—and that had happened only a few times since they'd been together.

His mother ended the call with a flurry of declarations—that his father sent his love, how much everyone missed him, and of course the point she never failed to make: everyone was praying for him.

When he hung up, Luke turned to Lori and studied her for a moment. She was small and well built, and he was used to sharing a bed with her. But he'd never really been attracted to her, not the way he'd been to Reagan.

She rolled on her side and opened her eyes. "What'd your mother want?"

"Just an update."

For a few seconds Lori looked like she wanted more details, but she let it go. A low moan escaped her, and she reached around and pressed her fist into the small of her back. "My lower vertebrae are killing me. I did a self-assessment and visualization on the way home, but the pain's still there."

Luke wasn't sure what to say. Couldn't she talk like a normal girl, just once? As intriguing as he'd found her in the beginning, these days more often than not she came across as a self-righteous, academic snob. Reagan never would've been so—

He caught himself, stopping the train of thought before it picked up steam. *Breathe, Luke . . . forget about her and just breathe.* "How was the seminar?"

Lori cast him an indifferent glance. "I didn't go."

Luke stared at the woman he was living with. "I thought you took off class to go." He waved his hands in the air. "It was supposed to be this big deal, remember?"

"So . . . I took off class and went to the doctor instead." She pulled herself up and locked eyes with him. "Is that okay with you?"

He drew in a steadying breath. "Listen, Lori, if something's wrong, you should've told me. Maybe I could help."

"I'm fine, Luke." She crossed her arms, and for the first time since Luke had known her, she looked young and helpless, more like a little girl than a college coed intent on changing the world. "It was just a doctor's appointment."

"All day?" He wasn't trying to fight with her, but she didn't look well. "What is it, the flu? a virus?"

"Look . . ." She was mad now. Her eyebrows came together in a sharp *V* as she stood and stared at him. "It's *my* body, okay? I find it offensive that you would even ask." She gave a sharp breath through her nose and turned toward their bedroom. Near the doorway she tossed him a final look over her shoulder. "And don't worry. It's not contagious."

Luke watched her go and felt no remorse. He headed for the window once more and stared out. Lately he spent half his time in front of that single sheet of glass, looking at the world outside their apartment, wondering how life had gone mad. What would make a person hijack a plane and fly it into a building full of people? That had been the turning point, really. His life would be forever marked by how it was prior to September 11. . . .

And how it was now.

He leaned his bare arm against the cold glass and tried to focus. Back cramps probably meant it was that time of the month for Lori. PMS was hard on her, though she hated to admit it. Some weeks she would wax on about the virtues of menstruation and how it empowered women. Other times she called it a curse, a challenge men knew nothing about.

Luke always wanted to laugh when she said that, but he didn't dare. If anyone knew about PMS it was a guy with four sisters. But Lori wasn't interested in his opinion—at least not on anything concerning a woman. He shifted and let his other arm rest against the glass. That had to be it, PMS, and maybe she'd been in for a checkup. Not that a checkup would take all day, but if she didn't want to tell him where she'd been, then so be it.

Right now, he didn't care.

He watched a car pull into the apartment parking lot and drop off a young couple. The two laughed as they waved good-bye and headed toward the front doors. Too bad Lori was sick. It would've been a great night to check out the action on campus. A concert, maybe, or a reading at the library. Life was about more than special-interest meetings, no matter what Lori thought.

Luke's mind drifted and he closed his eyes.

Where did Reagan live these days? With her mother in New York, obviously . . . the place she'd run off to on September 11. But was she happy? Had she enrolled in school and continued her education? Did she work at a café somewhere waiting tables or had she taken time off to mourn the loss of her father?

His words to his mother flashed in his mind: *"You did the right thing. She had to know someday."* Luke gritted his teeth. He wouldn't call Reagan—definitely not. Not when she knew how he'd changed. Not when she'd been so clear about his mother not telling him about her phone call.

Why had she called, anyway? Wasn't it enough that she'd refused his phone calls for months on end? *She* walked out on their relationship. What right did she have to try to find him now? He studied the sky above Bloomington and felt his anger dissipate. Maybe she needed to tell him something, something urgent. Maybe her mother had been hurt . . . or her brother.

He caught his reflection in the glass and realized how long his hair was. He used to wear it short, his style conservative and clean-cut. But Lori told him a man looked better natural, with long hair and a beard, that in the crucial academic years it was important not to stifle any of himself or the power within him.

So Luke had grown a mustache and a goatee, but he had drawn the line there. Beards bothered him, even if the lack of one left him powerless in his crucial academic years.

He took a step back and caught more of his reflection. Even now—months after he'd made the decision to become someone else—he had trouble recognizing himself. Wavy hair down to his jaw, the unruly goatee and wispy mustache. The only thing even a little familiar about himself was the look in his eyes, a look that even September 11 hadn't been able to destroy.

A look that told him the truth about his feelings. No matter how often he lied to himself, he would always love a girl with long, blonde hair and a heart of gold; a girl who once told him she wanted nothing more than to spend the rest of her life with him. A girl who would've been Reagan Baxter.

If only things had worked out differently.

CHAPTER FOUR

ASHLEY PULLED INTO the driveway at Sunset Hills Adult Care Home and grabbed the box of tea from the seat beside her. She was the manager now, and other workers shopped for the groceries. But the tea was something she took care of, something she had promised Irvel, Edith, and Helen. Ashley made sure the house was never without it.

Halfway up the walk she paused and took in the sight of the old house. Bathed in the sunlight of a rare warm spring day, the place looked quaint and quiet. The tulips were in full bloom again, but there was nothing memorable about the brick front. Nothing that would make a passing motorist stop and take a second look.

Yet beyond the front door was a world of pain and possibility, heartache and hope—and the sum of it had been exactly the therapy Ashley needed.

After all, she'd taken the job at Sunset Hills Adult Care Home working with Alzheimer's patients for one reason—to soften her own heart. She'd hoped that perhaps by working with society's frail and forgotten, she might somehow find herself, find the place from which she painted, the place she'd all but buried after her time in Paris. Yes, working at Sunset Hills had changed her.

That, and the nightmare of September 11.

Ashley had made peace with God and her past. In the process she'd started painting again. Beautiful pieces, portraits of the residents at Sunset Hills and landscapes of Bloomington's rolling hills and farmlands. She was averaging one painting every few weeks now. On a day like this she wished she could skip work and find a meadow of wildflowers where she could set up her easel.

But trouble filled the air from the moment she stepped inside.

The new girl, Maria, was serving breakfast to Helen and Edith, but Irvel's spot was empty. Ashley hung her sweater in the closet, went to the kitchen, and put the tea in the cupboard. From there she went to the dining room. "Where's Irvel?"

Helen waved a trembling hand in the air. "No one checks people anymore around this place." She gave the table a sharp rap with her hand. "I've *had* it."

Edith's had shook as she directed a forkful of eggs toward her mouth. Her words were quiet and more of a continuous mumble. "Hello . . . hello . . . hello . . ."

"It's okay, Helen." Ashley made her way around the table, all the while keeping her eyes on the new girl. "I've been checked."

Helen shot her a hard look. "Who are you? That's what I'd like to know. Showing up so late in the afternoon, and how do we *know* you were checked?"

"I was checked, Helen." The only time Helen was calm was after a visit from her daughter, Sue. Otherwise the Alzheimer's left her angry and suspicious, as she was this morning. But Irvel never missed breakfast, and Ashley felt a gnawing within her at the sight of the empty chair at the head of the table.

She followed Maria into the kitchen. "Where's Irvel?"

"I didn't want to talk about her out there." Maria lowered her voice to a whisper. She was a soft-spoken woman with a kind heart and a strong work ethic. So far she'd been wonderful with the five residents at Sunset Hills. "Irvel's sick. Her blood pressure is up, and the doctor ordered her to stay in bed today."

"Sick?" A pit formed just beneath Ashley's heart. "I'll check on her."

She headed down the hall toward Irvel's room and prayed that the situation with Irvel was minor. The residents at Sunset Hills were like family to Ashley. Bert, with his newfound ability to communicate and the saddle set up in his room for him to shine each day; Edith, who had screamed at her own reflection until Ashley removed the mirror from her bathroom; Helen with her mood swings; the newest patient, a woman who rarely left her bedroom; and Irvel.

They all mattered to Ashley, but Irvel was special. Irvel was her friend. Though it took the old woman time to figure out who Ashley was, and though some days she never quite did, Irvel was always genteel and hospitable, a woman with Southern charm and an insistence that her dead husband was still alive.

Ashley had framed a dozen old photographs of Hank and hung them on Irvel's wall. Then, a few months ago, she'd painted a portrait of the man. As manager, she'd been given full control by the owner to continue on with a type of care that allowed Alzheimer patients to live in the past. Past-Present, the method was called.

Now that no one reminded Irvel that her husband was dead, she'd been much happier. And much healthier. Until today.

Ashley took quick steps down the hall and into Irvel's room. The woman was awake, but her face was gaunt and her hands lay limp on the bedspread. Her eyes followed Ashley as she made her way across the floor to the edge of the bed. The air was hot and stale, and tinged with a sick smell.

"Hi, Irvel. I heard you weren't feeling so good." Ashley ran her fingers across Irvel's forehead and brushed back the wiry fringe of bangs.

"Yes, dear," Irvel swallowed, and the effort made her wait a beat before talking again. "Hank . . . Hank told me to rest for a while." She managed a lighthearted smile. "So here I am."

Ashley glanced at the woman's nightstand and saw a fresh glass of orange juice. "Are you thirsty, Irvel? Some juice, maybe?"

Irvel smacked her lips together and made a few swipes with her tongue at the pasty residue near the corners of her mouth. "Yes . . . that would be lovely, dear. And later maybe some tea."

"I brought peppermint tea today." Ashley held the orange juice close to Irvel and bent the straw so she didn't have to lift her head off the pillow. "Peppermint's your favorite, right?"

Irvel sucked hard on the straw and downed half the glass. She backed away from the straw. Juice trickled down her soft, wrinkled chin, but she made no move to wipe it off. Her eyes grew wide, and she looked at Ashley as if seeing her for the first time. "My goodness, dear. You have lovely hair. Has anyone ever told you that?"

"Not lately, Irvel." Ashley snatched a tissue from Irvel's nightstand and dried her chin. "Thank you for noticing."

As quickly as her energy level had peaked, it dropped, and the old woman settled deeper into the pillow. "Can't understand why I'm so tired." She peered at Ashley and made an attempt at another smile. "Hank leaves me here to have tea with the girls, and look at me. Too tired to get up."

"It's okay, Irvel. Hank wants you to get some rest."

"Yes." Irvel's words were slurring now, and she'd be out soon. As long as Ashley had known her, Irvel had been able to fall asleep in seconds when she was tired. "You're right. Hank likes when I get . . ." The old woman's eyes closed, and Ashley smiled at the soft snores.

She bent over and pressed a feathery kiss on Irvel's cheek. The woman's skin was soft and dusty, like the fuzz on a peach. When Ashley drew back, she studied Irvel. She couldn't be dying, could she? Irvel wasn't even eighty yet. She had lots of time, right? The woman's breathing was not quite steady and even slower than usual.

Before leaving, Ashley took Irvel's hand in hers and closed her eyes. *God, help her pull through this . . . please. Sunset Hills wouldn't be the same without her.* She laid Irvel's delicate hand back on the bedspread. "Good night, Irvel. Dream about Hank."

The rest of the day Irvel stayed in bed, while the others did more than their usual mumbling and wandering about. Lu, the owner of Sunset Hills, had hired a bookkeeper so Ashley could be with the residents. She enjoyed eating with the ladies and bringing Bert's lunch to him. She liked helping them with their showers and having tea with them in the afternoon.

But all day, nothing felt quite right.

It was Irvel's absence, of course, but it was more than that. Every few minutes Ashley caught herself thinking thoughts that had nothing to do with work. Why didn't Landon call more, and what kept him so busy? And what would happen when he'd finished his one-year commitment to the FDNY? Would he come home to Bloomington? And if so, would they pick up where they'd left off before September 11? Or had his feelings for her cooled?

And what about her paintings?

Landon had moved on with his life, but here she was, still hiding at Sunset Hills Adult Care Home. Meanwhile her house was practically bursting at the seams with artwork, pieces never seen by anyone but her and little Cole.

The fog of unsettling thoughts stayed thick around Ashley's heart long after she finished her shift and picked up Cole from her parents' house. Questions assaulted her the entire drive back to her own home.

Why was she different? Everyone else had a plan, a purpose. Brooke and Peter had their family and their medical practices; Erin and Sam were moving to Texas in the summer, and Erin already had a teaching job lined up; Kari had her modeling and Ryan his football coaching, and together they had sweet baby Jessie and a future so bright it was sometimes painful to look at.

Luke . . . well, he was the exception.

But all of her sisters had found that next phase in life and moved into it without looking back. So what about her? She'd come halfway, hadn't she? Gotten over Paris and found a faith she'd run from most of her life. She'd even figured out how to be a mother to the wonderful child who was her son. But deep within her a knowing existed—one that she'd been running from ever since she boarded the plane at the Paris airport. For three years she'd run from it, denied it, pretended it was only a hobby. But nothing made her desire go away.

She still needed to paint the same way she needed to breathe. Desperately, undeniably.

Up-and-coming artists were often featured on-line, and Ashley checked their Web sites to see what was being heralded as the next great body of work. She always left those moments with the same conviction: Her work was right there, as good as theirs. The colors subtle, striking; the subjects bathed in a kind of passion and emotion and light that sometimes took her own breath away.

So what was she afraid of?

And why hadn't Landon called more?

"Okay, baby, we're here. Get your backpack." She parked the car in the garage and helped Cole into the house. He sat on a bar-stool opposite her while she prepared to make scrambled eggs and toast for dinner. His little-boy conversation was the first thing that had cleared her mind all day.

"I did a good thing at Grandma's. Know what?"

"You picked up your toys?"

Cole giggled, and the sound settled Ashley's nerves. "No, Mommy, I haffa do that every day."

"Okay, then." Ashley set her whisk down and anchored her elbows on the counter between them. "What good thing did you do?"

"I prayed for my friend Landon."

Ashley felt her heart catch and stumble. "That *was* a good thing, Cole." She straightened and worked the whisk into the bowl of eggs.

"He told me to pray for him, remember, Mommy?" Cole flopped his forearms onto the counter and cocked his head at her. "So today I prayed lots and lots."

Ashley dumped the eggs into the heated frying pan on the stove. "Okay, Coley, I have a question for you." She looked at her son. "What made you think about praying for him today?"

"I saw the picture you made of me and him 'cuz it was in the living room and that's where I left my backpack."

"And the painting made you think of him?"

"No, Mommy, 'course not." Cole's giggle was pure delight. "I think about him all the time, 'cuz he's my bestest friend."

"He is, huh?" Ashley hated the way her heart got fidgety whenever she heard Landon's name, whenever she thought of the relationship he shared with her son. What if he didn't come back? What if she and Cole weren't part of his long-term plans? It was wrong to let her son fantasize about Landon this way. But nothing short of God could make her stop him.

"Yep." Cole made a little shrug. "But sometimes I forget to pray." His eyes lit up again. "That's why it was a good thing I saw your picture, Mommy. 'Cuz it made me 'member."

Ashley stirred the eggs for a moment. "Cole, do you think Mommy's paintings are good?"

" 'Course I do." He hopped down from the stool, skittered around the kitchen island, and grabbed hold of her legs. "Know what Grandma says about your pictures, Mommy?"

Ashley stiffened. She and her mother had covered miles of ground in the past year, but her parents had never seemed to think much of her artwork. When she was in high school, she'd show them a piece and they'd smile and nod. Then her mother would say, "Have you given much thought to what you want to study in college, dear? Those years are just around the corner."

When she chose art as her major, the comments changed. "Do you see yourself *teaching* art, Ashley, or maybe working at a gallery? You still have time to add a more practical minor, you know. Business or education, something like that."

Then there'd been the nightmare in Paris.

Her mother had fought the trip from the beginning. Ashley's father finally swayed her to allow it. When Ashley came back a year later, pregnant and ready to throw out her easel, her mother never said a word about being right. She didn't have to. Ashley's life made the truth painfully obvious.

Cole tugged on her again. "Mommy, did you hear me? Don't you wanna know what Grandma said about your pictures?"

Ashley dropped her gaze to her son and managed a weak smile. "Sure, honey." She held her breath. "What did Grandma say?"

"She said—" Cole's smile reached from cheek to cheek— "they should be in a usee'um."

"A *museum*, you mean?" Her mother wouldn't have said that, would she?

"That's what I *said,* Mommy." Cole skipped toward the back door. "A *usee*'um." He raised his eyebrows. "Can I play in the back till dinner?"

Ashley gripped the countertop and sucked in a quick breath. "Sure, I'll call you when it's ready."

When Cole left, Ashley turned off the burner beneath the eggs and wandered into her living room, the place where her paintings were piled three deep along the walls. Her easel stood in the far corner, a testimony to the truth that had plagued her all day.

Her dream was still alive.

As long as she was painting, it lived and breathed and some-times—on days like today—it sang within her.

Her mother thought her artwork belonged in a museum? Why hadn't she ever told Ashley she felt that way? Ashley couldn't re-member once when her mother went out of her way to see one of her paintings. Now she was raving about them to Cole?

A voice pierced Ashley's soul, one from a lifetime ago. Jean-Claude Pierre, sneering at the best piece she'd painted up until that point: *"It is trash, Ashley. Nothing more than American trash."*

She clenched her fists and gave a strong shake of her head. *No, that wasn't true. It isn't true. Take away the doubts, Lord. Make me believe in this . . . this gift you've given me.*

A Bible verse flashed in her mind like the whisper of springtime wind through the elm trees lining the street out front: *"Work hard and cheerfully at whatever you do, as though you were working for the Lord rather than for people."*

The words were a verse Ryan Taylor had talked about once when the Baxter family was gathered for dinner. It was the Scripture he used to motivate his players, even though technically God wasn't supposed to be mentioned at a public school.

But here . . . now . . . God brought the words to life for her and her alone.

Whatever she did, she must work at it with all her heart. Parenting Cole, tending to the residents at Sunset Hills Adult Care Home, earning a living for herself and her son.

And yes, even painting. Maybe *especially* painting.

She moved across the room to the painting of Landon and Cole, the one with Landon in his uniform and Cole looking like he'd found the greatest treasure in the world. It *did* belong in a museum, didn't it? On a wall between the works of other great artists.

Landon had followed his heart to New York City to fight fires, to the place where his best friend, Jalen, had begged him to come. After September 11, Landon knew Jalen was among the missing. But it took him nearly ninety days to find Jalen's body in the pile of rubble at Ground Zero. After that, Landon's dream changed.

"One year in New York," she could hear him telling her. "I'll do what Jalen would've wanted me to do and put in a year."

What was it she'd spent a lifetime saying? That she wanted to be a famous artist, have people line up to see her paintings and barter over who would pay thousands of dollars to take one home. She shifted her gaze and took in one painting after another. . . .

She'd taken digital photographs of each and catalogued them on a computer file. It was all there, wasn't it? If she wanted to make it as an artist, why was she hiding her artwork in her living room? Was that what God meant by working at it with all her heart? When no one—not even her mother—would ever see her work?

The answer rang clear in her mind.

Bloomington had a few galleries scattered among the quaint shops not far from campus. But the hottest spot, the one place other than Paris where she would've died to have her paintings hung, was New York City. Downtown Manhattan on Broadway or Fifth Avenue or one of the streets adjacent to Central Park and the Metropolitan Art Museum.

In that instant, Ashley knew what she had to do.

She thought about it while she returned to the kitchen and finished dinner for Cole. Thought about it after she put him to bed and throughout the long night when all she could imagine was how she would do it and who she would talk to and what she would say.

She had the next morning off, and by then, she had a plan.

With Cole busy out back, she sat at her computer, went on-line, and made a comprehensive list of galleries in New York City. Then she phoned them one at a time and explained her situation. She was an artist with experience in Paris and a roomful of original pieces.

The responses were varied:

"We're full."

"The gallery down the street's looking for new talent. Call them."

"Four years' gallery experience is a must before anyone here would be interested."

But Ashley didn't give up. For the next week she used every spare moment to contact galleries. With each passing day she fought discouragement, fought the memory of Jean-Claude's voice and the fact that she'd never been so bold as to take a single painting to even a local gallery since coming home from Paris. If she was going to work at it like Landon worked at fires—like Kari worked at helping people and Erin worked at teaching and

Brooke worked at medicine—then she could hardly let a few rejections stop her.

At the end of her second week of phone calls she got a bite.

"Do you have a Web site?"

A Web site! Ashley's heart jumped, and she had to slow herself down so her words didn't jumble. She had all the material for a Web site. It wouldn't take Erin's husband more than a few hours to put the digital pictures of her artwork onto a simple Web site.

"I should have it up by the end of the week." She closed her eyes and grinned. "But I can send you a few pictures of my work by E-mail if you want."

The woman at the other end yawned, and the sound of someone typing filled the line. "Umm, E-mail. Right, okay. Sure." She rattled off an address. "Send it to me and I'll get back to you in a few weeks."

Ashley hung up, E-mailed photographs of ten of her best pieces to the New York gallery, and seconds later had Sam on the phone, convincing him to come by after work and bring Erin. She'd serve dinner and visit with Erin while Sam put together a Web site for her.

"It's about time, Ashley." He was at work, but he didn't seem rushed.

"Meaning what?" She sat back in her chair, dazed by the number of calls she'd made that week.

"You're a brilliant artist." He hesitated. "I told Erin months ago you were crazy to keep those paintings in your living room when they'd make such a hit out in the world. I'd love to build you a Web site."

"You would? You did . . . you told Erin that?" She ran her fingers through her short hair. Why hadn't he ever told her? "You really think that?"

"The whole family thinks that." He chuckled. "But no one wanted to tell you."

Ashley's mouth dropped open. "The whole family?"

"Sure." Sam gave a loud exhale. "We've talked about it a lot, whenever you're not around."

"How come no one ever told me?"

Sam paused. "Want the truth?"

"Definitely." Ashley felt the color drain from her face. Her family had believed in her all along, but none of them had ever said a word.

"Because, Ashley, whatever happened to you in Paris must have been terrible. You came back a different person." The sincerity ringing in his voice made her grip the phone tighter. "If painting did that to you once, it could do it again. I guess none of us wanted to see that happen."

They finished the phone call, and Ashley stood and stared out the window at Cole. Painting hadn't made her unhappy in Paris. Her bad choices had. And now . . . now it was almost more than she could imagine. Her family *liked* her artwork, even thought it belonged in a gallery or a museum. But they'd never said anything for fear of harming her.

Ashley wasn't sure whether to laugh or cry. How much sooner might she have chased this dream if she'd thought they were even a little interested? Ryan liked her work, and Landon, of course. But it was easy to believe they were just trying to be nice. Her parents—those were her critics. And if they'd ever told her, even *once,* that she was good enough to make it, maybe she wouldn't have gone to Paris in the first place. Maybe she would've known she didn't need a year abroad, what with some of the finest galleries in the world right here in the United States.

She was still thinking about the craziness of it all that evening as she waited for Erin and Sam to arrive. They were five minutes late when the phone rang.

"Hello?" She cradled the phone between her ear and shoulder and leaned over to light a candle at the center of her dining-room table. Cole was playing with a Lego set a few feet away, and she gestured for him to pick it up and take it to his room.

"Ms. Baxter?" The voice had a New York accent. "I believe we spoke earlier today."

Ashley had spoken to more than fifty people that morning. She swallowed hard and carried the phone into the kitchen. "Yes . . . how can I help you?"

"You sent me an E-mail. I'm Ms. Wellington." She paused. "I must say, we were very impressed with the pictures of your art-work."

Ashley groped around for a barstool and somehow managed to sit down without passing out. The woman had said she wouldn't call for a few weeks. "Thank you, Ms. Wellington."

"My husband and I own a gallery here in Manhattan. He wanted me to ask you a question."

"Anything." Ashley's answer was quick. Too quick. She sent a slow breath through her clenched teeth. *Come on, Ashley, get a grip.*

"We are a serious gallery, Ms. Baxter. Our clients have no room for fraudulent work."

"I'm sure." Ashley pinched her temples between her thumb and forefinger. "What are you saying, exactly?"

"To be blunt, we need to know that the work in your pictures is original art. That you didn't copy them somehow or com-puter-enhance them."

Ashley started to laugh, but her hand flew to her mouth and she caught herself. "You want to know if my work's original?"

"My husband and I both want to know." From the tone in the woman's voice, Ashley realized that she and her husband must have been lied to before.

"Yes." Ashley's heart raced and she felt the floor fall away. "That's exactly how they look, and they're original. Definitely." She wanted to jump in the air and shout. So *what* if they had to ask hard questions? She had the answers. Besides, if they were worried about fraud, it could only mean one thing.

They loved her work!

"Well, then—" the woman cleared her throat—"we'd like you

to come to the gallery next week sometime and bring the following three pieces."

She rattled off the titles of three of Ashley's favorite paintings. Ashley grabbed a pencil and scribbled the information on a piece of scrap paper near the telephone. The whole time she worked to concentrate.

The woman hesitated. "Will that be possible?"

Ashley couldn't keep the room from spinning. She'd waited years to push ahead with her dream, and now . . . the news about her family, the idea of the Web site, the contact with dozens of New York galleries. And finally this phone call. Suddenly she realized she hadn't given the woman an answer and she stifled a giggle. *God, you did it. You did all of this.* "Yes, of course. I'll figure out how soon I can be there; then I'll give you a call."

"That would be lovely." The woman's voice was kinder than before. She gave Ashley directions to the gallery—a small, conservative shop in Manhattan's Upper West Side, not far from Central Park. "Ask for me at the front desk."

Ashley promised she would. The doorbell rang just as she hung up. She raced to the entryway, pulled on the handle, and stared wide-eyed at Erin and Sam.

"What is it, Ash? You look scared to death." Erin opened the screen door and stepped inside. Sam followed her and the two of them waited.

"You won't believe it!" Ashley took a few steps back and did a little jump-skip across the living room, her fists raised in the air. "I'm taking my paintings to New York City!"

CHAPTER FIVE

J OHN B AXTER RARELY worked nights.

He'd been a doctor in Bloomington for enough years that the younger guys at the office handled the on-call hours. But tonight was different. One of his patients—a man who served alongside John on the elder board at church—had undergone triple bypass surgery two days earlier. The man had been moved from the cardiac unit to intensive care, an upgrade that pleased John. But he wanted to make sure his friend was comfortable.

It was just before seven o'clock when he stepped off the elevator onto the third floor and headed for the nurses' station. A whiteboard posted on the wall nearby had the names and conditions of each patient in the unit. John glanced at the list and saw that his friend was doing better.

He was about to turn and head down the hall toward the men's room when something caught his attention. One of the names on the list was Lori Callahan.

Wasn't that Luke's girlfriend's name?

Why in the world would she be in the hospital? And in the intensive care unit, no less. He spun around and met the eyes of one of the nurses behind the counter. "Lori Callahan? Is she a young woman, twenty, twenty-one?"

The nurse studied the whiteboard for a minute. "Yes, I believe so. She's new to the unit, Doctor. Let me check." She sorted through a pile of files nearby and found the one she was looking for. "Yes . . . twenty years old, lives in an apartment off-campus." The nurse continued to scan the report. "Says here she's a full-time college student."

John bristled and took a step backwards. His son was living with a girl who was so ill she was in the intensive care unit at St. Anne's Hospital, and no one in the Baxter family even knew about it? John was a doctor, after all. He could've done something to help the girl if Luke had called.

Things must've been worse than John thought, the chasm between Luke and his family wider with every passing hour.

"May I see that, please?" John reached for the file. The girl probably had a bad case of food poisoning or pneumonia, maybe a bacterial infection gone haywire. College coeds didn't wind up in the ICU every day. He scanned the admit sheet, past her name and address—the address she shared with Luke—past her date of birth. Then, in less time than it took to blink, he found it— and his heart dropped to his knees.

It was impossible.

Lori Callahan was suffering from an infected uterus due to postabortion difficulties.

Postabortion?

The information had to be wrong, or maybe the girl wasn't Luke's live-in friend, because no matter how much he'd changed, Luke would never agree to something like this. John closed the file. His forehead was damp and his knees trembled. It had to be some kind of mistake.

The nurse was watching him, waiting for the folder. "Doctor, is everything okay?"

John handed over the file and steadied himself against the nurses' station. "Is anyone in with the girl?" If Luke had been a part of this, if the girl in the room was the same one he was living with, if he'd gotten the girl pregnant and agreed to the abortion, then he'd be in there, sitting by her side, holding vigil, desperate for her to turn the corner.

"No, Doctor, the young woman's had no visitors." She opened the file and flipped back a few pages. "Apparently she drove her-self to the emergency room earlier today. The notes say she didn't want anyone contacted."

"Very well." John backed away from the counter. "Thank you. I'll take a look at her before I go."

The nurse's eyes reflected curiosity, and for a moment John thought she might ask why he was interested in Lori Callahan, why reading the girl's file had caused him such concern. But nurses worked under a clear-cut code of respect for doctors, and the woman only nodded and returned to her work.

John headed down a hallway, his mind and body in a trance. Why had he come to the hospital tonight, anyway? He squinted, determined to escape the avalanche of fear coming down on top of him. His friend from church—that was it. He moved his legs in the direction of the man's room and found him sleeping. John checked his chart, inspected the incision down the center of the man's chest, then prayed over him.

The moment he finished, he couldn't remember a word he'd said.

Back out in the hall he went to the nearest rest room, darted inside, shut the door, and locked it. He fell against the wall and squeezed his eyes shut. The girl's diagnosis flashed in his mind again and again, like some twisted, evil taunting designed to make him crazy. Potent emotions swirled in his mind—grief and guilt and regret. Remorse and anger and desperation.

Lori had had an abortion?

What in the world was Luke thinking? How could he allow this, and then stay home while Lori struggled in the intensive care unit? Was that all the character his son had? All the faith and goodness he'd been able to muster after a lifetime under the

Baxter roof? Yes, things were much more serious than John had thought.

He'd assumed Luke's absence from his family, his decision to move in with Lori, had been a phase, some kind of extreme reaction to September 11. But he never figured it would lead to this.

John opened his eyes, took a few steps toward the sink, and gripped the ceramic basin. *Father, I never thought I'd be here. Never thought I'd be dealing with this, and, well . . . I don't know how to do it. Give me the right words when I talk to Luke. Make him hear me somehow. Please, God . . . please.*

The girl was hardly out of the woods. John wanted to check on her before he took the next step. And he *would* take it, no question about that. Maybe he'd lain too low for the past few months, letting Luke stumble along a path that ran straight to his own destruction. But the least his son could do now was be here with the girl. John would insist on that much, even if Luke resented him for interfering.

Steadying himself, John left the rest room and went to Lori's room. Hers was the bed nearest the door. John had never met the girl, because Luke wouldn't hear of it.

"Is she afraid of us, Son?" John had asked Luke the last time they were together—sometime back in January. "You've always brought your friends home for us to meet."

"Not this time, Dad." Luke's jaded laugh raked John's nerves. "You'll have her listening to your God talk in five minutes flat."

"That's not fair, Son. At least give us a chance."

But Luke was adamant. "I won't have you meet Lori until you accept both of us for who we are."

John took quiet steps closer to the bed and studied the girl. A friend of the Baxter family was a professor at Indiana University, and last semester he'd had Lori in his class.

"She's a fighter, John. An always-angry, cause-bearing campus activist." The man raised an eyebrow. "She's the last person on earth I'd picture Luke dating. And vice versa."

John studied the monitors and then shifted his gaze back to

Lori. She looked nothing like a fiery activist now. Her face was smooth and unlined, her eyes as peaceful and long-lashed as a twelve-year-old's. Somehow he'd pictured her taller, more like Reagan. But the young woman lying in the bed was barely five feet tall.

As John watched her, he realized something. This frail patient had become the enemy in his mind, the woman who wooed Luke away from everything he'd believed in, the one who convinced him to drop his moral convictions and move in with her, taking up causes and joining clubs he would've laughed at a year ago.

But the girl lying here was hardly the enemy. She'd merely bought into a pack of the enemy's lies, traded old-fashioned common sense for an answer that was really no answer at all. She was as much a victim of her own bad choices as Luke. And now . . . if she recovered from the abortion, she'd have a whole new set of lies to deal with.

John thought back to Lori's chart. Her temperature had spiked as high as 105 in the past hour, and it hadn't come close to breaking. The doctor on duty had her hooked up to fluids, painkillers, and big-gun, broad-spectrum antibiotics. The next twelve hours would be crucial. If the infection spread to her blood, they could lose her.

So where was Luke?

The girl stirred and a low moan came from between her dry lips. With a jolt, her face convulsed in a twisted mass of pain. John took her hand in his. "It's okay, Lori. You're going to be okay."

She stirred just enough that John thought maybe she could hear him.

Despite the months his son had spent with this young woman, John knew little more than that she'd been raised in an agnostic home that tended toward atheistic viewpoints, and that she was a supporter of many left-wing and New Age organizations and causes.

Still, two truths remained: She was God's child, and she loved Luke. And as such, John did for her what he would've done for any of his own children. He clutched her hand a bit more tightly, closed his eyes, and began to pray.

"God, I beg you to lay your hand of mercy on Lori and breathe healing into her body." His voice was a whisper, and the heat from her fevered body filled the air between them. "Help her survive this, Lord, and forgive her because—" His voice caught. The baby she aborted had been his grandchild, Luke's son or daughter, a baby none of them would ever know. Still, John had no contempt for her. "Forgive her because she's been lied to, God. And I'm sure she doesn't understand what she's done. Heal not just her body, but her heart. And forgive Luke, too. Thank you."

John straightened and let go of Lori's hand. Whatever reason Luke had for not being here, it wasn't good enough. John checked his watch, and it hit him that he had no idea where his son would be at seven-thirty on a weeknight.

He sucked in a breath and wiped the back of his hand over his forehead. Nerves had no place in what he was about to do. He would have to go in the strength of what he knew was right, and pray that somehow Luke heard his heart. Because John Baxter's days of sitting back and waiting for everything to work out were over.

Even if Luke hated him for it.

Luke's poli-sci book was spread open before him, but he couldn't focus on the words.

Something about the judicial system or the process by which a judge could be removed from his place on the bench. But Luke's concentration was gone, and this time it wasn't only his past that plagued him.

Lori was gone again, and he had no idea where she was. She'd spent Monday at the doctor's office, and Tuesday she'd stayed home with back cramps. PMS . . . it had to be PMS. He'd been right all along. But then this morning she was gone before he woke up. Her first class on Wednesdays was at ten o'clock. So where was she?

Luke spent most of the afternoon wondering. Was she seeing someone else? Getting involved in some club or group that demanded all her time? If so, why hadn't she told him? They'd agreed to have an open relationship. Lori said their inner beings couldn't be free unless they kept their commitment open-ended. Luke agreed, because who cared what Lori did? He wasn't in love with her.

But if she had something else taking up her time, the least she could do was tell him. He forced his eyes back to where he'd left off in the book, but three lines later he stopped. Not one word had registered, and not just because of Lori's strange behavior these past days.

But because of Reagan.

He pushed his chair back, planted his elbows on his thighs, and dropped his head into his hands. Why'd she have to call, anyway? Couldn't she have let well enough alone? She didn't love him anymore, hadn't since that night they were together. If she had something to say to him, she could've said it any of the dozens of times he'd tried to call her.

But now? What good could come of talking now? Did she really think he'd simply sit back and wait for her? That he'd keep going to church and believing God was good and chalk up her sudden disappearance to something that had never been meant to be in the first place?

Hardly.

Luke slid his chair closer to the table again. The poli-sci test was tomorrow at eight in the morning. He *had* to study or he'd never get a passing grade. He brought the book closer and found his place just as he heard a knock at the door.

He looked up and knit his eyebrows together. Who on earth . . . ? No one ever came over to hang out. And Lori would've used her key. A sinking feeling tightened around Luke's airways. It couldn't be his mother, could it? Twice before she'd stopped by with fresh-baked banana bread or a pile of mail.

"Mom," he'd told her the last time, "you've gotta call first. I deserve my privacy."

She'd promised him: no more surprise visits. So, then, what was this?

Luke stood, crossed the room, and opened the door. Standing a few feet back was not his mother but his father. For the briefest flash of a second, Luke almost went to him. Not because he wanted to hug him or be close to him or confide in him, but because his reflexes remembered that as the thing to do at a time like this. He'd shared a lifetime of hugs with this man, and it felt like the most natural thing in the world. He used to hug his dad every time they were together.

Not anymore.

"Hello." Luke held his ground, his tone a gruff mix of frustration and curiosity. His father had honored his wishes these past few months and stayed away. Luke couldn't think of a single reason why he would be here now. Even so, he stepped back and held the door open. "Come in."

"Thank you." His dad's businesslike tone bordered on angry.

Luke took the seat opposite his father in the living room and clasped his hands. "What brings you?"

"Lori." His father said the word so fast, it hit him like a sucker punch.

Luke's answer was equally quick. "She's not here." His dad had probably grown tired of waiting for Luke to come around, so now he was going to insist on it, have a chat with Lori, and explain that Luke had played at her house long enough. It was time to come home. He was about to tell his father how ridiculous that was when his dad leveled a gaze at him so intense it hurt.

"I know where she is." Disgust played across his dad's features. "I just came from there." He gave a sharp huff through his nose. "What I can't figure is what you're doing *here?*"

Luke narrowed his eyes. What was his father talking about?

60

How could he have just come from being with Lori? "Lori's still at school, Dad. I doubt you've seen her."

It took half a minute, but gradually, like the morning sun rising over the farms of Bloomington, a look of understanding dawned on his father's face. "You . . . don't know?"

"Know what?"

"How sick she is."

A laugh managed to slip from Luke's throat, but it was void of any humor. "What're you talking about?"

"Son, Lori . . ." He stood and paced a few steps away from Luke and then back again. "She's in the hospital, Son. She's very, very sick."

"She's not sick." His father had to be mistaken. "She was fine last night. You must have her mixed up with someone else."

His dad sat back down and stared at him. His eyes were as angry as Luke had ever seen them. "You think you know so much, big Luke Baxter, all grown-up and ready to make your own choices." His father paused. "Just so you know, a girl can get infected after an abortion."

Luke's mouth hung open and his heart pounded in his throat. An *abortion?* After an abortion? Was that what his father had said? "I . . . what do you mean?"

"It doesn't happen all the time." His father waved his hand in the air above him. "But once in a while the infection gets so bad . . . we lose the young woman."

Luke's teeth felt dry and pasty. "An abortion?" He licked his tongue across his lips. "Lori didn't have an abortion." It was all he could do to stay seated. "It . . . it must've been some other girl."

"Lori Callahan." His father's voice was loud and full of accusation. "Isn't that her name?"

"No . . . I mean, yes. I mean . . ." Luke got up and took four long strides toward the window. When he spoke next, he kept his back to his father. "That's her name but, Dad, it isn't her." He glanced over his shoulder. "She's at school."

The dawning on his father's face became full-fledged and the anger left his eyes. "She didn't tell you." The statement sounded as though it was as much for his own benefit as for Luke's. "I can't believe she didn't tell you." John blinked and when he spoke again, his tone was quieter, resigned. "Her chart had your address, Son."

Deep in Luke's gut, fear and anger battled for position, and the ensuing fight left him speechless. What right did his father have to come here like this? Was Luke a child, a bad boy who'd broken curfew or violated some other Baxter rule?

John stood and came closer, disappointment screaming from his eyes. "She could die, Luke."

No words came in response. Luke turned from the window, fell back against the frame, and hung his head. The depth of the situation was getting through. He'd gotten Lori pregnant, and she'd had an abortion. Was that why she'd been at the doctor the other day? why she hadn't told him? Yes, abortion was a woman's choice—at least that's what he'd come to understand in the past few months. But shouldn't he have had a say, too? He was the father, after all.

His dad was inches from him now, and he crossed his arms. "You need to get down there, Luke."

Luke jerked his head up. "Don't tell me what to do."

"Actually, Son, I believe I will." His father's eyes narrowed, and the sympathy faded. "I've sat back and watched while you've self-destructed. You've turned your back on everything that used to matter. God, then me, then the rest of our family." He worked the muscles in his jaw. "You've been rude and callous, and the few times you've talked to your mother you seemed to think you're the only one with any real understanding of the world." He paused long enough to grab a breath. "And right now I don't care what you think about me, Luke. I'm going to tell you the truth, the thing I should've told you months ago. You're running, Son . . . running from—"

"Wait!" The shouted word stopped his father midsentence, and Luke held up a hand. "You have no right to—"

"No!" John grabbed Luke's shoulder and gave him a shake. "*You* wait, young man. I'm still your father, and you'll listen to me even if you hate me for what I have to say."

Shock rippled through Luke's body. His father hadn't laid a hand on him since he was a young boy. Here, now, when Luke was a man making his own choices, he could hardly believe this was happening. He stayed frozen in place, his mouth open.

"Look—" his dad loosened his grip, but didn't remove his hand—"September eleventh didn't just happen to you, Luke. It happened to all of us. But here you are, acting like an insolent brat, pretending you believe that . . . that self-enlightenment garbage. As though you could use a class project to disprove God, or that spending your time with the academic elite somehow changes God's truth." Control was back in his father's voice. "It doesn't take much enlightenment to get a girl pregnant, Son."

Luke's entire body went stiff, and he spoke through gritted teeth. "Get out!"

"No." His father dropped his hand but held his ground. "You're scared and you're running, because all your life you had everything figured out, Luke. Kari was wrong for marrying Tim . . . Ashley was a disgrace for going off to Paris and getting pregnant. But not you, Luke. No, you had it all together. You were better than—"

"I don't need to hear this." Luke spun around his father, stormed across the apartment, and flung open the front door. "I said go!"

His father turned and headed toward him.

John Baxter was a gentle man, someone who lived out his convictions and whose strength was not illustrated with loud displays or confrontations. But Luke suddenly wondered if his father might throw him to the ground. His dad's face was red, and the veins near his temple stood out. When he was face-to-face with Luke, he stopped and locked eyes with him. "I know what you're running from, Luke. And until you figure it out, you don't need to worry about ordering me out of your life. I'll stay gone." His father took a step toward the door. "You've lost so much, Luke. Now you've lost a child. And you may lose Lori."

"I'm not running!" Luke hated the feelings fighting within him. Part of him wanted to stop his father before he left, fall into his arms and beg for forgiveness. But a greater part wanted nothing to do with him. "I'm a grown man. I don't need you telling me what to think."

"I won't." His dad took another few steps, never taking his eyes from Luke's. "When you're ready to admit what your choices have done to all of us, then we'll have something to talk about. Until then, you won't hear from me."

"Fine." Luke spat the word and then bit his lip. For a moment, both of them seemed frozen in place. Luke's very bones ached from the finality of the moment, but his heart refused to engage.

"Good-bye, Son." His dad leaned back on his heels, the fight gone from his voice. "No matter how long you stay gone, remember I love you. I've always loved you, and nothing—nothing—you do could make me stop loving you." His voice trembled. "When you're ready to come back, I'll be waiting."

Luke clenched his teeth and let his gaze fall to the floor. When it was clear he wasn't going to say anything, his father turned and headed down the hallway to the stairs. Luke waited, listening as his dad took the steps and headed into the parking lot. He stayed there as he heard his father's car start up and pull away.

The whole time, Luke didn't move a muscle. He reminded himself to breathe. Life would be better with his father out of the picture, less complicated. Besides, if the news was true, he had bigger issues to deal with. When he could no longer hear the sound of his father's car, Luke went inside, slipped his tennis shoes and sweatshirt on, grabbed his car keys, and headed for the hospital.

He *had* to think about something besides what just happened between him and his father. If Lori had gotten pregnant, why hadn't she told him? Besides, they'd used birth control every time, hadn't they? And how could she get an abortion without asking him? Not that he wanted a baby now, when he still had an entire year of college left. But didn't he have a say in the matter? And how could she be fighting for her life in the hospital without his even knowing about it?

Fifteen minutes later, Luke found her, just as his dad said. He stayed by her side but was unmoved by the sight of her.

"It'll be okay, Lori." Even as he whispered the words, he kept wondering why he'd moved in with her in the first place. How could he lie to her, saying he loved her when she was merely someone who helped open his mind and pass the time?

At nine o'clock a nurse came to check on Lori and announced her fever had broken. An hour later Lori's doctor declared her officially on the road to recovery. Sometime before eleven, Lori woke up and peered around the room until she found Luke.

"Hi." She smacked her swollen lips and reached for the ice water near her bed. "I guess—" she took a long sip—"you know why I'm here."

"Yeah." Luke moved closer. "How come you didn't tell me?"

Even in her weakened condition, Lori bristled. "I don't . . . have to tell anybody what I do." She took another swig of water. "It's my body."

"Yeah, but it was my baby."

For several seconds she said nothing. Then she sat up some and winced as she shifted. "No." She locked eyes with Luke and shook her head. "It wasn't."

Of all the things that had happened that day, this was the one that took Luke's breath away. She must've been delirious from the infection, dazed by the pain medication. She couldn't possibly have just said what he thought she'd said. He slid his chair closer to her bed. "What?"

"The baby wasn't yours, Luke." She released an exaggerated sigh and gripped the bed's side rails. "A couple months ago I was out late after the club meeting, remember?"

Luke searched his mind. He had no idea what she was talking

about, but he couldn't make his mouth work well enough to speak.

"Anyway—" Lori sounded bored—"it meant nothing. The group had a guest speaker, and the two of us went back to his apartment afterward for more discussion. We shared a few hours in bed, nothing more. Neither of us had protection, and I got pregnant." She blew a wisp of bangs off her forehead. "My fault, my body, my solution."

"Just like that?"

"Just like that." She managed a weak smile. "But thanks for caring enough to come."

Luke grabbed his knees and tried to keep from vomiting. She couldn't possibly be serious. Lori had shared a few hours in bed with a stranger? And neither of them had used protection. "What if he had a disease, huh? Have you thought about that?"

"He told me he didn't, and I believe him. His whole talk that night was on honesty and how freethinkers are released to be honest with others. I hardly think he would've lied to me." Lori rolled her eyes and settled back into the pillow. "Besides, you always use something, so it's not like you have to worry."

"My girlfriend's sleeping with some stranger, and it's not like I have to worry?" Luke's voice rose, and he had to stop himself from losing control.

"Stop, Luke." She was awake now, composed and unashamed. "We agreed not to be exclusive, didn't we?"

Luke slammed himself against the chair, closed his eyes, and let his head fall back. Not like he had to worry? What was she thinking? They might not have been married or even engaged, but they were living together. Didn't that mean anything? And if she'd slept with this . . . this stranger so easily, who else had she been with?

"I can't talk about it." Luke stood and walked out of the room. Somehow he managed to find his car and drive back to the apartment, but all the while he couldn't stop rehearsing the facts. First the argument with his father, and now this.

How could he stay with Lori if she was sleeping with other men? And why had he thought her ideas so grand in the first place? You couldn't use freethinking as a cover-up for cheating on someone. Suddenly his future with Lori was precarious and uncertain. In fact, everything about his life felt that way, with the exception of one thing. Whatever his tomorrows might include, there was one thing they would never hold again.

Contact with his father, the man who until a year ago had been his closest friend.

CHAPTER SIX

REAGAN DECKER FELT STRANGE from the moment she woke up.

Her stomach hurt, but not with the tight feeling she got whenever she had light contractions. This was different, lower and more pronounced. And her lower back hurt, even though she couldn't remember doing a thing to it.

Labor was an obvious possibility. It was the first of June, three weeks before her due date, but the doctor had said it could be anytime. Still, she'd talked with her mother about it after breakfast and she didn't seem worried.

"You'll know when it's time." Her mother had reached across the kitchen table and patted her hand. "True contractions can't be mistaken for anything else."

But the pain in her abdomen and the uneasiness that went along with it continued through the day and after dinner. Now it was seven o'clock, and the women from her mother's bunco group were arriving. Most of them were church friends, well-off women in their late forties who Reagan had thought would be harsh and judgmental about her pregnancy. Instead the group embraced her, offered to take her to appointments if her mother was busy, and a week ago they'd held a baby shower for her.

"Love is about honor," one of the women told her. "You've made a hard decision—a right decision. And by doing that you've honored your baby, your family, yourself, God. All of us, really."

Reagan moved into the kitchen and mixed a pitcher of sweet tea. As the months passed, she realized what the women meant by *honor*. Though she and Luke had been wrong to give in to temptation, having the baby was the right decision. And anytime someone did the right thing, God was honored. Not just God, but everyone involved.

"It's a benchmark of any relationship," her mother explained. "Showing honor to others." Tears had glistened in her eyes. "Your father treated me that way, always appreciating the good about me, taking time to make me feel special and wanted. It's something we tried to do for you and your brother, and now . . . you can show that same honor to your baby."

Reagan stirred the tea. A few scoops of ice and it would be ready. Those discussions about honor convinced Reagan to finally call Luke. If honor was truly the benchmark of any relationship, then she'd done a poor job with Luke. Running from him, ignoring his phone calls, pretending these past months that he didn't exist . . . it all had been anything but honoring.

Since hearing about how he'd changed, Reagan could only wonder. Was it her fault? Had he become disillusioned about God, tossed out his beliefs and convictions, and wound up living with another woman because she hadn't honored him? It was possible. No excuse existed for the way she'd behaved.

The voices in the next room were cheerful, and the conversation picked up. Reagan should join them, bring the tea and some glasses and pull up a chair the way she usually did when they played bunco. But the pain in her abdomen was worse, and she couldn't take a full breath. She scooped the ice into the pitcher of tea, stirred it, and leaned against the counter.

Her head swam, and the walls swayed like flags in a summer

breeze. She grabbed the kitchen sink. The porcelain was cold and the feel of it settled her.

Maybe she needed a glass of tea or water. Yes, water was bound to help. Dehydration could cause light-headedness and stomach pains, couldn't it? What was it her doctor had said? Keep hydrated, drink lots of water in the weeks leading up to her delivery, right?

As she turned and reached up to take a glass from the cupboard, a pain ripped from her lower-right side, beneath her swollen abdomen. Then the pain doubled in intensity. Reagan cried out as she fell to the floor. "Mom! Help . . . me."

Her energy faded, and she felt something warm and wet between her legs. Had her water broken? If so, what was the horrible pain sending shock waves through her body and down her legs? Was this a contraction? She forced herself to scream. *"Mom, come here!"*

The kitchen door burst open. Her mother raced to her side, the other women close behind, all of them wide-eyed as they took in the sight of Reagan on the floor. "Reagan, dear, what happened?"

"I . . . don't know." Reagan curled into a ball and tried to breathe through the pain. If this was a contraction, shouldn't the pain be easing? Instead the searing burning near her pelvic bone was getting worse. She squinted at her mother and shook her head. "I can't . . . stand it."

Before her mother could answer, one of the other women tugged on her arm and whispered something. Reagan couldn't hear much over the pain screaming within her, but she caught a few words: *bleeding . . . emergency . . . ambulance.* The entire group of women sprang into action.

Someone found the kitchen telephone and called for help, while two of the women ran from the room and returned with a stack of linens. Reagan's mother took a towel and laid it beneath her head; another one she pressed hard between Reagan's legs at the place where she'd felt the warm liquid.

Nausea suffocated her, and dark spots flashed before her eyes. What was wrong? Why wasn't the pain going away? "God, help me!" Reagan's words were weak. She couldn't have said them louder or with any more strength if she'd wanted to. Her energy was fading with every beat of her heart, and her next words were uttered without sound, in the most desperate part of her soul. *God . . . help. Don't let anything happen to my baby.*

The pain was terrible, and Reagan forced herself to think back. She'd attended childbirth classes with her mother, searched the Internet, and read everything she could find about having a baby. But nothing in all the literature she'd scoured had ever mentioned pain like this. And if she was bleeding . . . something must be terribly wrong, something that could mean trouble for her and her unborn son.

The black spots were coming together, making it hard to see, and the noises around her began to fade. "Mom . . ." Her voice was scratchy and low, too weak to do more than express the panic that had a grip on her throat.

Her mother squeezed her hand and leaned over her. Reagan could feel her presence, but she couldn't see her, could barely hear her. "Pray, Reagan. Everything's going to be okay."

She wanted to nod, wanted to believe that somehow, yes, everything would be fine. But the pain was beyond bearable, and she began to fall into a soft, fuzzy hole with no sides and nothing to grab on to. No way out. Everything in her cried to let go, to give in and let herself fall, and finally she couldn't fight the feeling. She closed her eyes and almost at the same time the pain eased.

Somewhere in the distance she heard sirens, but then, this was New York City. Manhattan. Sirens were always sounding somewhere. They couldn't be for her because she was only taking a nap, lying on her bed in the midst of a most unusual sleep. And she must've been dreaming, because the voices surrounding her were not clear-cut but muted, blurred together, not quite understandable. Sounds that sometimes accompanied dreams.

Reagan heard her mother speaking, but the words didn't quite make sense. Something about too much blood, and losing the baby or losing Reagan. The panic in her mom's voice was so real Reagan decided maybe she should wake up, brush off the dream, and let her mother know that everything was okay.

But no matter how hard she tried, Reagan couldn't lift her head, couldn't even open her eyes. She frowned. Maybe she wasn't dreaming; maybe she was in trouble. She wanted to pray but her mouth wouldn't work, and she couldn't remember the right words.

Quieter. Darker. More distant.

Reagan felt herself slipping further away from the sirens and voices and people gathered around her. The last thought she had was of Luke. He'd been her everything. The one she'd known she would marry. But somehow it had all gone wrong, and now she'd never see him again, never hold his hand or look into his eyes and tell him they had a son.

Worst of all she would never get to apologize for taking what had been so wonderful and somehow destroying it for both of them.

Landon Blake was at the station supper table when the call came in.

Pregnant woman hemorrhaging, one engine company, one paramedic team needed to an apartment complex east of Fifth Avenue. Another station was closer to the location, but those units were at a fire near one of the theaters. The call was a common one. Get to the scene, aid paramedics in the assessment and transport of the patient, and make the report.

Landon slipped into his turnouts and shouted across the station at his partner, Doug Phillips. Doug drove on-calls when the captain didn't come. "Make time, will ya, Phillips. We're ten blocks away, easy."

Five of them rode the engine to the call, and little conversation took place as they sped toward the apartment. Minutes later they burst through the door and were greeted by a group of middle-aged women, each of them pale-faced and frantic. According to radio reports, the ambulance was at least a full minute behind.

Most firefighters were trained as EMTs, emergency medical technicians, and on this call Landon's partner would get the nod. He was a medic, capable of handling any rescue.

"Where's the ambulance? Are you with the ambulance?" A heavyset woman in a red sweater stepped forward. "She needs a doctor."

"An ambulance is on the way." Landon was first in the line of firefighters who had entered the apartment. "Take us to the victim."

"This way." The woman led them into the kitchen. More women were gathered there, squatted on the floor in a circle around a young blonde woman lying in a pool of blood.

Landon made a quick assessment. First, the woman was very pregnant and very young, not much older than a teenager. And second, she'd already lost too much blood. He directed the women away from the girl, clearing enough room for them to work.

At the same time, another woman stood and faced them. She was crying and her teeth chattered as she spoke. "I'm her mother." Her words ran fast together. "She's . . . she's three weeks from her due date. Her stomach hurt today, but we didn't think it was anything, and then she was making tea and she collapsed here on the floor and started bleeding, and . . ."

Landon's partner took his position near the victim's side and felt her pulse. "Weak and thready." His words were too low for most of the people in the room to hear. But the urgency there was undeniable. "Possible ruptured uterus. We need to stop the blood."

A pile of towels lay nearby, two of which were already soaked red. Landon grabbed a clean one and pressed it between the woman's legs. It was then that he focused on her face, and the shock hit him dead center and almost knocked him back.

The victim looked like Reagan Decker, Luke Baxter's girlfriend. The girl who had ridden the bus to Manhattan with Landon in the hours after the terrorist attacks. He narrowed his eyes. It couldn't be her, could it? For one thing, Reagan wouldn't be pregnant. Landon tried to remember what Ashley had said about her brother. He was struggling . . . hadn't talked to Reagan, and something about his moving in with some wacky girl from school. Luke hadn't talked to Reagan once since she moved back to New York.

Then maybe it wasn't her; maybe it was a different tall blonde, one who looked like Reagan. He was about to ask her mother when his partner looked over his shoulder. "What's the victim's name, ma'am?"

The girl's mother was shaking harder now, looking like she might pass out. "Reagan. Reagan Decker. She's . . . she's twenty years old."

"Is there a husband, someone who should be called?"

"No." The answer was quick—too quick. "There's no one."

Landon pushed the towel harder against Reagan, and his stomach lurched. The dates were coming together. If she was almost nine months pregnant, then she got pregnant before September 11. Either that or immediately afterward, and Landon doubted that was possible. Which meant that maybe—just maybe—the baby Reagan was carrying was Luke's.

And Luke knew nothing about it.

Before Landon could give the matter another moment's thought, paramedics burst into the room and took over. An immediate determination was made that Reagan was critical, perhaps fatally so. She'd lost too much blood, and despite their efforts she was still bleeding.

Landon stepped back and watched them lift her limp, pregnant body onto the stretcher and carry her from the apartment. Her mother stayed close behind, her voice tight and pinched as she rambled on about Reagan's stomachache. "Because she had nothing wrong with her yesterday, and if something had been wrong yesterday, we would've taken her in right away. I mean, even with the blood this whole thing is strange because the doctor saw her a few days ago and told her she wasn't dilated at all and . . . she's going to be okay, right? I mean you can save the baby, right? Because . . ."

The group headed into the hall, leaving the firefighters, half a dozen women, and the terrible silence that always came in the wake of an emergency. Landon helped his partner pack up their equipment while the others from their engine company interviewed the women about what led up to Reagan's collapse. Any information would be included in the final report.

Landon walked through the next five minutes without registering any of what was being said. His mind was on Reagan— and the fact that unless God breathed a miracle into her, odds were against her surviving. The baby had almost no chance at all. And what about Luke? If he was indeed the baby's father, didn't he have a right to know what was happening?

Mrs. Decker's words came back to him: *"No . . . there's no one."* If Luke was the father, Reagan clearly hadn't intended to tell him.

When they were back in the engine, Landon's partner elbowed him as they pulled away. "You haven't said a word since we got here."

Landon swallowed and met his partner's gaze head-on. "I know the girl, Phillips. She's—" he stared out the window— "she's a friend from back in Bloomington."

His partner hesitated. "How good a friend?"

"Very good." Landon sucked in a slow breath and found Phillips's eyes.

"What about the baby?" Phillips's mouth hung open.

"I didn't know until today."

"So . . ."

"So . . . she's gotta make it."

CHAPTER SEVEN

THE REST OF LANDON'S shift passed in a blur of prayer and wild thoughts, and it was all he could do to keep from calling Ashley. If Reagan didn't want the Baxters to know, he could hardly break the news to them. Especially now, in the middle of an emergency. But what if the baby died? What if Reagan did?

He finished work at midnight, took a cab to Mt. Sinai, and there he got word about Reagan's condition. A woman at the front desk explained that she'd been upgraded from critical to stable. She'd delivered the baby, and she was in the maternity ward under close watch.

Landon exhaled for what felt like the first time all evening. He took the elevator to the right floor and found Reagan's mother staring through the glass at a roomful of babies. When he came up beside her he cleared his throat and nodded. "I heard she's doing better."

Mrs. Decker looked at him, her eyes swollen and red. "Yes, they stopped the bleeding. And the baby's . . . the baby's fine. A little boy."

"I'm so glad." Landon breathed a silent prayer of gratitude.

"You . . . you're one of the firefighters, right?"

"Yes. Landon Blake." He held out his hand and shook hers. "I just got off work."

"That was very nice of you to come down." She sniffed and pulled a wadded-up Kleenex from her purse. "It's a miracle, Mr. Blake. The doctors said we should've lost both of them, and that—" Her voice broke and she hung her head again.

Landon didn't know what to say, so he put his hand on her shoulder and waited.

"We couldn't take another loss. Reagan's father . . ." She held her breath until her emotions were under control. "We lost him September eleventh."

"I know."

His answer caused her to look up. "You do?"

"Mrs. Decker, I know the Baxter family. I'm a, well, a special friend of Ashley Baxter, Luke's sister." He hesitated and sank his hands in the pockets of his pants. "I moved here to work with FDNY after the terrorist attacks. Reagan and I were on the same bus."

"Then—" her face lost a shade of color—"then you know about the baby?"

Landon shifted his position and ran his tongue over his lower lip. It was none of his business. "No, ma'am. Not until today."

Reagan's mother looked into the nursery. When she met Landon's gaze again, desperation looked at him from her eyes. "Don't tell him, please. Reagan doesn't want him to know." She smoothed her hand over the wrinkles in her sweater, and her eyes pleaded with him. "It would only complicate things."

Landon wasn't sure what to say. The information was too new for him to sort through. That the baby was Luke's was obvious. But how could Reagan and her mother think it was better to leave Luke out of the picture? It *was* his child, and Landon was certain he didn't know. If he did, he hadn't told any of the Baxters, because if one of them knew, they all did. And Ashley hadn't said a word about it.

If Luke knew about the baby, he wouldn't be living with some girl he met at school. He'd be here—with Reagan. So why hadn't she told him?

Reagan's mother was waiting for an answer, and Landon could do nothing but give a polite nod. "Of course. That decision belongs to you and Reagan, not me."

Relief washed over Mrs. Decker's face. "I know it's . . . unconventional. But she tried to call him, and, well . . . Reagan has her reasons." She looked back at the nursery. "Thank you for respecting that."

Landon followed her gaze. He coughed twice and cleared his throat. "Which one is he?"

The woman pointed to a blue-capped infant near the window, red-faced and screaming mad. "He's a fighter. Reagan named him Thomas Luke."

"He looks perfect."

"Yes." The word came out part laugh, part sob. Mrs. Decker put her fingers against her mouth and shook her head. "Almost six pounds and completely healthy."

The baby lay beneath the incubator's warm lights, but he was breathing on his own. It was a scene Landon hadn't expected to see. After Reagan's blood loss it was truly a miracle either of them were breathing at all. He looked from the baby to Reagan's mother again. "Reagan's okay?"

"She had a partially ruptured uterus." Tears swam in her eyes again. "The rip was too jagged. They . . . they couldn't save it."

Landon had enough medical training, enough experience in emergencies to understand, and the knowledge kicked him in the gut and left him sick to his stomach. The doctors had performed an emergency hysterectomy. Reagan would never have another baby.

Reagan's mother dabbed at the wetness on her cheeks and sniffed hard. "She doesn't know yet. The doctor's going to tell her tomorrow, unless—" she looked at Landon—"do you think you could tell her?"

Landon wanted to look over his shoulder to see whom the woman was talking to. Certainly not him. He hadn't talked to Reagan in eight months! How could he tell her the worst news of her life? He coughed again, and the reality became suddenly clear. In the past nine months Reagan had been dealt one blow after another.

Obviously she and Luke went against their convictions about saving sex for marriage. And, given the dates, September 11 and the death of Reagan's father came right after that. She probably no sooner got back in New York City than she realized she was pregnant. She'd gone through the entire ordeal without ever telling Luke. If her mother was right, if she'd tried to call him, then she knew how he'd changed. That he had chucked his faith and was living with some girl he'd met at school.

Now this. Landon thought about the damage to Reagan's body, and a long breath eased from his throat.

No wonder Mrs. Decker wanted her to hear the news from him. The poor woman trembling before him probably couldn't handle sharing one more bit of tragedy. With Reagan's father dead, the other option was for a doctor—a stranger—to tell her what had happened to her body.

He shifted his gaze from Mrs. Decker to the baby in the incubator. How had everything between Luke and Reagan gotten so twisted? She must feel so alone, lying in a room down the hall with no husband, no support, no words of comfort or congratulations to mark the birth of her firstborn child.

The only child she would ever bear.

Landon looked at Reagan's mother. "Is she awake?"

Her mother gave a dainty sniffle. "Off and on."

"Tell you what . . ." Landon gritted his teeth for a moment. "Let her get a good night's sleep, and I'll tell her in the morning."

Mrs. Decker hesitated, and for a moment Landon thought she might reach out and hug him. Instead she clutched her purse more tightly to her waist, her smile falling far short of her eyes. "Thank you. I . . . I couldn't bear to do it."

"I know." Landon put his hand on the woman's shoulder again. "What room is she in? I'll say hi before I go."

The woman told him, and Landon found it easily. A person didn't need to work FDNY long to become familiar with the layout at Mt. Sinai Medical Center. He took slow, quiet steps as he made his way to the side of her bed. A light moan came from her, and Landon clenched his teeth. He couldn't decide which emotion was stronger. His anger at Luke for not trying harder, not flying to New York and forcing her to deal with the tragedies that had nailed them. Or his compassion for Reagan, so young and beautiful and heartbroken.

That probably was how Ashley felt when she came back from Paris.

"Reagan . . ." He took her hand in his and leaned over the bed. "It's Landon Blake."

She rolled her head a few inches in each direction before her eyes opened. For a while she said nothing, only squinted at him. Then another moan sounded from her throat, and she squeezed his hand.

"You're okay, Reagan. The baby's okay. Everything's going to be fine."

She seemed to realize who he was and what was happening. Her eyes grew wider and she made three desperate, pitiful shakes of her head. "Don't . . . tell him."

"Shhhh. I won't." He ran his thumb over her hand, his face two feet from hers and his voice little more than a whisper. "I promise, Reagan. This is your thing."

Her grip on his hand relaxed and her eyelids grew heavy. She nodded and fell back to sleep. Landon released her fingers. "Sleep well, Reagan. I'll talk to you tomorrow."

He didn't see Reagan's mother on the way out of the hospital. In fact, he didn't see much at all. He was too busy wondering about life and how random it could be. When he got outside, he waved for a cab and found a piece of sky between the buildings.

"Why, God . . . ?"

His words blended with the traffic and drifted in the wind. Why September 11? Why Reagan's father? Why Jalen? Why were Luke and Reagan apart when they should be sharing the joy and pain of what had just happened? And why—when he and Ashley had finally found a connection—hadn't he called her much lately? For that matter, why had he come back to New York City at all? The fire department didn't need him as much as Ashley and Cole did.

He still had six months before his year with FDNY was up, and then what? The captain talked about a promotion, but that would never work. Not when he couldn't go an hour without thinking of Ashley and all that awaited him back in Bloomington.

So why hadn't he called her?

A cab pulled up, and Landon slipped into the back. He gave the driver directions and slumped against the seat. The reason was the same now as it had been in those months after September 11. By not calling her, he spent less time looking at flight schedules on the Internet, less time wondering how he'd survive another week without her.

Besides, they still had no commitment, no promises or certainties about sharing their future, and that was his fault, wasn't it? She'd shared everything about her past, and what did he do? Gone back to Manhattan without making his intentions clear. As though somehow that would make their time apart less painful.

They pulled up at a stoplight, and Landon gazed out the window at shops that lined Broadway, barred and locked up for the night. The closest one had a lit sign that read G&G Jewelry.

G&G Jewelry.

The light changed. The cab pulled into the intersection and continued north as Landon was struck by a thought. Life was too short to waste it wondering about timing and distance and proper ways of doing things. Over the next four blocks his mind began to formulate a plan. He would tell Reagan the truth about her condition, and then sometime tomorrow afternoon he would call Ashley and see how quickly she could come to New York.

The next time he saw her he would leave no doubt as to his intentions. Even if the certainty of them would make the next six months unbearable.

CHAPTER EIGHT

REAGAN STARED AT the clock on her hospital-room wall and watched the second hand make its way around, one painfully slow tick at a time.

It was ten-fifteen in the morning, and the nurses said she could hold her baby at noon, after they made sure his temperature was stable. The reports coming in about him were amazing. He'd suffered some stress while Reagan bled, but his little body had lain just the right way against the jagged tear in her uterus, keeping her from bleeding too much and probably saving both their lives.

It was God's plan of course. He wouldn't take both her son and her father in the same year. Not when she'd already lost Luke. God knew how much she could take.

A gentle snoring sound came from the corner of the room, and Reagan looked over her shoulder. Her mother had stayed the night and had probably not fallen asleep until a few hours ago. She was sleeping soundly now, stretched out on a small vinyl couch and covered by a thin layer of white hospital blankets.

Reagan pushed herself up in bed, but the pain made her catch her breath. Whatever they'd done to sew her up, the pain was hard and pulsing. She would have to ask the nurse for more medication if she was going to be strong enough to hold Thomas Luke in a couple of hours.

A flash near the door caught her attention, and she saw Landon Blake enter the room. He was dressed in his uniform and held his hat in his hands. Reagan managed a smile, but she felt her heart skip a beat. How had Landon known she was here? And if he knew about her baby, then had he already told Luke? She silently ordered her questions to wait their turn.

"Hi." He crossed the room, glanced at her mother, and then took the chair closest to her bed. He kept his voice low. "How're you feeling?"

Reagan swallowed and gave a quick shake of her head. "What . . . what're you doing here?"

"I took the call last night." He leaned his elbows on his knees and met her eyes. "You were pretty sick."

She didn't know what to say. Her bed was in the maternity ward, and if he'd been one of the firefighters at the scene he obviously knew about the baby. "My . . . uterus ripped."

"I know." His eyes held hers. "I know everything, Reagan."

Cold fear climbed in bed beside her and she heard her teeth rattle. A conversation would be impossible until she asked him. "Have you talked to Luke?"

"No." Landon bit his lip, but his expression shouted out the question he wasn't asking: Why had she kept the baby a secret? "I haven't told anyone."

Reagan was silent, desperate for the right words. But in the midmorning light of day nothing would make any sense. She dropped her gaze to her hands as another wave of pain passed over her lower abdomen. "Can you get the nurse? It hurts so much."

Landon did as she asked, and ten minutes later, after the nurse had given her another dose of pain medication, they could talk again. This time Landon leaned back in the chair and asked the question she'd been dreading since he'd walked into the room. "Why, Reagan? Why haven't you told him?"

Across the room, Reagan's mother stirred and turned onto her side. Maybe if she woke up, she could help explain the situation. Whenever she and her mother talked about how she'd kept the baby a secret, her silence made sense. But here . . . now . . . "I didn't know what else to do." Her voice was small, and she turned and looked out the window.

"Look—" Landon touched her arm—"I'm here as a friend, not a reporter. You don't have to be afraid to talk to me."

Reagan drew a slow breath through clenched teeth and faced Landon once more. "It was all so complicated, after September eleventh, I mean."

Landon gave a slow nod. "For all of us." He hesitated. "I'm sorry about your father."

"Thanks." Moisture built in Reagan's eyes, and she blinked to keep the tears from spilling onto her cheeks. "Luke and I were so good, Landon. We had plans, intentions. We . . . we set rules so nothing would get in the way of us doing things right."

"Rules?"

"Yes." She sniffed and made her hands into fists. "We promised never to be alone in my apartment, but on September tenth . . ."

Landon's eyes registered the date. "A Monday . . ."

"Opening day for football, I think." Reagan sounded tired, and her insides tightened at the retelling. But she needed to talk about it, needed someone who would listen and care and not think her terrible for what she'd done. "We were supposed to play softball, but Luke didn't want to. Instead we went up to watch some game, I don't know, the Giants and somebody."

"Denver." Sadness tinged Landon's smile. "I watched the game at the firehouse."

"One thing led to another and then . . ." Her voice trailed off.

"That's okay, Reagan, you don't have to tell me." Landon's face was kind and unhurried, without a trace of judgment.

"No, I want to." She slipped her fists behind her and pressed them into her lower back. She'd been an athlete all her life, but no sport had caused her the kind of pain she felt now. A full breath eased out between her clenched teeth. "We were on the couch and my dad called, right in the middle of the worst decision I've ever made in my life. But you know what?"

Landon was silent, waiting.

"I didn't take the call. I figured—" a sound more sob than laugh came from her—"I figured I could call him back the next day. I had all the time in the world, right? What difference would one day make?"

He worked the muscles in his jaw and gave a single shake of his head. "He died the next morning."

Reagan rubbed her fingertips into her brow and paused a moment. If only her father had lived. He'd be here now, holding her hand, promising her everything would work out okay. "I never talked to him again. He—" she sniffed, and this time a tear rolled down her cheek—"he died before I could tell him good-bye."

Landon touched her arm once more, and this time he kept it there. "I'm sorry."

"Yes." She wiped the back of her hand across her face. "Me, too." She reached for the water on her bedside table and took a sip. Afterward she found Landon's eyes again. "I thought his death was God's way of punishing me. You know, that I should hide away at my parents' place and pretend I'd never met Luke Baxter."

"You were in shock." Landon shrugged. "All of us were."

"Did you ever find your friend, the firefighter?"

"Yes." Landon brought his lips together in a hard line. "Found his body almost three months later."

Reagan felt her shoulders slump. "I'm sorry." She looked out the window again. "It was such . . . such an awful time."

"Yes, it was."

"Weeks went by, and all we did was wait." Reagan watched a pigeon land on the windowsill outside. "One shovelful of dirt after another, and still we held out hope. This would be the day they'd find him, buried in an air pocket, hiding safely in the pile of debris waiting to be rescued. Day after day."

"Luke called you, didn't he?"

"Constantly." She leaned back against the pillows and stared at the ceiling. "At first it was part of the punishment. I was the most horrible person on earth, and my father died because of it. No way I was going to allow myself the privilege of talking to Luke. A few months of feeling that way, and I knew it was too late. Luke still called, but I wasn't the girl he'd fallen in love with. I was older and used and pregnant. Look how he treated Ashley when she came home from Paris." She paused. "I convinced myself a guy like Luke wouldn't want anything to do with me."

Landon nodded. "I guess that's when he sort of flipped."

"Yes." She lowered her chin and they locked eyes once more. "I finally got the courage up to call him two months ago. I figured maybe I was wrong, and what if he *did* care, what if he still wanted to work things out?" Her voice fell a notch. "And I thought he had a right to know about the baby."

"That's when you found out about the other girl?"

She nodded. "His mother told me. She said he'd met her on campus, and now they were living together, and that . . . that he'd walked away from his faith, his beliefs. Even his family."

For a while silence fell between them. The series of events since that night in her apartment was like a terrible chain she'd been forced to wear, one that grew link by link and sometimes made it difficult to walk without falling to her knees. The truth about Luke and the possibility that his choices were her fault were a part of the chain that weighed heaviest of all.

A part that at certain moments very nearly strangled her.

"You should tell him, Reagan." Landon clasped his hands and rested his chin on his fingers. "The baby's his, too."

"I know." Reagan covered her eyes with her fingers. "But he's living with someone else. What am I supposed to do? Force him away from this . . . this lifestyle he's chosen? And for what? Child support? A guilt trip?" She let her hands fall and looked at

Landon. "I couldn't do that to him. It's better this way. My name will be the only one on the birth certificate, and he'll never know the difference."

"Unless someone tells him."

Reagan could feel the heat in her cheeks, sense her blood beginning to boil within her. "That's not your place, Landon." Her tone was half terrified, half angry. "You can't."

"Not me, but someone else. People will find out, Reagan. You can't hide a baby forever. And one day your son will want to know."

She breathed hard through her nose and stared at her lap. "I have a lot of decisions to make, but that one is already made. I'm not telling Luke, and I don't want anyone else telling him." The feelings coursing through her were clear for maybe the first time. She was angry with Luke for what he'd done, for moving in with someone else so quickly after their breakup. If he cared that little for her, then he didn't have a right to know. She angled her head and lifted her chin. "The baby's mine."

"Okay." He glanced across the room at Reagan's mother, but she was still sleeping. "I'm not your enemy, Reagan. I won't say a word. But I pray you don't regret this."

"I won't." Her answer was automatic, and she forced herself to relax. Her body ached all over. "Sorry for getting upset."

"It's okay." Landon ran his tongue over his lower lip and cleared his throat. "There's something else I need to say. Something your mother wanted me to tell you."

Reagan stared at him, her face frozen. Somewhere deep in her soul she was sure about something. This couldn't be good news. Otherwise her mother would've told her and not asked Landon to do the talking. She waited, barely breathing.

Landon hung his head for a moment and rubbed the back of his neck. When he looked up, his eyes were deeper than before, and a new sadness shone from them. "You know what happened to you, right? About the torn uterus?"

"Yes." Reagan's mouth was dry. She didn't want to talk medical details with Landon. In thirty minutes they'd bring her baby in and everything would be all right. She shifted in bed and tried not to wince. "I bled pretty bad; at least that's what the nurse said."

"Very bad. We were . . . afraid we'd lose you, Reagan. The baby was sitting just right or we probably would've." When he narrowed his eyes, she had the impression he was trying to brace her for whatever was coming. He sucked in a slow breath. "When the doctors tried to repair your uterus, they found that the tearing was too jagged, the skin too torn apart for stitching."

Too torn apart? The words banged about in Reagan's head like loose bowling balls. What did he mean "too torn apart"? She'd had stitches—that much was obvious because of the pain in her lower abdomen. Also the nurse had told her not to make any sudden movements because of the incision.

Reagan looked at her hands. They were shaking, and her heart had stumbled into a rhythm she didn't recognize. If the tearing was too jagged then— She slammed her thoughts back into the box where they came from. "I . . . had stitches. I know I did."

"Yes." Landon slid closer to her bed and grabbed her hand. "Reagan, they couldn't save your uterus. It was too badly damaged. They had to remove it to save your life." He searched her face, and again he glanced briefly over his shoulder at her mother. "Your mom wanted me to tell you." He bit the inside of his lip and lifted one shoulder. "I'm so sorry, Reagan."

The room was shaking, or maybe it was her. The edges of things looked blurry and undefined, and a black-and-white pattern flashed in her mind every few seconds. The sounds around her dimmed, and all she could hear was the strange, irregular beating of her heart and the incessantly loud whirring of the hospital machines.

What had he said?

They hadn't been able to save her uterus? That couldn't possibly be true. He must've meant something else, that she'd suffered some kind of surgery that the doctors hadn't planned on, or that her recovery time was bound to be longer now. He couldn't have meant that they'd *removed* her uterus, because if they had . . .

Landon was still holding her hand, but he was looking down now, studying a spot on the hospital floor.

"I . . . I don't understand." Reagan hated herself for putting voice to her thoughts, but the truth would come no other way. She couldn't spend another moment guessing about what he meant. "You mean they had to . . . to operate on my uterus?"

Landon brought his head up slowly and gave a subtle shake of his head. "No, Reagan. They couldn't save it. You . . . can't bear any more children."

Reagan grabbed a quick breath and closed her eyes. She'd been standing at the edge of a cliff, and Landon's words pushed her over. Now she was falling, falling fast and hard with no way to stop, no way to catch herself. She hadn't died giving birth to Luke's son, but a part of her had. There would be no siblings for Thomas Luke. No brothers to play ball with. No little girl to play softball or volleyball with. No family gathered around the dinner table. Whenever she might meet the right man and fall in love again, she would never be able to share a child with him.

God, I can't bear this. Why . . . when you know how badly I want a family, Lord? Why?

Daughter, my mercies are new every morning. The night may be long, but morning will always come.

The words were the faintest whisper across her soul, a strangely real answer that placed its arms around Reagan and surrounded her with a peace she hadn't known in months. Nine months.

It was true, wasn't it? Didn't Lamentations make the promise right from Scripture? That though the night might be long and dark, morning would always come because God was nothing if not faithful. Indeed, his faithfulness was one of the greatest things about him.

Still . . .

No more children? Not ever? It was too great a blow to absorb all at once. When she opened her eyes, Reagan squeezed

Landon's hand. The news had shot a gaping hole through her heart, leaving wounds she would have to deal with the rest of her life. But at least her son had survived. God, in all his mercy, had given her that, and for now the baby's place in her life would have to be enough.

Her eyes found Landon's and she patted his fingers. Though she could barely see him through her fresh tears, she managed a smile. "Thanks for telling me."

He brought his other hand up and set it on hers, so that her fingers were sheltered on both sides by his. "Your mom didn't want you hearing it from a stranger."

"Be my friend, Landon. I could use one."

"Okay." Landon cocked his head. "You got it."

One more question stood at the doorway of Reagan's mind, and she couldn't keep it out another minute. "Have . . . have you seen Ashley?"

"Not for a few months." Landon's eyes grew softer. "But soon, I hope."

"You won't tell her?"

For a moment Landon pursed his lips and worked the muscles in his jaw. Then his expression softened. "No, Reagan. I promise. That's gotta be your call."

A shuffling sound near the door made them both turn and look. One of the nurses poked her head in and grinned. "Are you ready for your baby?"

Some of the sadness from their earlier conversation lifted, and Reagan couldn't contain her smile. "Yes . . . please."

She looked at Landon and squeezed his hand once more. "Stay, so you can see him?"

Landon cleared his throat and settled back into his chair. "I wouldn't miss it."

Before the nurse returned, Reagan's mother stirred and brought herself to a sitting position. "What time is it?"

"Almost noon." Reagan let a sad smile cross her features. "You're just in time."

"For what?" Her mother blinked twice, folded back the blankets, stood and stared, her eyes wide. "Reagan, is everything okay? The baby?"

"Everything's fine, Mom." Reagan shot Landon a sad look. "Landon told me about . . . about the surgery."

"Oh, honey." Her mother crossed the room and came alongside Landon. Then she bent over the hospital bed and hugged Reagan. "I'm sorry, sweetheart. So sorry."

"I'll be all right." Reagan's words were muffled in her mother's shoulder. She pulled back then and sniffed so she wouldn't give way to the sobs welling in her heart. "I have my son."

At that moment the nurse walked in pushing a bassinet. Bundled inside was a baby whose face Reagan couldn't quite make out. Landon slid his chair back so the bassinet would fit up against Reagan's bed. She peered inside and could neither speak nor breathe.

Her son was beautiful and tiny and perfectly formed. And the most amazing miracle was this: She could feel him in her soul, feel him growing and putting down roots with a fierce type of love she had never known until this day. The nurse stood by while Reagan's mother lifted Thomas Luke into Reagan's arms, and she cradled him close to her heart.

"Hi, Tommy. I'm your Mama." Reagan nuzzled her nose against his.

"He's so small." Landon peered over Mrs. Decker's shoulder. "Congratulations, Reagan."

"Thank you." She kept her eyes on her newborn son, and somehow she knew this little boy would fill her life with breathtaking moments. His first smile, first steps, first day of school. All of it—every moment—would be an adventure too amazing to miss.

And she knew something else, too. He would be beautiful, like his father. Blond hair . . . blue eyes . . . dimpled chin, and a personality that could hold a roomful of people captive. She knew it as clearly as she could see him now, for the first time in his young life.

The same way her mother and Landon must have known it. Because even as a wrinkled newborn, Thomas Luke looked exactly like his father. And though this moment was the greatest in all her life, though it was being indelibly written second by second across the tablet of her heart, Reagan couldn't help but feel another pang of sadness.

Luke had made his choice, and it didn't include her. Now he would never know this feeling, never hold this precious wonder child in his arms and understand intrinsically a new never-before kind of love. Luke would never know the bond between father and child. And though that truth was heartbreaking, the saddest part of all was this:

Neither would his son.

CHAPTER NINE

LUKE ALMOST KNOCKED her to the ground.

He'd finished his media law class and was barreling out of the building's south entrance when a woman cut in front of him. She was looking down at her cell phone; by the time she glanced up it was too late, and they collided smack into each other. The jolt sent her cell phone skittering across the floor—the phone in one direction, battery in the other.

He held up his hand and touched the woman's arm, making sure she had her balance. "Hey, sorry about th—"

Only then did he realize that the woman was his sister.

Brooke stared at him almost as if she were seeing a ghost. "That's okay." Her eyes narrowed, and she studied him over her shoulder as she picked up the pieces of her phone and slipped the battery back in place. "Luke?"

"Didn't recognize me, huh?" He forced a laugh, but even he could hear how tight and uncomfortable it was.

"Your hair . . . it's so long." She slipped the cell phone into her purse and smoothed a stray piece of hair into the loose bun at the back of her neck. Her voice was nervous and a little too friendly.

"And the mustache . . . the goatee. No, I didn't recognize you at all. How are you?"

"Good . . . real good." He took a step backward and stuck his hands into his jeans pockets. What was Brooke doing on campus? And why, out of all the people at school that day, did he have to run into her? Five months had gone by since he'd seen her or any of his sisters except Ashley. And he hadn't seen her since April.

An awkward silence stood like a wall between them.

Brooke cleared her throat and swung her purse back onto her shoulder. "I'm meeting a friend for lunch. She's a sociology professor."

Luke bit his lip and tried to remember. What was it Ashley had said? After not believing through most of their adult years, had Brooke and Peter bought into the whole God thing, too? Or were they still skeptical? Maybe he was the family's lone doubter these days. He couldn't remember, so he lifted his shoulders. "Sociology professors have it together pretty well."

"Sami Baker's a Christian. Maddie and her little girl are in the same Sunday school class at church."

Luke gritted his teeth and stared at the ground. Okay, so Brooke was a Christian now, too. Fine. He had a class to get to. He was about to wish Brooke well and be on his way, when she interrupted his thoughts.

"Can I make an observation?" Her tone was just short of condescending, the same way she'd talked to him back when they were little kids. Brooke was the oldest, and sometimes their mom had to talk to her about letting up on Luke. About not being his second mother.

He looked up and met his sister's eyes. "What?"

"You say you're doing well, but your eyes tell another story." She took a step closer and lowered her voice. "You walked out on us, Luke, all of us. And you think that's enlightenment? You think that's freethinking?" Anger flashed across her features. "I'll tell you what it is, Luke; it's a bunch of baloney."

The hair stood up on the back of his neck. "Wait a minute. I didn't ask for a lecture. I get enough of that from Dad."

"Come here." Brooke took hold of his arm and led him to a bench a few feet away from the stream of students heading for class. She gave him a light shake. "What has gotten into you, Luke Baxter?"

He jerked out of her grasp. "I could say the same thing to you. Last I knew, you didn't believe in God, and now you go to church? What sort of joke is that, Brooke? Terrorists crash a couple planes into a few buildings, some people die, and all of a sudden God makes sense?" He huffed and crossed his arms. "That's the bunch of baloney right there."

Brooke released a long breath. "I'm sorry. I shouldn't have yelled at you."

"Yeah."

"But look what you're doing, Luke. Don't you see? God's the only thing that *does* make sense now."

Luke held a single finger up. "That's where you're wrong, big sister." He gave a few chuckles. "I used to buy all that narrow-minded junk, but then I found a whole new world. A world where freethinking is a good thing and love can't be defined by rigid rules or an ambivalent God. Relationships are open, minds are open, and life is free to be lived whatever way seems best to you. Now *that*—" he shook his finger—"that makes sense."

"Bad things happen every day, Luke." Brooke's voice was much gentler now, and she reached out and tried to take his hand. When he jerked it away, she didn't give up. "Someone gets cancer, someone gets hit by a car, someone dies in a terrorist attack. Bad things happen, so what sense is there in freethinking? That doesn't bring order to life."

"And God does?"

"Yes." Brooke tossed her hands in the air. "Yes, a hundred times over. If this is all there is, then what's the point? If God doesn't exist, then neither do absolutes. No right or wrong, no moral compass. So why live, Luke? For the experience of it? Surely that sounds shallow, even to a freethinker like you."

"The thing about you God people is you're willing to build your entire life on a belief that can't possibly be proven. You should know that, Brooke. Those were your words, remember? Back before the world turned upside down?"

Brooke flinched at the reminder. "I'm sorry I ever said that." She lost some of her fight, and her gaze held a deeper look than he'd ever seen before. An undeniable something that hadn't been there before September 11. "I was wrong."

"How do you know?" He gritted his teeth. Why was he having this conversation? He was late for economics, and the professor was bound to make a note of the fact. "What makes you so sure, Brooke? When for so many years you didn't believe?"

She gazed up at the trees that marked the quad a few feet away. "The way an elm moves in time with the wind." She turned her head and stared at the sky. "The endless blue of the heavens." She looked straight at him. "The fact that you and I are here today. Out of all the people I might have run into."

He was silent a moment too long.

"You can keep up your New Age act, Luke, keep telling yourself that none of us matters and that living with that . . . that girl you met is the secret to happiness. But one day it'll be too late. People die, life changes, and sometimes regrets are all we have." She stood and straightened her jacket, her eyes never leaving his. "One day you'll have a family, Luke. When you do, when you hold your child for the first time, you'll believe again. And you'll know just how much your distance is killing Mom and Dad."

Luke's questions were gone, and in their place anger jabbed at him. He stood and gave his sister's arm a quick pat. "Thanks for the lecture, Sis. See ya around."

Without looking back, without apologizing for his behavior or giving her statement a minute's consideration, he spun and jogged to class. It wasn't until he was seated in his chair that he realized there was something he'd forgotten to ask Brooke. He wasn't sure why it mattered. After all, *family* was a loose term, and sharing a bloodline didn't necessarily give people a lifelong bond. At least that's what the guys at the Freethinkers Alliance had told him.

Still, he was suddenly desperate to know—desperate enough that if he could be sure he'd catch her, he would run back across campus to find Brooke and ask her if they ever figured out what was wrong with Maddie.

🌿

Ashley boarded the American Airlines jet just before seven on June 10.

In the past few days Landon had left her two messages, but his answering machine picked up each time she tried to call him back. Then Travelocity E-mailed her with a last-minute discount round-trip to La Guardia. That's when the idea hit her.

She'd go to Manhattan, take her paintings, and surprise Landon all at the same time. She hadn't told him yet about the call from the gallery, or that they actually wanted to sell three of her paintings. But this way she could get to the city, check in at her hotel, and drop by his station. If he wasn't working, she'd go to his apartment. She'd never been there, but she had the address, and any cabdriver would know how to find it.

Her parents had offered to take Cole, and now, forty-eight hours later, she was boarding an airplane.

Ashley made her way down the aisle and found her spot. A window seat. Good. A window would give her time to think, time to gaze at the heavens and feel a little closer to God. Time to wonder what he was doing by allowing her this opportunity in New York. And time to think about Landon and how good it would feel to see him again.

Ashley had E-mailed photos of her paintings to Ms. Wellington at the gallery. She'd chosen Ashley's favorite three paintings—favorites, that is, among those she was willing to part with.

"They're perfect," the woman told her. "I can't wait to see them in person."

The first was of her parents' house—not the one she'd painted that freezing winter day when Landon showed up and surprised her. But another one bathed in cool autumn light and anchored by an American flag billowing in the breeze.

The second was one of several she'd painted of Irvel, this one with Irvel gazing out the patio window of the Sunset Hills Adult Care Home. In her hand was a china cup of peppermint tea, and in her eyes, a longing for a man who would never again return to her. Something about the lines on Irvel's face, the pinched eyes gazing beyond the Sunset Hills yard, made her look almost lucid. As though she actually knew the truth about Hank just for a moment, and knew, too, that one day they'd be together again.

The third painting was of Landon, one of a few she'd painted after his time at Ground Zero. She'd seen pictures, watched the news, studied the photographs in magazines during that time. Several of her recent pieces depicted intimate looks at the people who had helped remove the piles of debris. A few times she'd given a firefighter Landon's face, his lanky frame, and sharp blue eyes. This painting was one of those, with Landon sitting on a park bench, head down, while workers carried on at a distant Ground Zero scene.

"Americana," the woman from the art gallery had called them. And they were—though years earlier Ashley never would have figured herself to paint anything but impressions. The funny thing was, in the months after taking the job at Sunset Hills, after living through the events of September 11, after finding her heart and faith in God again, all she wanted to paint were portraits of America.

Ashley settled back and gazed out the window. She was less worried about Landon now that he'd called twice in the past few days. He was obviously busy, and maybe he still saw their situation the way he'd seen it back when he was working Ground Zero. What was it he had said when they finally saw each other after that awful time? That he couldn't call her; wasn't that it? Otherwise he would've been on the next plane home to Bloomington.

She had no reason to think he felt any different. Yes, he was free to find other friends and even date or fall in love. But Ashley remembered the way he'd looked at her that night last summer when she'd told him the truth about what happened in Paris. She'd remember the look in his eyes as long as she lived.

No, Landon wasn't busy with another woman. He was just busy. Twelve-hour shifts, department softball games, and volunteer work at the hospital. An hour each day for jogging and weight lifting. He probably had time for little else but sleep and cleanup. And if she knew Landon, he was probably thinking about her at least as often as she thought of him.

The truly crazy thing was that she hadn't seen it sooner—how much she cared about him. She'd always thought he was too safe and structured, that he wouldn't be happy unless he had a nice little church wife, someone who volunteered for the women's bazaar and baked casseroles for the monthly potluck.

Yes, Ashley loved God now. In fact, he'd been her mainstay for nearly a year. But she'd never be a conservative little church wife. Not when she'd rather sit on a hillside and create magic on canvas.

"Something to drink?"

The flight attendant's voice caught Ashley's attention, and she turned from the window. "Water, please." She looked at her watch. She would arrive in La Guardia and go find Landon at the station. That would surprise him, and then she could take him to dinner and celebrate the fact that her paintings were going to be shown to the public.

Ashley took a small cup of water from the flight attendant and drank it in four long sips. The flight wasn't half full, and she had no seatmates, which was a good thing. She didn't want to share this moment with a stranger—or anyone else, for that matter. No one but Landon Blake. He'd believed in her art as far back as she could remember. Even before Paris, when they were juniors in high school.

"Your paintings are so good, Ash," he'd told her back then. He'd been admiring a work she'd done for an art class. "You'll be famous one day for sure."

Funny how she had blocked out much of her childhood, how she'd been a black sheep among the Baxter faithful. Even images of Paris were dim at best, relegated to the basement of her memory. But the image of Landon studying her class assignment and assuring her she'd be famous one day . . . that was as real and vivid as it was the day it happened.

She thought about Cole. She and her little boy were close now, and that was Landon's doing, too. His reminder that her son was the good that had come from Paris helped Ashley change her mind-set about her past. These days she enjoyed Cole so much, she'd even considered bringing him on the trip. But Manhattan was no place for a little boy, not when Ashley had business to do.

A yawn slipped, and she closed her eyes. She'd gotten up at three this morning to catch her flight, and a nap would be wonderful. She stared out the window at the distant, towering clouds. Who was she kidding? Sleep wasn't even a tiny possibility, not with her body trembling in anticipation. Not because she was about to realize a lifelong dream.

But because she was going to share it all with Landon Blake.

CHAPTER TEN

THE PAST TEN DAYS had been one miracle after another.

Reagan had brought Thomas Luke home four days after delivering him, and though it took another few days before she was able to get around, she was savoring every moment with him. The nickname she'd given him in the hospital stuck: Tommy. It suited him, now that she'd gotten to know him.

She woke up that morning feeling better than she had all week, and that's when the idea hit her. She called Landon at the fire station and asked if he could take a break late that afternoon.

"Sure." Landon's voice was kind, the way it was every time she'd talked to him since Tommy was born. "What's up?"

"It's a beautiful day, summer feels like it's here, and my baby hasn't had a walk in Central Park yet." She paused. "Wanna go?"

"Sure." She could sense Landon's smile over the phone lines. "I wouldn't miss it."

They planned to meet at five o'clock, Landon's lunch hour. She would bring Tommy's fold-up stroller, and they'd walk as far into the park as Reagan could handle. Her abdomen was still sore, but the doctor had cleared her for walking. As long as she didn't overdo it.

"Reagan, are you sure you want to go?" Her mother came around the corner and anchored her hands on her hips. "The baby's not even two weeks old."

"It's eighty-eight degrees out, Mother." She dressed her tiny son in a blue, one-piece, terry-cloth outfit and wrapped a lightweight flannel blanket around him. "I'll be with Landon; we'll be fine."

"I could come to help with the baby."

"No, Mother." Reagan smiled. "I'm fine by myself."

Over the course of her pregnancy, she'd watched mothers with newborns and wondered how she'd feel when they placed her infant in her arms. Nervous and unsure, she figured. Afraid she'd drop the baby or hurt him with some kind of clumsy move. But now that she had Tommy, now that she'd cared for him and cradled him and sung to him practically around the clock for the past week and a half, she was more at ease than she'd ever thought possible.

The only thing more natural than being with her newborn son would have been sharing the experience with Luke. But that was out of the question, and now that her initial adjustment to motherhood had begun, she tried not to think about him as much.

Her mother sighed and dropped to the closest chair. "It's strange, Reagan, watching you with a baby, knowing you're in charge of him." Her light chuckle drew a smile from Reagan. "I guess I don't quite feel like a grandma yet."

Reagan crossed the room, Tommy nestled in the crook of her arm, and kissed her mother on the forehead. "We'll be fine. Thanks for worrying." She straightened and gave her mother another smile. "It makes me feel loved."

"Don't ever doubt that." Her mom reached out and took hold of Reagan's wrist. "Be careful, honey. I mean it. The city's a dangerous place."

Until the moment she left the apartment, Reagan kept up the dialogue, assuring her mother that they'd be fine. She carried

Tommy down the elevator in a portable car seat, which would snap into the stroller frame once they arrived at Landon's station. Over her shoulder she had a diaper bag with more than enough baby supplies.

The bag was a gift from Landon, blue with tiny firefighter helmets on it. Reagan was glad for the chance to use it now, so he could see how much she appreciated it. She hailed a cab and struggled to buckle the car seat in, while the driver put the stroller in the trunk. After a minute or so she figured it out, then slid in beside her baby. She gave directions to the cabdriver and let her gaze settle on her tiny son.

He was sleeping, his fists tight, arms stretched out by his sides. How much easier these early days as a mother had been because of Landon. Though her mother was available to help her with the practical part of mothering an infant, Landon was there to hear her heart. He was the friend she'd needed, and she thanked God often for his recent part in her life.

The cab pulled away and headed south toward Landon's station. Sometimes she wondered if she felt more than friendship for him. Whenever her thoughts veered in that direction, she always steered them straight again. Landon belonged to Ashley, and he always would. He talked about her enough to make that clear. Besides, it wasn't Landon she longed for. She enjoyed his company, enjoyed calling him at the station and chatting with him between his calls. Being with him, talking to him, reminded her of Bloomington and made her ache for that time in her life.

But Landon, as good as he was, wasn't Luke Baxter.

She looked out the window and caught a street sign. Five more blocks and they'd be there. Her eyes found Tommy again and her heart sank a notch. No, it wasn't Landon Blake she wanted. Not hardly. It was Luke . . . the way he used to be.

Sometimes her desire to call him and tell him about the baby was so strong she had to sit on her hands to keep from dialing his parents' number. But usually the feeling was fleeting. Luke had changed. He was no longer the boy she'd known and loved, and so she never gave in to her feelings. Deep in her heart she knew she never would.

Because of that, Landon's friendship was a welcome diversion, a way of passing the time and knowing that someday she would connect again with a man. Someone kind and gentle, a man of faith with a deep love for little Tommy. Someone God himself would bring into her life.

And until then, she had this. Friendship with a man who neither judged nor threatened her. A man who had kept his promise by not telling the Baxters about her baby. All of which was more than she could've hoped for.

The cab pulled up in front of Landon's station, and she set about the ordeal of getting out and assembling the stroller. The instructions had shown that if she pressed a red lever, the frame would pop into place. Instead, something was stuck. With Tommy still buckled into the backseat and the driver glancing at his watch in the front, Reagan pushed the lever three times and then banged the stroller wheels on the ground.

Her veins felt hot with the rush of adrenaline.

The stroller had worked back at the apartment when Reagan practiced with it. But now . . . her mother was right; she shouldn't have taken this first trip without someone to help her. Now her baby was alone with the cabbie, and at any minute the man could take off. She'd never see her baby again, and there'd be no time to get the license-plate number, no way of knowing who the driver was or where he'd gone with her son—

Reagan's heart pounded, and she considered jerking Tommy out and setting his carrier on the sidewalk. But what if the cab pulled away and someone ran up and grabbed her baby? Wild thoughts shot across her heart and fell in an irrational heap.

She was about to flag down a stranger when she felt someone behind her.

"Need help?" Landon smiled and reached out for the stroller frame. "I saw you pull up."

Of course. Why hadn't she realized that? She was just a few

yards from the front of the fire station. She exhaled and tried to still her shaking hands. "I . . . I was about to give up." Reagan's cheeks were hot from the panicky moment. "I still have a lot to learn."

"One of the guys at the station has this kind for his baby. It's easy . . . watch." He gave the frame a quick jolt as he pressed the red lever with the toe of his work boot. The stroller snapped open and locked into place. "Voilà!"

"Show-off." She laughed as she paid the driver.

Landon unbuckled Tommy's car seat from the cab and popped the carrier into the stroller frame. He took the diaper bag from Reagan and nodded at it. "Nice choice on the bag."

The muscles at the base of Reagan's neck relaxed. "It's Tommy's favorite."

"*Tommy*, huh?"

"Yep." Reagan came up alongside Landon and stared at her still-sleeping son. "He can be Thomas Luke when he's older. Right now he looks like a Tommy, don't you think?"

Landon studied the baby for a moment and grinned. "Actually, now that you say it, he does."

Reagan drew a settling breath, and her heart rate returned to normal. She'd read a dozen books about parenting a newborn, but all of them referred to the job as a partnership. Teamwork. The way a pitcher and a catcher worked together in a softball game. One parent doing the feeding, the other restocking diapers; one parent getting the car seat from the cab, the other opening the stroller. Her anxiety from a moment ago reminded her how much she had yet to learn about *single* parenting.

She hugged her arms around her waist and shrugged at Landon. "You ready?"

"Not yet." He motioned his head toward the fire station. "I need to check out."

Reagan followed him into the station. A few firefighters were playing cards at a beat-up picnic table in the middle of the room. She held up her hand and flashed them an easy smile. As much time as she'd spent on an athletic field, she was always comfortable around a roomful of guys. "Hi."

Landon pushed the stroller up to the table. "Guys, this is Reagan." He tilted his head toward her.

Each of them lowered his cards and nodded at her. One of the guys stood and held out his hand. "I'm Doug, Landon's partner."

"Hi." For a fraction of a moment she wondered if the guys thought she was Landon's girl. It almost seemed they were seeing if she measured up.

"Cute baby." Doug peered over the table and into the stroller. Then he raised an eyebrow and shot a look at Landon. "You know this little guy?"

"Yep." Landon reached into the stroller and ran his finger over the baby's blond eyebrows. "This is little Tommy." He put his arm around Reagan and gave her a side hug. "We worked on Reagan the other night."

"Oh, the one who calls here sometimes." A knowing expression filled Doug's eyes. "You two were, uh, friends back in Indiana, right?"

"Right." Reagan smiled again, but this time she was certain Landon's partner had the wrong idea about the two of them. She took a few seconds to replay the conversation in her mind. Maybe she'd imagined the implication in the firefighter's voice. After her little freak-out by the cab, anything was possible. She swallowed her concerns and turned to Landon. "Ready?"

He glanced at the guys. "We're taking a walk in the park." He pulled the stroller back from the table and turned it toward the front door. "I'll have the pager if you need me."

Doug nodded. "Okay. Take care of your little guy there."

Reagan took a step toward Landon and stopped. *Your little guy?* Thomas Luke was *not* Landon's little guy. Reagan started to say something, to assure the guys at the station that the baby was hers alone, but she stopped. What would it hurt, just this once? To pretend she actually had a Landon Blake of her own, someone to admire her baby and help her with the stroller and take walks with her?

Besides, the last thing Reagan wanted to imply was that Landon didn't matter to them. She sighed, fell in place beside him, and headed toward the park. The whole notion was probably just her crazy imagination.

That, and a case of hormones gone wild.

CHAPTER ELEVEN

ASHLEY ARRIVED AT THE fire station at ten minutes after five. She'd checked into her hotel and left two of her paintings in the room. It was a simple place with a partial courtyard view in the Chelsea area, far from the heartbeat of the city. But it might as well have been a penthouse suite overlooking Central Park.

She'd finally arrived, finally been given the chance to showcase her art in a Manhattan gallery. And now she was about to show Landon the piece she'd painted of him at Ground Zero. She could already feel his arms around her, sense his glowing approval of her newest work. She couldn't wait to breathe in his excitement when he learned that her artwork would be sold right there in the city.

The cab stopped half a block from Landon's station. She wanted to walk the last fifty yards, take a few moments to inhale the city's life and passion and energy, soak it in so she could believe it. She climbed out of the cab and caught a glimpse of the sun through the trees and tall buildings. The day was perfect, warm and breezy, without the humidity that was bound to come in the next few months.

She used careful hands to lift the oversized leather art case from the trunk of the cab. Then she paid the driver and positioned herself square in the middle of the sidewalk. She was here; she really was. In the case was the painting of Landon, and in her heart, the chance of a lifetime.

Should she throw her arms out and twirl around, shouting her thanks to the heavens, letting anyone who saw her know that this was a moment she'd waited for her whole life? Ashley made a partial turn and saw the busy, distracted looks on the faces of most people. No, she'd keep the moment private, a celebration between her and God. And, in a few minutes, Landon.

Her skirt fell almost to her ankles, and her cotton tank top left her bare arms goose-bumped from the thrill of it. She fairly floated to the station, stopping just outside. It was a simple brick building, older than most around it, but it was the place where Landon had worked that past year, the place where Jalen had worked.

For a moment her enthusiasm dimmed.

The men she was about to meet had suffered much this past year. She would do well to keep her excitement contained, at least at first. Her fingers wrapped more tightly around the handles of her leather portfolio, and she drew in a slow breath. *Okay, God, lead the way. Let me know if Landon's been missing me the way I've missed him.*

She pushed open the door and saw half a dozen uniformed men playing cards at a picnic table. Almost at the same time, she caught a row of framed portraits of firefighters along one wall. Each of them contained a name and two dates.

One of them had to be Jalen. Ashley wondered which one.

A man at the table cleared his throat, stood, and gave her an approving smile. "Hello. Can we help you?" His tone suggested he was more than willing.

She flashed them a grin and positioned her case in front of her. "Yes. I'm looking for Landon Blake."

"Uh . . ." He shot a confused look at two men beside him. "He's taking a walk."

Across the table, a stocky firefighter looked over his shoulder. "You just missed him. They were pushing a stroller, headed for the park."

The first man kicked his stocky colleague under the table and frowned at him. Then he caught Ashley's eyes again and forced a smile. "You got an appointment with him?"

Ashley set the portfolio down on the floor and let it fall against her legs. What in the world were they talking about? Landon was on a walk with a baby? Whose baby? "Landon's out walking a baby?"

The men at the table exchanged a series of uneasy glances. The first firefighter stepped away from the others and approached Ashley. "The girl's his friend." The man shrugged, and something in his eyes all but shouted pity. "She came with the baby, and they . . . they went to the park. He was pushing the stroller." A tension-packed pause pierced the moment. "He'll be back in half an hour."

"What girl?" Ashley's head spun, and she ran her tongue along the inside of her lips. Landon—*her* Landon—was walking in the park with a girl and her baby? Whatever for? And how come Landon hadn't mentioned his friend to her? Nausea closed in around her. Was she going to have to excuse herself and find a bathroom? The surprise was going all wrong, and so far none of what the man was saying made sense.

She pinched the bridge of her nose and gave a few quick shakes of her head. "Has . . . has she been here before?" Ashley hated herself for asking, but she couldn't catch her breath until she knew what this craziness was about. When was Landon going to come bounding around the corner, sweep her into his arms, and kiss her the way she'd been dying to be kissed since their last time together?

The man took a step back toward the men at the table and shot them a nervous look. "She's called, right, guys?"

A few of them nodded.

"Definitely," one of them said. "Almost every day."

The man on his feet looked at Ashley again. "This was her first visit to the station." He crossed his arms. "The baby's young, a few weeks old."

Her stomach pain doubled. A few weeks old? That couldn't mean that . . . Landon never would've . . . her thoughts wouldn't stay together, and the floor beneath her felt like quicksand.

Before she could ask another question, the man held out his hand. "I'm Landon's partner, Doug." He hesitated. "And you're . . . ?"

She found her voice and tried to still her trembling fingers. "Ashley." She gave the man's hand a delicate shake and then took a step backward. This was the moment when Doug's eyes were supposed to light up in recognition, the time when he should've put his arm on her shoulder and grinned at her, told her that he'd heard so much about her and had always wanted to meet her.

But instead he only stared at her, his expression a mix of sympathy and interest. Ashley shifted her gaze to the others at the table, but they'd resumed their card game. Not one of them acted as if they'd ever heard of her. She swallowed hard and managed a quiet, disbelieving laugh. "I . . . I don't mean to pry, but whose baby are we talking about?"

The dark shadow that fell over the man's eyes told her everything she needed to know. She wanted to run, tear out of the building before this . . . this partner of Landon's could voice the truth. But she was stuck, her feet frozen in place. Her question had placed her in front of a firing squad, and now she could do nothing but wait for the bullets.

Doug lowered his brow and pursed his lips. He exhaled and gave a single sideways nod of his head. "I . . . I don't think Landon knew about him until we made the call."

"The call?" She was buying time, desperate for some logical answer.

"The young woman nearly died. She began to bleed, and we

answered the call. Landon knew her, and, well, he didn't say much but I got the feeling the two of them were close."

"And that's when he found out about the baby?"

"That's what he said."

The pieces didn't fit together. "What . . . what makes you think the baby's his?" Ashley could feel the rifles aimed straight at her heart, feel her hands tied to a post as she faced the squad of executioners.

Doug looked at the floor for a moment and then lifted his eyes to hers. "He just told us . . . a few minutes ago." He glanced at the other firefighters, none of whom were paying attention to their conversation. "He told us Tommy was his little guy."

The bullets hit then.

Ashley slumped as his words ripped their way through her heart and soul. Was she dreaming? Could she be standing here in Landon's fire station hearing the news that he had a baby? A newborn?

She grabbed two jagged breaths and opened her mouth, but no words came.

"Ashley, follow me." Doug closed the gap between them and led her by the arm into the next room. There he directed her to a worn sofa, and he sat beside her. "You don't look too good."

Heat radiated through her body, but she began to shiver at the same time. A fine layer of wetness broke out across her forehead, and she bit the inside of her lip. "He . . . he didn't tell me."

Doug's voice was kind, gentle. "Are you his girlfriend?"

The question stumped Ashley. They'd never made any real commitment, had they? Oh, they'd talked about being together at the end of his year, but he'd made her no promises. She hadn't wanted any.

She blinked and noticed that her eyes were dry. "No." She was too shocked to cry, as though the news had numbed a part of her. "We . . . we're friends. I just thought . . ."

Suddenly she couldn't sit with the stranger another moment. She didn't want his sympathy or anyone else's. Disappointment had knocked on her door before. Even a disappointment as devastating as this couldn't change the reason she was in Manhattan. Let Landon live his private life, and she would live hers.

She stood and nodded to Landon's partner. "Thank you." Her breathing had been shallow and uneven, but now she exhaled and some of the shock drained away. She brought her fingers to her face and dabbed at her forehead. It was cooler than before. "I have to go. I have an appointment uptown."

Doug followed her to the front door, mumbling something about waiting for Landon to come back, maybe talking to him herself. To each suggestion she shook her head, and when she was a few feet outside on the sidewalk, she held up her hand. "I don't want to see him."

Regret painted the man's features. "Should I tell him you stopped by?"

"No." Ashley gave a quick shake of her head. "Don't tell him a thing." She picked up her portfolio, walked through the door, and took four long strides toward the curb. "Taxi!" She waved her arm, and a yellow cab pulled over. Without turning around, she slipped her bag into the trunk, laid it carefully on its side, and slid into the backseat.

The cabbie shot her a look in the rearview mirror. "Where to?"

Ashley wanted to give him the location of her hotel, but she couldn't force out the words. Landon was walking in the park with some girl and a baby—a baby he'd fathered some nine months ago. With the cabdriver waiting, she did the math in her head and realized that he must've been with her those first few weeks after September 11, back when he'd rushed to New York City to find Jalen.

After spending the entire summer with her and Cole.

Memories tried to play in her mind, but she wouldn't let them. Not when she was still trying to make sense of everything she'd just learned. This was supposed to be one of her greatest days ever. The day when she would make her art debut in New York City and be reunited with Landon.

"Lady, where to?" The cabdriver's voice was short and frustrated.

"Umm . . ." She didn't want to be anywhere but here, spying at the front door of the fire station until Landon and his . . . his *girlfriend* returned with their baby. She had to see it for herself, had to see him cross the street pushing a baby stroller, had to see the way he looked at this girl, whoever she was.

She leaned forward and met the driver's impatient eyes. "Could you flip around and park on the other side of the road, maybe twenty feet down from here?"

The driver raised a single eyebrow. "This ain't a park bench, lady; it's a cab. Where to?"

"Look—" Ashley held up her hands. They had to get away from the fire-station door before Landon returned. "I'm serious. You can keep the meter running."

The driver shook his head. "Craziest place in the world." Then with a quick glance over his shoulder, he worked the cab back into traffic, made a right at the next street, and after a few turns pulled up along the opposite curb, just south of the fire station. "This work for you?" He looked at her in the mirror again.

"Perfect."

Ashley pressed her fists into her stomach and watched the stream of people heading toward them. Her heart beat faster than before, and she wondered at her sanity. What if he didn't come back for an hour? And how would she feel if somehow he saw her—watching him from the backseat of a cab?

She slid lower in the seat and narrowed her gaze. *Lord, how could this happen? I thought he was . . . I thought the two of us . . .* Her silent questions were too raw, too fresh, for her to consider hearing an answer. If Landon could lie to her about this, then how could they share even a friendship? She pulled her sunglasses from her bag and slipped them onto her face. She couldn't be his friend; it was that simple. Friendship was based on trust, and obviously whatever Landon had gone through after coming to New York, he hadn't been willing to share it with her.

Had he thought she'd never find out? Never learn that he'd fathered a child in his shock and grief after September 11? And what about Cole? How careless had she been letting her son grow close to Landon without knowing everything about him, without guessing that maybe he'd found someone else in Manhattan?

Come on, Landon, show your face. Let me see what you've done.

Another minute passed, and then she saw him. The girl beside him was tall and blonde, a scarf around her hair and dark glasses perched on her face. The sight of them together cut off her oxygen and made it impossible to inhale. Landon was pushing the stroller, smiling at the girl, looking every bit the proud father. Just like Doug had said.

"How much longer, lady?" The driver tapped on the meter. "Time's money."

"Wait!" She hissed the word and waved her hand at the driver.

Landon and his friend moved with the flow of traffic toward the crosswalk. As they did, Ashley got a better look at the woman. Her face held something familiar, something in her cheekbones and tall stature. The closer they came, the more certain she was that she'd seen the girl before.

Then, in a rush of recognition, Ashley's hand flew to her mouth.

It was impossible. Landon never would have . . .

The young woman looked like Reagan Decker—Luke's girlfriend.

Ashley lowered her glasses and stared at the girl, the way she held her head and smiled at Landon, the swish of her long blonde hair and the graceful way she kept pace with him.

No question about it, the woman was Reagan.

And as Reagan and Landon pushed the baby stroller across the street and headed into the fire station, a truckload of details landed squarely on Ashley's shoulders. The last time she'd seen Reagan had been at the bus station in Bloomington, the place where Luke had bid Reagan good-bye.

At that point they knew Reagan's father was missing, trapped in the rubble, and as a way of helping her get home, Luke had taken her to the station. The same place she herself had taken Landon.

Her head ached, and the cabdriver was tapping his steering wheel. "How much longer, lady?"

Ashley summoned all her strength and rattled off the intersection for her hotel. The driver sighed hard and jerked the cab into traffic once more. Ashley barely noticed. She was too busy putting together puzzle pieces that finally formed a complete picture.

Reagan and Landon had ridden the same bus to Manhattan that terrible day. In fact, they must've spent the night together either on the road or at one of the dozen bus stops between Indiana and New York. The two of them had probably sat together, sharing their pain and comforting each other.

Who could better understand what the two of them were going through than each other? Ashley stared out the cab window and tried to remember a single time when Landon had mentioned Reagan. There had been none. Surely after the long bus ride the two of them would have made a plan to stay in touch. So why hadn't Landon talked about it with Ashley? What reason did he have to hide the fact, unless . . .

Her mind sped around a blind corner and ran square into another set of facts, facts that until that moment had never had anything to do with Landon. After saying good-bye to Reagan at the bus stop, Luke had tried every day to contact her. Twice a day, sometimes three times a day.

But not once had she taken his call. Not one single time.

Ashley had seen Reagan and Luke together. They seemed made for each other. In fact before September 11, the Baxter girls had agreed that sometime in the next few years they would marry. So why—in the wake of her most devastating loss—would Reagan cut Luke out of her life?

And what about Landon? He hadn't called her from Ground Zero, had he? Not once. And when he came back, he'd been most excited that she'd been to church. What was it they'd said that last afternoon before he left for New York again? That there would be no promises; wasn't that it?

Still, she never would have guessed that he'd . . . he'd been with another woman. And Reagan Decker?

The past was as clear as if she were seeing it played on a movie screen. Landon and Reagan must have gotten close on the bus trip to New York. Then, once there, they'd found comfort with each other and somehow . . . one thing had led to another.

Landon had just come from Ashley, so he must've been confused, but clearly after being intimate with Reagan he'd been unwilling to call Ashley. The two of them were probably together several times a week—whenever he wasn't working at Ground Zero. And naturally Reagan wouldn't take Luke's calls. How could she, when she was sleeping with another man?

Again Ashley's stomach hurt. When Landon came back to Bloomington after finding Jalen's body, he must've been unsure if what he'd found with Reagan was real or part of the sorrow and tragedy of September 11. Maybe he didn't know until he got back to New York that Reagan was pregnant. In fact, he mustn't have known. Wasn't that what his partner said? He didn't know about the baby until Reagan's emergency delivery.

The two must've had a falling-out before he returned home to Indiana.

Ashley's defenses fell like scales from her eyes. Landon was in love with someone else, with Luke's old girlfriend. The whole picture was sharp enough to pierce her heart, and for the first time since learning about Landon's baby, she felt the burning of tears in her eyes. No wonder he hadn't promised her anything before he returned to Manhattan.

She was barely aware of her actions as the cab pulled up in front of her hotel and she paid the driver. She grabbed her art case, found her way to the room, and dropped into a chair that faced the window. The hotel was boxed in by buildings, the kind that killed her creativity.

Gone were the energy and excitement, the thrill of being a

part of the life and culture of New York City. She would meet with the gallery director, sign over her paintings, and fly home. Cole needed her, and she needed him. Him and her parents and the rest of her family.

She remembered a time when those very people had been her enemies, the ones who thought her strange and different and determined to live life on her own terms. But in the past year they'd become her greatest support. She dug her elbows into her thighs and let her head fall into her hands. What would they say now? When she told them that Landon was with Reagan Decker? And what about Luke?

A shiver ran down her spine.

Her brother had been through so much this past year. First realizing that prayers weren't always answered with a yes. And then losing Reagan, and walking away from all he'd believed in. What would this blow do to him? Ashley couldn't think about it.

All her mind would allow were thoughts of Landon and Reagan and the stroller they were pushing. Their smiles and casual way of looking so much like a couple.

And how very much she was going to miss him.

CHAPTER TWELVE

THEY WERE GATHERED AROUND the Baxter table, and Kari had positioned Jessie's high chair between herself and Ryan. Cole ate across from them, seated beside his grandmother. At four years old he handled his own dinner quite well.

They'd made progress on several aspects of the coming wedding, and now they were at a bridge in the conversation.

"I feel out of touch." Kari set her fork down and pushed her plate back. "The wedding's taken up so much time, I've barely kept up with everyone else."

"Ashley's in New York; you know that, right?" Her mother smiled from across the table. She'd made a Spanish casserole tonight, and the entire house smelled like melted cheese and tamale sauce.

"New York?" Ryan was cutting a chunk of chicken for Jessie. He looked at Kari, eyes wide. "You didn't tell me."

"I just found out this morning." Kari grinned. "A gallery wanted three of her pieces. They're going to put them up on consignment and see how they do."

"Mommy's gonna be famous!" Cole raised his fork in the air. "Right, Grandma?"

"Right, buddy." She tousled his hair. "And one day we'll see her paintings in a museum. Just like we've always said."

"Right!" Cole nodded and returned to his dinner.

"I had no idea she'd gotten a break." Ryan looked from the elder Baxters back to Kari. "You're serious?"

"Yep." Kari dabbed a napkin at Jessie's chin. "She has the appointment Monday morning."

"I always knew she'd make it. Her work is amazing." Ryan gave a few thoughtful nods. "Good for her. And let me guess—" he winked—"she'll see Landon while she's there."

"Landon's my friend!" Cole chewed a mouthful of food. "Mommy said she'd tell him hi for me. She took a picture of him."

"A picture?" Ryan looked from Cole to Kari's parents.

"A painting." Kari's mother smiled at Cole and patted his hand. "It's one of her latest pieces. Landon at Ground Zero, sitting on a park bench. It's—" she paused and shook her head—"it's breathtaking."

"So I take it they'll see each other." Kari's heart lifted like a kite on a spring day. How long had Ashley and Landon cared for each other without admitting it?

Her parents exchanged a knowing look, one that spoke volumes. John anchored his elbows on the table. "I'd be shocked if she didn't."

"Hey, how's Maddie doing?" Kari angled her head. She hadn't gotten an update on her niece in weeks.

"Brooke says she seems okay. No fevers for a while now." Kari's father took another bite.

"What about Erin? We stopped our counseling meetings, but everything seems fine." Kari sat back in her chair and watched Ryan feed little Jessie. Her daughter was nineteen months old now, walking everywhere, and looking less like a baby. Without question, Ryan loved her as much as if she were his own.

Her mother stood and cleared her plate. She looked back at Kari from the kitchen. "She and Sam have finalized their moving plans. They'll set out the morning after Labor Day so they won't miss our annual picnic at the lake."

Kari had known her sister would be moving. They'd made the plans almost a year ago, but with the terrorist attacks, the economy took a hit, and the company that wanted Sam in Austin, Texas, delayed their plans. Kari bit her lip. Erin still didn't want to move, but the last time they'd talked she was at least committed to making her marriage work. Whether in Bloomington or Austin.

"That soon, huh?" Ryan reached for Jessie's sippy cup and handed it to her. She took it, popped it in her mouth, and held it to one side, her eyes glued on Ryan. Kari grinned at her daughter's trademark sideways-drinking. They liked to say it was because she didn't want to miss anything.

Kari's father helped himself to another spoonful of the casserole. "Erin's Realtor found them a house in a good neighborhood."

"What about our wedding?" Kari cleared the other plates and joined her mother in the kitchen.

"They'll fly back for the weekend." Her mother motioned to the sink. "Set them there, dear. I'll clean up later."

Kari did as her mom said, and they returned to the table. "It'll be strange, having them so far away."

"The way it feels with Luke." Her mother lowered her gaze to the table for a moment, and when she looked up, weariness seemed suddenly etched in her expression. "I'm sorry. I shouldn't have said that."

Kari wanted to add something, but her throat was too thick. She might've been out of touch because of her approaching wedding, but things were worse with Luke. They all knew it.

"It's okay." Ryan set Jessie's sippy cup back on the table and took her from the high chair. She reached her arms around his neck and rested her head on his shoulder. "I think about Luke all the time. How is he?"

Kari caught her father's expression, and it cut her heart like a knife. "Not good, right? That's what Ashley said before she left."

Her father curled his fingers into fists and held his breath for a few seconds. "The last time I saw him he told me to stay out of his life." He exhaled hard and gave a shake of his head. "He's made some . . . very poor choices."

"*Poor*, meaning . . . ?" Kari looked from him to her mother and back again.

"It's not something I can talk about." Her father gritted his teeth and relaxed his hands. His shoulders slumped some as he took hold of her mother's fingers. "He needs as many prayers as you can send his way."

"He's still living with the girl from school?" Ryan soothed his hand over the back of Jessie's head, running his fingers through the mist of auburn curls near the nape of her neck.

"Yes." Her father looked at Kari. "I don't think he'll be at the wedding."

The news landed like a rock in Kari's gut. "He'll be there."

"He doesn't believe in weddings anymore, or marriage, or life-long commitment." Her father leaned back. "He said going to the wedding would make him a hypocrite."

"Who's feeding him this garbage?" Ryan kept his voice low, since Jessie had fallen asleep on his shoulder.

"The clubs he's involved with." Kari's mother clasped her hands. "Freethinkers Alliance, and who knows what others."

"Are you serious?" Kari couldn't take it in. The brother who once criticized Ashley for not owning a Bible now no longer believed in marriage?

"Completely." Her father nodded sadly. "He won't be at the wedding, Kari. He told me he didn't want to come."

"Then that's what we'll pray for. That he changes his mind." Ryan shifted Jessie to his other arm, and she made a soft cooing sound. "If he does, it could be a turning point."

"It's worth praying about." Kari's father's eyes looked damp. "Right now I'd rather think about Ashley. I wish I could be there to see her face when she walks in that fire station unannounced and asks for Landon Blake."

"He doesn't know she's coming?" Kari slid her chair closer to Ryan's and put her arm around him and her daughter.

"She wanted to surprise him." Her mother grinned, and the light was back in her eyes. "I have a good feeling about this trip. Maybe they'll both stop running and make some decisions."

"You think so?" Kari wasn't sure. Ashley had guarded her heart for so long. Besides, she didn't seem to be pining away while Landon worked his year in New York City. Between Cole, her job at Sunset Hills, and her painting, she gave no indication that she was longing for a serious relationship.

"I only know this." Her mother lifted her chin. "When she talks about Landon Blake, I can see straight into her heart. She's in love with him, and I think they're both going to realize the fact sooner than either of them had planned."

Kari's father winked at them. "Your mother's usually right about these things."

"Hmmm." Kari closed her eyes for a moment, and a dreamy feeling came over her. "To think . . . right now the two of them are celebrating her success and maybe realizing what they have together. Even as we speak."

CHAPTER THIRTEEN

IT TOOK ASHLEY UNTIL Monday morning to come to her senses.

But first she spent a miserable Sunday alone, tormenting herself with her wild imagination. That morning she found a cathedral and attended a morning service. Afterward, she browsed the shops in the Upper East Side, and every time she checked the mirror her look was the same. Distant, far off, untouchable. As if the pain she was wrestling with couldn't be brought to the surface or it would kill her. When she finished shopping, she strolled through Central Park and finally caught a late-afternoon performance of *Les Misérables*, before taking the subway back to her hotel.

The entire time she kept expecting to see Landon and Reagan. Had they fallen in love once Landon learned about the baby? Or did he have feelings for Reagan when he came to Bloomington last winter? Her heart hurt so bad she wondered if she was walking with her shoulders stooped.

Then, sometime during the night, a realization dawned in the darkest places of her heart. No matter what her eyes had seen,

Landon couldn't be in love with Reagan Decker. He hadn't come to New York and slept with Luke's old girlfriend. Definitely not. Whatever reason his firefighter partner had for thinking Reagan's baby belonged to Landon, there had to be a reasonable explanation.

Because Ashley knew Landon Blake was in love with her.

He'd been in love with her since they were freshmen at Bloomington High School, and he loved her still. No matter how few phone calls she received or how comfortable he'd looked walking next to Reagan and her baby.

She had an appointment at the gallery this morning, but she couldn't climb out of bed until she called Landon and let him know the truth. First, that she was in town; and second, that jet lag or overexcitement or insanity had kicked in and made her think the unthinkable.

The phone was on a nightstand next to her hotel bed. She picked up the receiver, punched in Landon's number, and waited while it rang. She was in New York for only a few days, and she'd already wasted a perfectly good Sunday worrying about Landon and Reagan.

A click sounded over the line, and Landon's answering machine came on. After the beep, she cleared her throat. "Landon, I'm in town and, well, something crazy happened, but everything's okay." She hesitated. "I can't wait to see you."

Next she tried the station, but the man who answered said Landon wouldn't be in until that afternoon. Ashley hung up and bit her lip. She had to find him, had to talk to him before his partner told him she'd been by. If that happened, he was bound to ask questions and figure out that she'd been given wrong information.

She tried his house again as she dressed, then a third time after she eased her paintings into the leather portfolio. As she walked from her hotel to the street outside, she chided herself for ever doubting Landon. An explanation existed; she had no doubt about it. She knew Landon as well as she knew her own name, and though he'd gone back to New York to complete his year of service with the FDNY, he had never stopped loving her.

She called Landon once more from a pay phone a few yards down the street from the gallery, but there was still no answer. A frustrated huff slipped from between her lips as she hung up the phone and strode the remaining few steps to the gallery door.

It was a few minutes after nine when she walked in, and immediately she was met by the director.

"Ashley." The woman beamed. "I'm Margaret Wellington. We've been quite anxious to meet you."

Memories of Paris flashed in Ashley's mind, and she could hear Jean-Claude Pierre, see him sneering at her work. *"Your paintings are nothing but trash, chérie. American trash."*

Ashley angled her head and smiled at the director. "Thank you."

The woman reached back toward the cash register and took hold of what looked like a check. "This is for you . . . for your expenses here in the city."

Ashley took the slip of paper, glanced at it, then swallowed. A thousand dollars? She fought the impulse to stare at it. "Thank you. This . . . it's very generous."

"Wait here, please. I want to introduce you to my husband. He runs the gallery with me."

The woman was wiry, with conservatively styled hair and an attitude of elegance. But something about her fell just short of snobby, a sparkle in her eyes that told Ashley Margaret Wellington might be wealthy, she might run with Manhattan's elite, but she had a passion for art that danced untamed within her.

Just as it did inside Ashley.

For the first time since stepping inside, Ashley looked around and savored the atmosphere. A real New York City art gallery, the kind of place she'd only dreamed of before today. An olive green candle burned near the front desk, and the air smelled of eucalyptus and something floral. Roses, maybe. The combination was subtly assuring and gave the gallery a lived-in feeling. The leather and mahogany furniture groupings, distressed wood flooring, and faux stone fireplace reminded her of someone's cozy den rather than a showroom where more than a million dollars in artwork must trade hands each year.

The gentle strains of Bach filtered through the gallery, and in every direction the walls were hung with breathtaking originals, artwork Ashley would've needed hours to fully appreciate. And here—in this posh setting beneath carefully positioned lights— her very own paintings were about to be hung.

Gratitude overwhelmed her and for the moment overshadowed her concerns about Landon. *God, you did this.* She closed her eyes and breathed in the reality of it all. She was here! In New York at a gallery that actually liked her work. "God, thank you . . . thank you."

Almost as soon as she whispered the words, doubt slipped through the back door of her heart and sneered at her. *Who are you kidding? They'll take one look at your work and wonder what they were thinking. It'll be just one more rejection, one more reminder that all you can paint is trash, Ashley Baxter. You're crazy even to be here.*

"Ashley." A click of heels sounded at the other end of the gallery.

Her eyes flew open, and the mockery in her head fell instantly silent. "Yes." She licked her suddenly dry lips and took a few steps toward the sound of the woman's voice.

Margaret Wellington appeared from around a display of nature scenes. "Ashley, there you are." She had a short man by the hand. He was mustached and had thinning hair, but he wore a smile that could warm a winter day. Ms. Wellington nodded to him. "This is my husband, William."

The man's eyes held a peace that set Ashley at ease. "Hello, dear. Nice to meet you." He pointed to her portfolio. "May we see what you brought?"

"Yes." Ashley ordered her doubts to stay quiet. She positioned her leather bag in front of her and slid the zipper open. Then, one at a time, she took out the three pieces. The one of Irvel first, then the one of the Baxter home, and last the one of Landon. She set each against the back of the nearest sofa and then stood to the side.

The Wellingtons studied each painting as though at any minute the images might spring to life and perform tricks. Ashley directed her eyes to the tips of her shoes. *They're going to hate them. They'll yell at me and tell me to pack them up and get out of their gallery. This is crazy. I shouldn't have come, shouldn't have wasted my time. Then I wouldn't have found out about Landon, and all of this wouldn't be happening, and none of it matters anyway because in twenty-four hours I'll be on a plane back to Indiana and—*

"You are in your twenties, is that right?"

Ashley started and looked up. "Yes, sir." She glanced from Mr. Wellington to his wife and back again. "Twenty-five."

"I have one question." He and his wife exchanged a knowing glance. She nodded, and he brought his attention back to Ashley.

"Yes, sir?"

His smile shone a floodlight on Ashley's fears. "How on earth were we lucky enough to find you first?"

I know the plans I have for you, my daughter. Plans to give you a hope and a future.

The verse flashed in Ashley's mind, and she held her breath.

"You are a budding master, Ashley Baxter. We want to price your pieces starting at three thousand dollars each."

Ms. Wellington was still talking, going on about the details and what percentage the gallery would keep and where they would position the pieces and how quickly could Ashley come back with more and when could they stage a public showing, but she couldn't focus on a bit of it.

It was as though she had lifted off the ground and floated ten feet above the gallery floor. She closed her eyes. She'd done it. The trip wasn't a waste, and she hadn't produced trash for these kind people. God brought her here because he had a plan for her life. A plan for her to paint and to mother Cole and to love her family. And maybe to be with Landon, too. As she realized this, she noticed something else.

The ghosts of doubt were no longer merely silent.

They were gone.

Landon had a half-day shift Monday, ten to two, all of which would be spent on training drills. The city had been fairly quiet lately, a few calls a shift, but nothing fully involved, none of the warehouse fires or high-rise apartment burns that made his heart race the way he'd come to love.

The way Jalen must've loved.

He took the subway from his apartment to the station and checked in just before ten o'clock. He wasn't on the schedule, but he needed to practice for the training. The chief had given him a manual of the drills they'd be practicing that day, but he'd barely glanced at it. Every time he tried to concentrate, all he thought about was Ashley. He'd called her three times last week, but she hadn't been home once.

Now he couldn't focus, and it was his own fault. He'd made up his mind to move forward with her—if she wanted to move forward—and nothing was like it had been before. Fighting fires was a job, after all, and couldn't compare with finding Ashley and asking her if it was time.

Maybe not for the ring and the wedding date. But for a commitment at least, a promise that never again would either of them have to wonder if the other was waiting or moving on with life. A decision that from now on they could share their feelings without pretense.

Landon grabbed a foam cup and poured himself some coffee. Black and strong, the way he liked it. If only she'd call back. He took a sip and swung first one leg, then the other over the picnic-table bench and sat down. The steam from the coffee felt good on his face, warm and soothing. Summer might be there, but until August the brick fire station was almost always cool—especially in the mornings.

"You look tired, Blake." Doug Phillips sauntered around the corner. He had a bagel in one hand and a plastic container of cream cheese in the other. He grabbed a knife from a basket on the table and plopped down across from Landon.

"A little."

"Me, too." He shook his head and tore the lid off the cream cheese. "Hate these early training shifts." He poked the air between them with the knife. "Don't they know we night guys need our beauty sleep?"

Landon chuckled. "I'm pretty sure they don't care."

His partner was quiet for a moment, intent on spreading a half-inch layer of cheese on his bagel. Doug was an older guy, assigned to the Lower Manhattan station as part of the personnel shuffle after September 11. He was raised in Queens and had an accent thicker than clam chowder. Five years and Doug would retire. As far as Landon knew, the man was counting the days.

"I feel the love down here; don't get me wrong," Doug had told him when the two of them first started working together. "But a guy'd be crazy not to see the danger in all this." He'd shrugged and an intensity he rarely revealed shone in his eyes. "I got a wife and two girls at home. When I work my last shift for FDNY, I'm outta here."

Landon took another sip of his coffee and spotted a training manual at the end of the table. He stood and pulled it closer, flipping it open to the table of contents. Better late than never.

Across from him, Doug was attacking the bagel, downing each half in three fierce bites. He was between swallows when he dropped his hands to the table and stared at Landon. "I gotta question for you."

Landon looked up from the notebook. "Shoot."

"Who's Ashley?"

His heart sat straight up in his chest. Landon closed the manual. "Why?"

" 'Cause." Doug shrugged. "No big deal. Just wondered."

"Wait a minute." He pushed the notebook back to the center of the table and gave a chuckle that held little humor. "You sit there with your bagel and for no reason, just for something to say, you ask me who *Ashley* is?" Landon worked to keep his tone light. "Then you tell me no big deal? You were just wondering?"

Doug stuffed what was left of the bagel into his mouth, chewed three times, and stared at Landon. "Yeah." He chewed twice more and swallowed. "That's right. No big deal."

Landon planted his elbows on the table and exhaled. "Look, Phillips, Ashley's very special. You can't just—"

"You're tellin' me." He gave a sideways shake of his head and raised a single eyebrow. "Girl's gorgeous."

"You mean . . ." A mix of panic and confusion swirled in Landon's gut. "You've seen her?"

Doug raised his hands and let them fall to his lap. "I shouldn'ta said nothing."

Whatever Doug was talking about, none of it made sense. Where would he have seen Ashley? And if she was here in New York, why hadn't she contacted him?

Landon stood and leaned over the table, resting his weight on his straight arms and clenched fists, his face inches from his partner's. "Look, this isn't a joke, Phillips. I'm serious. Where'd you meet her?"

"It's better you don't see her, pal." Doug crossed his arms and leaned back, placing more space between them. "Things are too new with you and that—" like a blind man, he raised his hand and groped about in the air between—"what was her name? The girl with the baby?"

"Reagan? The blonde who stopped by the other day?"

"Yeah, that's her." Doug slid down a few feet and leveled his gaze at Landon. "You need to keep your priorities, Blake. Neither o' them girls needs you two-timing; know what I mean?"

Landon was beginning to.

He eased himself back to the bench and pushed down the panic welling within him. He needed to clarify the situation regarding Reagan, but not until he got some answers. "Get back to the part about Ashley. How do you know about her?"

"Okay, look." Doug held his hands up, palms toward Landon. "I told her I wouldn't say nothin', and I keep my promises, okay?"

Landon had to grip the bench to keep from lurching across the table and shaking his partner. "Ashley lives in Indiana. If you saw her, I need to know about it. Believe me—" he glanced around the room—"if she came this far, she wants me to know." His voice fell a notch, the fight gone. "No matter what she said."

Doug frowned. "I feel funny about it. I promised her." He looked up and the two of them made eye contact. Gradually the angst turned to empathy, and Doug's shoulders slumped forward. "Fine. But don't tell her I told you."

A picture was forming in Landon's mind, one that riddled his stomach with knots. "She was here?"

"Yeah, the other day. Just after you and your girl went for the walk."

Landon felt the blood drain from his face. "My girl?"

"The first one, the blonde . . . with the baby." Doug shook his head. "Your life's a mess, pal."

"Did she see me? With Reagan and the baby?" Landon's throat was dry and he couldn't swallow.

"No." Indignation punctuated the word. Doug raised his eyebrows. "I told her. I said she'd just missed you. You and the girl were out with the baby."

The baby! Landon's stomach tightened. "What did you tell her about the baby, Phillips?" He was on his feet, moving one slow step after another around the table toward his partner. "Did you say something about the baby?"

Doug shrugged. "She asked."

"About the baby?"

"Yeah." He lowered his eyebrows. "I told her the truth. What'd you want me to do, Blake, lie to the girl? How was I supposed to know you was two-timin'?"

"I'm *not* two—" Landon fell back against the closest wall and stared at the ceiling for a moment. "Never mind." *God, where is she? What's she thinking?* He didn't wait for a response. Instead he lowered his chin and found Doug's eyes again. "What'd you tell her?"

"I told her it was yours." Doug stood up, crossed the dining area and tossed his crumpled napkin into the trash can.

"You *what?*" Landon gritted his teeth. "Reagan's baby isn't mine. She's a friend, Phillips. She used to date Ashley's brother."

Doug froze in place, clearly processing this newest bit of information. "But after the call, when the girl was bleeding and we were back in the truck, you said . . ."

"I said we were good friends."

"Very good friends."

"So that doesn't mean I'm the father of her baby!" Landon's voice rose.

"And then the other day you said he was your little guy, the baby." Doug's expression changed. He headed for the doorway, rolled his eyes, and brushed his hand in Landon's direction. "You got yourself into this, Blake."

"Wait!" Landon caught up to Doug. *"I didn't say he was my little guy; those were your words."*

Doug thought about that. "Fine. You didn't say anything different."

"So Ashley came here looking for me? And you told her I was out with a girl and a baby?"

"Your baby."

"Did she . . . did she say where she was staying? Why she'd come?"

Doug thought for a moment. "She had this—" he spread his arms out to either side—"this huge bag. Kinda thin and leatherlike. Big enough to hold blueprints, you know?"

Her art portfolio? Ashley came to New York with her portfoio? Landon's mind raced. Had she brought her paintings? But why? Was she looking at one of the galleries in the city, or had one of them found out about her? She hadn't said a word, but then maybe that's why she'd come to the station.

To surprise him.

Instead, the surprise had been all hers. Landon gripped Doug's shoulder. "Where was she staying?"

"She didn't tell me." His partner jerked his shoulder free from Landon's grasp. "You should be careful what you say."

"Forget it." Landon turned and went to the farthest chair he could find, a dilapidated recliner stuck in the corner of the den.

Doug was right; the mess was his own fault.

He dropped into the chair and leaned forward. His forearms rested on his knees and he clasped his hands. How could she have come at that exact hour? When Reagan was there? Why hadn't he been more careful with his words? He wasn't interested in Reagan; he just wanted to make her feel welcome, special. She was all alone in the city, a single mom, and still grieving the loss of her father.

Of course Landon had been kind. But look where kindness got him.

Now Ashley was somewhere in the city believing . . . what? That he'd come here last September and fallen for Reagan Decker? The idea was ludicrous, but what else could she think after his partner's explanation? He had to find her, had to clear this mess up before Ashley left without knowing the truth.

Landon pressed his fingers into his brow and tried to guess where she'd be. If she hadn't gone home yet, she could be anywhere. He closed his eyes and exhaled hard. *God, help me. Where would she be? Who would know how to find her?*

Then it hit him.

Her parents. They probably had Cole, and if not, they would definitely know about Ashley's trip, how long she was here, and where she was staying. He was on his feet as soon as the idea snapped into focus.

In the two seconds it took him to cross the room he tried to guess at what Ashley must be thinking. The image of her standing in the station with her art case, hearing the news from Phillips, was—well, it was enough to frighten her away again. Maybe forever. Even after she knew the truth, she might assume she wasn't right for him, that his life was in New York, that they had no future together. He punched in the numbers and held his breath. He needed to get the truth to Ashley as soon as possible, because he knew the way she had to be feeling, knew the panic in her heart and the uncertainty in her soul. He knew her as though a part of her lived and breathed within him.

Now he could only pray she knew him as well.

CHAPTER FOURTEEN

WHEN ASHLEY LEFT the art gallery she crossed the street and walked through Central Park again. She wanted to call Landon, but not until she got back to the hotel. Her heart was too full for her to do anything but bask in the glow of all God had done. The Wellingtons loved her work! Their reaction was more than she'd dared dream, and now . . . now it was all beginning to happen.

Sometime that evening she would share the good news with Landon.

Ashley clutched her empty portfolio and took slow steps along a gently curved path. The reservoir was to her left, and she watched a mother duck lead a string of babies down a muddy embankment into the water. The sun glistened off a thousand ripples. She leaned her head back, letting the breeze work itself across her cheeks.

She lowered her chin and stared at the people making their way through the park. Would this be the place she and Cole would one day move? So she could be close to the gallery, closer to Landon? Normally a scene like this would make Ashley want to pull out a sketchpad and capture the image on paper, then one day make it the subject of a painting. But this time it only made her think of Landon.

Everything was coming together. With Cole, with God. And now with her paintings. Later that night she would see Landon and know that things were right between them also. Yes, he'd been busy, but she could hardly hold that against him. He'd never been one to spend much time on the phone, and hadn't he explained it to her last winter? Talking to her only made him more homesick.

She kept walking and tightened her grip on the portfolio. The Wellingtons had given her paperwork to fill out, and while she'd worked on it, Margaret and William discussed framing options for her works. They agreed that the couple would make the final decision on choosing frames, and that once the pieces were ready, they'd be placed on the gallery floor.

"In a prominent spot," Margaret had added.

If the Wellingtons' impression of her work was correct, she'd be back to New York soon. In fact, if they were right, she'd all but crossed the line from amateur to professional, from uncertainty over how she'd provide for Cole to maybe making a living as an artist.

Just as she'd always wanted.

She wound her way back to Fifth Avenue, hailed a cab, and arrived at her hotel just as a business luncheon was letting out in a conference room off the lobby. She waited through three carloads of people before she finally squeezed her way onto an elevator and headed up four levels to her floor.

The noise from the elevator faded as she turned a corner and headed down another hallway to her room. She kept walking as she sifted through her bag for her key. When she looked up she was a few yards from her door.

Her breath caught in her throat.

A man was leaning against her door, his back to her. A few seconds passed while Ashley studied his build—the curve of his shoulders and the length of his legs—and instantly she knew. He must've heard her, because he spun around. When their eyes met and held, Ashley saw a raw kind of terror there that took her breath away and told her the thing she'd wondered about.

Landon's partner had told him about her visit the other day.

Without waiting another moment, she shook her head and held up her free hand. "Landon—"

"Ashley, it's not what you think." He cut her off, his words tumbling from his mouth as he took a step toward her. "Doug—my partner at the station—told you that the baby I was walking was . . . that he was mine."

She set her art case down and stared at him. "Landon . . ." A smile lifted the corners of her mouth. "I've been trying to call you all morning."

He ran his tongue along his lower lip. "Ashley, I'm not the baby's father." He held up his hands. "I promise you."

Her smile faded and she went to him. "I know."

His mouth was open, as if he still had a dozen ways of convincing her. But now his lips came together and he searched her eyes. "Who told you?"

"No one." She was inches from him now, her eyes lost in his. "I know you, Landon. And you never could've come to New York and slept with Reagan." She pressed her fingertips against his chest and gave him a gentle push. "Silly. You were worried for nothing."

"You mean you . . ." He exhaled and his eyes filled with relief. "He told you I was the baby's father, and you never believed it."

"Well . . ." Ashley lowered her chin and winced as she raised her eyes to Landon. "Maybe a little."

He traced his thumb along the edge of her jaw. "How little?"

She lifted her hands to her face and shielded her eyes. "I figured it out this morning." Her fingers parted and she peered at him. "It took me that long to get the upper hand over my imagination."

He laughed and caught her hands in his own. "At least you figured it out."

Two men entered the hallway from a few doors down, their conversation loud, their laughter, louder. Without saying a word, Ashley moved around Landon and passed her key through the door lock. A tiny green light flashed and she pushed it open.

"Let me take my portfolio in." She felt numb, as though the entire scene were some strange sort of dream. "We can talk down the hall."

He exhaled hard as they entered the room. "What a relief."

She tossed her portfolio near the pillows. Then they walked down the hall to where two sofas sat near a gas fireplace. They sat and turned to face each other.

Landon's mouth hung open, and his eyes never left hers. "When my partner told me . . ." He gave a shake of his head. His voice was quiet, but tinged with a desperate urgency. "I couldn't wait to see you."

"I tried calling you three times this morning, just in case he told you what he'd said." Ashley drew her knees up. His nearness was doing unfair things to her heart, and she bit the inside of her lip. "You . . . you don't know how hard it was to think that maybe you and Reagan . . ."

"I haven't been with Reagan or with any woman." His eyes caught hers and held them again. "In fact . . ." He laced his fingers along the back of his neck and uttered a low moan. When he looked up, his eyes told her all she needed to know about his feelings for her. "I missed you so much, Ash."

"Me, too." She slid back on the sofa. "Tell me about Reagan."

"We took a call that a pregnant woman was hemorrhaging. When we got there, I found out it was Reagan." The story spilled out as quickly as Landon could form the words. "That was the first time I knew she was pregnant. The first time I'd seen her."

Ashley sat cross-legged and waited.

"The bleeding was bad—real bad." He hesitated. "We almost lost Reagan and the baby, but later that night I went back to the hospital. It was a miracle. The baby was fine, and so was Reagan. Her mother asked me to come back the next day because, well—" he shrugged—"Reagan needed a friend, and I was willing."

Ashley felt a warmth in the center of her being. Of course Landon was there for Reagan—the way he would've been for anyone in that situation.

"Since then we've talked a few times, and the other day she asked if she could bring her baby by the station. She wanted to take him on his first walk."

"His first walk?" No question, Landon was telling the truth. But didn't he see how Reagan could've gotten the wrong impression from his attention?

Landon moved to the edge of his seat. "I feel so sorry for her, Ashley. She's a single mom, all alone out here. Her father's gone and everything about her life is upside-down." The intensity remained in his voice. "I wanted to help her."

"So you claimed the baby was yours?" For the first time since seeing him and Reagan, Ashley's anger stepped up and demanded to be heard. "That's how you helped her?"

"I didn't claim that." He stood and paced to the elevator door and back. His voice was louder, more frustrated. "My partner said something about him being my little guy, and I agreed." He huffed hard. "I didn't want to hurt Reagan's feelings."

She raised her eyebrows.

"It was stupid, okay? I wanted her to feel special, like I cared about her baby and his first walk and how she—"

"Stop." Ashley held her hand up. She closed her eyes and concentrated. Was he serious? Would he say something that careless? Around his buddies at the firehouse? "Okay, let me see if I have this right. You don't see Reagan for months after you both come to New York City. Then one night you take a call, and there she is, bleeding and in need of help, right?"

"Exactly." He sat down again.

"And the reason you've spent time with her since is because she needs a friend; is that right?"

"Right." Hope sparked in Landon's expression. He stared at her for a long time until the slightest chuckle came from him, a chuckle less humorous than painful. "Ashley—" he gave a few short shakes of his head—"I said good-bye to Reagan at the bus stop here and didn't talk to her again until the night Tommy was born." He turned to face her, reached out, and took Ashley's hands. "I could never have been with her."

"I know. I knew it as soon as I woke up today." A wave of regret at what she'd believed before this morning stirred up the sands of remorse and washed over her.

He slid a few inches closer to her. "I could never be with her, Ash. Not her or anyone else when—" his eyes shone—"when I'm so in love with you."

Love flooded her heart—a love so real and strong and deep it was almost painful.

"Ash . . ." The dimmest shadow fell over his expression. He released the hold he had on her and touched his fingertips to the side of her face. "I'm so glad you realized you were wrong."

His touch was silk against her skin, silk and butterfly wings. "I'm sorry."

"No." He nuzzled his cheek against hers. "It's not your fault; it's just . . . I don't ever want you to doubt me. Never."

She closed her eyes, soaking in the feel of him. "I couldn't have been mad, Landon, not even if it was true. When you left we agreed to wait, to not make promises."

He whispered against her face. "I know." She felt him trace the arch of first one eyebrow, then the other. "I regret that—" his finger moved to her cheekbone and down to her lip line—"more than anything else I've done."

"You do?" She blinked her eyes open. Her voice was still quiet, laced with desire and gratitude. She loved being here, lost in Landon's eyes, trapped in the power of the pull he had on her. A pull that grew stronger every time she saw him.

She could no longer stay still. Her fingers came up, and she wove them into his hair, making a delicate frame of her hands along either side of his face. They were alone except for the occasional footsteps in the hallway. "You regret that?'

"Yes." Landon sucked in a full breath and looked down at the spot where their hands were joined. "When Phillips told me what he'd said, I almost lost my mind." He pulled her into a hug. "I had to find you."

"How'd you know I was here?" She breathed the words close to his ear.

"I called your parents." He leaned back and clutched both her shoulders. The passion in his eyes faded, and an excitement burned there instead. "They told me about your paintings!" He gave her the slightest little shake. "I knew it, Ashley. One day everyone will know about your work." He stood and pulled her to her feet. "I'm so proud of you."

"You won't believe it, Landon." She couldn't keep the news in another minute. "They loved my paintings! They're putting all three pieces up in the gallery later this week, and they want more as soon as I can get them here."

"Of course they do, silly." He picked her up and twirled her around. "We have to celebrate!"

This was nothing like the conversation she'd expected to have with Landon. Her cheeks grew hot and a buzzing filled her head. *God, you worked it out after all. He's here, and he still wants me.*

So far Landon hadn't kissed her, but in the exhilaration of their excitement, he worked his fingers along the sides of her face to the back of her head and eased her up against him. In a way that she'd imagined every day since their last time together, he brushed his lips against hers. "Ashley, I love you." He kissed her slowly and softly, a tentative kiss of forgiveness and misunderstandings made right again. "No matter what else happens in life, that won't change." His breath brushed against her lips. "Not ever."

She hadn't wanted to cry about what happened. Years of being the Baxter bad girl had made her expect loneliness and loss. But here, in Landon's arms, the sting of tears overwhelmed her. He loved her. He was never going to stop. It was too much, more than she deserved.

She blinked away the wetness, and this time the kiss came from her, deeper and filled with a passion that only hinted at all she held inside, all she was still somehow afraid to let him see. "Landon . . ." Her lips moved over his again. "I can't believe we're here."

"Me neither." He brushed his nose against hers. His eyes saw straight to the most private places of her soul. "I prayed you'd understand about . . . about the mix-up with Reagan. But I was worried you might think it was some kind of sign that I wanted to be with someone else, or that you weren't ready for a commitment. Something weird like that."

"Weird?" She pulled back as a giggle slipped out. How wonderful to laugh with Landon, to kiss him. She pointed to herself. "Me, Ashley Baxter? Weird?"

"Yes, you." He twisted his face into a shape that made her laugh out loud. "Crazy girl . . . running all over town thinking I'd fallen for Reagan Decker. Even for a day."

At the sound of Reagan's name, Ashley pulled away a bit and looked at Landon. "Now *that's* weird. That she'd get together with someone so soon after leaving my brother."

Landon's expression changed, and he drew back. He met Ashley's eyes but said nothing.

Something strange seemed to be going on in Landon's heart, but she couldn't make it out. She brushed her fingers through her short-cropped hair and sat on the edge of the sofa. "You're not saying anything." She tilted her head. "I mean she and Luke were pretty serious before—"

Her stomach dropped, and it was as if the oxygen left the room. Just how serious *had* her brother and Reagan been? Her gaze fell to her hands, and she did the math again. If Reagan's baby was born at the beginning of June, that meant . . .

Ashley knew the trick. Kari had taught it to her when she was pregnant with Jessie. Don't count back nine months; count ahead three.

Ashley closed her eyes. *July . . . August . . . September.*

Which meant . . .

Her eyes flew open and she found Landon looking at her. "Is Luke the . . . ?" She couldn't bring herself to finish the sentence. It would be too awful, too horrible to know that her brother had pined over Reagan all those months, to know that he'd left life as he knew it to move in with Lori, whoever she was, all because he was dying of a broken heart.

And then to find out that—

"Landon." She slid closer to him. It would kill her brother to learn he had a son he never knew about. And what about their parents? "Tell me the truth. Please."

He took her hands in his. "Reagan doesn't want him to know." A sad smile lifted the corners of his mouth, but his eyes were flat. "I can't keep anything from you, Ashley. Maybe you were supposed to find out."

Ashley could swear she was being sucked into a churning riptide, tossed about beneath the water with no way to swim back to shore.

Luke was a father?

The baby Reagan had been pushing in the stroller was her brother's son, her own nephew?

Why hadn't she thought of that? Of *course* the baby was Luke's. How could she have believed for a minute that the baby was Landon's when she'd seen for herself how close Reagan and her brother were before September 11?

She stood and went to a nearby window. Her breath came in short bursts against the glass, and she let her forehead fall against the pane.

"Ashley." Landon came up behind her and put his hands on her shoulders.

"Of course." She looked straight ahead out the window, seeing nothing. She folded her arms and pressed them against her stomach. "It was so obvious. Why didn't I see it before?"

Question after question, all demanding immediate answers, churned inside her. What would Luke think? How angry would he be that Reagan had cut him out of her life after finding out she was pregnant with his child? What would this do to his current take on life, his current living situation, for that matter?

Most of all, why hadn't Reagan told him?

Not a few weeks ago, when the baby was born, but the moment she found out she was pregnant? Ashley might've been at odds with her brother for years prior to September 11, but afterward, they'd been as close as ever. She was sure he would've gone to Reagan, supported her, and stayed with her. Moved to New York, helped her through her pregnancy, and been a wonderful father to their son.

And today he would still be the Luke they all remembered. Humbled and human, yes. But Luke Baxter all the same.

"Tell me what you're thinking." Landon brought his face alongside hers.

She gave a few slow shakes of her head. "My brother's life is a mess and . . ." She turned and faced Landon, linking her arms around his waist. "It's his fault, but everything would've been different if she'd told him the truth."

"I know." He pursed his lips. "I wanted to call him, but she begged me not to. She knows about Luke . . . that he's living with another girl. She doesn't want anything to do with him, not for her or the baby."

"That's not fair." Ashley heard the strain in her voice. "Luke's the father."

They fell silent, lost in the sorrow of all that had happened. Then, slowly, a light dawned in Landon's eyes. "How long are you here?"

"I leave tomorrow morning." Sadness pierced her at the thought. She'd wanted to spend the weekend celebrating with Landon.

His mouth showed the hint of a smile. "What if you called her? You could say you were in town, that you saw her with me and asked and, well . . . now you know."

"So tell her the truth, basically."

"Basically." Landon flashed his teeth, his eyebrows raised in a hesitant smile.

Ashley grinned. Though this was the single greatest day in her career as an artist, she hadn't smiled for real until now. The combination—having Landon here, knowing he hadn't done something crazy with Reagan; receiving the high praise from the art gallery—all of it made for the most wonderful feeling.

But the problem with Luke remained. And it was a big one, one that would rock the Baxter world yet again. Because they were bound to find out. "Won't she be mad at you?"

"How can she be? You saw us together."

"True."

Landon pulled his cell phone from his jeans and flipped it open. "Her number's in my phone book." He punched a series of buttons and hesitated. "Here it is."

She raised her eyebrows. "Okay . . . call it."

He pushed the Send button and handed the phone to her.

Ashley held it to her ear and gripped it tight. Reagan would probably hang up on her, but so what? Ashley had less than twenty-four hours left in New York, and she wanted to meet her nephew. Now it was merely a matter of convincing Reagan to let her come.

She waited.

On the second ring, a woman answered. "Hello?"

"Hello, Reagan?" Ashley needed a drink of water. Her mouth was so dry she could barely talk.

"Yes."

"This is Ashley Baxter, Luke's sister." A pause planted itself between them. "I'm here in New York on business and, well, I wondered if I could see you?"

The silence on the other end was one of the loudest Ashley

had ever heard. *God, please, don't let her hang up. I know you want me to see her.* She waited, wanting desperately to believe Reagan would talk to her, hoping she would welcome her over to see the baby. But only one truth made itself known in that moment.

Whatever happened after this would be up to God.

CHAPTER FIFTEEN

REAGAN FINISHED THE CONVERSATION and hung up the telephone. Her hands were shaking and knots filled her stomach.

"Mom . . ."

Tommy was asleep in his crib, and she didn't want to wake him. Still, talking with Luke's sister had knocked the wind out of her, and she could hardly walk around the apartment looking for her mother. She put the phone down on the kitchen table and sat back in her chair. She kept her voice even and as loud as she dared. "Mom, come here."

A full minute later her mom pushed open the swinging door and made her way into the kitchen. "You shouldn't call out like that when the baby's—" she stopped short and stared at Reagan—"honey, what is it?"

Since September 11, none of the Deckers took life for granted. Reagan realized she probably looked awful. She felt cool and clammy, and she could see that even her arms had grown pale in the last few minutes. Her gaze fell to the table. "The phone call . . ."

"Who was it?" Her mother sat next to her at the table and gave a tender brush of her fingers over Reagan's forehead.

Reagan looked up. "Luke's sister."

For a moment Reagan watched the emotions make their way across her mom's face. Shock. Fear. And finally a stunned sort of calm. "She knows?"

"Yes." Reagan ran her tongue along her lower lip. Her throat felt like it was lined with cotton balls. "Landon told her."

"He promised you he—"

"No." She held up her hand. This wasn't Landon's fault; she couldn't have her mother believing it was. Not even for a minute. "She came here on business and saw me with Landon. She figured it out, Mom."

"Okay." Her mother drew in a sharp breath through her nose and lifted her chin a few inches. "Does Luke know?"

"Not yet." Reagan's head ached, and her heart beat so hard within her she could feel it in her temples. It was her own fault, really. She had stuffed her feelings in brown bags and stored them in the cellar of her soul. Now she needed to sort through them and see what was there—what she could keep and what had to be tossed. And what simply needed repair.

Before she could do any of that, her mother folded her hands on the kitchen table and looked hard at her. "Reagan, I told you it would come to this." Her voice was kind but unbending. "Luke should've known from the beginning."

"I couldn't tell him." Tears filled Reagan's eyes and the image of her mother blurred. "He thought—" she waved her hands, looking for an answer that dangled just beyond her—"he thought I was a nice girl, Mom. The kind who would wait, and . . ." She let her hands fall. "After that night, I didn't want to look at him because—" a sob caught in her throat and she paused until she could find her voice—"because I wasn't that girl anymore. I wasn't pure."

Her mother leaned forward and searched Reagan's eyes. Her voice was thick, as though she, too, wanted to break down and cry. "Reagan, don't you see?"

She grabbed three jerky breaths. "What?"

156

"Neither was he."

For a long while Reagan stared at her mother. Neither was he? Slowly, like sand slipping through her fingers, her mind let go of everything she'd believed about Luke. And for the first time since they'd said good-bye at the Bloomington bus depot, she could see clearly.

Luke wanted his girlfriend pure, but he'd wanted himself that way, too. Reagan covered her face with her hands and allowed herself to return to that time when she'd been Luke Baxter's love. He was so strong and intelligent, dedicated to truth and making right choices. But one thing about him had bothered her.

He had been utterly unforgiving.

Whether with Ashley and her bad choices, or with his older sister who had chosen to distance herself from her family's faith, Luke was always critical, even harsh. So when she and Luke fell that Monday night, she'd been certain he'd think of her the same way—weak, unfaithful, unworthy. What she *hadn't* considered was that he would feel the same way about himself.

Her mother cleared her throat. "It's true, Reagan."

She let her hands fall away from her face. "You think . . . he's more upset with himself than with me?"

"Well—" she tilted her head—"probably not." She bit her lip and was quiet for a moment. "I've thought about him a lot, and I'm guessing he's most mad at God."

"That much I'm sure you're right about." A memory flashed into Reagan's mind of Luke boarding the airplane next to her the time they flew to New York to visit her family. He had been talking about his sisters and their failings.

"God's pretty easy to figure out," he told her. They were making their way through the jetway to the airplane, and he grinned at her. "Live life right, and it all goes your way. Mess it up, and God lets you live with your choices."

She'd wanted to ask him what he meant by that. Surely he couldn't have meant that bad things never happened to people who lived their lives for God. But in the rush of getting their seats and storing their carry-on luggage, she'd never asked. Not until after she moved back to Manhattan did she realize that Luke meant *exactly* that.

Yes, he must've been angry with God. What else could have spurred him to abandon his beliefs and move in with some girl he'd met at college?

Reagan clasped her hands to stop their shaking. "Every time he called I found a reason not to talk to him."

"I remember." A sad smile played on her mother's lips. "Whenever I asked, you didn't want to talk about it. Then after we found out about the baby . . ." She shook her head. "I figured he'd done something you weren't willing to forgive."

"No." Reagan sniffed and ran her fingertips across her cheeks. "It was the other way around. I'd done something I was sure *he* couldn't forgive."

"How could you think that?" Her tone was gentle, kind.

Reagan knew the answer as well as she knew her name. She'd thought about it every day since. Sometimes every hour. Luke's phone calls were his way of dealing with his guilt, but she always knew what would happen if she talked to him. He'd tell her he was sorry, and maybe for a few calls after that he'd make small talk. Then he'd fade out of her life and write her off.

The same way he'd written off his sisters.

"You both made a mistake that night." Her mother tried again. "But how could it have been more your fault than his?"

"Because—" Reagan leveled her gaze, her eyes dry—"Luke wanted me to take the call."

Confusion wrote itself over her mom's face. "What call?"

"Dad's. He called after the Giants game, and we were . . . we were on the couch and already, well, already involved." Reagan's voice cracked. "I think Luke wanted the phone call to be our way out. He told me to answer it."

"And you didn't?" Understanding filled her mother's voice. Understanding, but no condemnation.

158

Reagan's eyes fell again. "I said I'd call him back the next day." She pursed her lips. "And then . . ."

"Even when Luke called all those times, you figured he'd hold that night against you?"

"Yes." Her answer was barely audible. She had thought that, but what if she'd been wrong? What if he was more upset with himself, with God? What if he wanted to find a way back to how things used to be with her? "Mom, did I make a mistake?"

Her mother's exhaled breath fell just short of weariness. "The thing about God, Reagan, is that he already knows the answer." She leaned closer and gave her a kiss on the forehead. "And no matter what mistakes you make, no matter what promises you've broken, God will still make good on his."

Reagan thought about that. Her mother was talking about her special Bible verse, the one engraved in wood at the bottom of a framed photo of her that hung above her bed. Her parents had given it to her when she was a small girl, back when the photograph inside the frame was that of a towheaded, gap-toothed kindergartner. Every year when she brought home her picture packet from school, her mother took the piece down, opened the frame, and slipped in the new photo. Then she put it back together, held it so Reagan could see it, and together they read the Scripture aloud.

The memory lifted, and she locked eyes with her mother. "I know the plans I have for you, says the Lord . . . plans to give you a hope and a future . . . and not to harm you."

Her mother smiled. "Exactly."

"Even now? After all I've done wrong?" Reagan narrowed her eyes. The pain was still so fresh. Whole months had gone by without her giving a single thought to the idea that God had plans for her, or that somehow the future wouldn't harm her.

A knock sounded at the door, and they both turned toward the sound. "Yes, Reagan." Her mom patted her hand and nodded toward the door. "Even now."

CHAPTER SIXTEEN

ASHLEY STEPPED BACK from the door and leaned against Landon.

The sick feeling was worse now than before, but Ashley wasn't about to turn back. Not when she was sure this was where God wanted her to be. The pieces were too perfectly aligned. First that Landon would happen to be the firefighter who responded to Reagan's emergency, then Ashley's seeing Landon and Reagan together.

Ashley had no doubts; God wanted her here. What would happen after that, she couldn't begin to guess.

"You okay?" Landon leaned his head closer to hers.

"Yeah." She gave him a quick kiss on his arm. "Thanks for coming."

He looked at her, and she could almost read his mind. He wanted to be here with her; the talk they needed to have about each other would have to wait until after this meeting.

The door opened and Reagan tried to smile. Her cheeks were tearstained, and her swollen eyes held raw fear. Ashley's heart quieted immediately. She took the first step and hugged Reagan for a long while. Irvel and her friends at Sunset Hills had taught her the importance of hugs, that sometimes an embrace said more than words ever could.

When she drew back, Ashley looked at Landon and then at Reagan again. "Thanks for letting us come."

Landon came up alongside her. "I'm sorry about all this."

"No." Reagan gave a quick shake of her head. "It happened for a reason. I have to believe that."

They made their way into the living room. Ashley couldn't help but admire the place. It was spacious and beautifully decorated. A portrait of Reagan and her family hung over an ornate gas fireplace. Reagan's father had been tall, with friendly eyes. Ashley tried not to stare at the image as she found a seat next to Landon. Reagan sat across from them.

Ashley and Reagan's earlier conversation had been brief and to the point. Since then Ashley had thought of a dozen questions she wanted to ask. But she needed to take them slowly.

"I must look like a wreck." Reagan ran her fingertips beneath her eyes and uttered a sound that fell short of laughter. "Your phone call . . . well, I wasn't expecting it."

Ashley blinked. Had Reagan thought she could raise the baby to adulthood without ever contacting Luke? She swallowed her amazement and glanced through a door into a hallway and then back at Reagan. "Where is he?"

"Sleeping. He should be up any minute."

Landon slipped his hand in hers, and Ashley squeezed his fingers. She found Reagan's eyes again. "How's he doing?"

"Great." She stared at her hands and twisted her fingers together. Maybe the small talk was making her nervous. All of them knew the issues that lay ahead.

Ashley couldn't wait another minute. She used her mothering voice, the one she spoke in when her son needed reassuring. "What happened, Reagan? Can you tell me?" She looked from Landon to Reagan again. "You and Luke were so . . . I never thought . . ."

162

Reagan shook her head, her eyes still down. "The whole thing was crazy, something we never meant to happen." She looked up and fresh tears made her eyes glisten. "It happened September tenth, while we were watching the Giants game." Reagan hesitated as though she might say something else, but then she brought her lips together.

Pushing the girl would be neither kind nor helpful, so Ashley took her time with the next question. "Okay, now, Reagan, help me here." Ashley slid forward in her seat and felt Landon tighten the grip he had on her hand. "You came home and probably didn't find out you were pregnant for several weeks, right?"

"Yes."

"So why didn't you talk to Luke? Why didn't you take his calls?" Ashley kept her tone even, nonthreatening. "He phoned every day, didn't he?"

A jagged sigh slipped from between Reagan's clenched teeth. As she looked up, a teardrop rolled down her cheek, and she stopped it with her fingertips. "You, Ashley, of all people—" her gaze was direct, her eyes locked on Ashley's—"should know why I didn't want to talk to him."

Ashley was about to protest, to assure Reagan that she could think of no reasons why the girl would summarily cut Luke out of her life. But a realization took shape in her heart. He'd done the same thing to her, hadn't he? When she returned from Paris, pregnant and alone. For years he talked to her only out of necessity, and then without so much as a hint of kindness.

Luke hadn't understood failure, but there were some things he'd known even less about. Grace . . . forgiveness . . . mercy.

A rush of sorrow filled Ashley's heart. She released Landon's hand and moved to sit next to Reagan. "I'm sorry." Their eyes still held. "I never thought about that."

Without any words, Reagan slipped her arms around Ashley's neck and the two of them hugged. Tears came for both of them then. Hadn't that been the hardest part of coming home from Paris? Luke's cold response, the way he'd written Ashley off as unworthy of the Baxter name? He'd refused to treat her as anything but an outcast. Reagan had seen that treatment firsthand.

No wonder she hadn't taken his calls.

Ashley pulled back and searched Reagan's eyes. "He's not like that anymore, Reagan. I don't think—" she sniffed—"I don't think he would've treated you like that. I really don't."

Landon coughed twice and motioned toward a door. "Can I get some water?"

"Sure." Reagan gave him a quick glance.

Ashley watched him go. He knew his way to the kitchen, but clearly he'd told her the truth. He was Reagan's friend, nothing more.

Reagan dried her cheeks with the backs of her hands. "Nothing was the same after that night." She paused and slid back a few inches on her seat. "Within an hour I became like any other girl. Cheap . . . easy . . . used." She sniffed again. "I knew Luke would never think of me the same again. Even if he did call."

Landon returned with three glasses of water and three coasters. He passed them out and took his seat again.

Ashley barely noticed. "Did Luke tell you that? Did he say anything to make you think his feelings for you had changed?"

"I just knew. Luke wanted everything perfect, and after that night it wasn't. It never would be again."

Some of Reagan's story filled in the missing pieces in Luke's recent history, the part Ashley hadn't understood but had somehow known was there. She remembered how quiet Luke had been in the days after September 11. He'd had a reason, of course. Reagan's father was among the missing, feared dead. But something else had bothered him, and now Ashley understood.

She looked hard at the woman next to her. "September eleventh changed him, Reagan."

"That's what your mother said." Her expression fell, and she focused on a spot near her shoes. "He's forgotten who he was."

"His life's a mess." Ashley's heartbeat picked up. This had to be the reason God wanted her to see Reagan, to let her know about the other changes. "But something else is different." She hesitated. "Remember that afternoon at the bus stop?"

"Yes." Reagan looked up. "Landon told me you'd taken him."

"Right." Landon coughed again and cut into the conversation. "Reagan and I sat by each other on the bus and tried to guess whether you and Luke would see each other in the bus terminal."

"We did." Ashley had never told this story to anyone but her parents. Not even to Landon. He hadn't been home long enough to get those kinds of details last winter. She grabbed a quick breath. "Luke . . ." She shook her head, overcome with sorrow for her little brother. He'd tried so hard to be good, and that day at the bus station had been proof that his heart of tenderness hadn't died when she returned from Paris.

And nothing since then could've made it die either.

Landon and Reagan were waiting. She swallowed and found her voice. "He cried and hugged me . . . like a little boy. The way he hugged me a long time ago, when I left for Paris. He told me he was so sorry." She looked at Reagan. "He's been broken ever since you left, Reagan. And in that one hug I felt his heart again. Scared and unsure and hanging on because he knew when he let go, your bus would be gone. And nothing would be the same again."

Tears spilled onto Reagan's cheeks again. "So . . . you and Luke are okay?"

"Yes." Ashley slipped an arm around her shoulders and smiled through her tears. "He's made a lot of bad choices; I can't disagree with that. But I watch his eyes when someone mentions you, Reagan. He still loves you." She blinked back the wetness. "He's scared and lonely and confused. He's a lot of things, but he has nothing against you. That much I know."

In another room a baby's cry filled the spaces between them. At the sound of it, Ashley's breath caught. The lusty cries belonged to her brother's son. A child who was Cole's cousin, a Baxter. She removed her arm from Reagan's shoulders and patted her knee. Her voice was a ragged whisper. "May I see him?"

Reagan nodded, and a single, small sob escaped from her throat. She brought her fingers to her lips, stood, and left the room.

When she was gone, Landon took her spot, nestling himself close against Ashley. He kissed the side of her head and whispered in her ear, "I love you."

Ashley pressed into him and turned so they were facing each other. Somewhere in the back of the apartment, the baby stopped crying, and Ashley's heart skipped a beat. She would meet her little nephew soon, but right now all she could think about was Landon.

So many feelings vied for her attention. Her brother's pain . . . the son he knew nothing of . . . Landon, so close, so real, his presence filling her senses, but for so short a time. She took his chin in her fingers and leaned up until their lips met. Their kiss was laced with sadness and lasted only a few moments. When she drew back she studied his eyes, willing him to see how she cared for him, how she would freeze this moment and stay here beside him forever if she could.

"I love you, too." She kissed him again, but the sound of footsteps made her drop her hands and sit back.

Reagan entered through a doorway at the other end of the room. She was carrying the baby, bundled in a blue blanket. The pain and guilt had fallen from her expression. Instead undeniable pride filled her eyes, and the hint of a smile played on her lips. No matter what else had gone wrong for Reagan, one thing was certain.

She loved her baby.

Ashley stood and saw her nephew's tiny hands stretch above the blanket, his fingers moving in that graceful, angel-boy way, the way Cole's had moved when he was a newborn. Landon stayed seated as Reagan walked up.

"Here." She held out her son. "His name is Thomas Luke, but I call him Tommy."

"Thomas Luke." Ashley's voice cracked as the name sounded

on her lips. She'd been too shocked to ask about the baby's name, and now here she was, staring into the face of her brother's namesake, his firstborn. She reached out and took the baby, cradling him in her arms as her heart melted with the warm, bundled-up weight of him against her chest.

That first look, the first moment when she allowed her eyes to fully take in the sight of him, made her lips part and caused her next breath to come sharp and fast. Photographs of the Baxter kids as babies hung in her parents' house. And looking at Luke's son was like watching her brother's baby picture come to life.

He looked exactly like Luke.

"Oh, Reagan." Ashley lifted her eyes. "He's beautiful."

"I know." Reagan's smile filled her face now, and even her swollen eyes couldn't dim the joy exploding in her heart over this child of hers. This child of Luke's.

Next to her, Ashley felt Landon give her leg a gentle squeeze, his way of telling her he cared about what she was feeling. But he remained seated, so very Landon, leaving this moment to her. Her eyes found the baby's face again. As long as she lived this picture would stay with her, his full lips and pale blue eyes, the white blond fuzz of his eyebrows and the shape of his head.

The baby blinked and looked at her, and suddenly she was four years old again, cradling her little brother, whispering to him.

"Hi, Wuke-y. I'm your big sister, Ashwee." Ashley grinned at the memory. Back then, all her Ls sounded like Ws. *"I'm going to be your bestest sister and you know what? I wuv you so much, Wuke-y."*

The memory was maybe her earliest of all, holding Luke, loving him, promising to be his best sister. And now, as Luke's son studied her face, she sensed him becoming a part of who she was, her heritage.

"Hi, sweet boy." She nuzzled her face against him, and thoughts came that she couldn't bring herself to voice. *I hope I get to see you grow up, little baby. And that this isn't the last time I'll ever hold you. I hope you'll get to know your daddy someday.*

She straightened and brushed her knuckles against his tiny hand. As she did, he gripped her little finger. Ashley stared at the spot where they were connected and willed the child never to let go, never forget that he had a family not just here in this Manhattan apartment but also a thousand miles away. She leaned close to him again. He smelled of new life and baby powder. She soaked in his nearness, his breath mingling with hers as she kissed his cheek.

A sudden, sad thought came to her. Her father and Luke weren't speaking, so even if this baby did meet his father, the chance existed that he might never meet his grandfather. Might never have the chance to run in the fields outside the Baxter house or skip rocks in the stream out back.

Please, God, bring Luke home. Restore our family . . . please.

A shadow stretched over the moment. Where was Luke now? How would he feel if he knew she had held his son before he did? What pain would it cause him to discover he'd fathered this baby? Most of all, how could she return to Bloomington and not tell him after seeing his son, feeling him in her arms? Thomas Luke couldn't grow up without a father, without Luke's ever knowing about him, no matter what Reagan thought.

For much of the next half hour, Ashley held her brother's baby. Too soon the visit ended and she had to hand him back to Reagan.

Landon led her to the door, and Reagan and the baby followed. They stopped in the foyer to say good-bye.

Ashley came up beside Reagan and took a final look at Thomas Luke. Her eyes met Reagan's, and Ashley hesitated. "You have to tell him." She let her gaze fall to the baby once more. "Luke needs to know he has a son."

Landon anchored himself at Ashley's other side and remained quiet except for his occasional cough. He hadn't been able to get rid of the cough he picked up at Ground Zero.

Reagan took a step backward. "Luke is living with someone. Everything would be a mess for all of us if I told him now."

Ashley didn't blink. Instead her voice fell a notch, and she kept her gaze locked on Reagan's. "And everything will be a mess for your son if you don't."

Reagan bit her lip, and for a long while none of them said anything, but clearly Ashley's words had hit their mark. The tears in Reagan's eyes told her that much.

"I'll tell him." Reagan leaned closer to her son and wiped her cheek on his blanket. "When the time is right I'll tell him. Until then—" she looked from Ashley to Landon and back again— "please, don't tell anyone else. I . . . I need to figure things out myself. Okay?"

Ashley wanted more time to consider Reagan's plea. Minutes ago, when she'd been holding Thomas Luke, Ashley knew exactly what she'd do when she got back to Bloomington. She'd drive to Luke's apartment and tell him the truth. He was a father. He needed to get on an airplane, get to New York, and take his rightful place in Reagan's life.

Whether Reagan wanted that or not.

But now the pain and fear, the guilt and uncertainty in Reagan's eyes made Ashley hesitate, if only because they reminded her of herself, the way she'd looked and felt when she returned from Paris. Her choices up to that point might have been bad, and she might not have had a clue where she was going from there, but Cole was her son, and she wanted to make the decisions that impacted him.

Ashley closed her eyes. When she opened them, she gave Reagan a single nod. "Okay." A ribbon of pain tied itself around her heart. How long would Reagan wait? How many days or weeks or months? How many years even before Luke would know about this child if she, his bestest sister, didn't tell him?

Reagan relaxed her hold on Thomas Luke and gave Ashley a look of gratitude that convinced Ashley she had made the right choice. "Thank you." She ran her tongue along her lower lip. "I'll tell him. I will tell him. Just give me a chance to make a plan."

Ashley took the few steps that separated them and hugged

both Reagan and the baby. "I will." She looked at Luke's son one last time and uttered her next words without looking at Reagan. "But hurry, please. This might be how God brings Luke back."

They said their good-byes, and not until she and Landon were down the hallway near the elevator did Ashley's tears come in earnest. Landon wrapped his arms around her and held her even after the descending car came and left.

"Luke needs to see him." Her words were muffled, spoken into Landon's denim shirt.

"God knows that." He kissed the top of her head and tightened his hold on her.

"God knows it—" Ashley searched Landon's face—"but does Reagan?"

CHAPTER SEVENTEEN

A SHLEY AND L ANDON ate dinner at Casey's Corner in a quiet booth near the back of the café. Then they walked across Central Park, and she took him to the gallery. It was closed, but her paintings were there. The one of Landon on the park bench at Ground Zero hung in the center of a window display, and Ashley's other two were positioned not far beyond as the central part of another display.

"Ashley—" Landon had her hand in his, and he took a step closer—"it's unbelievable."

Her cheeks grew hot, and she rested her head against his arm. The work was one of her best, maybe her very best. Standing next to Landon now, admiring it, she saw it in a new light. "Thanks."

"Your heart shouts from every stroke." He did a half turn and searched her face. "I mean it."

Her heart shouted from every stroke? How crazy had she been to look past this man? Ashley gave his hand a light squeeze and met his eyes again. "No one else sees that."

"You're wrong, Ash." He looked at the painting in the window again. "Your work's wonderful." He chuckled. "That's why it's here."

"I don't mean that." She leaned against him. "I mean you're the only one who sees my heart in every stroke."

She hadn't seen Landon's apartment, and he took her there after the gallery. For an hour they talked about the Baxters—Kari and Ryan's wedding, Erin and Sam moving to Texas, Brooke and Peter's precious Maddie.

It was almost midnight when Ashley stood and wandered around his living room. He had a framed photo of Jalen and himself, and another of her and Cole. Hanging on the wall was a picture Cole had colored for him back before September 11. The view out his window was of a teeming intersection not far from the lights of Broadway.

"It's nicer than I pictured." She turned and caught Landon watching her. He'd slipped an instrumental disc in the CD player, and something familiar and melodic filled the room. With a flick of a switch he softened the lighting so that a subtle glow lit the rim of the room. She raised an eyebrow. "Much nicer."

"Jalen's parents bought it for him. They knew I was coming to work with him. They'd just paid to have it fixed up before . . ." He gave a boyish shrug of his shoulders. Sorrow played with his expression. "They charge me barely anything to stay here."

She angled her head. Her heart was still full from the day's wild ride of emotions. "You miss him."

"Yes." He slipped his thumbs into his pants pockets and moved toward her, his eyes locked on something just outside the window. When they were shoulder to shoulder, he coughed twice and cleared his throat. "Every time a call comes in I think what it would've been like, you know?" He turned slightly and his eyes found hers. "If he'd lived . . . if September eleventh hadn't happened."

She nodded. "I think about that, too."

He looked out the window again, and his arm brushed against

her shoulder. "Five minutes before that first plane hit, he had his life all figured out." His eyes met hers again. "Makes you wonder."

"When you came home those few days last December . . ." Ashley looked over her shoulder at the city below before she continued. "You said you thought you'd feel him with you on every call, at every fire." She paused and found his eyes once more. "Is it like that?"

"Sometimes." His eyes narrowed. "I'm doing the job he loved. I can feel him looking over my shoulder from his place in heaven, asking God to keep me safe."

Ashley leaned against the windowsill so she could see Landon's face, see all of him, taking a mental picture to last her until next time. Whenever that would be. "Is that why you don't call?" Her tone was soft, curious. "Because you're living Jalen's life for him?"

Landon's shoulders drooped a few inches. For a while he said nothing, only looked at her, searching her eyes the same way she searched his. Looking for answers that maybe didn't quite exist. "I don't know." He took a step closer, never losing the hold he had on her eyes. "I ask myself that all the time."

Ashley was quiet.

Finally, she understood. He hadn't called because he hadn't let go of Jalen, hadn't made the decision to let go of his dream of fighting fires alongside Jalen in New York City. And since he'd committed to the department, pining over Ashley would be senseless.

At last the pieces fit together; the picture was clear.

Landon came to her and slipped his arms beneath her elbows, around her waist. "I'm sorry." He drew her to him, but held his face at a distance so he could read her eyes. "I just want the year to be over."

She didn't have to study his features to memorize the look of him. His image had long since been painted on the canvas of her heart. Still she raised her hand, and with gentle, childlike strokes she brushed her fingers along his brow and down the side of his face. "You're beautiful, Landon." She felt a sad smile play at the corners of her lips. "You want life to be good and right and fair. And when it isn't, you remain unchanged." A barely audible laugh came from her. "It's amazing."

"No." He pressed his face the slightest bit against her hand, as though any contact had to be enjoyed in their brief time together. "Winning your heart, Ashley. *That*—" he tapped her once on the tip of her nose—"was amazing."

She giggled, and colors splashed across the moment. How wonderful, having a reason to laugh when the moment wanted so badly to be sad. "I was a brat."

"You were."

"I think Irvel changed me."

"God changed you." Landon cocked his head. His eyes sparkled the way they always had when he and Ashley were together, even back when their time together was limited to whenever they might run into each other.

"Yes. God did it." She brought her other hand up and framed his face with her fingertips. "But he used Irvel."

The moment changed, and her senses were suddenly on high alert. She was here, a thousand miles from home, alone with Landon in his dimly lit Manhattan apartment with smooth, seductive music playing from the CD player, filling her senses with possibilities.

He eased his hands up her lower back and they came together. The kiss left them breathless, and Ashley saw a passion in his eyes deeper than anything she'd ever known. Before they could kiss again, he took a small step backward and cupped her chin with his hands. "I have . . . haven't I, Ash?"

What was he talking about? She bit her lip and gave a few quick shakes of her head. She wanted one thing—to be close to him again, kissing him, forgetting the time and the place and the danger of the moment. Passion colored her tone. "You have what?"

"Won your heart?" Landon's voice held a barely detectable question mark.

Ashley came to him again. After months of silence, her answer demanded voice. "Yes, Landon." She'd feared just such a moment since Paris, yet here she was. And nothing in all the world could've felt more right. She gave him a simple kiss. "My heart's all yours."

Once more their lips met. For a long while they let themselves be carried on a wave that surged above the shore of common sense. But then he took her hands in his. His fingers trembled and his breathing was ragged, but she saw determination in his gaze. "I . . . I can't do this."

His words landed them safely on the beach. "It's late." She sucked in a steadying breath. "I need to go anyway."

"When do you leave?" He still had hold of her hands, and he worked his thumbs across her knuckles.

"Seven-fifteen."

"I work at six."

She wanted to ask him if this was it, if they wouldn't see each other again for another six months. But instead she breathed a silent prayer, a thanks to God for giving Landon the sense to take a step backwards. Whatever the future held, they would do it God's way and believe—in the process—that he would one day give them all they'd ever dreamed of.

"Remember last time we said good-bye?" Landon was trembling less now, in control again.

"We agreed to make no promises." Her heart held its breath. Something about this time with Landon felt miles deeper, more certain. But she wouldn't ask for a commitment, even now. "Right?"

"Right." His voice was quiet. The passion remained, even if it was no longer calling the shots. "Let's do something different this time."

"Different?"

"I don't ever want to lose you, Ash. I never want—" his eyes darted around the room, as though he was searching for the right words—"I never want you to wonder about my feelings for you, never want you to imagine me walking with some girl and a baby and wonder if I've found someone else."

She smiled and let her fingers play lightly against his palms. "I was stupid, that's all."

"No." He shook his head and something serious flashed in his eyes. "I was wrong to leave you like that last time. Especially when all I want is to go home with you and start life the way I want it to be."

"So . . . ?"

"So, I promise you, Ashley, here and now." He brought her hands to his lips and kissed first one, then the other. "I'm coming home for you. I'll finish work here in New York, and then I'm coming home. And if a day goes by between now and then when I don't call you, you'll never have to wonder again."

"Landon . . ." Something old and fading in her wanted to object, to make him aware that he owed her nothing, that she wasn't worthy of his love let alone his commitment. But a louder voice echoed in her soul, assuring her that this was part of God's plan, part of the future he had for her.

Maybe even the biggest part.

She closed her eyes for two seconds and opened them. Then she did it again.

"Okay, now you're acting like Irvel." Laughter danced in his words, and he raised his eyebrows at her. "What are you doing?"

"Convincing myself—" she laughed as she opened her eyes— "that I'm not dreaming."

The call came as she was on her way to the airport the next morning. She barely had time to snag her phone from her purse before it stopped ringing.

"Hello?"

Static rang across the line, and a voice tried to rise above it. "Ashley . . . tell you . . ."

"Excuse me?" The traffic outside her cab made it impossible to hear. "I think we have a bad connection." She pressed the phone against her ear and ducked her head closer to her knees. "Could you repeat that, please?"

The static grew worse. ". . . to tell you . . . from Paris—"

Then the call went dead.

Her mind raced over the few details. Someone from Paris? With something to tell her? A cold chill ran down Ashley's spine. She closed her phone and returned it to her purse. The caller had used part of her name. Otherwise she would've suspected it was a wrong number. But why Paris? She'd left nothing of herself back in Paris. No artwork, no friendships, no promises to return. And today—reveling in the glow of last night with Landon—she needed no reminders of that time in her life.

The call haunted her all the way to La Guardia, but with every few blocks she worked on her memory of it. Maybe the voice hadn't said Ashley, but something else. *Actually,* maybe. Yes, that had to be it. *Actually, I can't hear you . . .* or *Actually this is the wrong number . . .* or *I have the wrong number, actually.*

Actually was a common word, wasn't it? Or maybe it was *as we.* Maybe the caller said, *As we all know, this is a wrong number.*

Ashley wore the thought for a while, but it didn't quite fit. Someone from Paris—of all places—had accidentally dialed her cell phone number? Was that even possible?

She was still uncomfortable when she boarded the plane. Instead of pleasant convincing thoughts about wrong numbers and words that sounded like her name, she began going over a dozen reasons why someone from Paris would call her. The impossible existed, of course. Someone at the gallery where she'd worked had remembered her art and wanted to display it. Or maybe they needed an American to run the desks again.

But her memories of Paris were hardly laced with compliments for her artwork or of happy moments behind the gallery desk helping English-speaking customers.

They were completely taken up with the dark days of Jean-Claude Pierre.

And any phone call from Paris was enough to turn her stomach. The possibilities balanced like an avalanche positioned directly over her chest, so that even thinking about them made it almost impossible to breathe. She never wanted to think about Paris again, not as long as she lived. Not when her entire being wanted only to think of Landon Blake.

And the fact that—after a lifetime of feeling unloved and unwanted and unable to love back—she was finally standing on the brink of happily-ever-after.

CHAPTER EIGHTEEN

THE FREETHINKERS MEETING was just getting started when Luke walked in through the back door. He slipped into a seat along the side, halfway toward the front, and slid his backpack under the chair. Then he glanced around. Had to be more than a hundred students packing the room, but Luke wasn't surprised. Lori had told him the speaker would clear up any lingering doubts he had about her occasional wanderings. The talk today was on "Open Love—Relationships That Work."

He didn't want to miss a minute of it.

He opened his notebook and took a pen from his backpack. The speaker looked to be in his thirties, short hair and nice clothes. The look of a company president or a doctor at St. Anne's. The man's voice was smooth, his smile cool and confident. Further proof that Lori was right. This way of thinking wasn't way-out or crazy. It was practical and more common all the time.

No matter what the great Dr. Baxter thought about it.

"Relationships can be painful. How many of you have seen that?" The speaker moved up to the first row of seats and made eye contact with several students.

A few hands lifted, and a general murmuring of agreement passed over the room.

"That's because too many people work their relationships by the world's rule book. A rule book of morality and rigidity." He stopped and lifted his chin. "Freethinking means we take a hard look at a situation, we think outside the box, which lends freedom to all situations." He paused. "Including love."

He went on to talk about a relationship he'd had his first year of college. "The two of us were exclusive, playing by somebody else's rules." His gaze roamed the audience. "But she met a guy in her biology class, and a week later we had the breakup scene." He turned and walked to the other end of the room. "Tears and apologies and sadness, all completely unnecessary."

Luke pictured Reagan. They hadn't had that scene, but they might as well have.

The speaker stroked his chin. "Now, what if we'd been freethinkers?" He let the idea hang in the room for a moment. "Love wouldn't be boxed in by a list of archaic rules."

He asked for two volunteers, then chose a girl and a guy from the middle of the room. When they were up front, he had them face each other and act out a scene like the one he'd just described.

The couple looked uncomfortable at first, but after a few awkward lines, they relaxed. "I met someone," the girl said. She shrugged for effect and earned a few laughs from across the room.

"Really?" The guy raised his eyebrows. "Someone you like?"

"Yeah. I like him a lot."

The speaker stepped in and gestured toward the couple. "Work it now; think outside the rules."

"Okay." The guy looked to the speaker for encouragement, and then back at the girl. "That's cool, because there's a girl in my math class I've wanted to hang out with."

The girl took a step closer and winked. "Maybe we could double-date."

The students burst into a spontaneous bit of applause and laughter, and the speaker waved the volunteers back to their seats.

He punctuated the air with his finger. "Perfect!" When the laughter died down, he continued. "We laugh because we're so entrenched in society's way of thinking." He spoke with his hands, his eyes wide with conviction. "Freethinking takes time. But doesn't it make sense in relationships?"

Freethinking makes sense in relationships. Luke scribbled the words across his pad of paper. Doubts poked pins at his conscience. How had he felt when he found out about Lori's abortion, that she'd been with another man? Betrayed. Upset to the point of almost leaving her. But since then she'd talked at length about love the same way the speaker was talking now.

Free . . . open . . . a way of expressing self through physical intimacy. One person could never be enough for a task that involved. Luke wasn't sure.

"Think about yourself, your creative inner person." The speaker's voice rose. "Could one person really meet those needs, the innate desire within you to share your body with another?" He stopped and raised an eyebrow. "Now don't mistake what I'm saying for irresponsibility. You owe it to yourself and anyone you share yourself with to use protection. That goes without saying. But within those safety bounds, free love, freethinking is very possible."

He began to list the reasons why open relationships worked best. Multiple partners increased a person's ability to make love interesting and satisfying to all partners. With freethinking, guilt and regret and sorrow were eliminated from the formula of love.

"Now tell me that doesn't sound like a better deal than what the traditional rule book offers."

Luke felt himself nodding along with the others in the room. This was exactly what Lori had been talking about, and maybe she'd been right. What did it matter if she'd spent an afternoon or an evening with someone else? The experience would make her a better lover, so why should he care?

The speaker stopped in the middle of the room and pointed at them. "Tell me this. If loving one person is right, how can loving *more* than one person be wrong?"

Once more a niggling thought scratched at the door of Luke's conscience. Something about sexual immorality and God's plan for love. Luke gritted his teeth, banished the thought, and tuned back in to what the speaker was saying.

"I challenge you to live life on your own terms, not by someone else's rules." He made eye contact with a few of them. "Love . . . life . . . your bodies. They're meant to be shared. And a year from now you'll never have to dread a broken relationship again."

For a moment Luke tried to imagine what the great Dr. Baxter would think of this speaker. That he was blind, probably. Walking in darkness, ignorant of the truth. Lost. Luke used the end of his pen to scratch the back of his head. How long had it been since he'd seen his father? Two months, maybe? Yes, it'd been that long. For a moment—even though the speaker was going on about his challenge—Luke could do nothing but think about his dad, his mom . . . his entire family.

Did they miss him? Were they sorry for being so judgmental? for running him off and forcing him to make it on his own? Luke scribbled a series of circles around the holes in his notebook paper. If their faith meant anything, shouldn't they accept him for who he'd become? not expect him to live life on their terms?

Nothing freethinking about that.

And his dad, of all people, a man with more education than anyone in the family. He should understand the need to challenge life, to find nontraditional answers, to push the envelope on why life existed. His dad's training was in biology and medicine, after all. Disciplines with provable theories and exact formulas.

How could the man believe God was behind all of life when

science had so many answers? A strange ache settled across his chest, and he wished he could see his father again. Just for an evening or an afternoon.

Luke shook his head. *What's your problem, Baxter? Your old life held no answers; why question the new one?*

Return to me, Son. I have loved you with an everlasting love. Return even now.

Luke straightened in his seat and gave a slight shake of his head. Who said that? The words had been whispered, as though someone was standing behind him, leaning close to his ear. He glanced over his shoulder. The student behind him gave him a strange look and focused his attention back on the speaker. Luke slunk down and turned to the front of the room again.

If the kid behind him hadn't said it, then who?

Back when he'd been duped into believing the whole Christian thing, he'd imagined a voice like that all the time. Daily, even. But it had grown softer with time, and Luke hadn't heard even a whisper in months. Why would his imagination dredge up such a thing now? at a Freethinkers meeting?

Luke bit the tip of his pen. Probably as a reminder. He would have to attend many more meetings like this one before the habits of his upbringing faded into nothingness and gave him the true freedom he sought.

The speaker was wrapping up, and Luke looked at his watch. Lori was out tonight, studying at the library with some friends. He hesitated and stared at the notes in front of him. Then, in a gradual morphing of grays and blacks and muted colors, the image changed, and it wasn't notes he was seeing at all, but faces. His father's . . . his mother's. Ashley's and Kari's.

Reagan's.

The ache in his heart worked its way through his body, even to the tips of his fingers. He begged his mind to change channels, think of something else. *Anything* else. But their images remained, and he heard none of the speaker's concluding remarks.

The images of the people who once made up his world had

come more than once, and each time hurt more than the last. At first Luke thought the pain came because the faces of his past made his new lifestyle hard to swallow. But now—in a room full of freethinkers, at a time when he wanted so much to embrace this new way of seeing life—now he understood the ache in his heart.

It wasn't only that his past flew smack in the face of his present. Rather, his memories gave him the strangest feeling, a feeling he allowed for just a fraction of a second before sending it scurrying back to the cave from which it came: That he wanted to do an about-face, set out at a dead run, straight past the piles of hurt feelings and words he regretted, and on into yesterday.

Before the detours he was taking made it impossible to find his way back.

John was more tired than usual but he couldn't sleep.

Elizabeth snored softly beside him, so he crept out of bed and made his way down the hallway to the living room and his old blue recliner, the chair where he liked to read his Bible and take in the newspaper on occasional summer mornings. Sometimes, on nights like this, he would settle back in the chair and look straight ahead at the mantel above the fireplace, at the framed senior portraits of his five children.

Brooke . . . Kari . . . Ashley . . . Erin . . . Luke.

Normally Elizabeth took on the role of family worrier, but tonight John felt uncomfortable in his own skin. The humidity was up, and even his heart beat out of sync.

Ashley was just home from New York, but they hadn't gotten a chance to talk. When they did, he would have to tell her about the phone call. Some woman from Paris, who'd spoken to him in broken English. She needed to talk to Ashley, and when she learned Ashley wasn't around, she pressed further. A cell phone or hotel, some other way to reach her. The call was critical. He'd questioned her about the nature of the matter. But the woman hadn't shared the details other than one: It was critical she talk to Ashley.

He'd planned to tell Ashley the moment she got home. But she'd breezed in earlier today and collected Cole, stopping barely long enough to make small talk. Yes, they'd liked her paintings; yes, they were displayed at a gallery in Manhattan; yes, she'd seen Landon.

Then she thanked him and Elizabeth and left with a round of kisses and promises to come by sometime that week.

John stared at her photo now, the one she'd fought against her last year of high school.

"Come on, Dad, the whole senior portrait thing's outdated." She'd rolled her eyes and flopped down on the sofa that still stood next to his recliner. "Can't you just take any old picture and put it in a frame?"

John and Elizabeth had insisted, and Ashley rose to the occasion. She looked stunning in the picture, her eyes a curious mix of pain and rebellion and the briefest glimmer of hope.

Was it his imagination, or had she been in more than the usual hurry earlier today? His heart told him things she hadn't. That whatever happened in New York, some of it she hadn't been willing to share.

His eyes moved to Erin's picture. Dark-haired with a rounder, plainer face, Erin's eyes told of her hesitancy, her desire to be accepted. More than the rest, she enjoyed being around family. How well would she do after Labor Day, when she and Sam headed off to Texas? Last fall their marriage had been in trouble, and now, certainly, the greatest tests were ahead. If they'd been able to have a baby, perhaps the move would be easier. At least Erin would have family of her own to take with her.

John studied his youngest daughter's face. *Lord, give her a child. Please, Father.*

Sometimes when he prayed he could practically hear God echoing a reply in his soul. But not tonight. Tonight he felt only the assurance that God had heard him, and somehow, some-time, God would answer.

His eyes rested for a beat on Kari's photograph. She was well and happy and about to marry a man who had been her heart's love since the two were teenagers. *Thank you, God. Thank you for delivering her, for redeeming her from the pain of her past.*

But what about Brooke?

John looked deep into his oldest daughter's eyes. She believed now, at least somewhat. She and Peter attended church, which had to be some indication of their changing beliefs. But Brooke and her husband were so private, rarely sharing about the faith that might or might not be going on in their home. And though they were more open to learning about God now, they didn't seem as close to each other as they'd once been.

A sigh found its way up from John's heart. Sometimes, when he couldn't stop fear from lighting on the windowsill of his soul, he imagined what might happen if Maddie had been sick. Really sick. If the fevers and constant bouts of illness had led to something devastating and deadly. What would Brooke and Peter have thought of God then? If September 11 had affected them all so profoundly, what about the death of a child? One of their own.

John rubbed his fingertips into his brow and fear took flight.

If he'd learned one thing over the years as a parent and a doc-tor, it was this: Worry did no good. In his early days—back when he wasn't sure how he would get through med school, and even a decade ago when he wasn't sure whether Elizabeth would survive her bout with cancer—he'd armed himself with truths from Scripture.

Truths that had a way of clearing the windowsill.

He closed his eyes and let the words run like a soothing stream of water over the parched areas of his heart. *"Do not be anxious about anything, but in everything, with prayer and petition, give your thanks to God, and the peace of God, which transcends all understanding, will guard your hearts and minds in Christ Jesus."*

How many times had those words brought peace at such a moment?

But this night was different. He wasn't worried, just full. Full of thoughts about whatever the future might hold for all of them. Or maybe that was worry dressed in curiosity's clothes. His eyes shifted to Luke's picture.

Ah, Luke, my boy. Where are you now? Tears poked pins at John's eyes, and he knew, deep within, that this was the reason he couldn't sleep. It was bigger than worry and curiosity combined. It was a desperate fear, a terrible longing for his little boy. Not the type of fear that merely lighted on the windowsill of his soul, but one that consumed it.

A sound interrupted his thoughts. He turned toward the doorway and saw her standing there in her navy satin robe, watching him. "Elizabeth . . ."

"I felt your absence." She came closer and took the spot on the sofa nearest him. Her gaze left him and found the photos on the mantel. "This is *my* job, John."

He studied their son's picture. "I know."

"It's Luke, isn't it?"

"Of course." He leaned forward, shifting so he could see his wife. "Remember how he was as a child?"

"The light of your life." Elizabeth looked at him, and the sadness in her small smile nearly broke his heart. "You two were inseparable. Every day he did something to amaze you."

John looked at his son's photo. That was exactly right. Luke was the most easygoing child, so much so that discipline was rarely required. A memory tapped lightly on the door of John's heart, and he willingly opened it. . . .

Luke was with them in the church parking lot, and for some reason Elizabeth had gone ahead toward the main building. The Baxter kids were taught to never cross a parking lot without an adult. Breaking the rule would mean punishment.

"Stay with us," Elizabeth always told them. "Drivers are looking for adults, not little people."

But that morning, without looking, Luke set off at a flat run after Elizabeth. He made it halfway to her when he ran right in front an oncoming Jeep. John's scream was lost in the screeching of brakes. Somehow the Jeep stopped in time—just inches from Luke. By the time John and Elizabeth reached him, their son's face was pale, his eyes wide.

They thanked the driver of the Jeep and held tight to Luke. John had been about to scold him when they realized he was crying. No, not just crying. Sobbing. Gulping, heartfelt sobs that shook his shoulders and back.

Elizabeth mouthed something to John about Luke's being afraid. Obviously that was the source of his tears. So John stroked his son's back. "Are you crying because you're scared?"

The boy pulled back and rubbed his eyes with his chubby fists. "N-n-nooo." Luke's tears came harder then. "I'm n-n-not afraid."

"Then what is it, Son? Did you get hurt?"

"Daddy—" Luke's response still rang clear in John's memory—"I'm sorry I didn't obey you." He flung his arms around John's neck and grabbed hold of Elizabeth's dress slacks. "I'm sorry, Mommy and Daddy."

John pulled himself from the past and stared at Elizabeth. "Remember the parking-lot incident, back when Luke was five years old?"

A soft laugh played in Elizabeth's tone. "More worried about disobeying than dying."

Other memories came then, tiptoeing up the steps of his mind and slipping in before he could stop them. The way Luke had imitated everything John did. Once when Luke watched John pull weeds from Elizabeth's garden, Luke went out the next morning and pulled up every single baby carrot plant.

"I got your weeds, Mama," he sang out when he came back in the house that morning. He pointed to his shirt, stretched out and folded up, overflowing with baby carrot plants. "Just like Daddy."

As he got older, Luke adored his sisters, and when one of them got in trouble for picking on him, he would brush off the offense. "It's okay," he'd tell John. "Don't be mad at her; she didn't mean it."

In his early teens, if John wore his Indiana University shirt to a picnic, Luke wore his also. For most of high school Luke even toyed with the idea of med school so that one day he could work at St. Anne's alongside John. In the end, Cs in math and science kept him from that.

From early adolescence, Luke had brought every troublesome thought, every curiosity, every goal and plan and dream to his father. He also explained the reason he didn't do drugs or drink as even some of his church friends did. He feared it would damage that special something he shared with John.

"We're not like other sons and fathers," Luke told him one day. "You're my best friend, Dad."

John turned to his wife, and the memories lifted. "When Ashley got back from Paris—" he paused—"that's when he started changing."

"Yes." She gave a slow nod, and her eyes held a shadow of pain. "His standard was so high."

"Why didn't we see where it would go? How damaging it was to expect perfection of people?"

"I thought it was a stage." Elizabeth shrugged with one shoulder. "Residual from a lifetime of making mostly good choices."

This was ground they'd covered a hundred times since Luke left home, but the signposts were only clear now in light of how the events in his life had played out. Luke's faith before September 11 reminded John of a pond that had formed in their backyard once after heavy rains. The creek behind their house overflowed, and at a glance it looked as if a formidable lake had appeared where land had been a day before. But an hour after the rains stopped, the lake disappeared.

"What happened to all that water?" the children asked him that day.

"It looked deep because it was so big," John answered. "But it wasn't deep at all, maybe only an inch."

The shallow pond vanished the moment the rain stopped, the same way Luke's faith collapsed right alongside the Twin Towers. What looked like an ocean of conviction and belief was nothing more than the shallow pond of self-righteousness.

"John." Elizabeth's voice sounded tired, worn out. "It's after one."

"I know." He looked at Luke's picture again. For a long moment he was silent, refusing to free the thing that wouldn't take wing, the thing that hunted his soul like a lion and made sleep all but impossible. The fear he had never voiced.

"What if—" his tone was more desperate than sad, and he turned to Elizabeth once more—"what if he never comes back?"

CHAPTER NINETEEN

A SHLEY FELT LIKE one of the patients here at Sunset Hills.

The information about Luke's son made her distracted and distant, and each night she went to bed knowing that tomorrow had to be the day. That finally Reagan would make the call or fly out with Tommy in her arms. If she called, then the moment Luke knew the truth, he'd fly to New York, maybe even tell his family what he was doing.

Ashley was at work that June afternoon, a week after returning from New York. Twice she'd tried to call Luke, just to feel him out, to see if Reagan had called him. But both times he'd been gone, so she'd left a message.

If the knowledge of Luke's son wasn't enough to distract her, she'd received word from Margaret Wellington that one of her paintings had sold already. They were sending her a check in the mail and wanted her to hurry with the next three. She and Cole had gone to dinner with her parents to celebrate, and that night she'd spent an hour on the phone with Landon.

Ashley calculated that if she sold three pieces in two months, she could consider quitting her job at Sunset Hills. If she wanted to. But as long as Irvel was living, she definitely didn't want to. Irvel and Edith and Helen and Bert—they did too many wonderful things for her heart.

She stirred the chicken soup and tested it with her finger. Residents at Sunset Hills ate their soup warm, not hot. Less danger of burns that way. She took the pot and a tray of buttered toast to the table and went to find the residents. Bert was eating with them now, and though he still spent most of the afternoon in his room polishing his saddle, he enjoyed company for lunch. He was more talkative these days, but more confused also.

It took Ashley a few minutes to get them all seated. Irvel at the head of the table, as always, with Helen on one side and Edith on the other. Bert sat at the other end. Before Ashley could say the prayer, Irvel pointed at Bert. "You're a very nice old man." She used her finger to draw invisible circles in the air for emphasis. "But I'm glad you're at that end."

Helen shot Irvel a look. "What's wrong with him?" She raised one eyebrow in Bert's direction. "Is he a spy?"

"I got a saddle." Bert gave the women a shy smile. When none of them responded, he looked at Ashley. "I got me a nice saddle."

"Yes, Bert. Very nice."

"Very nice." Edith gave a series of slow nods and stared at the table in front of her. "Saddles. Very nice."

"Spies use saddles." Helen had seen her daughter, Sue, the day before, so she wasn't angry or confrontational, but she definitely was nervous. She eyed Irvel. "Don't spies use saddles, Agnes?"

Irvel took a slow look over her shoulder, as though Helen might be talking to someone standing behind her. Then she looked at Helen and patted the woman's hand the way a mother might pat the hand of a confused child. "Dear—" she paused for effect—"I'm not Agnes." She pointed at Bert. "And he's not Hank." She dropped her voice to a whisper. "Hank gets jealous of gentlemen callers."

Ashley doled out the soup and let her mind drift. Little had changed at Sunset Hills, and the flow of conversation was com-

fortable. Ashley's Past-Present method of dealing with the patients—letting them live in the time frame where they were most
comfortable—had helped them. Irvel's doctor had figured out a
different batch of daily medication, so she was up and doing
better. For now, anyway.

Ashley was about to serve herself when a knock sounded from
the other room. Her eyes found Irvel's. "I'll be right back."

"If it's Hank, ask him to join us." She winked at Edith. "Hank
loves a good bowl of chili."

Helen dropped her spoon. "No one told me we were having
chili. My mother's the one who makes chi—"

The voices faded as Ashley rounded the corner and headed for
the front door. She opened it and found her father, wearing dress
slacks and a short-sleeved shirt. She smiled and opened the door
wide. "Hi."

"I had an hour between patients." He stepped in and hugged
her. "Thought I'd drop in and see the Sunset Hills gang."

"They're in the other room." Ashley nodded toward the dining room. "Everyone's in fine form."

More than once her father had marveled at the improvements
the residents had made under Ashley's care. He'd dropped in two
other times to see for himself the easy way each of them handled
daily routines now that they weren't being forced to live within
the confines of reality.

"Come on." Ashley grinned and led the way. When they
reached the table, Ashley stood near Bert and put her arm
around her father's waist. "This is my father, everyone. Dr.
Baxter."

"Dear," Irvel leaned across the table, bringing herself a few
inches closer to Ashley. "I don't think anyone's sick."

"Everyone's fine." Her father took the chair between Edith
and Bert and rested his forearms on the table. "I'm here for a
visit."

"Doctor visits are very expensive." Irvel gave a slight shake of her head and raised her eyebrows at the others. "Maybe if we pitch our money together."

Helen lowered her brow and looked from Ashley to her father and back again. "He's safe." She gestured toward Ashley. "That girl checked him, right?"

"Right." Ashley gave her father a quick grin. "He's been checked."

Burt had finished half his soup, and now he took his napkin and began making slow, deliberate circles on the table near his bowl. It was Ashley's signal that he'd had enough interaction. He was ready to get back to work, rubbing oil into the saddle she'd positioned in his room last winter.

Over the next thirty minutes, Ashley helped Bert to his room and the three women to their recliners in the living room. When they were all settled, she and her father slipped out front and headed for the porch swing, something Lu, the owner of Sunset Hills, had purchased that spring.

"For when you need a sanity break," she'd explained to Ashley. "And because it makes the house look more like a home."

Ashley and her father sat in the swing and set it gently in motion. "Beautiful day." Her father stared past the roses in bloom along the walkway, through the full trees to the blue sky beyond.

"They say July is supposed to be a scorcher."

Her father nodded. "Makes me glad Kari and Ryan are waiting until the end of September to get married." He tilted his head back some. "Fall looks better on Bloomington than most any other place in the country."

Silence fell between them, and Ashley marveled at how comfortable she felt. God had changed her, no doubt. He'd given her Sunset Hills and convinced her to share her past with Landon. Now she had no skeletons in her closet and no intention of wasting another minute of life. She and Cole were closer than ever, and even her parents seemed to have forgotten that she was the family outcast.

A bluebird landed on the grass a few feet away. It looked at them and hopped three times before taking to the sky again. Ashley breathed in the smell of jasmine and damp grass. "Even with the humidity, I love summer."

"Me, too." Her father used his feet to give the swing another push. Then he turned slightly and looked at her. His voice was casual, his expression relaxed. "Can I ask you something, Ashley?"

"Sure." She angled her body so she could see him better.

"How come you didn't say much about your time in New York?"

"New York?" Ashley tried not to let the alarm show on her face. Had he somehow found out about Luke? If so, why had he waited until now to ask her about it? She swallowed and gripped the heavy chain that held the swing. "I thought I did."

Her father sucked his cheek in a little. His eyes lit up the way they did when he was teasing her. " 'Fine . . . good . . . fantastic.' " He paused. "My daughters usually have more to say than that."

Ashley's shoulder muscles eased some. Good. He was looking for conversation, not a confession. "I guess I was in a hurry to get Cole home." She uttered a laugh, but it sounded tinny, anxious. "We're reading the Junie B. Jones books, you know. Takes about a half hour each night."

"I sort of thought you'd tell me about the phone call."

Again Ashley's heartbeat doubled. She met her father's eyes and tried not to sound interested. "What phone call?"

"You know . . ." A breeze drifted through the trees and brushed through the spaces between them. "The one from Paris."

Ashley let go of one fearful possibility—that her father somehow knew about Luke's little boy—and jerked her mind in a completely different direction. This wasn't about Luke; it was about the strange call she'd gotten before leaving New York.

She twisted her face up. "You mean the wrong number? The person called once when I was on my way to the airport. I heard every other word, so I figured it was a mistake."

Her father stared at her. His feet went still and gradually the swing slowed down. "It wasn't a mistake, Ashley." He leaned over his legs. "I would've said something sooner, but I assumed she got through to you."

"Who?" Ashley's throat felt tight.

"The woman from Paris." He searched her face. "That's partly why I wanted to come by—to see what she said. Why it was so critical that she find you that morning."

"What—" Ashley ran her tongue along her lower lip—"what did she want?"

Her father gave a sideways shake of his head. "At first I sort of figured maybe she'd seen your Web site." He smiled at her. "It's beautiful, Ashley. Your work is wonderful."

She felt the corners of her mouth climb up her cheeks. "Thank you, Daddy." For the briefest instant, Ashley allowed herself to bask in the sunlight of her father's praise. Then she did the only thing she could think to do: put the Paris phone call on hold. She stood and held up a finger. "I have to check on them." She tiptoed through the open door and glanced around. The women were still sleeping, and no sounds came from Bert's room. She waited another few seconds, then rejoined her father.

"So," she caught his eyes again, "you think Paris might be interested in my work? After I've been gone for so long?"

"That's what I thought at first." He hesitated. "I asked the woman if I could take a message, and she said no. She said it was critical that she talk to you personally. After that, I wasn't sure what she wanted." He reached out and patted her knee. "That's why I'm here. I thought you could fill in the details."

"I know nothing." Ashley sat a little straighter and gave the swing a small push with her feet. Why in the world would someone from Paris call? And what critical thing could the woman—whoever she was—possibly have to talk about?

Ashley realized her father was watching her, catching every emotion as it filtered across her face. She laughed softly. "If it's that critical, I'm sure she'll call back."

"Yes, I suppose." He paused, searching her eyes. "It just seemed strange. I . . . I didn't want it to be about Cole."

There it was, out in the open.

The dots Ashley had refused to consider, let alone connect—that somehow someone from Paris knew about Cole. With the frightening possibilities suddenly as clear as a summer morning, she could do nothing but let the questions come.

Had Jean-Claude Pierre changed his mind? The artist had sneered at her the last time they spoke, suggesting she get an abortion, telling her he wanted nothing to do with *her* child. Cole couldn't have been the only illegitimate child he'd fathered, not when he looked at sex as merely an artistic form of exercise.

So what had he done now, hired an attorney? Had the woman called in an effort to find her and track down Jean-Claude's son? Ashley wasn't sure, but she didn't think he'd be entitled to visitation rights after being out of the boy's life for so long. Of course, he had plenty of money if he wanted a legal battle. So was that it? Had he changed his mind, and now he wanted a son?

The idea terrified Ashley like nothing ever had.

"Maybe—" her father's voice brought her back from the edge of a cliff, a canyon of fear that knew no bottom—"it's about some bookkeeping detail, something you could help them with. That could be it, couldn't it?"

Hope gave her a burst of air and helped her catch her breath.

"Yes." The more she thought about it, the more she liked the idea. "Yes, that could be it."

Why hadn't she thought of that before? In fact, that's exactly what it had to be. She'd been privy to dozens of office books, especially where the English-speaking customers were concerned.

Her father stood and stretched. "That makes sense." He held his hand out and helped Ashley to her feet. "They probably have a new bookkeeper, someone who wants to know how you handled things, something like that."

"Probably." Ashley gave her father's hand a squeeze. She put the call from Paris out of her mind.

"How are things with Landon?"

Ashley's heart melted. "Good." She dropped her chin and felt her eyes sparkle as they hadn't yet that day. "Very good, really."

"I miss seeing him around." Her father's smile was kind, and he gave Ashley a hug.

"Me, too." She stepped toward the front door of the house.

"You're talking more these days?" He didn't know the details that she'd shared with her mother, but obviously he knew more than he usually let on.

"Yes." Ashley's cheeks grew hot. "Much more."

Time was when conversation about her and Landon would frustrate her, make her feel as though everyone in her family was trying to plan her life. But now, mention of Landon and the relationship they were building warmed her heart.

"Well—" he headed down the sidewalk toward his car—"tell him we said hi."

"I will."

Her father stopped and turned then, halfway down the walk. "Does he ever see Reagan?"

Ashley's heart flew to her throat, and she put her fingers near her neck so she might find her voice. "Um . . . I'm not sure." She shrugged, hating the lie. "Manhattan's a big place."

"Yes." Her father nodded, his eyes wistful. "Well, ask him sometime." He gave her a lopsided grin, one that didn't disguise the sadness in his expression. "I still think things would be different for Luke if he and Reagan would . . ." His voice drifted. "Just ask him sometime, okay?"

"Okay."

Her father waved again and went to his car. He was a tall man—tall and proud, with the gait of a thirty-five-year-old. At least that was how he used to look. All his life he'd been the strong one, especially when things didn't turn out the way they'd planned. When she came home from Paris pregnant with Cole . . . when Kari's husband left her . . . and when Tim was murdered by that crazy college kid.

But this—the loss of Luke from his life—was sapping the strength from him, a little more each day.

Throughout the afternoon, as Ashley finished her shift at Sunset Hills, she hurt at the burden her father bore, how he missed Luke all these months. But that didn't hurt as much as the fact that she held the information that might make everything right again—and she couldn't do a thing about it.

CHAPTER TWENTY

THE FEVERS WERE BACK, and Brooke had never felt more helpless in all her life.

It was Monday morning, just twelve hours after the family had gathered at the Baxter house for little Hayley's third birthday. Maddie was fine at the party, riding her tricycle up and down the long driveway, calling out to Cole to catch her as she pedaled.

Now she lay beneath her bedsheet burning up. It was her moaning that had awakened Brooke sometime before five that morning and brought her to Maddie's side. She'd been sitting by her, patting her head with a cool cloth and praying ever since.

Brooke sat on the edge of her daughter's mattress and glanced across the room at Hayley. Their younger daughter was sitting cross-legged, watching the scene through wide, worried eyes. "Mommy, is Maddie sick again?"

"Yes, honey." Brooke clenched her teeth. "She has a fever."

Hayley tilted her blonde head and bit her lip. "God's going to make her better, Mommy, right?"

"Yes, sweet girl." Brooke refused to hold the question up and analyze it. "God's going to make her better."

Hayley slipped out of bed and padded over to Brooke's knee. "Can I get dressed?"

"Sure." Brooke led the way to the girls' closet. She pulled out a short-sleeved pink pullover and found a pair of light denim shorts in one of the dresser drawers. Hayley had changed much in the past year. Where Maddie was quiet and conservative, Hayley was the adventurer, their independent daughter. It wasn't enough to keep up with Maddie; she wanted to do everything faster, better, more completely than Maddie.

Even if she was nearly two years younger.

Brooke helped her into the clothes and ran a brush through her hair. Fine, golden hair, just like Maddie's. She was tying Hayley's Cinderella tennis shoes when Peter stuck his head into the room.

"How is she?"

"Hot." Brooke wasn't sure why, but her husband's attitude irritated her. If he cared so much, why hadn't he been in here for the past two hours, holding vigil by their daughter's bed, praying for her? The way Brooke had been.

"How hot?" He entered the room and stood near Maddie. He studied her for a few seconds, and then looked at Brooke again. "Did you take it?"

"No." Brooke straightened and patted Hayley on the back. "Go on, honey. You can stay in the playroom until breakfast, okay?"

"Okay." Hayley flashed her a carefree grin and then grabbed hold of Peter's legs on her way out of the room. "Maddie's sick." She craned her head back so she could see Peter's eyes. "Make her better, okay, Daddy?"

"Okay, pumpkin." He gave Hayley a smile that Brooke recognized as decidedly plastic. "Go play now, all right?"

Hayley skipped from the room, humming a happy song. When she was gone, Peter looked at Brooke. "Why didn't you take her temperature? A detail like that could help us figure out what's wrong; you know that."

"Listen—" Brooke felt the hair on the back of her neck rise— "I don't need you telling me what do to, Peter. I'm a doctor, too." She lowered her voice so the anger in her tone wouldn't wake Maddie. "I can tell a child's temperature within half a degree." She planted her hands on her hips. "She has about a hundred and three, okay? How's that going to help us figure out what's happening to her?"

Peter's hard breath fell just short of a huff. He sat next to Maddie and touched her forehead with the back of his fingers. "She's hotter than that now."

"Okay, so if you're so worried, tell me this." Brooke took a few steps closer. "How come you weren't in here sitting beside her all morning?"

"Because you were." His answer came sharp and fast. "And if you're such a good doctor, you should've been able to handle it without me. That way at least one of us can go to work today."

Brooke wanted to scream at him. Was that all he cared about, that one of them made it to work? She was about to open her mouth, about to shoot something quick and mean back at him, when she caught herself.

Just yesterday Pastor Mark preached on love. The type of love Christ had for his people. Patient and kind, gentle and not easily angered. The way she and Peter always loved before they started attending church. So why were they arguing more in the past few months? And how come they hadn't made love or even kissed in more than a week? With Maddie sick, they needed each other more than ever, but instead of drawing close they'd allowed a tension to build between them. Sometimes Brooke felt she was living with a stranger.

God, where are you in all this?

Love one another, my daughter. As I have loved you, so you must love one another.

A chill ran over Brooke's arms. This was her favorite part about her new relationship with God. Sometimes when she'd utter a prayer, she'd feel an answer whisper across the plains of her heart. It wasn't an actual answer, audible words from God like Moses heard at the burning bush. But a feeling, a thought. A timely Scripture that reassured her God was right there beside her. Within her soul, in a place where she would never be alone.

The verse that filled her heart now was the one Pastor Mark talked about just twenty-four hours earlier. He'd started his sermon with the idea that God asked just one thing of his people: that they love each other. Then Pastor had gone on to describe love—love the way God designed it.

She felt the fight leave her. "I'm sorry." Tears stung her eyes. She lifted her hands and let them fall to her sides. "Go get ready for work, Peter." She crossed the room and put a hand on his shoulder. "I'll stay with Maddie."

"She has an appointment at ten o'clock with Dr. Ruiz." Peter's voice was more controlled, and he kept his eyes on Maddie. "I called a few minutes ago."

Dr. Ruiz? "Why him?"

"Because he handles internal medicine, and he's the best in the state. I want a closer look at her blood count. Maybe we've overlooked something."

"She's been well for months, Peter." Brooke stared at him. "Maybe she has the flu."

"We'll let Dr. Ruiz decide."

Brooke wasn't sure how to feel about that. Peter could've asked her first, could've made a plan that they would follow together. Instead he'd booked the appointment without discussing it with her, and that lit the fires of her anger again. They ran tests on Maddie early last spring, when her fevers came in a cluster. Blood panels and lung X rays and throat cultures. Always the results were the same. Her white count was elevated, but nothing more. Of course Brooke understood the potential danger. She was a doctor. She knew that fevers of unknown origin combined with a high white count were often the first symptoms of leukemia.

But this was Maddie's first day sick in months. So why would

Peter make the appointment with Dr. Ruiz? Didn't he trust the care the two of them could give her? Was that it? He figured they didn't know what to do about their sick little girl so they needed Dr. Ruiz?

When she didn't say anything, Peter cleared his throat and turned to look at her. "I'm not waiting this time, Brooke." His eyes were more lined than before, and he looked as if he'd aged five years in the past one.

"I don't want to wait either, Peter, but infectious diseases? We don't even know if her count's high."

"Ruiz can tell us. And he'll check for things we never looked for: intestinal anomalies, parasites, and—" he paused, and when he spoke again he said the one word they'd refused to say, the one they'd kept from their vocabulary since Maddie had started getting fevers—"cancer."

"She doesn't have cancer." Brooke had to fight to keep the frustration from her voice, battle to make herself treat her husband with love.

"Okay, but it can't hurt to run some tests. As a precaution." Peter held his hand up to her. "I'm sorry, Brooke. I hate this as much as you do."

She sniffed and wiped at a tear on her right cheek. She'd wanted desperately to believe in God, to live her life knowing that he was in control, watching out for them, loving them. But if Maddie had cancer . . .

Peter stood and pulled her into a hug. "I'll call your mom and see if I can drop Hayley off at her house on my way in." He kissed her once on the forehead. "Then I'll meet you at Ruiz's office."

She lowered her gaze to the floor and gave a slight nod. "Okay."

"Hey—" he lifted her chin until their eyes met again—"if the fevers are back, we have to get this figured out. It's what we would do if she were anyone else's little girl."

Brooke's mouth hung open. She couldn't deny that. "You're right." She pulled away from him. "Go get ready for work."

When he was gone, Brooke went back to Maddie. She could hear Hayley in the next room, still humming and talking to her baby dolls. Peter's words ran through her mind again. He was right. If Maddie had been any other child, they would've recommended her to a specialist months ago, when the fevers were practically constant.

So why hadn't they contacted Dr. Ruiz back then? The answers were ugly and terrifying all at once. Because they'd figured anything Maddie might need, they could provide. Tests . . . medicines . . . blood work. Neither she nor Peter was a specialist, but they could order tests. And so in their great belief in themselves they'd failed to do the one thing that might've helped Maddie months ago.

Call another doctor.

She reached out and took Maddie's limp, hot hand in her own. Their tiny daughter was so precious, so much a part of their lives. What would she and Peter have between them if it weren't for the girls? A life of commonalities, yes. A shared interest in medicine and an appreciation for Bloomington and the beauty of Indiana University.

But love?

The kind of love Pastor Mark talked about? Gentle and kind and unconditional? In the deepest part of her soul Brooke was sure she'd known that type of love only twice in her lifetime. With Maddie, and then with Hayley. Not with Peter or her parents or anyone else except the little blonde girls who ran and played and laughed and lived.

All at the very center of Brooke's existence.

CHAPTER TWENTY-ONE

JOHN HEARD ABOUT the appointment from Elizabeth. Just after nine o'clock that morning she called his office and said she had Hayley for the day.

"Maddie's sick again. A fever, higher than before." Her pinched voice was clear evidence of her anxiety. "They're taking her in to Dr. Ruiz at ten today."

The news hit John like a load of bricks beginning to descend on his shoulders. "She's been well for so long."

"Brooke and Peter are worried. She has no other symptoms."

"Fever of unknown origin." He held his breath. "Just like before. I'll meet them over there after the appointment."

"I've heard of the doctor."

"Ruiz is the best in his field." John squeezed the bridge of his nose and sensed his prayers lifting to heaven before he could even voice them. "Pray it's nothing, Elizabeth."

"I am."

At ten-thirty, John took a series of hallways and catwalks to the building where Dr. Ruiz had his practice. John still had his lab coat on as he entered the office and nodded at the receptionist. He explained that he was looking for his granddaughter, and the woman checked a stack of charts on her desk.

"She's five years old?"

"Right." John leaned against the counter, willing the fear to leave his heart. Kids got fevers, sometimes without any explanation. Besides, her white count hadn't even been checked this time.

The woman glanced at her computer screen. "Looks like they've admitted her to St. Anne's for testing." She paused, her expression more serious than before. "She's running a hundred and four, Doctor."

A hundred and four? This wasn't the answer he'd expected. He was supposed to drop by, see that Maddie's fever had broken, and give Peter and Brooke a reassuring hug. Dr. Ruiz should've stuck his head out to shake his hand and smile about the obvious answer for Maddie's latest fever. A flu bug, nothing more.

But apparently Ruiz was worried.

"You're sure?" John took a step back. "She's at the hospital?"

"Yes." The woman looked at the computer screen again. "Dr. Ruiz is with them."

John thanked the woman and prayed as he made his way to his car. He didn't want to call Elizabeth yet, not until he knew something more, but he called his own office manager and asked her to clear his schedule for the next few hours.

He arrived at the hospital and found Maddie's room in a matter of minutes. As he approached her door from out in the hallway, he could hear Brooke and Peter talking. The sound of their voices made him stop. They were quiet and angry, and though he couldn't make out what they were saying, he had no doubt they were fighting.

Dr. Ruiz approached from the opposite direction. The two men nodded at each other, and John explained that Maddie was his granddaughter.

"I'm admitting her for a few days, trying some IV antibiotics on her. The big guns." The doctor pursed his lips. "According to her records, her white count's much higher than before."

"How high?"

"Over ten thousand."

The number was another brick added to the load forming across his shoulders. Ten thousand? Numbers like that had to be taken seriously. "An infection?"

"We'll see." He held his clipboard close to his body and looked toward Maddie's room. "You know the routine. If she responds to antibiotics, we look for the source of infection. If not . . ."

The doctor didn't need to expound on the possibilities. John patted Dr. Ruiz's shoulder. "I'm going to see her now."

"Okay." He paused before turning back toward the nurses' station. "We should know something in the next three days. During that time we'll try a few broad-spectrum antibiotics."

"And we'll pray." John managed a partial smile.

The two promised to talk soon; then John entered Maddie's room. Immediately Brooke and Peter stopped talking. The hard expressions on their faces told John he was right. They'd been fighting. Not far from them, Maddie lay beneath the hospital blankets. She looked small and pale.

"Dad." Brooke came to him and gave him a kiss on his cheek. "They're running tests."

"I talked to Dr. Ruiz out in the hall." John hugged her and went to Peter, who stood a few feet away near the foot of Maddie's bed. He held out his hand and Peter took it, but with none of his usual warmth. "It'll be a few days before we know anything, right?"

"Right." Peter was grim-faced, and he didn't meet John's eyes. Instead he stared at Maddie and took gentle hold of one of her feet. "We should've taken her to a specialist months ago."

"Fine." Brooke fell hard into a chair by the head of Maddie's bed. "What he's trying to say, Dad, is that this is all my fault." Her voice was tinged with equal parts sarcasm and fear. "I thought *we* could order whatever tests she needed." Another huff. "Peter deferred to me, and we didn't bring Maddie to a specialist until now." She crossed her arms. "Peter thinks it's all my fault."

"That's not what I—" Peter stared at Brooke. "Forget it." He waved his hand at her and strode from the room.

John looked from Maddie to Brooke. Something about the way Brooke and Peter had spoken to each other told John this wasn't the first time they'd had such clashes. And that whatever was at the root of their anger toward each other was dangerously deep.

He cringed at the blow of another brick.

Brooke gripped the rails on Maddie's bed and hung her head. "Sorry." She looked up enough to meet his eyes. "I wish you hadn't seen that."

He moved toward her and placed his hand on her shoulder. "Is it Maddie? Is that the problem?"

Brooke gave a slight shake of her head. "I don't know. We were at each other all the time when she was sick before."

"Sickness will do that." John pulled up another chair and sat beside Brooke. "Your mother and I went through some of that when she got sick. The first month after they found the lump, when they knew it was cancer, we fought over the smallest things."

"I didn't know that." Brooke sat back in her chair. "When . . . how did it change back again?"

"Well—" John turned so he could see his daughter better— "we met with a counselor, someone your mother's doctor recommended. The man was a Christian, and he told us something we haven't forgotten since."

Brooke was quiet, searching his eyes.

"He talked about the Scriptures reminding us to return to our first love. I know the verses are talking about our returning to Christ, but the counselor thought the principle could be applied to marriage as well. He reminded us of Scriptures that urged a husband and wife to find delight in each other. See, we're supposed to keep going back to our love for each other, that wonderful, heart-pounding love that drew us together. But returning isn't a onetime thing. It's a constant returning. Day after day after day. Returning to each other with a thirst that can never be met without a fresh supply of water. With that attitude, any couple could survive the hills and valleys of life together."

"Hmmm." Brooke still had hold of the bed rails. "I like that." She lowered one hand to Maddie and slid forward so she could stroke her daughter's blonde head. "But what if you aren't sure you have anything to return to? What if you were classmates and friends, and before you knew it you were married with children?" She turned and looked at him again. "What if you never once loved each other the way you love your children, Dad? What then?"

"If you don't know how to return to each other, you do the thing that comes first, Brooke."

She waited, tears glistening on her eyelashes. "What?"

"You return to God."

John spent almost an hour with Brooke. Maddie's fever was down a bit by the time he left and headed outside to use his cell phone. His first call was to Elizabeth. He explained the situation, careful not to let her hear the depth of his concern, the same way he'd been careful with Brooke. He didn't want either of them to worry about the thoughts that kept demanding his attention.

If tests showed that Maddie had cancer, it was possible she might never leave the hospital. Possible that these were her last days. And if that was true, the rest of the family would find out soon enough.

But one of his children would never know unless he was told in straight, blunt detail just how serious the situation might be. The moment he finished talking to Elizabeth, he called Luke.

It was just after noon, and Luke was having lunch with Lori at their apartment, something they did every Monday after classes and before the afternoon clubs and meetings that often took them in different directions. It was the first time either of them had taken a full load during summer, but doing so meant graduating a semester early and getting to law school that much sooner.

Besides, Luke's life revolved around campus now. He worked at the cafeteria and had a leadership role in three clubs that met during the summer months.

He and Lori were teasing each other about some girl who'd been calling for Luke, when the phone rang. Luke was up first. He pointed at Lori and chuckled. "It's not her . . . she's not interested, I'm telling you." He checked the caller ID and saw words that made him cringe.

Baxter, John.

"You get it." His smile faded as he handed the phone to Lori. "I don't want to talk."

She glanced at the caller ID window on the back of the phone and raised an eyebrow at him. "You have to face him, Luke." She whispered the words as though somehow his father would hear her from wherever he was making the call.

The phone rang a third time.

"Just answer it. Please." He and Lori had been doing better these days. She was completely recovered from her infection, and though they agreed that seeing other people was the free and right thing to do, they'd developed a friendship that appeared fairly exclusive. In bed and out.

Lori hit the On button and held the phone to her ear. "Hello?" She paused for a moment. "Uh . . ." Her eyes caught his and she held her hands in the air for a moment. She cleared her throat. "He's out right now. Is . . . is there a message?"

Luke sat and watched her, searching her expression for some clue as to why his father was calling.

She lowered her brow and gave a slow nod. "I see. Yes, I'll tell him." Pause. "I will. I'll have him call you when he gets in."

Lori said good-bye, clicked the Off button, and stared at him. "Your niece is in the hospital."

Seconds passed and a single thought anchored itself in the deep waters of his mind. If something was wrong with Maddie, then he had to get to her, had to see her and hold her the way he'd done every week when he'd lived with his parents. He needed to run from the apartment, jump in his car, and make his way to the hospital fast. His legs tightened, and he could feel his feet tense in anticipation of his going.

Surely he would go.

But before he could lift himself off his seat, he pulled the anchor and let his mind sail to another place. The muscles in his legs relaxed. "Maddie?"

"Yes." Lori's eyes looked troubled, even disappointed. "Luke, you need to go. No matter what your family thinks of you." She hesitated. "Your dad said she might have something serious."

Luke steeled himself. "She needs the others, not me." He picked up the sandwich on his plate and paused. "I'd make everyone uncomfortable."

"But your father said she was—"

He held up his hand. "I'm allowed to think the way I want, right?" His voice echoed off the plaster walls. "Isn't that what we're being taught?"

"That doesn't mean you stop caring about the people you love." Her voice was soft. She stood and grabbed her purse. "Freethinking is about *more* love, not less." She stared at him. "Something happened when I was in the hospital, Luke. Something I haven't told anyone." Her eyes welled up and she coughed to clear her throat. "Your dad came and held my hand. He prayed for me, and you know what?" Her tone matched his now. "I might not believe in prayer, but I know one thing for sure. Your father is a great guy. He should've hated me. But he stood there and prayed for me. He—" her voice cracked—"he told me everything was going to be okay."

Luke couldn't think of anything to say.

Lori gave a sad shake of her head. "That's the man you're running from, Luke? It doesn't add up."

She left without saying another word, and Luke stood and crossed the apartment to the window. He stared out and let his forehead fall against the glass. His father prayed for Lori? Even knowing who she was and the role she'd played in leading him away from the Baxter family? Even when he'd thought the baby she'd aborted was his?

A sinking feeling pushed at the edges of his gut. His father must still think that. After all, he'd done nothing to make him believe otherwise.

He grabbed hold of the windowsill. What had happened to him? What had he become after months of letting go of everything he'd believed? After allowing those in the know to reshape his thinking to a level that should've been higher and more freeing, his life was more meaningless than ever before.

"Freethinking is about more love, not less." Lori's words sounded good, but it was crazy, really. Freethinking meant he could avoid his family if he wanted to. According to freethinking, whatever thought he went with was the right one.

But was that true?

If so, how could cutting off his family—something perfectly acceptable in freethinking—be more loving?

The alternative, of course, was the worldview he'd held before. The belief that God was, and is, real and that he cared enough to stay with a person every minute, every day, for a lifetime. Could any belief be more archaic? Amazing that it took something like September 11 to open his eyes.

But if freethinking didn't make him more loving and if God's love wasn't real, then what was? What foundation did he have to stand on?

Minutes turned into half an hour, and still no answers came. None at all. Life was strange and dark and empty and alone. And for just a moment Luke was certain that somewhere across Bloomington in a hospital room at St. Anne's, a little girl he still loved had to be feeling the same way.

Strange and dark and empty and alone.

A towheaded, blue-eyed wonder child, whose laugh when she raced him down the driveway at the Baxter house was like wind chimes in a summer breeze. He called her Little M, and she called him Uncle Lu-Lu.

He held his breath and wished for a minute that he still believed in God, still had the confidence to know without a doubt that he need only ask God for heaven to hear and for Maddie to be well again.

If only he could believe just one more time.

CHAPTER TWENTY-TWO

ASHLEY TOOK THE day off so she could set up her easel at her parents' house and paint. The country scenes—especially those with flags—were favorites with the New York gallery, and Margaret Wellington had called again to report that a second of Ashley's paintings had sold.

A humid blue sky hung over Bloomington that morning, and Ashley set up a hundred yards from the house. Cole had made friends with a neighbor boy, who had joined Cole in a game of soccer on the grassy field between her easel and the front door. Every now and then they'd leave the ball and play hide-and-seek near the big elm tree out front, or sit together on the bench beneath the branches and sing songs. Ashley could barely make out the words, but the songs were happy. That was all that mattered.

For as long as she'd loved painting, Ashley had wondered what it would feel like to live the life she portrayed on canvas. A life filled with light and hope and unforgettable colors. After coming home from Paris, her life had been more like a solid black sheet than one of the Americana portraits she loved to create. A black sheet punctuated with a single piercing yellow dot: Cole.

But not anymore.

"Mom! Watch this!" Cole stood beneath the tree. He lowered his head, ran fifteen steps, and tumbled into a series of somersaults. When he stood up, he did a victory dance and held both fists high in the air.

"Wow, Cole, you're the best tumbler in the world!" Ashley blew a wisp of bangs off her forehead and wished for a breeze. The day was getting hotter. If the humidity didn't let up a bit she'd have to move inside.

"I can do it, too!" Cole's friend set off running.

Ashley stared at her painting and realized that was just what it needed. Not just the house and the flag, but two rough-and-tumble boys playing near the tree in the foreground. She set her brush down and reached for her pencil. With feathery light strokes she sketched in the images of one boy somersaulting while the other celebrated.

The drawing took less than ten minutes. Ashley leaned back and admired it, but something wasn't quite right. She blinked and then it came to her. One of the children needed to be a girl. Yes, an older girl. Because that was the very tree where she and Luke had played. That way this painting would capture a precious slice of their childhood.

Ashley worked on the images, penciling with almost invisible lines. Artists all worked differently, but for her, the picture had to be sketched first. Once the framework was in place, the colors would come. Usually fast and with a rush of emotion. And that was a good thing. Because with work and Cole and time with her family, Ashley couldn't take months on end to finish a piece the way some artists did.

In fact, the faster and more focused her work, the better it was. As though she needed to transfer all that was in her heart to the painting before a single color or brush stroke was forgotten.

By the time two o'clock rolled around, Ashley had nearly completed the painting. A bit more pale gold and cream in the summer field, and she'd be finished. They said good-bye to Cole's friend, and since no one was at the Baxter house, Ashley gathered her things, set the drying painting on her easel in one of the upstairs bedrooms, and helped Cole into the backseat of the car.

When she pulled away, Cole reached his hand up onto the console between the two front seats. His sign that he wanted to hold her hand. She took his hand and sent him a quick smile over her shoulder. "Did you have fun?"

"Yes." He yawned. "I like when you have a day off, Mommy."

"Me, too." Ashley pictured Irvel and the others, how much they needed her but how little they missed her—if at all—when she was gone. "If I sell enough pieces, maybe I won't do anything but play with you and paint."

"Are *pieces* and *paintings* the same thing?" Cole's voice was tired. "Because if you mean Lego pieces, Mommy, I'll give you some to sell. If you would be home more."

Ashley's heart melted at his words. "Actually they have to be paintings, but thanks. I'm glad you were willing to share."

"Yep." Cole tapped his foot against the back of her seat and then stopped. "Know what, Mommy?"

"What?"

"I miss Landon. When's he coming back home?"

Ashley bit her lip and steered the car onto the two-lane highway. That was the question, wasn't it? He had a few more months before his year was up, but what about after that? As often as Ashley and Landon were talking now, they still hadn't made a decision on that. When exactly was Landon coming back to Bloomington, and if he wasn't, what were they going to do about it?

She kept her voice even. "It'll still be a while, honey." There wasn't much else she could say. "I miss him, too."

"He loves us, huh, Mommy?" Cole leaned forward and craned his neck.

"Yes." Ashley caught his eyes and felt a smile warm her expression. "Very much."

They were home in ten minutes and Cole headed for the backyard. Ashley set her things down in the living room and checked the messages. There were three.

She hit the Play button and leaned closer so she could hear.

The first message was from William Wellington at the gallery in Manhattan. Her third and final painting had sold in what was a record time for any artist they'd showcased. When could she get another three paintings to them, and how long before she could supply them with twelve to fifteen pieces? They wanted to feature her in their annual fall show.

Ashley closed her eyes and gripped the counter. All three paintings had sold! It really wasn't a fluke or a quirk or anything else. People actually *liked* her work, and not just any people. New York people. Manhattan people. Buyers who could've chosen from dozens of galleries and artists. *God, thank you . . . thank you.*

For an instant, the Bible verse from Jeremiah flashed in her heart. The one about God knowing the plans and hopes he had for her. Ashley treasured the notion in her heart, believing every word. She had Cole and Landon, Sunset Hills, and now her painting. All of it was playing out just as God had planned it, and that left her in awe.

The machine beeped and the next message began. "Hey, Ash, it's me." Landon's voice was smooth, kind, even through the speaker of a tinny answering machine. "I had an idea." Pause. "Call me, okay. I miss you." A smile sounded in his tone. "You *and* Cole."

Ashley tilted her head and grinned. The downside to how well things were going with Landon was how badly she wanted to get on a plane and return to New York City. Rather than waiting for the third message, she hit the Stop button on the machine, picked up the phone, and punched in Landon's cell phone number.

He answered on the first ring. "Hey, I knew you'd call."

She sat on one of the dining-room chairs and stared out the window at Cole playing on the swings out back. It hadn't been twenty-four hours since her last conversation with Landon, and already the time felt like an eternity. "You knew, huh?"

"Yeah." Traffic sounded in the background. "I figured you'd go to your parents' house, paint a masterpiece and, oh, about one o'clock you'd start missing me. You and Cole would head back home, get my message, and voilà. Here we'd be."

"Where are we?" Ashley's tone was soft and teasing.

"In the middle of Central Park, leaning against a tree, reading a book, and wishing Ashley would call."

"I see." She muffled a giggle. "Sounds like we're having a wonderful time."

"We would be—" the laughter in his voice faded—"except I miss you so much."

"Yeah, it's weird, isn't it?" She stretched her legs out and her movement caught Cole's attention. He waved and she did the same. "Every day feels like forever apart from you."

"How's Cole?" Landon's voice was softened some by what sounded like wind through the trees.

"Good. He asked about you today."

"He did?"

"Yeah. He wants to know when you'll come home."

Landon paused for a second or two. "Tell him I feel the same way."

She sat a little straighter and peered into the living room, the place where she stored her paintings. "Have you seen Reagan? I forgot to ask you yesterday."

"No. She's keeping her distance."

Ashley sighed. "She hasn't called Luke; at least I don't think so. I've put a few calls in to him, and I think he'd tell me if he'd heard the news. In fact I'm sure he would."

"It must be killing you." His voice was tender, compassionate. "Knowing about the baby and not saying anything."

"It's impossible." Ashley tapped her finger against the receiver. "If she doesn't say something soon, I don't know. Luke has a right to see his baby."

They were silent for a few beats; then suddenly Ashley remembered. "Hey, guess what?"

"You're moving here with Cole next week?"

Her heart lurched at the idea, but she put the thought of it on hold. "Besides that."

"The Metropolitan called; they want your work in the front room?"

Her head fell back as a ripple of laughter made its way up from her throat. "Nothing quite that big."

"Okay, sorry." The silliness faded from his voice. "What?"

She hesitated. "The gallery called. They sold my third painting."

"Ashley!" He did a loud hoot. "All three already?"

"Yes." She leaned forward and rested her elbows on her knees. "They want to feature my work at their fall show. I can't believe it."

"I can." He was breathless, maybe more excited than she was. "So when'll you be here?"

"Be there?" She loved this, the way their phone calls were filled with play these days. They'd wasted so much time. "You mean with my next paintings?"

"No, with Cole and your suitcases." He paused and the teasing faded from his tone. "I'm serious, Ash. I've thought about it a lot since you left. What if you and Cole moved here?"

"Landon, you know I—"

"Wait." Fresh possibilities colored his voice. "Hear me out. The two of you move here. We get married and find a house in the country where you can paint. I commute to work for the fire department, and you'd be less than an hour from the gallery. It could work—" he paused long enough to grab a breath—"couldn't it?"

Ashley heard the words he wasn't saying. It was something he'd mentioned a few days ago. "You got the promotion?"

"The captain called this morning." His words were slower now, measured. "They want me to train for lieutenant."

Two distinctly different emotions filled Ashley's head. Pride over all Landon had accomplished at the department in so short a time, and raw fear over what the news meant for their future. She grabbed hold of the brighter of the two. "Congratulations,

Landon." It took all her effort to sound as happy for him as he had sounded for her. "You'll be chief one day if you stay in New York."

His answer came without hesitation. "I won't stay without you, Ash. I can't." Distant carnival music sounded in the background, an ice cream vendor maybe. "Nothing matters to me more than being with you."

Ashley stood and sauntered to the dining-room window. Cole was playing with a yellow truck, pushing it along the wooden railroad ties that bordered his swing set. "A house in the country, huh?"

Landon chuckled. "With a gorgeous view in every direction."

She'd never seriously considered such an idea, and much about it concerned her. First, New York was expensive. Finding a house like that, one that would be just an hour's commute to the city, might be next to impossible. But more than that, if they stayed in New York, if Landon stayed with the FDNY, then the possibility would always exist that what happened to Jalen could happen to him.

And now, after figuring out what she felt for Landon, she couldn't fathom losing him. Not for any reason.

But God held the number of their days, didn't he? And Ashley had never been known for playing it safe, taking the most cautious path. Life was found by risking, wasn't it? So why not move to New York, especially when the gallery wanted to feature her work?

"Ashley?" Another wind gust sounded in the distance.

"Can we do this . . . can we talk about it when I come?"

She could almost see his smile. "When?"

"The gallery wants me out there in the next few weeks. The first week of August, maybe, when I can bring them another batch of paintings." A burst of sunlight colored the moment. Whatever she and Landon decided would be the right thing. Whether they were in New York or Bloomington, it didn't matter. As long as they were together. "Let's talk about it then, okay?"

"Okay." A smile filled his voice. "I'll be waiting."

She closed her eyes, remembering the last time they were together, the way his arms had felt around her. "Hey, do you have a minute to talk to Cole?"

"My best boy?" He sounded happier than she'd ever heard him. "I have all day for Cole."

Ashley knocked on the window, pointed to the phone in her hand, and motioned for Cole to come in. A minute later he rounded the corner into the dining room, his eyes wide. "Landon?"

She nodded and handed him the receiver. Then she relaxed in the chair and watched her son talk with the man she loved. Cole told him about the worm he'd found beneath a rock in the backyard and how he'd been the somersault champion earlier that day at his grandma's house. When he was finished talking, he walked around the dining room, grinning and giggling at whatever Landon was saying to him. Finally Cole nodded. "Okay, love you, too."

Ashley took the phone and gave Cole a kiss on the top of his head. "Go play." He skipped off and she held the receiver to her ear again. A dozen thoughts played on the tip of her tongue. How grateful she was that Landon loved her son, how amazing that he had been the one to teach her to appreciate Cole in the first place; how badly she missed him and wished they could be together.

But she settled on the one that took precedence over all of them. "I love you, Landon Blake. I love you so much."

He chuckled. "Why do I wish the next passing jogger would pinch me?"

"What, you don't believe it's real?" The giggling returned to her voice. "Okay, then listen to this: I love you. I love you. I love you." She cradled the phone close to her, as though somehow the action might bring him closer as well. "I'll never stop loving you."

His tone grew serious again, quiet and as deep as the ocean. "I love you, too, Ashley. But then—" he paused—"I always have."

When their call ended, Ashley returned the receiver to the base and saw the flashing 1 in the window of the answering machine. She'd forgotten about the last message. Almost as an afterthought, she pushed the button and turned toward the cupboard. She grabbed a glass and was filling it with water when the voice came on.

"This is Marie from Paris. I run the gallery where you worked several years ago. Your family gave me your number."

Ashley turned off the faucet, spun around, and stared at the machine.

"I have some information you need to have. It is crucial that you call me." The caller rattled off a phone number before the message ended.

Ashley set her glass of water on the counter, grabbed a pen and a pad of paper from the drawer near the telephone, and played the message again. This time she wrote down the number and for the longest time, she merely stared at it.

Common sense told her this was about some paperwork issue from her time at the gallery. But a knot formed in Ashley's stomach, and her hands trembled as she picked up the phone. After so many years, would the gallery contact her about some bookkeeping issue? Would they even care about a detail they'd let go for so many years? And why the urgent phone calls?

She punched in the numbers, then lifted the phone to her ear and waited. From the backyard she could hear Cole's silly-heart voice singing as he played in the heat of the afternoon.

Doubts—dreadful doubts—hung above her like so many swords, questions about Jean-Claude Pierre and the possibility that this call involved him or the fact that he was Cole's biological father. But she stayed still so none of the swords would fall and slice her to pieces.

A ringing sounded in her ear once . . . twice. *God, let this be nothing, please.*

"*Bonjour.*" The voice belonged to a man.

Ashley cleared her throat and wondered if he spoke English.

"Hello." She returned to the seat near the window and focused her attention on Cole. "I need to speak to Marie, please."

"Marie?" The connection wasn't great, but she could understand the man. *"Oui, oui."*

Half a minute passed while Ashley waited. Then a woman came on the line, the same one who had left the message earlier. The same woman who had once, a lifetime ago, told Ashley her art wasn't welcome in a Paris gallery. "Hello, this is Marie." Her accent was stronger than Ashley remembered. "How may I help you?"

Ashley looked down and noticed that her knees were knocking together. "This . . . this is Ashley Baxter. I'm returning your call."

"Oui, I've tried to reach you. One minute, please. It is busy; I must go where it is quiet." The background noise gradually faded to silence. "There. Now we can talk."

For the briefest moment, Ashley wondered if her father was right. Maybe Marie had stumbled onto her Web site and somehow come to see her paintings in a new light. Maybe she wanted to offer her a chance to show her work there in Paris. She held her breath and waited.

"Ashley, I have not so good news for you."

The room tilted. Ashley steadied her gaze on Cole. "What . . . what is the problem?"

"You remember Jean-Claude Pierre? The artist featured at our gallery when you were here?"

"Yes." Ashley's heart was in her throat, and she could barely concentrate. *Get it out, woman. Just say it.*

"He is dying."

The moment the words hit her, Ashley was seized by a wave of fear and nausea. Jean-Claude? Dying? Of what? And why would the news involve her? Before she could ponder that, before she had time even to inhale, the woman continued.

"Jean-Claude's doctor prepared a list of names, people to call with the details." She hesitated, her accent thick. "You, Ashley, are on the list."

"I . . . I don't understand." The voice was hers, but she was a million miles away. Somewhere in Central Park, sitting beside Landon, kissing him, whispering promises of forever to him. She opened her mouth and forced another few words through her lips. "I haven't stayed in touch with Jean-Claude."

"Ashley . . ." The woman waited and for the first time, her voice held a modicum of sensitivity. "Jean-Claude is dying of Acquired Immuno-Deficiency Syndrome."

A rushing sound filled Ashley's senses, and Marie's words ran together. Immuno something . . . a deficiency of some kind? A syndrome? What did that have to do with her? And why did Marie sound so grim? Ashley dug her fingernails into her brow. From outside Cole waved at her and flashed her a lopsided grin.

She waved back and somehow found her voice. "I don't know what . . . what you mean."

The woman sighed, and the weight of that sound hit Ashley from a continent away. "It is our law that doctors do what they can to alert people who . . . who have had contact with the patient."

Ashley wanted to run, but nowhere offered her an escape from the freight train bearing down on her. She was stuck on the tracks, her feet anchored in cement, with no way out. She tried again to understand. "Jean-Claude has . . ."

"He has AIDS, Ashley. I'm sorry."

AIDS? Jean-Claude has AIDS?

Ashley made it through the rest of the phone call, stood, and then collapsed against the window. She couldn't cry, couldn't scream, couldn't do anything but stare out the window at Cole and consider the only questions that still mattered.

Had Jean-Claude gotten the virus before or after her time with him? And if it was before, if she'd been carrying the deadly disease all this time, how much longer until she herself would die?

Thoughts of Landon tugged at her attention, but her mind was too busy with Cole. She held her hand up to the window and watched him chattering happily to himself, playing without a care in the world.

"Cole . . . ," she whispered. "What have I done?" Another thought hit her, this one more terrible than the others. If she'd been infected, what about her child? It was possible, wasn't it? That this would affect Cole, too? Her gaze froze on him, and she slid to the floor.

The freight train hit then.

Everything hopeful about her future was suddenly and swiftly taken from her, obliterated on a line of tracks that led back five years. Back to a small art gallery in Paris and a series of decisions from which there now seemed no escape, no hope, no return.

Not for her or Cole or Landon.

Not for any of them. Not ever again.

CHAPTER TWENTY-THREE

JOHN TOOK THE CALL from Brooke just after noon.

"Dad, come quick." Her serious tone spoke volumes. "Some of Maddie's tests came back. I need to talk to you."

It took John a heartbeat to catch his breath. They'd been waiting for word about Maddie for five days now. "I'll be right there."

It was all he could do to keep himself from speeding. Obviously they'd found something; otherwise Brooke wouldn't have wanted to talk to him.

Fifteen minutes later he rounded the corner into Maddie's hospital room and found the place full. Brooke, Peter, Dr. Ruiz, and three other physicians John recognized as new specialists on staff.

The tension between Brooke and Peter still seemed thick, but John turned his attention to his daughter. "How is she?"

"Dad . . ." Brooke pulled herself away from the group. Her eyes glistened as they met his. A catch sounded in her voice when she tried to talk. "She . . . she doesn't have cancer." Her forehead fell against John's chest, and he wrapped his arms around her.

John silently thanked God before taking the time to exhale. He stroked Brooke's back and closed his eyes. His words were soaked in relief. "God is good."

"Yes." Brooke sniffed and looked up to study his face. "He heard my prayers. Not only is Maddie responding to the antibiotics, but Dr. Ruiz thinks he's found the problem." A happy sob came from Brooke's throat, and she lifted her fingers to her mouth. She let her arms fall to her sides, took a step back, and shook her head. "It's the simplest thing, Dad."

Dr. Ruiz approached them and gave John a confident smile. "The problem's in her bladder." He slipped his hands into the pockets of his white lab coat. "An anomaly in her system causes it to never completely drain."

"Reflux." John crossed his arms.

"Exactly." Dr. Ruiz looked from John to Brooke and back again. "Which makes her prone to a type of infection that rarely presents with anything but a high fever and high white count. Each bout damages her system, but it looks like we've caught the problem in time. The damage is minimal and reversible."

Brooke gripped John's forearm. "We can have a procedure done to correct the problem. It's an outpatient laser surgery." She shrugged and a few happy tears slipped onto her cheeks. "And that'll be it. No more fevers, no more sickness. Mystery solved!"

Maddie stirred in the bed beyond them and blinked her eyes. John watched her look about the room until her eyes fell on him. "Hi, Papa." She yawned. "What're you doing here?"

John went to her and took her hand in his. He was overwhelmed with gratitude, struck by God's goodness, barely able to find his voice. "Hi, sweetheart." He bent over and kissed her cheek. "I'm hearing the good news that you're getting better."

She grinned. "I *feel* better."

Dr. Ruiz checked the chart in his hand and directed his attention to Peter. "Let us know when you'd like to schedule the procedure. The sooner the better."

The doctor didn't need to spell out the reasons.

Any time a child succumbed to an infection as swift and powerful as the one that had been attacking Maddie, there were risks. The infection could spread throughout her system and move into her bloodstream. If the right antibiotics weren't administered quickly, she could even die. Now that they'd found the source of her problem, the procedure to repair her bladder should be done as soon as possible.

Dr. Ruiz and the other doctors left the room, and John looked at Peter. His attention was on Maddie, so John shifted his gaze to Brooke. She rolled her eyes and gave a slight shake of her head. However good the news about Maddie, it hadn't eased things between Brooke and Peter.

John caught Brooke's eye. "Have you told your mother?"

"No one." She grinned. "I wanted you to hear it from Dr. Ruiz before we told the family."

A long breath made its way from John. He'd been terrified about what they might find wrong with Maddie. Now she could be home in a day or so. The joy of that news was still making its way to the corners of his heart, replacing the fear that had built up there.

"Well—" John ran his hand over the back of Maddie's head— "Papa's gotta run. I'll call Grandma and let her know you're feeling better, okay?"

"Okay." Maddie grinned. "Tell Cole I'll race him next time I'm over."

John's heart swelled. "I'll tell him, sweetie." He looked at Peter. "Congratulations."

Peter nodded. "We should've done it sooner. Then she wouldn't have any kidney damage."

"It's reversible, Peter!" Brooke tossed her hands up, her voice a study in controlled frustration. "Didn't you hear Dr. Ruiz?"

"It doesn't matter." He flashed her a pointed look. "I wanted this two months ago, but you thought I was crazy."

No wonder things were tense between them. John opened his

mouth to tell them both to let it go, to celebrate the victory at hand, but he stopped himself. It wasn't his place, not with his adult married children; not unless they asked his advice. He gave a little cough and took a few steps toward the door. "I'll let the others know."

"Thanks, Dad." Brooke walked to him and hugged him once more. In a voice that was barely audible she whispered, "Pray for us."

John nodded and waved at Peter. "See you soon."

"Yeah." Peter dug his hands in his pockets and moved to the spot near Maddie's bed.

The hallways were empty as John made his way off the floor and down to the lobby. Whatever strain Maddie's illness had placed on Brooke and Peter's marriage, it seemed silly to nurse it now when they'd received such wonderful news. How different the scene would've been if the news had been something terrible—cancer, even.

John shuddered.

He was near the front doors of the hospital when he spotted Ashley heading up the main walkway. Probably coming to visit Maddie. When she didn't see him, John came to a stop and studied her. She looked upset, as though she were carrying the world's troubles in her purse. For the first time in months, she looked like the old Ashley, her arms clutched tight to her waist, eyes dark and brooding.

She came through the front doors before she saw him; then she, too, stopped. She flashed him a smile that didn't even pretend to be genuine. "Dad, what're you doing here?"

"Brooke called me." He crooked his arm around Ashley's neck and gave her a quick kiss on her cheek. "They got Maddie's test results."

"And . . . ?" Ashley froze, her eyes locked on his.

"It's a problem with her bladder. They'll need to schedule a procedure, but otherwise she'll be fine." He shook his head. "It's wonderful news."

"Oh, Dad . . ." Ashley's expression softened. "I was so worried."

"We all were." John bit his lip. "The possibilities were terrifying."

Something flashed in Ashley's eyes, anxiety, maybe, or fear. But this time her smile was more genuine. "I'll have to stop up there and congratulate them. They must be so relieved."

"Isn't that what you're here for? To see Maddie?"

The question seemed to catch Ashley off guard. She thought for a moment and gave a few quick shakes of her head. "No . . . I mean, yes. That, too."

"What else?"

She shrugged and uttered a single, quiet laugh, one without a trace of humor. "Just some tests at the lab. Routine stuff." Her gaze shifted down a hallway a few yards away. "It's down that way, right?"

"Right." John searched her eyes. Something about the way she was acting wasn't quite right. "What's the test for?"

"Nothing, really." The laugh again. "Actually I requested it. Just a blood workup—cholesterol, blood sugar, mineral check."

No matter how old his children got, John was always interested in their health. He lowered his brow and tried to keep his tone casual. "Have you been sick?"

"No, Dad." Ashley patted his shoulder. Her voice told him he was worrying about nothing. "Everything's fine. I hate needles, that's all. It's been a few years since I had it checked. No big deal."

"Okay." He took her hand and gave it a gentle squeeze. "You're coming tomorrow, right?"

"Kari's shower?" This time her smile reached her eyes. "Of course. We'll all be there."

They said good-bye.

John's heartbeat slowed to normal. The ordeal with Maddie clearly had him on edge, as though some sort of tragedy was right around the corner. If not with her, then maybe with Ashley or Landon or Elizabeth.

He made a mental note. That night when he brought his cares

233

to God in prayer, he'd have to talk about this. Anxiety would get him nowhere, and whenever he sensed himself losing the battle to his worries, it was time to ask God for another dose of peace.

In this case, maybe two or three doses.

❧

Ashley turned down the hallway and headed for the lab, but it wasn't until she was sure her father was gone that she stopped, dropped to a nearby bench, and covered her face with her hands.

Was she crazy? How could she have her blood tested here at the hospital where her father saw patients and knew every doctor on staff? She should've gone to Indianapolis or one of the small towns between here and there, a place where no one would know her.

She drew in a slow breath and let her hands fall to her lap. Yes, that's what she would do. Her mother was watching Cole. She could call and say she had a few extra errands to run, ask her mother to watch him a little longer. She'd convinced herself that since blood work was confidential, her father would never find out. But of course he would. He might get curious and ask her doctor or check on the results himself. He would have access to her files, for goodness' sake.

Her legs were wobbly as she headed back to the lobby. She went up to Maddie's room and passed on her congratulations to Brooke and Peter—neither of whom seemed overjoyed with the situation. Then she gave Maddie a kiss and said her good-byes.

Forty-five minutes later she drove into the parking lot of a small regional hospital outside of Indianapolis. In her hands she had her doctor's orders for a complete blood workup, including an HIV test. The hospital was older and smaller than St. Anne's, and the grounds weren't as well kept.

Ashley found the lab and presented her papers.

"Wait here." The tech disappeared through a door behind the counter.

Five minutes passed, and Ashley's heart beat strangely within her. *Beat, beat.* Silence. *Double-beat.* Silence. *Double-beat. Beat. Beat.* A layer of perspiration broke out on her forehead, and black dots circled the air in front of her. What was happening to her, and why did she feel so light-headed? What was she doing? Getting her blood drawn at some strange hospital because she didn't want anyone to see her? The entire ordeal was a nightmare, as though it were someone else's life and not her own.

She had a friendship with God now. She treasured Cole and loved Landon. She wasn't supposed to hear that Jean-Claude Pierre was dying of AIDS. It wasn't possible.

An image came to mind. Jean-Claude crossing a Paris street, arm in arm with a young blond man in the days after she'd stopped seeing him. Hadn't it occurred to her then? Buried deep beneath the surface of her soul, hadn't she known that if Jean-Claude was that promiscuous, she herself had already been put at risk?

The tech was back. "Follow me." She led Ashley through a different door to a counter with three partitioned sections. A stool stood in front of each of the three. "Take the first seat."

Ashley set her purse on the floor and slid the stool out from the counter. Carefully, mindful of the fact that she still felt faint, she swung herself onto the cushioned seat.

"Someone will be right with you." The tech was neither rude nor welcoming. A robotic figure in some kind of bizarre drama.

Another three minutes passed, and a woman appeared from an adjacent room. She slipped on a pair of gloves and set a tray of vials and needles on the counter in front of Ashley. "Quite a few tests, huh?" Her voice was kind, but she looked tired, worn-out, as though she'd been through much in her life.

"Yes." Ashley managed a smile. "It's part of a checkup."

The nurse scrutinized the paperwork. "Sort of far from home for a checkup."

Ashley and the woman locked eyes, and in that instant Ashley knew. The woman understood why she was here, why she had driven forty miles to have her blood drawn.

"It's okay." The woman rested her hands on the counter. "No one's more confidential than we are." She pointed at Ashley's left arm. "Set it up here and make a fist."

Ashley wasn't sure what to say. Part of her wanted to confide in this nurse, tell her how terrified she felt and how she'd just learned that a man she'd slept with was dying of AIDS. But the truth was so horrible, she could barely voice it to herself, let alone to a stranger. Instead she lifted her arm onto the counter and squeezed her fingers together.

The woman wrapped a lightweight rubber tube around Ashley's upper arm and met her eyes again. "This stuff make you queasy?"

"No." Ashley shook her head. "I'm fine."

Her words echoed in her soul. Fine? She was fine? Nothing in the world was fine. Two days ago she was camped out in one of her Americana paintings. But now . . . now her life—and maybe Cole's—hung in the balance. Scared to death, yes, but definitely not fine.

"If it bothers you, turn away." The nurse swabbed a wet cotton ball over the faint blue lines that ran along the inside of Ashley's arm.

Ashley said nothing. She watched the woman slide a needle into her vein, hitting the mark on her first attempt. Instantly a stream of red blood moved up the needle. The liquid was rich looking, and Ashley narrowed her eyes, willing herself to see whether something existed there that would wreak deadly havoc on her life.

The nurse finished with the first vial, wrapped an identification sticker around it, and began to fill a second. As she did, Ashley was struck by the irony.

The blood filling the glass vial sustained her life.

But quite possibly it was the very same stuff that would destroy her. A positive test would effectively remove Landon from her life. She loved him too much to subject him to risk—physical or emotional. No, she'd thought that much out the night she received the news. If she tested positive for HIV she would break things off with Landon forever.

Then there was Cole. If she got sick and died in the next few years, she'd leave him with no parents whatsoever. No one to call his own, except her folks—and though they were healthy, no guarantees existed to assure they'd live long enough to see Cole safely out on his own.

Other scenarios existed, scenarios that had made it difficult for Ashley to sleep these past few days, difficult for her to speak with her family or Landon or even Cole. What if Cole had the virus? What then?

She bit the inside of her lip and watched as the nurse filled the third and final vial. When she was finished, she pulled the needle from Ashley's arm, pressed a piece of gauze over the small hole, and wrapped a piece of clear tape over it. "Keep that on for an hour."

"Okay." Ashley watched the woman place the three filled vials on the tray and start to turn back toward the adjacent room. "Wait . . ."

The nurse turned around. "Yes?"

"When . . . when will I know?"

"Things are slow this week." The woman cocked her head. "It's Friday. Give us a call Wednesday or Thursday. We should have it all back by then."

Ashley had made the decision to get her paintings to New York soon—in case the tests turned up something. She'd fly out next Thursday, and though she hoped to have the results by then, she would've gladly waited a year for them. Every minute she didn't know was one more she could pretend she'd never had to come here, that she'd never received the phone call from Marie, never heard that Jean-Claude Pierre was dying.

Fear took the seat beside her and buckled up on the way home, reminding her that until she received a negative test, she might as well assume the results would be positive. After all, Jean-Claude obviously lived his loose lifestyle long before she went to Paris. She should've seen it. He'd been too willing to take her out that first night, despite the fact that he was married.

Commitment hadn't been in Jean-Claude's vocabulary.

She wondered how he'd remembered her, why he'd found it in himself to give the doctor her name. Certainly if he'd made the rounds as widely as it appeared, she was merely another conquest, a passing fancy.

Something else occurred to her. Maybe it was God's will that she find out. For the past three days she'd wondered about God, how he figured into this latest devastating turn her life had taken. Was he punishing her? Letting her know that though he forgave her, she would still have to pay for her sins? And with what? Her relationship with Landon? Her son's health? Her life?

But now—despite fear's running commentary that her life was over, that she'd never love or laugh again because she was about to get sick and die a horrifying death alone—now she was able to think about God differently.

Maybe he'd given Jean-Claude a divine ability to remember her name so that she would run out and get tested. That way she could have either peace of mind or the wherewithal to protect Landon.

"God, are you there?" Her whispered words sounded above the breeze filtering in through the car vents.

Fear unbuckled itself from the passenger seat and slipped out the window.

God, I figure this . . . all this is a punishment from you. But— tears filled her eyes and she blinked to clear her vision—*but my friendship with you is too new, too sweet, and I can't believe it. If I have this . . . this virus, it's because of my choices, but not because you're punishing me. Right, God?*

For a while silence filled the car. Ashley was no longer afraid, but she couldn't quite hear God, either. *Are you there, Lord? How am I going to get through this if . . . if . . .*

She remembered the words from Pastor Mark, words she'd shared with Landon several times in the past few months. They came from Romans, chapter eight: *God works all things out for the good for those who love Him.*

All things.

The words soothed Ashley's soul the way a stroke of yellow might soothe a stormy sky in one of her paintings.

All things for the good. Is that right, God? All things? Even this?

Daughter, yes, even in this I am with you . . . your rock and your strong fortress.

Ashley gripped the steering wheel more tightly. "God?"

She recognized some of the words from a Bible verse, one that Cole had brought home from church last Sunday. He'd learned a song about God being mighty and powerful, a rock and a strong fortress. Cole liked the fortress part, because his Sunday school teacher had taught them to bring their arms up in a fighting position for that part.

The words were something else, too. A whisper that seemed to come straight from heaven. What was it Landon said? That if people were quiet enough they could hear God, hear him warning them, directing them. Comforting them.

"His voice is still and small," Landon told her. "Sometimes more of an impression than actual words. And if we don't get real quiet, we won't ever hear it."

For the first time in three days, Ashley's smile came from within. Almost as if a lighted match of hope had been tossed into the dark cavernous places of her soul. Jesus loved her, and no matter what the test results brought, he would see her through. In fact, as she drove into Bloomington and on toward Clear Creek and her parents' house, she was sadly calm about all but the worst part of her situation. And that thought troubled her enough that when she pulled into the driveway she had to wait until she stopped crying before she could go in and get Cole.

Yes, God would be with her even if she tested positive, even if she got sick and died of AIDS. She would never lose God.

But she would lose Landon . . . and Cole.

The very idea made her weep, and her tears put out the small flame of hope and opened the door to fear once more. Nothing she could do would change the high stakes that lay ahead, the life changes that might swiftly come if her blood tested positive. She could do nothing but pray and wait.

And know for certain that the next six days would be the longest in her entire life.

CHAPTER TWENTY-FOUR

LANDON HAD WORKED the early shift that Friday, and now that he was off he had things to do. Huge things.

A few hours earlier he got hold of Reagan and convinced her to commit to a meeting. The two of them had spent time together before Ashley's visit, and Landon was certain she needed a friend as much now. Maybe more.

He ran a few errands, and it was just after six o'clock when he stopped by her apartment. Not only did he want to see the baby and encourage her to tell Luke, but he also wanted to show her something.

She opened the door and let him in. For the first fifteen minutes they talked about little Tommy, how quickly he was growing and how he was looking less like a newborn and more like a baby.

"See—" Reagan held him up, her smile taking up most of her face—"he's filling out. And his eyes are more alert, don't you think?"

"Definitely." Landon did a gentle tug on the baby's foot.

"And he looks even more like Luke."

It was true. The little boy was a miniature of his father. Landon leaned back against the sofa opposite Reagan. "You haven't told Luke yet." It was a statement rather than a question.

"No." Reagan cradled her baby closer to her chest and met Landon's eyes. "I'm afraid."

That made sense. The last time Reagan and Luke talked was at the bus station in Bloomington, the afternoon of September 11. Everything that could've changed had done so in the months since. "What scares you most?"

Reagan kept her voice quiet, but it held a strain that hadn't been there before. "I have no right to expect anything of him, Landon. After I let so much time go without answering his calls." She clenched her teeth and shook her head. "Okay, so he has a son. But he's moved on, and maybe hearing from me would make him more angry. Maybe he'd yell at me or tell me he hated me or hang up on me."

"Reagan—" he leaned forward and rested his forearms on his knees—"you'll never know if you don't call."

"Sometimes I wish someone else would tell him—you, maybe, or Ashley."

Landon gave her a crooked smile. "She'd do it today if you gave her the go-ahead."

"I know." Reagan tilted her head and studied her son. "But that's just part of it."

He waited.

She lifted her eyes again. "Maybe I don't want Luke in my baby's life. If he's got this—" she hesitated—"this wacky way of thinking, that there's no God, no faith, no truth, then what happens when Tommy's older?"

"You mean old enough to understand his father's viewpoint?"

"Exactly." A desperate sigh escaped her. "I can't imagine letting my son spend summers or holidays with Luke only to have his mind poisoned."

Landon gave her a few seconds to cool off. When he spoke, he kept his voice kind. "You're right; that's scary." He clasped his hands. "But Luke's still the baby's father."

"I appreciate what you're saying, Landon, but I'm not sure." She kissed her baby's cheek. "Lots of kids go through life without a father. Look at Cole."

"Cole . . ." A grin worked its way up Landon's cheeks before he could stop it. "That's the other thing I wanted to talk to you about."

"Cole?" The baby began to cry, and Reagan rose to her feet. She bounced him just enough so that he settled back down again.

"Yes, I think in the not-too-distant future he's going to have a father after all."

Reagan stopped bouncing. "Landon!" She stared at him. "Did you ask her?"

He stood and came to her, reached into his pocket, and pulled out a small velvet box. "I've been saving for three months." His fingers worked their way between the crack of the box, and he opened the lid. "I had it custom-made."

Reagan gasped and transferred Tommy's weight to her right arm. With her free hand she took the box and studied the ring that lay inside. "Landon, it's beautiful."

He gazed at the ring, the solitaire at the center and the three small diamonds on each side. One set of three as reminders that the life ahead of them would only be strong if it included both of them and God. The Bible was clear: a cord of three strands is not easily broken. The other three diamonds represented the family they would be the moment they exchanged vows. Not because Landon was obligated to be a father for Cole but because he wanted to.

With all his heart.

He met Reagan's eyes, and his voice was thick. "She's coming Thursday with more paintings." The longing in Landon's heart swelled until he could barely breathe. "I love her so much, Reagan. I'm going to ask her then."

"To marry you?"

"Yes." He looked at the ring again and chuckled. "Think she'll like it?"

"My goodness, yes, Landon. It's beautiful." She looked at it for a moment longer before handing the box back to him.

He closed the lid and slipped it back into his pants pocket. "I'm not sure I'll survive till then."

"I didn't realize the two of you had, you know—" a light shrug played on her shoulders—"that you'd gotten so close."

"We've talked about marriage, but I still think she'll be surprised."

Reagan looked at Tommy and then back at Landon. "He's asleep. I'll be right back." She turned and headed through the doorway down a hall. When she came back, she took her spot on the sofa. "Kari and Ryan are getting married in September; is that what you said before?"

Landon nodded. "They're having the ceremony and reception at the Baxter house—setting up a few tents and inviting maybe a hundred and fifty people. Close friends and family."

"Sounds beautiful." Something wistful hung in Reagan's tone. "Then you and Ashley." She blew out softly through her nose. "Looks like life is working out pretty well for the Baxters."

The implication was as clear as the image she made, her heart twisting in pain across from him. He cocked his head and waited until she looked up. "Except for Luke, right?"

"Yes." Tears fell onto her cheeks, and she brushed at them with the back of her hand. "I'm sorry. I . . . I wasn't going to do this." She sniffed and searched his eyes. "Sometimes I want to call Luke so badly. Tell him he has a son and beg him to get on the next plane to New York."

"The thing is, Reagan, you'll never know." Landon paused. "Unless you ask him."

She crossed her arms. "Pray for me, will you? That I'll get brave enough to call him. He has a right to know. And whatever happens after that, I have to believe it's for the best."

Later that night, looking out the window of his apartment, Landon got hold of Ashley and told her about the meeting with Reagan. "I think she's close." He squeezed his eyes shut, forcing himself to make small talk. The proposal was already on his tongue, begging for release. "She knows she needs to tell him about the baby."

"Good." Ashley's tone was flat. "We need to pray."

Landon stared at a piece of sky wedged between two buildings. What was that odd note in her voice these past few days? "You okay, Ash?"

"Fine. Just tired. Sorry."

"You're still coming Thursday, right?"

"I have my ticket."

Maybe whatever he was hearing in her voice was his imagination. His concerns hung like so many cobwebs in his mind, and he batted at them, knocking them down so he could concentrate. "Did you decide which pieces you're bringing?"

"Another one from Sunset Hills, a painting of Bert with his saddle. Then two new ones—one of a girl and boy playing outside the Baxter house, and another of Cole sitting on the bench beneath my parents' tree, blowing bubbles into a summer breeze."

"Mmmm." He settled back in his chair. "I can picture them, Ash. Don't give them to the gallery without showing me first, okay?"

She gave a soft laugh, but even that sounded strained somehow. "You're too nice, Landon."

"I'm honest." He let his chin fall to his chest and with his free hand he rubbed the muscles in the back of his neck. "The question here is whether *you're* being honest."

She hesitated a beat too long. "About what?"

"I'm not sure." Landon brought his head up again. "I just know that for years I've been able to read you—even if you weren't willing to be read." He exhaled. "And right now I can hear something in your voice. Something I can't read without seeing your eyes."

Again her answer was quick. Too quick. "I'm fine, Landon. Really."

He let it go. They wound up their conversation and said their good-byes. It wasn't until after they hung up that he caught something he'd missed at first. She hadn't told him she loved him. It was the first time in weeks, and it troubled Landon enough that he had half her phone number punched in again before he could stop himself.

Ashley was probably just being Ashley. Worrying that she wasn't right for him, or that even though he'd told her he was committed to her, somehow he was having doubts. Something like that.

The idea made him smile as he stood and returned the phone to the kitchen. Just six days until he would see her again. Six days. And after that she would never again have to worry about the future, because she wouldn't be wearing her doubts on her sleeve the way she had for so long.

She'd be wearing his ring.

CHAPTER TWENTY-FIVE

ASHLEY CALLED THE HOSPITAL laboratory six times Wednesday, but her results weren't in yet. Finally late that afternoon, the woman who answered recognized her name.

"You were in here last week . . . from Bloomington, right?" Her voice held a hint of compassion.

"Yes." Ashley raked her fingers through her hair. "I need the test results as soon as possible. I've got a . . . a business trip tomorrow."

The woman hesitated. "We don't usually do this, but I'm working tomorrow morning. If they come in I'll give you a call. That way you don't have to keep checking."

"Thank you." Ashley noticed she was shaking again. Something she'd been doing off and on since hearing the news about Jean-Claude. "Do you need my cell number?"

"Uh . . ." There was the sound of papers shuffling. "No, I've got it."

"Can you call me even if the results aren't in tomorrow morning? Whenever they come?"

"Sure." Something in the woman's voice told Ashley she'd

been there before, waiting breathlessly for results that would perhaps set the course for the rest of her life.

On Thursday morning, Ashley was still thinking about the woman, her willingness to break protocol, her kindness. She tossed her suitcase and the portfolio with the three paintings into her car and hurried Cole to her parents' house. Their good-bye was more emotional for her than usual, because chances were the next time she saw her son, she'd know at least a part of what the future held for them both.

Ashley got into her car without looking back. She arrived at the airport two hours before her flight, got through security, and found a seat at the gate.

The entire time her cell phone was never farther away than the pocket of her rayon blazer. She was glad the call hadn't come while she was saying good-bye to Cole or driving to the airport. The news might've been more than she could handle at either of those times.

Now, though, seated and waiting for her flight, she was desperate to know the results. She brought the phone out and studied it. No missed calls. For a moment she waited, willing it to deliver the news that she was fine, her tests perfectly normal.

But an hour passed. Her boarding call had just been given when her cell phone rang. She yanked it from her pocket, giving quick furtive glances to the people around her.

She checked the caller ID window and felt her throat grow thick.

It was the hospital.

Ashley looked down and let her forehead rest in her hand. Privacy . . . she needed privacy. She flipped the phone open and held it to her ear. Her voice was soft and jerky, as though the call were some part of a covert operation. "Hello?"

"Ashley Baxter?" It was the nurse who had drawn her blood.

"Yes." She closed her eyes. Her heart was racing so fast she could barely get the word out.

"I spoke with you yesterday about calling when your test results came in." The nurse's voice was measured, unreadable. "I got them a few minutes ago."

Breathing wasn't possible. Ashley's voice was weak and breathy. "It's . . . it's negative, right?"

"No." The woman paused. "I'm sorry. It's positive."

The woman was still talking, going on about having the test done a second time, and how a positive test wasn't always accurate, and that Ashley needed to see a doctor immediately to plan a course of treatment.

But the words became a blurred mumbling. Ashley's eyes flew open, and she nearly dropped the phone. A spot by the window was less crowded, and she walked toward it. She was dizzy, sick to her stomach; a rushing sound filled her brain.

It was positive? Her blood had tested positive for HIV?

"Ms. Baxter, did you hear me?" The woman's voice was tinny and distant.

Ashley realized she'd let the phone slip partway down her cheek. She lifted it back to her ear. "Excuse me?" Her body was taking over for her because her heart and brain had checked out. They seemed paralyzed, unable to believe it was possible, certain that this moment was merely one more in a run of bad dreams. Nightmares.

"Ms. Baxter, do you have a doctor you can contact, someone who can help you get a second test and a treatment plan?"

Did she have a doctor? Ashley squinted and let her body rest against the full-length window. "A doctor?" She gave a few hard shakes of her head. Her father was a doctor, after all. She swallowed. "Yes, I have a doctor."

"Final boarding call for Flight 27 to La Guardia." The voice sounded throughout the gate area.

Ashley jolted into sudden awareness. She was about to miss her flight. A cough lodged in her throat, and it took a few seconds for her to speak. "I . . . I have to go. Thank you." She slammed her phone shut, slipped it back into her pocket, and hurried the last few steps back to her bags. Five minutes later she found her spot on the airplane, a window seat in a row that was, once more, otherwise empty.

The shock was so devastating, she couldn't concentrate. She handed her art case to a flight attendant, who promised to keep it in a special storage area. Then Ashley turned her cell phone off and leaned back in her seat.

She was positive for HIV?

It wasn't even remotely possible. Not now, not when in a few hours she was supposed to meet Landon at La Guardia, spend the evening celebrating her return, and savor his hugs and kisses, the feel of him in her arms.

Breathe . . . you have to breathe.

She ordered herself to inhale, but nothing about the process seemed to be working. Ashley sat straight in her seat, and her gaze darted down the aisle toward the nearest exit. She had to get off, had to get a mouthful of fresh air or she'd suffocate.

But it was too late. Already the doors were shut, and the flight attendants were talking about the safety features of the plane and oxygen masks dropping if a change of pressure occurred. For a crazy moment, Ashley considered tearing at the paneling above her head, grabbing the oxygen mask, and gulping mouthfuls before she passed out.

Breathe. Get a breath. Hurry!

She sucked in, but the cabin seemed filled with something thick and stale that stuck in her throat. She knew what was happening. Her lungs were no longer capable of taking in air. Panic tightened its grip, and she clutched at the armrests on each side of her seat. "Help me." The whispered words were lost in the hum of blowing air and jet engine sounds. "God . . . help."

Her body was taking her straight into a panic attack, one that threatened to send her to her feet, running down the aisle, clawing at the exit doors.

"God . . ." She closed her eyes and the dizziness worsened. The jet engines roared now, and the plane began to taxi down the runway. Faster . . . faster . . . faster . . .

I can't breathe. Her words were silent now because she was out of air. *God, I have to get off. I'm going to die.*

Suddenly a memory flashed in her mind. She'd had panic attacks before. Back when she was twelve years old, the year she entered junior high and realized she wasn't gossipy and giggly like the other girls. The year they cut her out of their social circle and moved on without her.

She'd be lying in bed, and without warning her heart would leap into her throat. Her temples would pound, and she'd feel like she couldn't breathe. The same way she felt now.

Ashley took in three quick gasps, none of them meeting her need for oxygen. The picture of herself as a girl developed some. Scared to death, she always ran to her father, and he would talk her back to a place of sanity.

The rushing in her temples grew fuller as she struggled to make sense of her thoughts. What was it her father told her? Breathe out. Her lungs felt as heavy as lead, stiff and unwilling to cooperate. The plane was lifting into the air, making her crazy with the need to get off the plane.

She closed her eyes, pursed her lips, and blew out. A whisper of air left her mouth, but the feel of it reassured her enough to keep her seated.

She opened her eyes and stared at her hands. Again she blew out. Again and again, all without even trying to draw a breath. Another infusion of calm filled her veins. Understanding dawned—she'd been hyperventilating. Of course. In the panic of the moment, of the terrifying truths about her life, she panicked and sucked in air without letting any out.

What else had her father told her? Breathe in through her nose. Slow and easy, through her nose. She widened her nostrils, sucked in a small bit of air, and felt her lungs respond.

Once more she brought her lips together and blew out, longer this time. Slower. After ten minutes, she felt her body regain control. But not her mind, not her heart and soul. She was HIV-positive. The more the words ran through her head, the more their meaning sank in, leaving her sick and defeated. At least the panic attack had passed, and though her fingers still trembled, she could breathe again. She was no longer desperate to get off the plane.

God, give me something to hang on to.

Ashley looked out the window and squinted at the brilliant blue reflecting against the upper side of a field of puffy cumulus clouds. No answers flashed in her heart, but rather a knowing. God had promised that he knew the plans for her life, good plans. Maybe not the plans she'd had for herself, but good plans all the same. Whatever happened.

In the past few days she'd researched HIV on the Internet. What she'd found was more encouraging than she'd expected. Positive test results were no longer a death sentence. Doctors could help people now—the basketball star Magic Johnson had taught them that much.

A statistic on-line caught her eye the other day in light of the awful waiting period she'd just survived: 10 percent of those infected with HIV would get AIDS, and 10 percent of those who developed AIDS would die because of the virus. And the medicine cost less than ever before—a few hundred dollars a year.

Whatever it cost, whatever it did to her lifestyle, she would fight to stay healthy and well. For Cole. He needed to be tested, of course, though she'd read on one of the Web sites that if he had the virus, doctors would've discovered it when he was born.

Still, she wanted to be sure.

The life she and Cole shared was all she had now, because involving Landon in such a nightmare was something she simply wouldn't do. Marrying him would involve a physical relationship, which would always hold the risk that he would somehow become infected. She'd always believed he deserved someone better than her, and that was never more true than it was now.

Ashley blinked and breathed out again. The panic was gone, but in its place was a sorrow deeper than the ocean. A long time ago Kari told her something about love, a definition that had stayed with Ashley: "Love is a decision." A decision that some-times meant making hard choices. That was certainly true now.

She loved Landon. Saying good-bye to him would be the most difficult thing she'd ever done.

She'd go to New York and meet with him. She'd tell him about her test results, apologize, and insist they break off their relation-ship. She'd tell him good-bye, even if it killed her, and then she'd take her paintings to the gallery and explain that because of per-sonal reasons she could no longer have a showing in the fall.

All of that lay ahead of her when she arrived at La Guardia.

Suddenly she was no longer desperate to get off the plane. Rather she wished she could stay on it forever.

⋙

The moment Ashley walked off the plane Landon knew some-thing wasn't right.

She came to him, hugged him. Even kissed him, but not the way she'd kissed him when she left. When he asked her about it, she shrugged off her lack of energy and blamed it on being over-tired. They shared a quick lunch, and then he rode with her to her hotel.

He'd expected her to have a glass of iced tea with him at one of the cafes in the lobby. But instead she begged off, explained she needed to spend time with her work, catch up on her sleep, pre-pare for her meeting with the gallery owners the next day.

Before she headed to her room, she showed him the new pieces. They were breathtaking, each of them. Landon could hardly believe it had come to this, that her work was being fea-tured in a Manhattan gallery, and that the gallery owners had completely fallen in love with her.

Not that he could blame them.

The night passed slowly, as did the day.

Just before seven o'clock on Friday night, Landon positioned himself at the center of the Hyatt lobby near a standing floral arrangement and locked his eyes on the bank of elevators. The gallery was walking distance from the hotel, and the owners had put Ashley up here this time. Last night when he and Ashley discussed tonight's dinner, they'd agreed that the hotel restaurant made the most sense.

Besides, it was across the street from Central Park.

If things went the way he expected, he had plans for after dinner. A romantic walk south through the park to the place where horse-drawn carriages lined the street. Together they'd snuggle in the back of a carriage and spend an hour seeing the park by moonlight, talking about their wedding plans, and dreaming of a future together.

A future Landon had all but given up on just a year ago.

He glanced at his watch and shifted his weight. The occasion warranted something new, so he'd bought a pair of black dress slacks and a short-sleeved, pale blue, button-down shirt at a shop on Fifth Avenue.

The ring was in his pocket.

His thoughts ran a hundred miles an hour while he kept his eyes glued to the elevators. Maybe they'd settle in New York after all. Fighting fires for the FDNY had gotten into his blood, just the way Jalen said it would. He was healing from the loss of his friend, a little more each day. Twice during the past week he'd taken a call, rolled on it, helped put out a fire, and handled the cleanup without ever once imagining that he was doing the work in Jalen's honor, keeping Jalen's memory alive.

No, more often lately he was working for himself, savoring the rush, enjoying making a difference in a city of seven million people. A city in desperate need of firefighters. Where every call could mean life or death. And now that he'd been offered a lieutenant's position . . .

A future in New York City seemed to have God's fingerprints all over it.

One of the elevator doors opened, and Ashley stepped out. The sight of her made him gasp just a bit. Her outfit, a sleeveless

254

gray top and black pants, was silky and moved with her. She was striking, and people around her took a second look as she passed. The guys at the fire station thought she looked like Winona Ryder, and she did. But something in her eyes was deeper, more loving than any starlet's.

She saw him and smiled, clutching a small bag to her side, making her way closer. He reached into his pocket and felt the velvet box. *God, bless this night. Make it special so the two of us will remember it forever.*

When she reached him, she slipped her arms around his neck and hugged him. "Hi." She pulled back and smiled.

"Hi." He caught something in her expression—regret, maybe, or fear. But just as quickly it was gone, and he dismissed the idea. He put his arm around her waist and drew her closer. "So tell me what happened."

"Today? At the gallery?" Her eyes shone, but something tired remained in her expression. "It went great. They loved the new pieces."

"And you promised them three more in a few weeks, right?"

There it was again—something strange in her eyes, something he was certain he'd seen. A sorrow, almost. But what could she possibly be sad about? Her life was playing out like some kind of magical dream.

When she said nothing, he angled his head. "You aren't waiting until fall, are you?"

She bit her lip and let her gaze fall to his chest. "I'm not sure."

"Hey—" he lifted her chin with his fingertips—"you have to come back sooner." The feel of her in his arms was intoxicating. He leaned closer and kissed her, slowly, with a passion that went way beyond desire. "I missed you, Ash."

"Me, too." Her eyes closed, and this time she moved her lips over his. The contact was brief, but it let him know for certain that she loved him the way he loved her.

He drew back and studied her. "You look beautiful."

"And you." Her voice was breathy, and she raised an eyebrow as she took in his new outfit. "Nice."

"Thanks." He grinned and pointed to the restaurant. "I made reservations."

His hand found hers, and he led the way across the lobby. The place was dimly lit, with candles and linen cloths on each table. A maître d' led them to a high-backed leather booth in a quiet corner, several spots from the place where a pianist was playing a slow Lionel Ritchie number.

They sat across from each other and looked at their menus. Landon was too excited to eat, but he didn't want to give away the surprise. He scanned the items and then looked up and caught Ashley's eye. "Hungry?"

For a moment, it looked as though she might shake her head, but then she nodded. "Sure."

Throughout dinner they talked about the gallery and the break in the humidity, which had made for gorgeous Manhattan weather. Landon asked about Kari's wedding shower, and Ashley told him every detail, how all her sisters were there and how the guests insisted Kari replay her story of meeting Ryan and falling in love with him.

"When the shower was over, the four of us sorted through Kari's gifts and stayed up talking until after midnight."

"That's one thing I always knew would happen." Landon tore off a piece of his dinner roll and popped it in his mouth.

"What?" Ashley studied him over her iced tea.

He finished chewing and swallowed. "The four of you girls would wind up being friends." He could feel his eyes sparkling. The moment was getting closer. As soon as the waitress cleared their plates, he was going to reach for the ring.

He focused on what he'd been saying. "I remember when you thought Brooke didn't care about you or Kari or Erin. When any of you might not have been getting along." He felt the corners of his mouth rise. "But you Baxters have too much love to stay apart for long."

"That's why the Luke thing is killing us." She narrowed her eyes. "All of us."

Landon reached his hand across the table and took hold of her fingers. "You know what's going to happen, don't you?"

She ran her thumb over his and looked deep into his eyes. "What?"

Again he sensed a heaviness there. Something wasn't right. But soon things would be better than they'd ever been for either of them. Then the strange fleeting sadness would be gone from Ashley's eyes for good.

He forced himself to concentrate. "Reagan's going to call Luke." Landon hesitated. "He'll go to her, and they'll fall in love all over again. Then he'll return to your parents and make everything right. He and Reagan and their son."

She smiled. "Sounds very storybook."

"That's the thing about the Baxter family." Landon gave a light chuckle. "No matter where life takes a strange twist or turn, the final chapter always works out." He hesitated. "Look at Maddie."

"Yes." Ashley brought his fingers to her lips and kissed them. Her eyes never left his. "It always works out, but not always how everyone thinks it will."

Landon blinked. Why did he have the feeling they were talking in riddles? He kept his fingers woven together with hers and told her about his time with Reagan. "This time I think it will, Ash. Not the way they're worried it might, but the way everyone thought it would a year ago."

The waitress cleared their plates, and they turned down dessert. When they were alone, Landon eased his hand from hers and slid it into his pocket. For a long time he stayed that way, his hand wrapped around the tiny velvet box, his eyes captured by hers.

When he finally spoke, his voice was filled with an emotion deeper, different than any he'd ever known before. "Ashley, I have something to ask you."

Then, as her mouth fell open and before she could say another word, he slipped the velvet box from his pocket and placed it on the table where they could both see it. Even in the warmth of the candlelight, Landon could see the blood drain from Ashley's face, see her expression go from shock to dismay to something that looked like sheer terror. And for the first time since he'd had the ring made, Landon considered something he'd never even fathomed before.

What if she said no?

CHAPTER TWENTY-SIX

THROUGHOUT THE ENTIRE EVENING, Ashley had kept her composure.

When she stepped off the elevator and took in the sight of Landon, all six-foot-four inches looking like he belonged on the cover of a calendar. When she came near and breathed in his cologne and the faint mint of his breath. A moment later when they kissed. She'd even remained calm throughout dinner, when she knew her announcement was coming, that they had less than an hour to share together this way. Less than an hour.

For all time.

Through all of it she kept herself from breaking down, forced herself to enjoy the evening with him since it would be her last. But when he brought out the velvet box, the ground beneath their table tilted wildly out of control. Her cheeks flashed hot, and then she felt the blood drain from her face and neck.

"Landon . . ." His name came out as a faint cry, a plea for help. She stared at the velvet box and shook her head. "What . . . are you doing?"

Disappointment splashed across his features, and she hated

herself for ruining this night. Along with everything else her positive blood test would take from her in the years to come, it wanted this night first. This moment.

"Ashley, I . . ."

His voice faded, and he brought his lips together. Instead of talking, he opened the box and held it up so she could see what lay inside. Her breath gathered in her throat and stayed there. It was a ring—an engagement ring. A solitaire surrounded by three smaller diamonds on each side, all set in the most brilliant white gold she'd ever seen.

She reached out and let her fingertips play over the top of the stones, and almost without realizing it she began to shake her head. Her eyes lifted to Landon's, and she hated the pain she saw there, the raw mix of confusion and anger and frustration.

Tears filled her eyes and spilled onto her cheeks before she could stop them. "Landon, I can't . . ."

He stood then, holding the box, and slid around the table to the seat next to her. "Ashley, I haven't even asked you." His voice was a strained whisper, racked with questions he must've been afraid to ask. He set the box on the table and took her face in his hands. "I've been planning this for months." He swallowed, but still his tone was tight, almost desperate. "Last time we talked I told you we should get married and you . . . you seemed okay with it."

"Landon . . ." She let her face fall forward just enough to rest in his hands. As she did her tears came harder and she closed her eyes. *God, deliver me from this. I can't bear it.*

The time had come to tell him the truth.

He must've taken her silence for acquiescence. "Ashley, it's okay to be nervous. Maybe it's too soon. I just thought we could make a plan now so that when I—"

"Stop." She opened her eyes and lifted her head from his hands. For a long while she searched his face, his expression. He had to know, before he went another moment thinking that somehow she doubted her feelings for him or that she wasn't sure about the life they might've shared together. She took his hands. Her fingers eased between his, and together their hands fell to the table between them.

"Ashley . . ." His expression looked stricken, tight and pinched, almost worse than it had the afternoon of September 11 before he boarded the bus for Manhattan. "What is it? What'd I do?"

"Not you, Landon. I love you more than life." She gave his fingers the gentlest squeeze and forced herself not to fall into his arms and weep for the sadness exploding within her. "It's *me*." She clenched her jaw. The simpler she could make the news, the better. "Something's happened."

"What?" The ring box still lay on the table, cold, untouched. "Whatever it is, we'll work it out."

Her tears came harder, silent and steady. She shook her head and sniffed. A flood of sorrow the size of Niagara Falls was pressing at the door of her heart. If she didn't hurry, none of what she had to say would make sense. For several seconds she closed her eyes and held her breath. Then—as she'd done on the airplane the day before—she exhaled through pursed lips. And somehow she found the strength to meet his eyes once more.

"Tell me, Ashley." With slow movements he loosened one of his hands from hers and took hold of the linen napkin still stretched across her knees. He dabbed a corner of it beneath her nose and along the outline of her jaw. Then he set the napkin down, leaned forward, and kissed away the tears from first one eye, then the other.

Ashley melted beneath his touch, but it took only a few seconds for her to stiffen, sit straighter as his hand found hers once more. It was wrong to wait, but she didn't know where to begin. *How* to begin.

Landon searched her face and tried once more. "I've known the best and the worst about you, Ashley Baxter. Whatever it is, just tell me."

She'd prepared for this moment since getting the news more

than twenty-four hours ago. She'd known then that when she told him, he would insist on maintaining some kind of relationship. A friendship, maybe—or even an engagement—something they could take one week or one day at a time.

But she'd made up her mind. Landon was young and kind and impossibly attractive. She would not have him waste time on her when they could never have a future together.

She sucked in a slow breath and held it for a moment. Her heart was racing, but that was okay. Whatever happened next, she had to tell him. "Several days ago—" her eyes found his—"a woman from Paris called me. She . . . she said she'd been asked by a doctor to contact a list of names."

Confusion reigned in Landon's eyes. "From Paris?"

"Landon . . ." Ashley's mind was spinning. She tightened her grip on his hands and struggled to find the words. "Jean-Claude is dying of AIDS."

A series of emotions flashed across his face: shock . . . disbelief . . . horror . . . and finally hope. "It's been years since—"

"Landon." She let her gaze fall again. His eyes were too kind and deep, and she needed a few seconds to build up the strength to continue. When she looked up, her vision was blurred by fresh tears. "I took the test last week." The pause that followed was the longest silence in her life.

"And . . ." One emotion remained in his voice now. A raw kind of fear that knew no bounds.

"It was positive."

There. She'd said it, and now nothing between them would ever be the same again. She let her chin fall, let her eyes find the place where their hands were linked. When she spoke, her tone was so broken she barely recognized it. "I'm sorry, Landon."

For several seconds he said nothing. Then his words rushed out, as though by asking questions, by searching for answers, he might somehow change the situation. "Tests can be wrong, Ashley. Where'd you have it done?"

Before she could speak, he had his own answer. "Wherever it

was, it doesn't matter. Mistakes happen. Besides, even if it *is* positive, there are options these days. Drugs . . . medicine. It's not like it used to be, you know that, right, Ashley?"

"Don't, Landon." She freed one of her hands and brought it to the side of his face. Her fingers moved along his cheekbone, down the length of his jaw, memorizing the feel of him. "It's over." The tears spilled onto her cheeks again. "God wants me to move on, return to Cole, and figure out some kind of treatment." The lump in her throat felt like a grapefruit. "I have to let you go."

"No!" A controlled anger shook Landon's voice. "I want to marry you, Ashley. We'll find a way to make it work, we have to, no matter what happens."

She let her hand fall to her lap. In her rehearsal of the conversation that was taking place, she had imagined a dozen things. That he would tell her it was a mistake and insist on another test; that he would promise her he still cared, still wanted to be in her life even if she was HIV positive.

But she had never expected a marriage proposal.

Seconds passed, and she could do nothing but stare at him, allow him to fill her senses while she marveled at the man he was. The man he'd always been. But his goodness made her decision all the more firm. A man like Landon deserved a wonderful life, a healthy girl with a future ahead of her, a woman without a sordid past who could give him a family and a lifetime of happiness.

And he'd find that woman only one way.

If Ashley climbed onto an airplane bound for Indianapolis and never looked back. Not ever. No matter what he thought he wanted, that would be the best thing for him, the thing that would prove her love for him like nothing else she could ever do.

"Ashley, what are you thinking?" Fear was back in his voice. "I don't care about the test."

She closed her eyes one more time, and when she opened them she felt more composed. Her mind had been made up since she'd learned about Jean-Claude. Now they needed to find some place where they could say good-bye.

She caught his gaze and held it. "Can we get out of here?"

Landon swallowed, his eyes wide. He returned to his place on the other side of the table, pulled a credit card from his wallet, and set it at the edge of the table. Neither of them said anything while the waitress ran his card and returned the check to him.

He signed it, stood, and reached for Ashley's hand. Before they left he took the velvet box from the table, closed the lid, and slid it back into his pocket. She didn't have to ask him how he felt. The hurt was written clearly across his face, screaming from his eyes.

The news she'd given him tonight had devastated him. And what was about to come figured to be even worse.

When they were in the hotel lobby, he turned to her and searched her face. "Where?"

"The lobby near my room." She blinked. "We need to be alone."

In silence, their hands linked, they rode the elevator to the eighteenth floor. Once in the small, nearly dark sitting area, she turned and faced him. "Landon, it's over. All of it."

He shifted his weight from one leg to the other, and twice his mouth opened as though he wanted to protest. Finally he reached for her hand again. "Ashley, this is crazy. I've loved you as long as I can remember." His eyes drilled hers, begging her to understand. "A blood test isn't going to change that."

She wanted to break down and cry, to pull him close and tell him it hadn't changed her feelings either. But that would make the eventual good-bye worse. *Love is a decision.* The words played over in her mind like a song she couldn't forget. In her decision to love Landon, the last thing she could do was appear unresolved.

With her free hand, she took hold of his arm, her gaze direct and unwavering. "It changed it for me."

He searched her face, her eyes. "Ashley . . ." Tiny beads of sweat dotted his brow. "That's not fair. You love me . . . you *know* you love me."

"Yes." Her voice was a broken whisper. "I love you. But God

wants me to let you go." She bit her lip to keep it from quivering. "It's time, Landon, that's all." She moved her hand from his shoulder to the side of his face before burying her fingers in his dark hair and drawing him close. Her lips brushed against his cheek, his lips, and then she pulled back.

"You're panicking." His eyes were dark with desire. "We'll take it one day at a time; I can do this, Ash. Give me a chance."

She went to him then, allowed him to draw her into an embrace that said all they couldn't bring themselves to speak. He clung to her, begging her to work it out with him, but she could feel her body stiffen, resolute. Nothing would make her change her mind.

Her love for him was that great.

"Landon." They separated, and she refused another wave of tears. "When I leave tomorrow, don't call me; don't come after me." She kept her eyes on his, ignoring the sobs that welled within her. "Honor that, please."

He slid his hand in his pocket, and she guessed he was fingering the velvet box. Tears gathered in his eyes, tears that hadn't been there even when he returned from Ground Zero, from finding Jalen.

After a long while he sniffed hard and looked deep into her soul. "If you need time, I'll give it to you." He reached for her hands; then he kissed her one last time. He was breathless when he found her eyes, and his words were directed straight to the center of her being. "I'll let you go, Ash, but only for now. Until you have time to catch your breath. But one day . . . one day I'll return to you, and then you'll know."

She wanted to disagree, to insist that he forget such thinking because it would hurt them both when it didn't happen. But she couldn't stop herself from going along with it. She swallowed hard. "Then I'll know what?"

His eyes shone, and Ashley wished she could freeze time, wished she could collect her easel and a blank canvas and capture his look in case this moment was the last they'd ever share together. "Then you'll know what God's really telling you."

Ashley watched him turn and walk toward the elevators a few doors away. He pressed the button, then turned and leaned his shoulder against the wall, his eyes never leaving hers. When the door opened, he mouthed the words *I love you*.

Then he was gone.

Ashley stepped back and dropped slowly into an overstuffed chair. The heaviness of her heart was such that she couldn't stand up under it another moment. She buried her head in her hands and released the tears that had built there.

She wanted to scream, rail against the consequences that had come upon her now, just when life was coming together. And then—for the first time that night—the truth about Landon's plans hit her full force. He'd bought her an engagement ring! He'd been planning to propose to her, and if she'd never heard from Marie in Paris, this night would've been her most wonderful ever.

At this very moment they would've been kissing and laughing and admiring her ring. In the glow of candlelight, they would've talked about a wedding date and announcing the news to their families. Especially to Cole.

Somehow she struggled to her feet and found her way to her room. Thoughts of her son made her tears come twice as hard. Landon was his best friend. Her bad choices in Paris had cost Cole any chance at a father, all possibility of a normal life. They might even cost him his mother as well. Or his own life.

God, the sorrow is too great. I can't survive it.

She sucked in three quick breaths and willed the convulsing in her chest to stop. Tears still streamed down her face, but she stared out a distant window, found a piece of the sky, and set her gaze there. Where God lived. As bad as things were, as awful as they might become, she had done the right thing. The thing God wanted of her.

She loved Landon enough to let him go, and now God would

show her how to get on with life, how to figure out a way to live with her diagnosis. He would show her, because that was what he promised in Scripture—that he knew the plans he had for her, and that he would work all things out to the good. Even if she didn't see proof of that until heaven.

Gradually her tears slowed. A part of her ached to call Landon, to tell him it was all a mistake and that yes, of course she wanted to marry him. But she ordered herself to be strong, to stand by the decision she'd made. God alone knew what lay ahead for her. Somehow he would see her through.

Ashley fell into bed sometime before ten o'clock. When she did, she was surprised that though she felt buried beneath her sorrow, devastated, and afraid of the future, her heart wasn't broken as she'd thought it would be. Where her heart had been she felt a hollow empty hole. A cold, dark, nothingness.

And in that instant she understood why.

When he left, Landon Blake had taken more than her hopes and desires. More than the future she'd dreamed of sharing with him. He'd taken the thing that would forever be his alone.

He'd taken her heart.

CHAPTER TWENTY-SEVEN

LUKE HAD HIS BACKPACK flung over his shoulder, and he was almost out the door when the phone rang. He glanced back and considered letting the machine get it. But sometimes his boss at the cafeteria called this early to see if he wanted an extra shift. Money was tight, and since it was his day off, he took a few jogging steps back inside and grabbed the receiver.

"Hello?"

"Luke . . . it's Ashley."

"Hey." He glanced at his watch and ordered himself to be patient. "What's up?" Other than his mother, only Ashley made an attempt now and then to keep in touch with him. July had flown by, and she hadn't seen him in weeks. But she wouldn't look shocked at his appearance, wouldn't roll her eyes at his long hair and what was now a full-grown beard, the way Brooke had.

Ashley knew what it was to be the single Baxter going against the grain.

"Luke, we need to talk." Her tone was rock hard. "What time are you finished with classes?"

Luke blinked. "Am I in trouble?"

"No. Sorry." Compassion leaked in between her words. She exhaled hard. "We just need to talk."

"One o'clock." Luke's mind raced. Was something else wrong with Maddie? Ashley had given him the good news about her a few weeks earlier. But if it wasn't their niece, then who? What? In all the time since he'd left home, Ashley hadn't sounded so serious. "Wanna come here?"

"No." Her answer was quick, certain. "Remember that big willow tree near the math building? Let's meet at the bench beneath it."

"Okay." A handful of questions played on his tongue, but Luke swallowed them. It was probably something about his father. Maybe Ashley had decided to play peacemaker, in which case the meeting would be a waste of time. Unless his father accepted him the way he was, Luke wanted nothing to do with him. "I gotta run."

"Ten after one at the tree?"

"Right. See ya." Luke hung up, shifted his backpack higher on his shoulder, and jogged out the door. His first class was in eight minutes.

The morning passed in a blur of reviews for final exams, slated for the end of the week. By that weekend, summer classes would be over, and he'd have a month off until fall.

It was a few minutes after one when he jogged across the campus and turned left toward the math building. Ashley was already waiting for him at the bench beneath the willow, just as she'd said. She turned when she heard him, and their eyes met.

He walked the last few steps and was still breathing hard by the time he got to her. She looked as beautiful as ever, but her eyes were older. As though there were things about her life she hadn't shared with him. The possibility poked pins at his conscience. Why did he keep such distance—especially from her?

She stood and held out her arms, and he hugged her for a long time. When they pulled apart, he took in the length of her and gave her a partial smile. "You look good, Ash."

"Check out your hair." She ran her fingers along the base of his neck. Then she tickled his beard. "I almost didn't recognize you."

He shrugged. "I needed something different."

"That happens." She sat back down and patted the spot next to her. "Sit."

He eased his backpack onto the ground and dropped to the bench. "This is about Dad, right?"

She stared at him, her eyes serious and sad. Sadder than he'd ever seen them. "No." Her expression softened some. "I mean, yes, Dad's missing you. But that's not why I'm here."

He cocked his head. "This isn't about asking me to come home?"

Ashley shook her head. "No, Luke. It's so much more than that." Her gaze was as intense as the summer sun. "What I'm about to tell you, I promised Reagan I would never say. But—" Her voice caught, and for a moment she brought her fingers to her lips.

"Hey!" Luke put his hand on her shoulder and leaned a bit closer. "Ash, what is it? What's Reagan have to do with it?"

"Life is funny, Luke." She sniffed. "You think you have things all figured out, and then life throws you a curveball. Know what I mean?"

Luke could see himself in Mr. Decker's office high in the World Trade Center, Reagan standing beside him as they laughed about some play they were going to see that night. He blinked. "Yeah, I do."

She inhaled slowly through her nose. "I'm sick, Luke." She gave a brief shake of her head. "I tested positive for HIV."

For a split instant he wanted to yell at her, shake her, and tell her never to say anything like that again. But almost as quickly the facts began to register. First, she wasn't laughing. And second . . .

He felt faint, sick to his stomach, but he found his voice. "Was it . . . was it Paris?"

"Yes." She hung her head and her chin trembled. When she

looked up, tears filled her eyes and there was a pleading in her voice. "No one knows yet. Just you and . . . and Landon."

"But, Ashley—" his heartbeat doubled—"it's been such a long time. Are . . . you sure?"

"I haven't been to the doctor yet, but the blood test was positive." She bit her lip. "Anyway, that's not why I came."

He tried to remember what she'd said the last time they'd talked. Something about going to New York and taking some of her paintings to a gallery in Manhattan. She hadn't mentioned spending time with Landon, but that figured. He lived there, after all, and the two of them were friends. Good friends. Reagan lived in New York City, too. No wonder Ashley was thinking about his old girlfriend.

Luke gritted his teeth. He'd missed a lot since moving out. He didn't have a clue what was going on in his sister's life. Now she had HIV, and anything could happen. She could get AIDS and be dead in a year or two.

The thought made his head pound.

Until now his choices this past year had made him feel free in a proactive sort of way. If life couldn't be explained with faith and a belief in God, then at least he was doing something to figure out a different explanation, a different philosophy. A different religion. Wasn't that the point of the clubs and meetings, the Freethinkers Alliance? But here, now, in light of Ashley's admission, the past year felt anything but freeing.

It felt ugly and selfish and ignorant.

Whatever she wanted to tell him about Reagan, the news was nothing to what she'd just said. She had HIV?! She was his favorite sister. She couldn't be sick. He closed his eyes and let his head drop into his hands. An image flashed across the expanse of his heart. He and Ashley, maybe five and nine years old. She stood behind him, helping him hold a basketball the right way.

"Like this, Lukey." She'd given his right elbow a gentle nudge so it came in toward his body some. "Now bend your knees and push the ball up."

He did as she told him. The ball made a perfect arc up toward the basket and swished neatly through the net. "I did it!" He could see the little boy he was back then. Fist raised in the air, he flew into Ashley's arms, and the two of them jumped up and down together.

He blinked and stared at his lap as the memory lifted. She'd always loved him more than any of the others, but after Paris he'd treated her like . . . like he hated her. How many years had they lost because of his narrow-minded Christian views? And how many years would they have left if she got sick now?

"Ashley, I'm so sorry." He looked at her, and with his free hand he reached for her fingers. "You need to tell Dad. He . . . he can help you. They can do a lot more these days."

"I know." She was quiet for a moment, and the muscles in her jaw tensed. "Listen, that's not why I came. The HIV convinced me I had to tell you the truth." Her eyes searched his again. "Luke, I saw Reagan."

He was still reeling from the news about her health. Now what? Another attempt at getting him to call Reagan? Most of the Baxter family seemed to believe if he'd only get ahold of Reagan, he'd be the person he'd been before.

"You . . . saw her?" A burst of adrenaline shot through his veins, and his fingers trembled. He didn't have time to question his reaction, why he was feeling this way when he'd convinced himself he no longer cared about Reagan, no longer loved her. "When? What did she . . . did she call you?"

"She and Landon are friends now." Ashley ran her tongue along her lower lip and gripped her knees. "I can't believe I'm telling you this."

Luke held his breath. So she'd seen Reagan. Was that enough to cause her this kind of anxiety? He rested his arm on the back of the bench. "What aren't you saying?"

She planted her elbows just above her knees and covered her face with her fingers. "Luke—" slowly she dropped her hands and stared at him—"she has a baby."

Everything around him seemed suddenly frozen. Sound . . . movement . . . time. All of it stopped so he could concentrate on the single word screaming at him, echoing through his heart and soul.

Baby?

He remembered to breathe, but he could feel the blood leave his face, sense his skin becoming cold, clammy. "Ashley . . ." His voice sounded strange, as if someone else were talking for him. "What do you mean?"

"I *mean* . . ." She straightened and turned so she was facing him. Her brow lowered, and her struggle was written across her face. "She has a *baby.*"

He stared at his sister, searching her eyes for any sign of teasing or trickery. But her expression shouted the fact loud and clear. It was true. He stood and took four long strides away from the bench. With his back to Ashley, he grabbed fistfuls of his hair and stared at the sky. Reagan had a baby? How was that even possible? She hadn't been back in New York a year yet.

Then, like a slap across the face, it hit him. He spun around and walked the distance back to Ashley. "Tell me Landon's not the father."

A sad laugh played on her lips. "That's what I thought."

"He's not?"

"Luke—" her face grew more intense than before, and her eyes pleaded with him to understand—"the baby's *yours.* Your son."

He felt his heart fall from his chest and hit the ground. Tears stung his eyes, and his jaw dropped as he sucked in a sharp breath.

The baby was his?

How could the baby possibly be his? The truth cornered him, staring at him until he forced himself to look. As he did, denial stepped aside. What was he thinking? Of *course* the baby was his. Reagan would never have been with another man after their brief encounter. Not in the wake of losing her father.

The bench looked a long way down, but he dropped to it and felt the dirt beneath his feet turn to liquid. His mouth opened, but for the longest time no sound came out, no words. Nothing that could adequately convey what he was feeling, this strange disconnected sense that all of life had ceased and yet at the same time it was racing ahead at warp speed.

"I wasn't going to . . ."

Luke closed his eyes and gave a light shake of his head. Two streams of tears fell onto his cheeks and ran into his beard, but he couldn't lift his hands to wipe them. They'd been together just one night . . . one time. He'd lost track of how many days he'd tried to call her, and then finally he'd given up.

Never . . . never once had he considered that she might have gotten pregnant. That she'd returned to New York terrified, devastated at the loss of her father, only to find out that she was carrying a child.

Their child.

How must life have been for her? What did her mother think, learning about Reagan's situation so soon after Mr. Decker's death? And what about her pregnancy? Had she been alone with her concerns, her fears? Had the delivery gone smoothly, or had it been a difficult birth? Questions lined themselves up at the front steps of his mind, as far out as he could see.

His fingers tightened into fists, and he pressed them against his eyes. "Reagan." Her name was more of a moan, and he let his head drop again. He clasped his hands at the back of his neck and stared at the ground. *I should've been there, Reagan. Why didn't you tell me? How could you keep this from me?*

Ashley was saying something, something about Reagan. Her words ran together like a rush of waves crashing in a stormy surf. He lowered his hands and forced himself to concentrate. If Ashley had seen Reagan, then she must have some of the answers.

"Luke—" her voice was patient, gentle—"are you listening?"

"Yeah." He nodded and another wave of tears spilled from his eyes. "Sorry. What?"

Ashley hesitated. "I was saying that she wanted to tell you herself." She put her hand on his shoulder and squeezed. "But I couldn't wait. It's been . . . well, it's been too long." Tears glistened in her eyes, too. "Your little boy needs you." She tilted her head. "Reagan, too."

A whole new rush of possibilities slammed around Luke's mind, and he needed answers more than air. "Did you see him?" A sob was lodged in his throat, and he could barely work his voice. "The baby, I mean?"

For the first time since their meeting, a smile lifted the corners of her mouth. "He's beautiful, Luke." A sound came from her that was more laugh than cry. "He looks just like you."

The moment Ashley said the baby—*his* baby—looked like him, the idea became more than a source of shock. It became truth. He squinted, his entire body shaking. "I'm . . . I'm a father?"

"Yes." Another laugh slipped from her throat, and this time her eyes sparkled. "You have to see him."

Again the questions practically sent him to the ground. What would the Baxter family say now, now that he'd gotten Reagan pregnant and had a son? As soon as they knew, the pretense of his past would be gone forever. They'd know it wasn't September 11 that had changed him.

It was September 10.

The onetime good-boy image would be gone for good. What would his parents and sisters think, and what would Pastor Mark at church say when he found out?

More than that, why should he care even a little *what* they thought?

"Luke, talk to me."

He'd let himself drift again, oblivious to whatever Ashley was saying. "It's too much . . ." He fell against the bench and dropped his head back this time, shielding his eyes with his hands.

His questions took a different direction, one that pretty much knocked the wind from him. If he had a son, then he needed to see him, needed to see Reagan and find out why she'd kept the truth from him. But what did that mean for his freethinking future?

No doubt Reagan hadn't stopped believing in God. If he visited her now, wouldn't she expect him to become a part of the baby's life? Her life, even? Luke stopped the stream of questions long enough to consider that.

The thought sent chills down his spine—but chills that were more good than bad. He'd never stopped loving her, missing her. But he could hardly pretend to share her faith. Freethinking meant he had the right to his own viewpoint, separate from hers. What if that made her turn away from him again? This time maybe forever? Would that be fair to him, fair to the baby?

Worst of all was a truth that stood like a fortress between this moment and his future: He was nothing like the young man he'd been when he was dating Reagan. They'd had everything in common before that awful Monday night, and now they had nothing but memories.

Memories and a baby boy.

He thought back to when he was five or six years old. Ashley had taken him by the hands and spun him in circles three feet off the ground until his feet flopped behind him. The sensation was like flying, exhilarating and dizzying, but eventually her hands grew tired, and she dropped him. Luke had hurt his head and bruised his knee.

He felt the same way now. Spinning high and out of control, but this time he was a hundred feet in the air—dizzy and afraid and breathless. With no way to tell what would happen when he hit the ground. At some point pain was bound to hit, pain that came with not knowing about Reagan's pregnancy, not being there in New York to share the past year with her. Not seeing his son born. Not knowing whether he'd ever hold him, or watch him grow up, toss a ball with him, or teach him to drive. The kind of pain that would make his gut ache and place a mountain range along his shoulder blades.

"What're you thinking?"

His sister's voice broke through to him, and he lowered his head enough to see her. Answers to most of his questions would come in time. But his sister had to know the answer to at least this one: "What's . . . what's his name?"

Relief muted the concern in Ashley's expression. "Thomas Luke." Her voice was a gentle whisper. She searched his face. "Reagan's calling him Tommy."

Thomas Luke? She'd named the baby after her father . . . and after him?

Luke could do nothing but stare at Ashley. He would somehow survive the coming days, months. Years. Because the moment he'd heard the boy's name—heard his own name as part of it—the questions stopped, and his heart found its way back into his chest. He knew this because where there had been numbness, for the first time that afternoon he felt pain.

A massive, suffocating pain that made him doubt he could stand up under it. Pain bound to stay with him, holding him captive until something very special and amazing happened.

Until he held his son for the first time.

CHAPTER TWENTY-EIGHT

HIS PLANS CAME TOGETHER with amazing speed and clarity.

Ashley promised she wouldn't tell anyone else in the family about the baby, and after that Luke went home and spent the night on the sofa, lost in thought.

By morning, the shock had worn off.

In the light of day he did what any freethinker would do: He charted a course of action with his head and believed that at some point his heart would follow. For the next four days he attended class and took his finals, just as he'd planned. Not once in that time did he sleep with Lori, and twice she asked him about it.

"I need space," he told her. "Something I'm going through."

Since his talk with Ashley he'd known that no matter how liberal-minded he planned on becoming, the idea of an open relationship, multiple partners, and sex as self-expression simply didn't hold water.

The entire notion was insane. That he'd bought into it even for a time made him doubt his ability to think—freely or otherwise. Before they went their separate ways, Ashley told him about the man who was Cole's father. By the sounds of it, he could've been a guest speaker for the Freethinkers Alliance— different partners every few weeks, sex for recreation. Whatever felt good.

But look where it got Ashley. Not enlightened and freed from society's rules, but saddled with a virus that could kill her.

No, he couldn't stay with Lori another day. He didn't love her, and even after months of trying, he didn't see life through the same, strange glass she did. Now, after four days of thinking things through, his heart had indeed followed. He was certain about his decision. Thursday night he called Ashley and asked if she would put him up until he found someplace else to live.

"That way I can see Cole more," he told her. "And take a trip to New York. Whaddya think?"

Sweet relief filled her tone. "I'll be waiting for you."

On Friday, when Luke and Lori met back at the apartment for lunch, he knew what he had to do. He couldn't even *call* Reagan, let alone run off to New York City, while he was still living with Lori Callahan.

She opened the refrigerator and grabbed a loaf of bread and a plastic container of some pasty thing. Hummus, maybe, or fresh-ground almonds. Something earthy. Lori had given up eating meat now and joined Vegan Outreach, another campus club. The food she was buying this month was all soy, texturized vegetable protein, and seaweed. Things Luke had never considered eating.

"Animal fat clogs the channels of cooperative thought," she told him a few weeks back. "We need to free animals of that burden."

Luke had stared at her and wondered why he'd ever moved in with her in the first place. Eating healthy was a good thing—his parents raised him that way. In fact most of the time his mother ate a vegetarian diet. But more and more, Lori saw every aspect of life as some sort of enlightenment opportunity.

He watched her now as anxiety gnawed at him. How would she take the news? Not that he was sad about it. Not at all. He also wasn't hungry. A leftover cheeseburger sat in the fridge, but he would wait until later to microwave it. Better to avoid a lecture on freeing the cows.

She set her lunch plate on the table and sat down across from him. "Not hungry?"

"I'll eat later." He leaned his forearms on the oak finish. "Hey, Lori . . ." His mouth hung open, but the words got tangled up in his throat.

A small pile of the pasty stuff sat on the side of her plate, and she was dipping some strange-looking vegetable into it. She stilled for a moment and lifted her eyes to his. "Yeah?"

Luke hesitated, but only for a heartbeat. "I'm moving out this weekend."

She wrinkled her nose. "Moving out?"

"Yeah." He dug his fingers into the palms of his hand. "Taking my stuff."

"On a trip?" Her tone was a mix of confusion and mild amusement. "Just bring a suitcase."

Luke stroked his chin. "I'm not taking a trip, Lori." He exhaled hard through his teeth. "I'm leaving. Moving out."

Lori set her vegetable down and stared at him. "You mean for good?"

"Yes." He pursed his lips and tried to read her reaction. "It's over."

"Oh." She sat up a little straighter and lifted her chin. "What . . . did the almighty Baxter family get to you? Convince you I was a bad influence?"

Lori had spoken badly about his family before, and he'd always agreed. If she said they were controlling, he could think of a hundred times when he'd been controlled. When she called them ignorant, he found himself nodding along, remembering the times when they'd believed and prayed even when God—if there was a God—did nothing at all.

But now her remark wedged itself like a shard of glass between the newly softened crevasses of his heart. How dare she say that about them? The "almighty Baxter family"? He clenched his fists a bit tighter. "Look, Lori—" his voice sounded calmer than he felt—"this isn't about them; it's my call."

"No!" Her indifference turned to anger. "It *is* about them." She waved her hand in the air, as though she were searching for a hook to hang the blame on. "A freethinker would know that relationships have ups and downs."

"This isn't a down time, Lori."

"Of course it is." Luke heard something in her voice he hadn't heard before: panic. Lori was nothing if not confident and collected, completely sure of who she was and where she was going. "You're mad about my night with that guy, the abortion. The whole thing."

As soon as she said the words, Luke knew she was wrong. All he felt about those events was relief. A sense of deep gratitude that he hadn't been the father, and a strange sadness for the unborn baby. A sadness not in a moral sort of way but because the baby had never had a chance.

Sort of like Reagan's father.

What he didn't feel was jealousy or anger. Not even a bit. Luke cocked his head and willed her to make this simpler for both of them. "Those were your choices; I'm fine with that." He reached out for her hands, but she jerked them onto her lap. "It's just time."

The anger in her eyes changed to a deep, almost childlike sadness. "What about—" she gave a light shrug—"what about freethinking, different partners, the perfect relationship?"

With each passing hour, the idea of such an arrangement sounded more ludicrous. Sickening, almost. "What are you saying, Lori?" His tone softened, and his voice fell a notch. "That you'd rather have me stay and date other people?"

"Yes." Her answer was quick, and when her eyes met his he saw tears. Tears, where he'd never seen them before. "We're made for each other, Luke." Her eyes grew wider, as though she were searching for the perfect way to explain herself. "We'll have hard times, of course, but we stay together because freedom is such an . . . an intrinsic part of our love. We have no reason to leave each other."

Luke leaned back in his chair and studied her. So that was it? Love meant having no reason to leave each other? He inhaled slowly and narrowed his eyes. "We do, Lori. We have lots of reasons."

"What?" She crossed her arms, her face gripped with disbelief. "Name one."

"Well . . ." He hadn't wanted to hurt her, but it was too late to lie about the fact. "I'm in love with someone else."

Three seconds passed, and Lori sniffed. "Okay, so date her. That doesn't mean you have to move out."

"Lori . . ." He shook his head and made a sound that was more moan than laugh. "Who are you kidding? This whole open-relationship garbage is wrong, and you know it." He leaned forward and tried to speak straight to her heart, to a place he hoped hadn't really bought into the worldview she claimed so strongly. "Love—the kind of love that keeps two people together through the years—was never meant to be shared casually."

Her mouth hung open. "See?" She spread her fingers on the table between them. "This has Baxter morality written all over it."

Luke worked the muscles in his jaw. He still didn't believe in God, didn't want to speak to his father, and couldn't see himself in the Baxter family ever again. But here, now, he could say nothing to refute her. "Okay . . . maybe. And if it does, I'm okay with that. When I get married I don't want to wonder whether my wife is out late because she's sleeping with some other guy. I want it to be me and her. Just the two of us. Forever." He studied her face. "Whatever you call it, that's what I want."

At first Lori looked like she might agree, maybe even beg Luke to think of her as that woman, the one he might marry and love exclusively forever. But then her eyes grew hard. "Fine." She stood and cleared her plate. When she spoke again her back was to him. "Be gone by Saturday afternoon. I have plans that night."

Her words were meant to hurt him, convince him that she wasn't damaged by his decision. Luke gave a slow nod and said nothing. If she wanted to feel that way, he could let her. "I'll be gone by this evening." He lifted his hands and rubbed slow circles into his temples as he stood. He needed to find his suitcase and pack. If he was lucky, he'd be finished in less than an hour and on his way to Ashley's.

Luke watched Lori, her back still to him. "Hey." He cleared his throat. "I'm sorry."

She spun around, and her expression betrayed her sorrow. "It's Reagan, isn't it?"

Luke crossed the kitchen and stopped at the doorway to the living room. "Yeah." He slipped his hands in his pockets and met her gaze. "Yeah, it is."

"You're going to be just like them, Luke." She leaned against the counter. "Just like your father and your sisters, all the people you didn't want to be like."

"We're supposed to *think* about everything, right?" He anchored himself against the wall. "Think outside the box and go with our feelings, isn't that it?"

"Exactly."

"So . . ." He hesitated. "That's what I did. I thought outside this—" he drew an invisible square around himself—"this box I'm in, and you know what I found?"

She stared at him, waiting for him to continue.

"I don't have to agree with my family." He took a few steps backward. "But their kind of love isn't so bad. Not if I think outside the box."

The next hour went by quickly.

Luke found his suitcase. When it came down to it, he didn't have much at the apartment. The furnishings all belonged to Lori or her parents. He'd merely thrown some clothes together when he moved in with her.

With each passing minute, his plans grew clearer. Ashley used priceline.com, didn't she? She could help him book a ticket and maybe—maybe—he could leave tomorrow morning. Or at least by Sunday. Waiting around in Bloomington would do nothing to span the distance between him and Reagan. Him and his son.

Still, his doubts remained. The hardest part was trying to imagine what Reagan would say. She obviously knew about his decision to leave his family and move in with Lori. His mother had told her that much back when she called in April.

That was something else. Her phone call made sense now. Obviously she'd called to tell him about the baby. But when she found out how different he'd become, she begged his mother not to mention her phone call.

If that was how she felt then, why would she feel any different now? She could slam the door in his face, refuse to let him into her life or their baby's life. After all, he was coming fresh from living with another girl. He couldn't blame her if that's how she reacted. Nothing about him was the same as it had been before that awful September evening. He grabbed a stack of blue jeans and set them in the bottom of his suitcase. Not even the way he looked.

He was about to take a handful of shirts from the closet when the idea hit him. There wasn't much he could do about the way his beliefs had changed, his thoughts about humanity and his doubts about God. But at least she could recognize him.

His bathroom items were still in a cupboard near the sink, and he went to them. As he reached for the cupboard, he caught a glimpse of himself. Shoulder-length, thick hair, scruffy mustache and beard.

Why had he thought he needed to look like a sixties throwback to hold views that differed from those of his parents? He looked like a vagrant. Like one of those homeless guys who hung out near the freeway on-ramps on summer days in downtown Indianapolis. He scowled at himself. Then he stooped down, opened the cupboard, and found what he was looking for.

An old razor and his electric shaver.

He hadn't shaved since moving in with Lori, but now he held the razor to his jaw and made a smooth, methodical stroke. He attacked his face until most of the longer hair was gone. Next, he plugged in the shaver. Five minutes later, not a trace of the beard and mustache remained. Before he took his things to Ashley's house, he'd do something else—stop by the cheap hair salon near the university and get a cut.

As he cleaned up the chunks of beard that lay on the counter, he caught his look in the mirror once more and the image shocked him. For months he'd seen himself as someone entirely different than the boy he'd been the year before. Different address, different views, different feelings for his family. But now, as he studied his reflection, he saw the Luke he'd left behind. Not only along the clean-shaven lines of his chin and jaw and lips.

But in the soft light in his eyes as well.

CHAPTER TWENTY-NINE

KARI HAD BEEN LOOKING forward to this day for a month.

She and Ryan had been swamped with family get-togethers and dinner parties and wedding details almost constantly since they'd announced their engagement. Now summer was almost over, and they still hadn't taken a day for themselves. Because of that, they made this plan.

One week before the big Labor Day Baxter picnic, they'd slip away—just the two of them—and spend a day fishing at Lake Monroe. The way they'd done so often back when they were teenagers, back when they knew as surely as they knew the seasons that no matter what else happened in life, the two of them would be together.

They chose a Saturday because Ryan was using the weekdays to run his high school football players through weight training and drills. And though it would be busier than usual on the shore, Kari wasn't concerned. She and Ryan wouldn't be on the shore. They'd be on Ryan's boat, lost somewhere out in the lake in a place and time where the past would feel whisper close, and the future a heartbeat away.

The morning dawned bright and warm, and just after break-fast Ryan knocked on the door.

"Daddy's here, Jessie." Kari raised her eyebrows at her daughter as she headed toward the front of the house. They'd been teaching Jessie to call Ryan by the name she was bound to call him the rest of her life. Ryan already had the papers in order, and once they re-turned from their honeymoon he planned to start the adoption proceedings. By this time next year, it would be official.

He would be Jessie's father.

Jessie scampered to the door. When Kari opened it, her daughter held her hands up and gave Ryan a toothy grin. "Daddy!"

Ryan looked tanned in his tank top and shorts, much like the boy who had first captured her attention so many years ago. He leaned close and gave Kari a quick kiss, then he bent over and swept Jessie into his arms. "How're my favorite girls?"

Jessie brought her hands to his face and touched his cheeks, his nose. "Daddy love?"

"That's right, baby." He nuzzled his cheek against hers. "Daddy loves you."

Kari watched. Would she ever get used to seeing Ryan Taylor loving her daughter, claiming her as his own? How good God was to let their painful past come to this. She grabbed a bag with juice drinks and diapers and playthings for Jessie and nodded to-ward the door. "We're ready."

"Good." He shifted Jessie to his other side and pulled Kari into a quick hug. His eyes met hers, and his love for her was as real as his presence. "I can't wait to get out on the water."

They took Jessie to her parents' house, and Kari gave her mother instructions about naptime and Jessie's favorite foods.

"Where's John?" Ryan raised his eyebrows as he moved past Kari and her mother.

"Out back." Elizabeth took Jessie from Kari's arms. "Working on a few loose sections of the porch railing. He wants the yard perfect for the wedding."

Ryan headed outside and Kari turned to her mother. "Is Cole coming over?"

A curious look filled her eyes. "I'm not sure. Ashley hasn't been around much."

"But it's the weekend. Doesn't she usually bring him over so she can paint outside?"

"Usually." Her mother gave a slow shake of her head. "But something's eating her. Ever since she got back from New York."

"The gallery took her paintings again, right?" Kari ran the back of her finger absently over Jessie's cheek. The baby had her pacifier and was enjoying being held by her grandma.

"Definitely. They want more, as many more as Ashley can get them."

Kari shrugged. "Maybe she's stressed. I mean, she's still working at Sunset Hills, and now to have to produce like that. Her art's never been something she's had to churn out."

"That could be it." Jessie squirmed and stretched her arms toward the floor. "Okay, little one." Kari's mother set the little girl down and patted the top of her head. "You're as busy as your mother was at that age." Her eyes lifted to Kari's, and she hesitated. "To be honest, Ashley's worrying me. As much as she's struggled in the past, these should be the best days of her life. She and Landon are doing well; her art's being discovered. She has a great relationship with Cole and us and the rest of you." She hesitated. "Her distance lately doesn't figure."

"Maybe she's upset about Luke." Kari cocked her head. "I think the two of them still talk."

"If they do, she doesn't tell us about it."

Kari paused. "He still hasn't called?"

"No." Her mother's eyes grew misty and her smile faded. "Your father misses him so much."

A flash of anger stilled the busy places in Kari's heart. "Maybe I need to talk to him."

"He won't take your call. The last few times we've tried, he doesn't answer the phone."

"That's ridiculous." Kari put her hand on her mother's shoulder. "I'm sorry, Mom. I didn't know it had gotten that bad."

"He'll come around." She forced a smile and took a few steps toward Jessie. "I have to believe that. Your father believes it, too."

"If Ashley comes by this afternoon, tell her to hang out and wait for us to get back. Maybe she knows something." Kari heard the back door open and turned to see Ryan and her father coming inside.

"Today's the big lake day, huh?" Her father came to her and gave her a kiss on the cheek. "You two have a great time." He winked at Ryan. "Don't spend the day talking about mints and party favors."

An hour later they were in Ryan's boat, pushing off from the dock at the country club. It was just before ten o'clock, and they had the entire day together. Kari took the seat at the back of the boat and stared at the tree-lined shore as they idled out toward the lake's center.

"It's gorgeous." She made her voice loud enough for him to hear. "I should've brought my sunglasses."

He took his off and held them up. "Want these?"

"No, thanks. I have a visor in my bag."

"Okay." He slipped them back on and opened the throttle.

It felt like a lifetime ago that she and Ryan went out on this boat on a cool winter day, back when Tim was still alive, back when he was living with one of his college students. Now his killer was about to have his day in court, and the newspapers claimed it would be an easy win for the prosecution.

They were halfway across the lake when Ryan reduced their speed and gave his seat a partial turn so he could see her. "What're you thinking about?"

It was early, and this far out the lake was quiet. Kari leaned her head to one side and smiled at him. "Life . . . how strange it is. How sad about Tim and the college kid who killed him. The boy's trial starts in late October. At least that's what the district attorney told me last time he called."

Ryan directed his gaze toward the front of the boat once more. They still had a way to go before they reached their favorite spot, so he opened up the throttle and crossed the water to a quiet cove near the distant shore. It was a place they'd come to before, in Ryan's rowboat as kids, and then when Kari's world was so uncertain.

Ryan cut the engine and faced her fully. "I wish they didn't have to use you as a witness at the trial."

"It'll be brief." Kari stood and stretched. She made her way to the chair beside his and turned so their knees were touching. "They want me to make it clear that Tim didn't have an idea he was being stalked. That the guy was definitely lying in wait, that he surprised Tim."

"I know." Ryan leaned back and angled his face toward the sun. "I just wish you didn't have to do it. The past few years have been hard enough."

Kari rested her elbows on her knees and laced her fingers together. "The past several months haven't been that bad."

"True . . ." Ryan looked at her and a smile played on his lips. She couldn't see his eyes through his sunglasses, but she could still read his expression, the way he felt about her. "Who would've thought we'd have this day?"

"Even after Tim died, I figured you'd move on." She drew a slow breath and closed her eyes. The breeze off the lake played against her face and eased the hectic pace they'd fallen into lately. "As though somehow I'd already lost my chance to love you."

He took gentle hold of her legs and rubbed his thumbs along the sides of her knees. "Crazy Kari girl. You always assumed the worst."

They were quiet, and Kari's memories returned with a rush. She looked at Ryan and saw he was watching her. "I was thinking about my graduation party."

He smiled, but even now a tinge of sadness played on his expression. "We were both so stupid."

"We were." She settled back against the boat chair and

covered his hands with hers. She tilted her chin and looked at him again. "When was the first time you knew you loved me?"

Ryan let his head fall back some, and a teasing look played at the corners of his lips. "Really?"

"Yes." Kari pulled her legs up beside her and leaned on the arm of the chair. "Do you remember?"

He pursed his lips and gave a slow nod of his head. "Like it was yesterday."

"So tell me." An eagle soared overhead and disappeared into the trees that bordered the cove.

"Okay." He gazed at the spot in the sky where the eagle had been. "I had that truck, the one I drove back in high school."

"Mm-hmm." She loved this, sitting here suspended in time, walking through a million yesterdays.

"That one summer—you were fifteen, I think—I'd park it in my driveway, and you and I would climb in the back and watch the stars."

"We'd sit shoulder to shoulder for hours." A smile filled her heart at the memory.

"And one night, I'm not sure what we were talking about, but it was late, you had to get home. And before you left, I leaned over and kissed you. Remember?"

"Yes." Even now Kari savored the moment as clearly as if it had just happened. Her cheeks tingled, and she absently ran her fingertips over them. "I couldn't sleep a bit that night."

"I liked you before that . . . being with you, hanging out at the lake. Playing catch in the street." He wove his fingers between hers and gave her hands a slight squeeze. "But after that kiss, I knew you had me. I couldn't stop thinking about you. I never did."

"Really?" The sun was moving higher in the sky. Kari shaded her eyes so she could see his face better.

"Never, Kari girl." He leaned forward and worked his fingers along the side of her face, deep into her hair. "Okay." His voice fell a notch. "Your turn."

Kari put her free hand around his neck and kissed him. Not a long kiss, but one filled with passion all the same. The passion of remembering the places where their love first began. When she drew back she leveled her gaze at him. "You want to know when I first fell for you; is that it?"

"Yep. I bet it was the time the guys and I noticed you at the drinking fountain your first year at Bloomington High."

"Wrong." She moved close to him again and rubbed her nose against his. Then she sat back and took hold of the chair's arm-rests.

"When I brought you flowers on your sixteenth birthday?" Ryan raised an eyebrow.

"You really don't know?" A lighthearted laugh made its way up from Kari's soul. How could he not have seen it?

He leaned hard against the back of his chair. "No clue."

"It was the barbecue."

"The barbecue?"

"The one where we played football out front after we ate. The day my family moved in down the street from yours."

Ryan thought for a minute. "But we'd only just met that day."

"Exactly." Kari took his hands in hers again. "That's when I knew I'd love you forever, Ryan Taylor. The first time I ever saw you."

He stood and lifted her to her feet. Together they moved toward the side of the boat and he sat on it, drawing her close. "Come here, Kari girl."

She came to him easily, slipping her arms around his neck. "I thought we'd never be apart after that."

Ryan brought his lips together. "We wouldn't have been if I'd been thinking straight." He lowered his brow, and she could see his heart despite his sunglasses.

She pulled herself closer to him and let her forehead fall against his. "It doesn't matter. It's behind us."

He was quiet. "I feel weird sometimes, talking about how glad I am that things worked out for us."

"Because of Tim?"

"Yes." Ryan eased back and traced her cheekbone with his thumb. "As long as I live I'll be sorry about what happened to Tim. In a certain way, you know?"

"Of course." Kari relaxed her hold on him and leaned sideways against his leg. "Me, too."

"When Jessie's older, I want her to be able to talk about him." He paused, and the gentle lapping of water sounded against the boat. "Because *he* was her daddy first."

A lump formed in Kari's throat. She waited until it was gone before voicing the words that stirred in her heart. "That means so much to me, Ryan. After—" she swallowed hard—"after the way Tim treated me, I know you didn't think much of him. But he was my husband . . . Jessie's father. The fact that you respect that means more than you'll ever know."

"I didn't understand at first, but remember that day at the lake, the last time we were here?"

"Yes." She drew a slow breath.

"You didn't kiss me that day. Know why?"

"Of course." Another boat sped by a ways off. A moment passed before the sound faded.

"You told me love was a decision, and that you'd decided to love Tim the day you married him." Ryan ran his fingers lightly down the length of her bare arm. "Until that day I didn't really understand love, Kari. And when I moved away, when I took the job coaching the Giants, it was because I was making a decision to love you back. The way you wanted to be loved. In a way that respected what you had with Tim."

"I didn't see you again until Jessie was born." The memories— all of them—were still so fresh, living still in the hidden places of her heart and refusing to die.

"God showed me that I could love you better by letting you go."

She smiled, awed even now that they were here, together. "And when you returned?"

"I made a decision to return. Because God showed me that your time alone was over, and that my decision to love you—to *always* love you—was something I could do right here beside you. For the rest of our lives."

"I'll love you forever, Ryan." Her emotions were raw, and she wasn't sure why. Maybe because of all the yesterdays they'd walked through that morning.

"I can't wait till we're married." A cloud passed over the sun, and without the glare, Ryan took his sunglasses off and tossed them on the captain's chair. His eyes met hers, and the depth there equaled what she was feeling.

"Me, neither."

"Because then I can watch you fall asleep and wake up beside you every morning." His fingers framed her face once more. "The way I've always wanted to."

Their lips met. When he pulled away, he locked eyes with hers and spoke to a place deep within her soul. "Have you written it already? What you're going to say?"

"Weeks ago." Kari didn't blink. The moment was too sacred for anything to interrupt it.

"Me, too." He searched her face and swallowed. "Whatever else is going on that day—the bridesmaids and flowers and music and dinner. All the distractions . . . just know that I won't be thinking of anything but you and how much I love you, Kari girl. How much I'll love you for the rest of my life."

A fish jumped from the water a few feet from the boat and flopped back beneath the surface. They both looked at it and Kari laughed. "We're not getting much fishing done."

"Know what?"

"What?"

Ryan eased her close once more and kissed her again. This time it lasted long, and Kari was barely aware of anything but his touch, his lips against hers. When he released her, his voice was barely a whisper. "I didn't even bring the poles."

CHAPTER THIRTY

LUKE'S PLANE WAS COMING in just after six that night, and Reagan still couldn't believe it.

He called her the night before from Ashley's house. At first she hadn't known what to say. The conversation started with his begging her not to hang up. "I need to see you, Reagan. I know about Tommy."

She hadn't known whether to drop the phone or cling to it. When she finally found her voice, it hadn't sounded even remotely familiar. "Luke?"

"Reagan . . . I can't believe it's you."

After all the months of convincing herself she'd made the right decision—knowing that she couldn't tell him about the baby, and finding out that he was living with someone else—hearing his voice set the record straight once and for all.

Her feelings for him were as strong now as they'd ever been. No matter how hard she'd tried to distance herself from him, her heart had not forgotten.

Luke went on to tell her very little, really. He'd left the girl he'd been living with and moved in with Ashley. He'd booked himself a flight and would be in New York Saturday night.

Reagan wasn't even a little upset that Ashley had told Luke. She'd been too stunned to do anything but give him directions and tell him simply the way she was feeling. "I . . . I can't wait to see you."

She did the calculations and figured that by the time he landed and got his luggage, then found a cab and made his way to their Upper East Side apartment, it would be eight o'clock.

It was seven fifty-five now.

Tommy had already eaten, and she'd dressed him in a light blue knit outfit. He was cradled in her arms now as she sat in the chair closest to the front door. Her mother was working in the kitchen; every now and then she'd peek in and ask Reagan a question.

Reagan stared at her watch and tried to still her racing heart. Two more minutes ticked past, and her mother entered the room again. She was drying her hands with a dish towel.

"You okay?" She crossed the room and came to stand near Reagan and Tommy.

"You want the truth?" Reagan shifted Tommy to her other arm and leaned forward.

"You're scared?"

"To death." She let her eyes fall to her sleeping baby. "He wants to see his son. I got that much." Her gaze lifted to her mother's. "But what about me, and what about the way he's walked out on his family and his faith—all of it? We don't even believe the same way anymore. So what happens after we say hello?"

They heard footsteps outside the apartment. A pause and then a hesitant knock at the door. "Well—" her mother took a few steps backward—"you're about to find out."

Panic seized Reagan's heart, and her knees wobbled as she stood. "Pray for me, Mom . . . please."

Her mother nodded and turned back toward the kitchen. They'd talked about this moment a dozen times since last night, and agreed that it should be hers and Luke's and Tommy's alone. When she was gone, Reagan went to the front door and took hold of the handle.

Okay, God, be with us. We're going to need a miracle.

❧

By the time Luke reached Reagan's door, he could barely breathe, let alone think straight. Just days earlier he'd been living with Lori Callahan. Now he'd moved his things into Ashley's place and here he was—in New York City—about to see Reagan for the first time in almost a year.

Adrenaline coursed through him like a drug.

He'd told himself much on the plane ride to the East Coast. First, that he wanted to apologize to Reagan for not being more persistent. He had wanted to be sensitive to her grieving period, but when she hadn't taken his calls week after week, he should've come to her. And he hadn't.

He wanted her to explain why she'd refused his calls. He'd searched his heart for hours since learning about Thomas Luke, and the answers never quite made sense. Okay, so she was upset by her father's death. And yes, the pregnancy had to have been a shock. Especially since she'd made a very clear-cut commitment to wait until she was married before having sex.

The disappointments and heartaches had stockpiled, one on top of the other. But still . . . couldn't she have taken his call? Just once?

And then, when she'd known the truth about him, how he'd changed and moved in with another girl, couldn't she have cared enough to call? Even as a friend?

So this meeting had a lot of issues to cover.

He also wanted to apologize for moving in with Lori. No, he didn't owe Reagan any explanation. After all, she'd been gone for months by the time he'd moved in. But still, it was wrong. He never loved Lori. When he looked back at the situation now, he admitted he'd never even liked her all that much. So in honor of all he'd shared with Reagan, he should've waited. And for that he was sorry.

But there was one thing he wouldn't apologize for: the way he believed now.

His belief system was something he owned, something that belonged to him, regardless of how shocking it might seem to her. Yes, he wanted to see her, and yes, he wanted to be a father to Tommy. But even if they found their way back to the place where they loved each other again, nothing could convince him God was real. The freethinkers might've had some wacky ideas, but they'd at least set him straight on that much.

God—some Creator taking care of his creation, investing in their daily happenings, looking out for their future—was a nice, fuzzy idea. But it was all folklore and fantasy. His freethinking meetings had taught him at least that.

Back on September 11, Luke had begged God to let Reagan's father live . . . to let things work out okay for her and him, for the two of them together. But his prayers—prayers uttered in a moment of direst need—had fallen on deaf ears.

If God had been real, he would've heard the prayers of Luke and a million other people that day. He would've kept the Twin Towers from falling. Even if he'd had to hold them up with his almighty hands.

Instead things had played out randomly, the way all of life— Luke saw now, in hindsight—always played out. That fact made it impossible for him to have a relationship with his father— which was something else Reagan couldn't change his mind about. His father thought him lost and confused, brainwashed. The man didn't have a bit of respect for the way Luke believed.

And so he and his father would find their own way in the world, and Reagan couldn't do a thing about that. If Luke and she found common ground, he would be straight with her. He planned to never set foot in a church again, never pray or read a Bible. And never contact his dad.

If Reagan wanted to do those things, fine. She was entitled to her way of thinking. Maybe in time she'd even come to see things his way. That God couldn't possibly exist.

Anyway, those were things they'd have to talk about, and none of them made Luke feel even a little bit at ease. But despite all the difficult things that lay ahead for him and Reagan, he felt something else. Pure, indefinable joy. Because no matter how he'd changed, one thing had remained firmly the same.

He loved Reagan Decker.

He wiped his palms on his jeans shorts, cleared his throat, and knocked. On the other side of the door he heard muffled voices, and then silence. The faint sound of footsteps drew closer, and then the door opened.

Time stood still as he took in the sight of Reagan. Everything about her was exactly the same—her long, blonde hair was pinned in a messy pile at the top of her head, and her body was as fit and leggy as ever. But when he caught her expression he saw something different.

Her eyes were older. Years older.

His gaze dropped, and he could feel his breath catch. Cradled in a blanket in her arms was a baby he couldn't quite see. He took a step forward, wiping his palms against his shorts. "Reagan . . ."

She lowered the baby and adjusted the blanket. The infant stirred and opened his eyes just as Luke took another step closer and leaned down.

Then, in a moment like none other in his life, Luke looked into his son's face. Seconds passed. Something both deep within him, and yet close to the surface, began to melt. Sudden, unexpected tears filled his eyes and spilled onto his cheeks, and a handful of truths stood in a row, suddenly clear and eager to be examined.

First, Ashley was right—the baby looked just like him. His skin was honey and cream, and his blond eyelashes went on forever. As Luke's did in pictures he'd seen of himself at that age.

Luke wiped the back of his hand across his own cheek; then, with a single delicate brush of his finger, he touched his baby's cheek.

That's when the second truth made itself known: He had a son. He actually had a son! An unbelievable explosion of awareness went off in his heart and continued on into his soul. Luke Baxter had a son! The eyes blinking back at him belonged to a child who would forever be a part of him and a part of Reagan. A part of his parents and her parents. A child who bore his name and always would.

Another truth stepped forward. No matter what happened between Reagan and him, he could never walk away from the baby in her arms. He was the boy's father, and though he hadn't been sure what that meant until now—watching the baby, connecting with him, feeling his heart and the baby's become one—he was convinced. He would walk around the world to spend an hour with this child.

And that brought about another obvious fact: This feeling—this amazing connection—had to be the way Luke's father felt about him when he'd been born. For an instant Luke closed his eyes and tried to imagine the baby before him grown-up, defiant and angry, setting out to make his way in life. No matter what words the child in Reagan's arms would ever say to him, Luke could never forget the way he felt right now. The deep, never-say-die kind of love that filled him . . . that his father must've felt every time they'd fought or parted in anger over the past year.

Luke's heart did an about-face. No matter what their differences, he needed to make things right with his father. Maybe not today or tomorrow, but sometime soon. He squeezed his eyes shut. *Dad, I'm sorry. I've been an idiot, Dad, I didn't know.*

His thoughts fought for position. Luke blinked his eyes open and remembered to breathe. His looked at Reagan. "He's . . . he's beautiful."

"Thanks." It was her first word since she'd opened the door. "Ashley says he looks like you."

"He has your nose." Luke lifted his eyes and let himself get lost in Reagan's gaze. The connection there was almost strong enough to bring him to his knees.

Reagan smiled down at the baby. "Look at him."

Luke did, and he saw what Reagan was looking at. Thomas Luke was cooing in his direction, waving his tiny fingers in the air above his face and grinning, almost as though he knew this was his father standing there, staring at him with such awe.

"Baby . . . I'm here." Luke's voice was choked. He held out his hand and let the tips of his fingers brush against his son's.

And that's when one last truth stepped up and announced itself—a truth Luke couldn't have denied if his life depended on it. Because, no matter what he'd been thinking in the seconds before knocking on Reagan's door, looking into the face of his son and feeling the very fiber of his being connect with a child that was his own made something utterly clear.

What this newest truth meant for his future, the future of his son and the girl he still loved, Luke wasn't sure. Most of his doubts were still firmly in place, but as he followed Reagan into her apartment, as he hugged her and cried with her and told her he was sorry a hundred times over, he was as certain of this final truth as he was of anything in all his life.

God had to be real.

Thomas Luke was living proof.

CHAPTER THIRTY-ONE

JOHN BAXTER'S CHEST ACHED, and he blamed it on being more tired than usual.

Never mind that they'd finished moving the blankets and picnic baskets and Frisbees and place settings from the car and set them up on the beach. Forget the fact that Elizabeth was sitting beside him, and that playing on the shore a few dozen yards away were the people he loved most in the world. They'd brought thirteen people with them to the Baxters' annual Labor Day picnic this year.

But it was the fourteenth that John missed.

And with Sam and Erin leaving in the morning, John was pretty sure he'd never again spend a Labor Day on the shores of Lake Monroe with all his children present.

Once Erin and Sam spent their first year in Austin, they planned to vacation early next summer. With Erin teaching, by the time Labor Day rolled around again, the two of them would have to be back home getting ready for the following school year.

John stretched out in his beach chair and glanced at Elizabeth. "Sorry."

She raised an eyebrow. "For what?"

"For not talking much."

"You said you were tired." She reached over and covered his hand with hers.

A long breath eased from between his lips, one that seemed to come from the bottom of his feet. "That's not all."

The whisper of a gentle wind off the lake played in the tree branches behind them. Elizabeth made a slight turn in her chair and met his eyes. "I know."

He hesitated for a moment. "What do you mean?"

"I mean you're sitting here thinking about Luke, wondering where he is and how come he isn't here. Knowing that wherever he is, he knows it's Labor Day . . . knows he's missing our picnic, but that he's chosen to stay away all the same." Her voice was calm, steady. Soothing, the way it always was. "And you're thinking about Erin and Sam leaving tomorrow."

He stared at her for a long while. How many times had he sensed this bond between them, known for certain that she truly was part of him and he a part of her? Elizabeth could read his thoughts, his heart, as easily as he could read hers. And no matter how far apart their daily dealings took them, they always returned to this . . . this not knowing where she stopped and he began. This quiet place where oneness wasn't something they tried to find but rather simply was.

A slow chuckle sounded in his throat.

"I'm right." It wasn't a question. She turned and looked at Cole, Maddie, and Hayley chasing each other in the gentle surf.

"Perfectly." The laughter faded and he studied his wife's profile. "Where do you think he is?"

"I'm not sure." Unshed tears made her eyes glisten in the waning afternoon sunlight. "With Lori, I guess."

They were quiet for a moment. Elizabeth was right, of course. Luke had to be with Lori, maybe at some club event convincing himself that his family was no longer worthy of his attention.

After a long while John let his eyes lift toward the sky.

"God—" he hesitated, sensing the very real presence of the king of the universe—"wherever our boy is, please bring him back to us." His voice cracked when the weariness within him was more than he could bear. "We miss him so much."

❧

Luke's biggest revelation of the week took place in a rental car twenty minutes out of Bloomington.

Until then, he could hardly believe the changes that had happened in his heart this past week. He and Reagan had talked for hours that first night, while he held Tommy and tried to convince himself he was really in New York City holding his son and talking with the only girl he'd ever loved.

They'd agreed on almost everything. That they'd been foolish to let so much time pass, that she was sorry for keeping her pregnancy from him, and that no matter what happened next, they never wanted to be apart again. They'd even talked about getting married.

The thing that remained a struggle for Luke was the idea that God had allowed the tragedy of September 11. He and Reagan went round and round on that, and always she said it was simply her father's time to go. Same with the other people who died. All people have a last day on earth, and that was it for the people in the Twin Towers.

But Luke was still troubled.

Why bother to pray if God was going to do his own thing anyway?

They'd agreed on something else. That Luke needed to make things right with his father, needed to come clean with him about what had happened between Reagan and him in the hours prior to the attacks on America. And he needed to tell his parents about the baby.

"Are you afraid?" Reagan asked him two nights ago. "To see them . . . after so much time?"

"A little." They had been sitting side by side, with Tommy lying across both their laps. "I've been such a jerk." He'd gazed at
her eyes and wondered how he'd lived without her for so long.
"What if things are never the same again?"

"They will be, Luke." She leaned close and kissed him on the
cheek. "I know your dad, remember? Things will be fine. But
you need to go to him."

That conversation moved Reagan and him to get on her family's computer and book another flight—this one round-trip to
Indianapolis.

He'd landed an hour ago, rented a car, and was now headed
for Lake Monroe. Suddenly traffic slowed and narrowed to one
lane. Ahead he could see two fire trucks and at least two ambulances. The flash of lights told him that something bad had happened. Maybe even something deadly.

One car at a time made its way past the area. As Luke pulled
up close enough to see the accident, he caught sight of the car. It
was an SUV of some kind, lying on its side, crushed almost beyond recognition. Two other vehicles were pulled off to the side,
both with serious dents, but less damage. To the side of the SUV,
three people huddled together, all of them weeping. At that moment one of the ambulances pulled away, sirens blaring.

That's when something else caught Luke's attention, and he
glanced toward the other waiting ambulance. Two paramedics
carried a stretcher toward it, but they weren't in a hurry. Luke
saw it more clearly then. His eyes grew wide; his heartbeat
quickened. On top of the stretcher was a body.

A covered body.

Luke swallowed hard and filed past in the stream of traffic,
but when he was a mile up the road he pulled off at a gas station,
parked his car, turned off his engine, and dropped his head
against the steering wheel. When he closed his eyes he could see
it: the totaled car, the paramedics with the body suspended between them.

Just minutes ago the person on the stretcher was driving

down the same road Luke had been on. Heading to an afternoon barbecue or telling stories to the family as he drove down the highway. Maybe he'd been to the lake with friends or on a business trip. Or maybe he'd merely been out to the store for a bag of groceries or a can of paint. Whatever his reason, he couldn't possibly have known that in the blink of an eye he'd be lying on a stretcher, dead.

The image played again and again in Luke's mind, and it occurred to him that he'd seen it somewhere before. Fire engines . . . ambulances . . . paramedics. Covered bodies on stretchers.

Then he remembered where.

On TV footage after September 11. Body after body after body.

Slowly, with other cars coming and going past him, the realization grew in Luke's mind. Not a news flash exactly, but something that hadn't hit him quite this way before. Ever since the collapse of the Twin Towers, he'd been blaming God for not coming through.

But for the person in the crushed SUV, today was even more tragic than September 11. That person's day of reckoning, of tragedy and terror, happened on a sun-soaked highway late in the afternoon of a beautiful Labor Day. The person's last day on earth.

Tragedies happened every day: murders . . . rapes . . . car accidents. As Reagan said, everyone had a last day, a time when their hours would be over and they'd be called to judgment. Luke gripped the steering wheel and lifted his head enough to look out over the dashboard.

Suddenly Luke's realization hit full force: God hadn't hijacked the planes that day. He hadn't flown them into the World Trade Center or encouraged the terrorists to do so. What God *had* done, Luke realized, was give each person free will. Not so much freethinking, but the freedom to make choices—either good or bad, right or wrong.

He closed his eyes again and remembered something his mother had told him in the weeks after he left home. The Hound of Heaven wasn't about to let him go easily. Luke blinked, and in a flash the events of the past few days screamed at him. Had his mother been right? Was God the one who'd been chasing him all those times when he couldn't find peace?

God, are you there? Are you . . . are you mad at me?

A car squealed out of the gas-station parking lot, but when the sound faded, Luke felt something stir in his soul. A voice even quieter than a whisper.

Son, I have loved you with an everlasting love. Return to me. Return to your first love.

Once, a lifetime ago, thoughts like those would have echoed loudly in Luke's heart, making him certain God was there beside him, talking to him. But now . . . was it his imagination? Wishful thinking, maybe, or a beacon of contrived light to help him find his way through the dark?

A dampness gathered at the corners of Luke's eyes. How could he return to God when he'd made such a public mockery of the faith he'd been raised with? His family, his father had honored his choice to set out on his own, to explore the options a fallen world offered. They'd honored him and loved him even while he made plans to cut them out of his life completely.

He hung his head. *God, I'm pathetic. The worst son ever. I'm not even sure I remember how to love.*

Return to me, my son.

Luke blinked his eyes open and looked around. The voice had stirred in the private places of his heart, the places that hadn't forgotten—no matter how much his mind had willed him to forget—what it was to love God.

Not only did God exist, but he hadn't given up on Luke Baxter. Even after every horrible thing Luke had done to leave God behind.

A Bible story came to mind—something from a sermon he'd heard on the radio long before his world turned upside down. Jesus was talking to his friends after many of his followers had turned away. Tension must've filled the air as Jesus looked at those who remained and asked simply, "Will you go, too?"

Peter's answer rang through Luke now—even after such a long time away from the Bible: "Where would we go? You alone have the words of eternal life."

Hadn't that same dialogue played out across America this past year? Wasn't Christ's question to his followers the same one indirectly posed to all of America on September 11? With so many across the United States already turning away from God, Jesus might as well have peered at his followers through the veil of smoke over New York City and said, "Will you go, too?"

Some—Kari and Ryan, Peter and Brooke, even Ashley—answered the way Peter had thousands of years earlier. "If ever I needed God it was after September 11," Brooke told him once. "Faith helps everything make sense."

But others . . .

Luke's chest ached and he sat up. He relaxed his hold on the wheel and stared at his hands. How could he have run from God? What was he thinking? That somehow he'd find something more stable, more comforting? That peace and perfection and answers to the evil on earth might exist in something other than faith in God? Why hadn't he had the rock-solid belief of Kari or Ryan or his father?

Or Peter . . .

Luke's eyes widened. Peter. Simon Peter—the one who so firmly looked Jesus in the eyes and declared, "Where else would we go?" was the very same man who would deny Christ hours before his death.

Not once, but three times.

Peter—the one who swore that all the others might scatter, but he never would—was the one whose voice Jesus heard when he came into the courtyard after being beaten . . . the voice denying he'd ever known Jesus.

Understanding wrapped itself around Luke like a blanket. Peter knew he could turn nowhere but toward Jesus, yet barely a season later he blatantly denied Christ in front of a crowd of people. The very same way Luke had done this past year. Time and time and time again.

Lord, forgive me. What have I done?

A hundred memories screamed at him, times when he'd counted himself among those most doubting of God, those outright against God. He winced as he remembered arguing against the Creator for his class project, the one he'd worked on with Lori. There he'd been, proclaiming the benefits of humanism and encouraging others to think for themselves, not to believe the faith of their families.

So strong was the stance he'd taken against God that he'd taught himself to dislike everything about his past, his faith, even his family.

An image of the last time he saw his father flashed in his mind. He could hear himself, almost as clearly as he must've sounded that day in Lori's apartment, yelling at his father, ordering him to leave, demanding that he mind his own business and stay away.

Just as clearly he could still hear his father's reply: *"I've always loved you, and nothing . . . nothing you do could make me stop loving you. When you're ready to come back, I'll be waiting."*

"Dad . . ." He whispered the word, but it banged around the inside of his car like a scream for help. "Dad, I didn't mean it."

Luke felt a stabbing in his heart, a pain as raw and gripping as if God himself were squeezing it, wringing out the anger and unbelief and bitterness. The pain was worse than anything Luke could remember, but it was something else, too.

It was freeing.

He closed his eyes. *God, I've done everything wrong, broken every promise I ever made to you . . . to my family. But I understand now. I do. There's nowhere else I want to turn. You hold my future, God. Please forgive me.*

Almost immediately the tightness in his heart eased, and he felt a dawning on the horizon of his soul. It was a feeling he recognized, one he hadn't known for a year but that he'd never forgotten.

The feeling of forgiveness.

Forgiveness and newness, hope and a second chance. They suddenly loomed as big as all his tomorrows strung together.

He savored the feeling. Then finally he started the car engine. The best part about the story of Peter was that for all his early boasts of strength and for all his dismal denials, God never gave up on the man.

And now Luke was sure that even after the debacle of the past year, God had not given up on him either.

Luke pulled out onto the highway and thought about the Baxter annual Labor Day picnic taking place at the lake. None of them knew he was coming, and if they were angry at him, it would be his own fault. But maybe—just maybe—they cared enough to give him another chance. He'd know soon enough.

Lake Monroe was ten miles down the road.

※

Life had already ended, but still Ashley was forced to go through the motions.

Walking along the beach at Lake Monroe. Playing Frisbee with Cole. Building a fort of twigs and rocks and leaves with Maddie and Hayley. Offering to help her father with the barbecue. All of it a series of disjoined actions, completely robotic. As though someone had scraped out her heart and soul and mind, and replaced them with enough mechanics to go through the motions of life, but nothing more.

Ashley sat on the shore and watched Kari and Ryan, hand in hand, standing with their feet in the water. They would be married in just three weeks, and then Kari's storybook life could continue as though it had never been interrupted.

What about me, God? Who will be there for me?

A recent memory of Irvel played in her mind. The woman had been sitting on the edge of her bed smiling, nodding her head.

"What is it, Irvel?" Ashley stepped into the room. Irvel's blood pressure was still unstable much of the time, and Ashley had wondered if the woman was having a seizure.

But Irvel had turned to her and grinned. Then she waved like a little girl looking at her mother from her place at the kinder-garten table. "Hi. Guess what?"

"What?" Ashley had come closer and put her hand on Irvel's shoulder.

"Hank's here with me." She raised a shaky hand and motioned at the pictures adorning her wall. Pictures of Hank. "He loves me so much." She gave a happy shake of her head. "Isn't that won-derful?"

Ashley thought about Landon and swallowed an ocean of sor-row. "Yes, Irvel. Hank is a wonderful man."

Ashley had assumed she and Landon would find their way into a relationship like the one Irvel had shared with Hank. But now . . . now Ashley's future seemed as ominous and empty as a city parking lot at nightfall.

In the midst of the terror she felt about her future were a handful of lies that made her feel disconnected, even more like some kind of machine with a key in her back. When she first re-turned home from Paris, she'd been adept at keeping secrets. It had been her way of surviving. But not anymore, and the things she wasn't saying were making every moment an effort.

She'd known about her positive blood test for weeks, and still only Landon and Luke knew the truth. Her parents, Kari, Cole—even her doctor—didn't know yet. She simply hadn't found the strength to tell them. Doing so would make her situa-tion so much more real. Her announcement would start a clock ticking, the one that would count down the days until she either responded to treatment or fell victim to the virus.

And the secrets welling within her were hardly relegated to her blood test only. No one else knew that she'd contacted the

Wellingtons in New York City and told them she wouldn't be bringing them any more art. She explained only that she needed to be closer to home, more focused on her private life. A local gallery not far from the university would handle any paintings she might sell.

Also, she was keeping quiet about Luke. No one knew that he'd moved in with her and Cole—though she suspected Cole would say something any day. The others didn't know anything of Luke's son or the fact that he was in New York City with Reagan.

Everything about her life was a lie, and all of it so monstrous she wasn't sure how to begin to tell the truth. But however it happened, the truth had to come out. She couldn't live like this much longer.

"Mommy, play catch with me!" Cole came tearing down the sloping grassy shore, a softball in his hands. "Let's do the dropsy contest. We have to beat our record."

Ashley lifted herself from the shore and dusted off the back of her shorts. *Dropsy* meant they'd count the number of times they caught the ball without either of them dropping it. Their record was twenty-two.

"Okay." She was dying inside, but she grinned anyway. "We haven't broken it all summer, but maybe—"

Cole tossed the ball to her. "One."

She caught it and flipped it back to him. "Two."

They kept up the pattern, and Ashley let Cole count by himself. She was too busy thinking about the biggest lie, the thing that most affected her heart: the idea that she and Landon were still together. Only she knew the truth.

They were finished. Forever.

Landon had honored her wishes. He hadn't called her or made any contact since she left Manhattan. Obviously, as difficult as it had been for him, he'd thought over her situation and agreed that breaking up was the most sensible thing to do. He was a thousand miles away, so a friendship was out of the question.

Besides, they could hardly pretend to be friends after tasting love, after knowing the strength of their feelings.

"Eighteen." Cole's voice rose a notch as he caught the ball and tossed it back to her. "Nineteen."

Ashley pressed her toes into the cool grass and pictured Landon, the way he'd looked the last time she saw him, telling her he loved her from the hallway elevator near her hotel room. He needed to move on. She could offer him none of the stability and future he deserved.

The irony was unbelievable. All her life she'd known she was wrong for Landon. She'd fought his attempts at a relationship and convinced herself that she didn't feel anything but friendship for him. Then—just when she finally realized how wrong she'd been, just when she'd recognized how very much she longed for him and loved him—the blood test came. And with it, a full-circle trip right back to the way she'd felt in the beginning.

She was all wrong for Landon Blake.

"Twenty-two!" Cole caught the ball and jumped up and down with it. "Here we go, Mommy. It's the dropsy record!"

Maddie and Hayley stopped collecting pretty rocks and came over to watch them. They stood a few feet from Cole, their eyes wide, ready to celebrate if Cole gave the signal.

He tossed the ball to her, and though it was a little to the side, Ashley lunged for it and caught it with one hand. "Twenty-three!" She held the ball high and turned to Cole. He was dancing in a circle, moving his fists back and forth in the air and shouting, "We *did* it! We broke the dropsy record!"

Brooke's two girls formed a circle with Cole, and the three of them held hands and did a dance that got faster and faster until they collapsed in a pile on the grass, giggling and tickling and talking all at the same time.

Ashley watched them, but all she could think was *God, what'll happen to Cole if I don't make it?*

Something near the parking lot caught Ashley's attention, and she turned. A man was walking their way, and at first she figured she had to be wrong. Her heartbeat picked up and her mouth hung open. It couldn't be—he never would have come here, not when he was supposed to be in New York.

But as he came closer she was convinced beyond any doubt.

Her brother, Luke, was making his way down the grassy hill toward the place where her parents were setting up dinner.

CHAPTER THIRTY-TWO

JOHN WAS REACHING into the cooler, pulling out the bags of preformed meat patties, when he noticed Ashley, Kari, and Ryan staring at something behind him. Before he had time to turn around, Elizabeth touched his elbow and nodded toward the parking lot.

"Did we leave something in the—"

He never finished his sentence.

Because when he looked over his shoulder to the place where his family was focused, what he saw made his heart take wing. There, walking toward him with slow, deliberate steps was Luke. And for the first time in a year, he wasn't scowling or smirking or rolling his eyes.

He was smiling.

Luke . . . his son—his only son—was walking toward him, faster now than before, his entire face lit up.

Beside John, Elizabeth uttered a quiet gasp and took hold of his arm. "John . . ."

"It's okay." He looked at his wife and patted her hand. "Let me."

His knees shook and his feet moved like lead, but he took a step toward Luke, and then another and another until just a few yards separated them. It was then that John could see something else, something besides the once-familiar smile.

His son was crying.

"Dad . . ." Luke held out his hands and stumbled the last few steps as he fell into John's arms—and into an embrace that held fast for what felt like a moment and a lifetime all at once. Luke was a bit taller than John, but he buried his face in John's shoulder, clinging to him the way he'd done when he was a boy.

John wanted to say something, but words could never have captured the tidal wave of emotion crashing around his heart. Instead he held on, rocking Luke, letting him sob as he spoke a string of apologies into John's T-shirt.

"I'm sorry, Dad. I didn't know what I was doing. . . . I'm so sorry."

"It's okay." John whispered the words, because a whisper was all that would squeeze past the lump in his throat. "You're home now, Luke. It's okay." He drew back and squinted. The boy must've been crying for a while before getting to the beach, because his eyes were swollen and bloodshot.

"I can't believe I'm here. I thought . . . I was afraid you wouldn't want me anymore."

John tilted his head and placed his hand along the side of Luke's face. "You don't know how I've prayed for this moment, Son."

"Yes." Luke gulped back another sob and gave a strong nod of his head. "Yes, I do know. Because I've prayed about it too."

John blinked, but before he could say anything, he heard the shuffling of feet behind him—many feet. In a slow rush of bodies and arms and cries of "Welcome home, Luke," and "Thank God you're okay," and "We missed you," each of the Baxters—even the youngest grandchildren—formed a circle around John and Luke. They pressed in close for a hug, an embrace that erased time and told all of them that no matter how far they strayed, they would always be welcomed home.

Tears came for most of them, until Cole popped his head up near the center of the circle. "Hey—" he looked at the faces around him—"what about Papa's hamburgers?"

Laughter softened the moment, and they drew back enough to see Luke, to study him and let him see how much he'd been missed. John had a dozen questions, but they would come later. He was about to wave Luke toward the barbecue pit when Luke held up his hand.

"I've made a lot of bad choices this year, and I'm sorry." He sniffed hard and stood a bit straighter than before. "I owe each of you an explanation." He looked at the ground, and shame shadowed his features. When he lifted his face, a seriousness flashed in his eyes. "But first, I have something to tell you."

John wiped his cheeks and waited. Whatever Luke wanted to say, it was important. And apparently it couldn't wait another minute. John watched Luke and Ashley exchange a look, and he had a strong feeling that whatever Luke was about to say, she already knew.

Luke cleared his throat and let his eyes travel to each of his siblings—Brooke and Peter, Kari and Ryan, Erin and Sam, Ashley—and finally to Elizabeth and John. "Reagan and I have . . . we have a son."

The words were out, but their reality was floating somewhere in the breeze above them. Elizabeth looped her arm through John's and leaned on him, but John wondered if he could hold her up. What was Luke talking about? Reagan was in New York. Luke hadn't seen her since September 11.

A son?

The idea was as impossible as Luke's presence among them that day.

The three young Baxter cousins had scampered off a few feet down the hill, tired of the adult conversation. But the others maintained their places. Ashley shifted her gaze to the ground, while the others' mouths hung open. None of them seemed to know what to say.

Elizabeth recovered first. "Luke . . . whatever do you mean, honey?"

Luke made small circles in the dirt with the toe of his tennis shoe. When he met their eyes again, he was more composed, and something close to hope cast a light over his expression. "Before Reagan left for New York, the two of us—" he dropped his gaze again before looking up at John—"the two of us let things go too far." His look shifted to Elizabeth. "I didn't know about the baby until two weeks ago, when Ashley told me."

John looked at his daughter and saw relief mix with a hint of guilt. So she *had* known. Thank heaven Luke had felt comfortable talking to one of them. He turned back to Luke and waited.

"When I found out I had a son, I broke things off with Lori and moved in with Ashley. But then I went to New York." He hesitated and let his gaze go around the circle again. "I've been there for the past week."

"So you really have a son?" The question came from Kari, who still had a sleeping Jessie cradled against her shoulder.

"I do." For the first time since his initial walk down the hillside, Luke grinned. "His name is Thomas Luke and—" he looked at Elizabeth—"he looks just like me, Mom."

Elizabeth covered her mouth, and this time she closed the distance between herself and Luke with a long hug. When she pulled back, tears sparkled on her cheeks, and she made a sound that was mostly laugh. "When do we get to meet him?"

"I'm not sure." Luke moved a step closer so they could all hear him. "He's with Reagan in New York still. It's a long story, and, well, I'll tell you all about it later. But I knew Sam and Erin were leaving tomorrow and I had to be here." His eyes met John's and held. "One last time, so we could all be together."

The evening passed too quickly, but through every minute Luke knew he'd found his way home. The people he'd grown up loving the most had saved a place for him at the table, believing he'd come back one day. And now he had.

It was obvious from his family's reaction that Ashley hadn't said anything to them—not about his leaving Lori or moving in with her and Cole, or having a baby in New York City. And obviously not about her blood test. Before the end of the night, he pulled her aside.

"Have you seen your doctor?" They were packing up after the picnic.

Ashley gave a nervous glance at the others up the hill. "Not yet."

"You haven't told Dad?" Luke held a stack of folded beach chairs. "Come on, Ash."

"I will." Her tone was low, agitated. "Give me time, Luke."

"Dad can help you." He stopped and stared up the beach to the place where Cole was helping Maddie carry a pail full of rocks toward the picnic table. His eyes found Ashley again. "You owe it to Cole."

"Fine." She began trudging up the hill toward the others. "I'll tell him tomorrow. After Erin and Sam leave."

Luke took a few steps then stopped. "Wait."

"What?" She paused long enough to look at him over her shoulder.

"Have you heard from Landon?"

A terrible sadness fell across Ashley's face, and she gave a slight shake of her head. "We're finished. I told you that."

"He hasn't called?" The truth of that awed Luke. From everything Reagan had told him, Landon had planned to marry Ashley. It was hard to believe he'd given up so easily. Even in light of Ashley's blood test.

"Look, I asked him not to." Ashley's eyes welled up. "I asked him to get on with his life. That's what he's doing."

Luke followed Ashley to the car. An hour later, everyone gathered at their parents' house, except Sam and Erin, who still had last-minute packing to do. When they were all seated around the living room, Luke admitted how crazy he'd been to believe for a single day that God didn't exist.

"When did you know?" His mother sat curled up next to his father on the old plaid sofa. Her tone was curious, without a hint of condemnation.

"The moment I looked at little Tommy."

Kari chuckled across the room and leaned her head on Ryan's shoulder. "Kids have a way of doing that to you."

"That's for sure." Brooke nodded. She and Peter sat on the same sofa, but not next to each other.

"Okay." Luke looked at the faces around him. He hadn't been sure he'd tell them this part, but the time seemed right. "You want the rest of the story?"

His mother's left eyebrow lifted a bit. "There's more?"

"Quite a lot, actually." He rubbed his hands together and released a nervous chuckle. His eyes found his father's. "Reagan and I are getting married on Christmas Eve. We'll have the wedding in New York."

A collective sigh seemed to make its way around the room. Nothing audible. Just a feeling that he'd done something very good. Had he been part of a conversation like this any time in the past year, their reactions would've irritated him. But now the quiet response told him something he was just realizing: If he was true to himself, his reactions would almost always mirror theirs. Because he was a Baxter. He'd been raised to do what was right, and he'd been happiest when he lived that way. When he didn't . . . well, he was plain old miserable. The way he'd been for most of the past year.

His mother made a polite cough and caught his attention. "What about school?"

"School." Luke nodded. He and Reagan had thought through every detail, and his education was certainly part of the picture. "I'll transfer to one of the universities in New York City, but not until after we get married. I'll take next semester off and work to save some money." He glanced around the room. "I took a full load this summer, so taking time off won't set me behind."

Again his mother had a question. "Where . . . where will you live?"

Luke sensed that his announcement—the part about moving away—was hardest on her. "With Reagan and her mother—in her brother's room until after we're married." The smile he could feel tugging at the corners of his mouth was a sad one. "We talked about waiting until after our wedding for me to move there, but I can't do it. I'll move there in a few weeks. After Kari and Ryan's wedding. I don't want to miss a minute with Reagan and Tommy."

"Wow." Kari grinned at him from across the room. "That's wonderful, Luke."

Ryan nodded. "You'll love Manhattan. At least until Tommy gets older."

"That's the other thing." Luke avoided his mother's eyes. "When I finish with my bachelor's, I want to go to law school. Reagan and I figure we'll stay in New York for at least the next five years." He paused. All of this was fine for him, but the news was bound to be a surprise to his family. "We'll live on campus. Reagan wants to be close to her mother."

"That's wonderful, Son." His father slipped his arm around his mother's shoulders. "Tell Reagan we love her. We can't wait to see the baby."

"She wanted to come, but—" Luke looked at his hands and then back at his father—"she was embarrassed. She feels like everything that happened last year was her fault."

"Poor girl." Ashley's tone was gentle. "You made your own choices."

"I told her that. But she felt funny. Like she wouldn't know what to tell all of you."

The conversation continued until long after midnight, and after the others went their separate ways, Luke pulled his father aside and apologized again.

"I need to tell you . . . about Lori's abortion." Luke crossed his arms. "The baby wasn't mine, Dad. I wanted to say something sooner, but not in front of everyone."

His father blinked twice and shook his head. "But you were living with her."

"We had . . . an open relationship."

He expected his dad to say something about Lori then, something negative and no doubt accurate about her strange way of thinking, the strange way Luke had been thinking.

Instead his father pulled him close and hugged him. "I feel like a new man."

"You do?"

"Yes." He leaned back and grinned. "I have my son back."

The next morning, just after sunup, Luke woke to the smell of pancakes and coffee and the sound of his mother in the kitchen. The voices coming from the next room told him that the others had already arrived for the farewell. Sam and Erin wanted to be on the road by eight o'clock.

He sat up and stared out the window at the familiar front yard and big oak tree, the winding driveway, and the American flag. For a few seconds he closed his eyes and rested his head on the back of the sofa. What if he hadn't talked to Ashley that afternoon on campus? What if he'd been too stubborn or too certain that his crazy new way of thinking was the only one worth holding to?

The idea sent a shiver through him, and when he opened his eyes he saw something that was bound to have the same effect on everyone who had already gathered at the Baxter house. Sam and Erin had just arrived.

And that meant good-byes were less than an hour away.

Breakfast was over, and John could sense the shift in his family's emotions.

Sam and Erin had made the rounds, taking time to tell each

person good-bye, making promises to call and visit and pray for each other. Sam was talking to Peter and Ryan in the family room, while Erin had a last few minutes with the girls. John and Elizabeth sat at the dining-room table watching the exchanges.

"Austin's just a few hours by plane." Erin hugged Kari, and then Ashley and Brooke. "Every few months we'll have to have a weekend together. Just us girls."

"Hey . . ." Luke walked up and reached his arms around Ashley and Erin. "Brothers like weekend getaways, too."

"Don't forget us moms." Elizabeth rested her chin on her hands and smiled at their children.

"Fine with me." Erin laughed, despite the faint mist of tears in her eyes. "We can have a reunion every month if you want."

Elizabeth stood and headed for the kitchen. She took a mug from the cupboard and a box of tea bags from a nearby drawer. John watched and knew she was struggling. She was doing a fine job of pretending, but this was hard on her. He followed and leaned against the wall a few feet from her.

"You okay?" His voice was too quiet for the others to hear him. He cocked his head and studied his wife.

Elizabeth dropped a tea bag into the mug and turned on the burner beneath the old kettle. "I'll be fine. They'll be back in a few weeks for the wedding."

"Still . . ." John gazed at their adult kids, still gathered in a circle laughing about something. "It's hard, letting them go." He looked at Elizabeth. "It was hard when Kari went to New York and when Ashley went to Paris."

"But this is different."

"Mm-hmm." John crossed his arms. The breakfast dishes were piled in the sink, and he made a mental note. After Erin and Sam left, he'd do them so Elizabeth could have a break. He looked at her again. "It's more permanent."

"And then Luke . . ."

Now they were getting somewhere. John had figured Eliza-

327

beth was dealing with more than Erin and Sam's move. "I still can't believe he's here."

"He'll be gone again in four weeks." Elizabeth turned to face him, and he saw her tears. She had promised Erin she wouldn't break down this morning, so no wonder she'd come into the kitchen. Elizabeth sniffed and brushed her fingertips beneath her eyes. "We just got him back, and now he'll be leaving." She lifted one shoulder. "It's hard, John. I have to be honest. Everything's changing."

Sam entered the dining room and raised his voice loud enough for all of them to hear. "Okay . . . we're off."

The kids were already out front playing, but now Kari took Jessie from her playpen, and the group followed along behind Erin and Sam. Outside there were more hugs, and this time a few tears. Cole and Maddie and Hayley clambered around for kisses and then scampered off again to play.

Kari squeezed Erin's shoulders. "You'll do just fine. I know it."

"Thanks." Erin sniffed and uttered a quick laugh. "I'll be back in a few weeks for your big day."

"You'll make it, Erin. Believe, okay?"

"I will."

John wasn't sure if any of the others heard their exchange, but he'd been standing nearby. He figured it had something to do with the Bible studies Kari and Erin had gone through together the previous year, back when Erin had considered leaving Sam rather than moving to Austin. The glowing look in Erin's eyes told John that whatever had transpired during those meetings, the result had been miraculous.

The moment was ending, and Sam gave Erin a look as he held up his watch. They needed to leave if they were going to get to their hotel before dark. Sam gave them a final wave and slid into the driver's seat. At the same time, Erin looked at the faces around her and smiled. Her eyes were watery, but they held none of the desperation she'd felt back when Sam first announced they'd be moving.

"Bye, everyone." She took her seat and rolled down the window. "See you soon!"

The Baxters stood as a group and watched Sam and Erin's car head down the drive, turn left, and pick up speed down the two-lane highway. They waved until they could no longer see their car.

Kari and Ryan said good-bye next. They had final wedding arrangements to make with the photographer. At the same time, Brooke and Peter gathered up Maddie and Hayley and said something about having chores to do at home.

The group dwindled to just Luke and Ashley, and John saw them whisper to each other before Luke headed inside with Cole. They were barely out of earshot when Elizabeth fell in beside Luke and linked arms with him. "So tell me about your little boy. . . ."

John wasn't in a hurry. He took slow steps toward Ashley, but the closer he got the more sure he was that something was wrong. Dark shadows fell across her face, and the smile she'd had for Erin a few moments earlier was long gone.

"Hey, Ash . . ." He came up to her and put his arm around her shoulders. Maybe if they spent an hour together doing dishes, she'd open up about whatever was bugging her. Whatever it was Luke had flashed her the look about. "Let's go see if your mom needs help in the kitchen."

But instead of walking with him, Ashley remained firmly in place. John stopped and turned to her. "Ashley? What is it?"

The color drained from her face, and for a long while she didn't seem to be able to speak. When she did, her tone was strained and breathy, as though saying the next words was taking all her effort.

"Dad . . . I have something to tell you." She hesitated and her knees buckled just a bit. John took hold of her elbow, and she leaned into him. Tears filled her eyes and spilled onto her cheeks, but finally she found her voice again. "What I'm about to tell you . . . will change everything. For all of us."

CHAPTER THIRTY-THREE

THEIR WEDDING DAY DAWNED with full sun and mild humidity. Kari's house had sold a while ago, and she and Jessie had moved her things into Ryan's house a week earlier. They were staying at her parents' house, in her old room, until after their honeymoon. Then they'd move in with Ryan.

Kari yawned and looked around the room where she'd first dreamed of marrying Ryan Taylor. For a few minutes after she woke up and registered the weather, Kari just lay there and remembered.

She thought how she'd looked down and found her heart gone the afternoon when she met Ryan for the first time—how they'd hung out together for several summers after that, fishing from his rowboat on Lake Monroe and skipping rocks from the shore. Hadn't she known back then that one day they'd be together?

The detours, of course, had been impossible to predict. And even a year ago she couldn't have guessed they'd be here now. But they were. And what she was about to do brought up every memory of Ryan she'd ever had.

He'd been her first kiss, first dance, first crush. But that day at

Ryan's parents' barbecue she'd felt the same way she did now. That she wouldn't really have her heart back until the two of them were together forever.

As they'd be after this evening.

From out back she could hear the caterers with their trucks, already getting things ready in the tent. The wedding was scheduled for three o'clock this afternoon, and a gazebo with a floral arch had been set up the day before. Chairs were placed evenly on both sides of the makeshift aisle, and pots overflowing with jasmine framed the entire setting.

After months of planning, hours of discussion, and a million phone calls, Kari could hardly believe September 21 was here. She and Ryan would spend tonight at a hotel in Indianapolis, and tomorrow morning they'd fly to Seattle. Ryan had kept the honeymoon plans a surprise, and last night after the rehearsal dinner, he'd given her a card with the details inside.

They were taking an Alaskan cruise, following the Inside Passage on a Holland America ship that catered to newlyweds. For seven days they would see grizzly bears and bald eagles and whales as they traveled up and down the Alaskan coast. Apparently September was the best time to go. Ryan had booked a cabin with a balcony and a Jacuzzi tub.

Kari climbed out of bed and slipped into a pair of shorts and a T-shirt. She had a hundred things to do before three o'clock, including packing for their honeymoon. As difficult as it had been, they'd waited for this day, saved themselves because that was what God wanted of them. And because they wanted to keep him first in everything about their marriage.

Though her wedding day was bound to be a day she'd remember all her life, the details seemed less pressing. Because sometime tomorrow she and Ryan would be on a plane to Seattle and after that, an Alaskan cruise. It was all she could think about. The two of them married, alone together on an adventure that would take them through both the daytimes and the nighttimes.

She could hardly wait.

The hours flew by, and shortly before three o'clock, Kari's father found her and her mother in the bedroom, in front of the mirrors they'd set up so the girls could get ready. Ashley, Erin, and Brooke were dressed and talking in excited whispers out in the hallway.

They'd been put on lookout, in charge of making sure the guys headed out to the tent first. Erin had just flashed the signal, so Kari took a final look in the mirror. Her mother was beside her, fixing one of the ringlets that hung on either side of her face.

"Now there's a picture." Her father entered the room with slow steps, his eyes fixed on both of them. His black tuxedo was a bit tight around the middle, but he looked fantastic all the same. He stopped and gave a shake of his head. "As long as I live I'll remember this."

"Hi, Daddy." Kari grinned at him in the mirror. "You look great."

"But you, my dear—" he came up alongside her—"you look radiant."

Her mother took a step back and admired the dress. "It's perfect, honey."

"Thanks." Kari had found the dress in Indianapolis, not long after Ryan proposed to her. It was white satin with a fitted bodice and short, puffy sleeves. The skirt was simple and straight, floor-length and cut longer near her heels, where it formed a subtle train. Her veil flowed along her back almost to the floor, and a hairdresser had come that morning to pile her hair on her head in a mass of ringlets.

"Guys, it's five to three." Brooke poked her head into the room. "Everyone's in the tent."

"Okay." Kari looked from her father to her mother. "Here we go."

Her father linked arms with her and leaned close, his voice a whisper. "I can't wait to see Ryan's reaction when you come down that aisle."

✣

The tent was full, the guests seated, and Ryan and Pastor Mark stood near the front, waiting for the procession to begin. An organist set up in the back played Pachelbel as a hush fell over the small crowd.

"Ready?" Pastor Mark leaned toward Ryan. Pastor had a Bible in his hand, and his smile went from ear to ear.

"For the past two decades." Ryan winked and turned his attention to the back of the tent.

When Kari's mother poked her head through the flaps, Luke was at her side instantly. He held out his arm, linked it with hers, and led her down the aisle. Ryan felt a lump in his throat as he took in the scene. Luke's return to the Baxter family had been nothing short of a miracle, the answered prayer they'd all sought God about in the past year.

Watching Luke now, it was impossible to tell he'd ever been gone. That's how good God had been to them. Ryan shifted his gaze to the back of the tent again. This time, Luke brought Ashley, leading her to her place at the far end of the altar area—the bride's side. Then he moved to a spot not far from Ryan.

Peter and Brooke came down the aisle, and then Sam and Erin. Both couples parted at the place where Pastor Mark stood and then veered off toward their designated places.

The children came next. First Cole, the ring bearer, dressed in navy pants and vest, with a white shirt and tie. His blond hair was neatly combed, and his steps were sure and proud as he carried the satin pillow down the aisle.

Not far behind him were the girls—first Hayley, then Maddie. Each of them wore a frilly white dress and carried a basket of rose petals. They looked like angels, and as they walked they took delicate handfuls of the petals and scattered them on the white walkway.

Hayley stopped halfway down and waved at Brooke. "Hi, Mommy! Am I doing good?"

"Yes, dear." Brooke mouthed the words and flashed the okay sign at her youngest daughter.

Hayley seemed to understand that she wasn't supposed to be talking. She dropped her voice to a loud whisper. "Can I keep some of the flowers, Mommy? Please. They're too pretty to drop on the ground."

Muffled laughter came from the guests, and a few people snapped pictures of the sweet child. About that time, Maddie caught up to her. "Keep going, Hayley. You're almost there."

Ryan smiled at Maddie's encouragement. How wonderful that she was healthy now. She'd had her procedure three weeks ago, and everything had gone well. She hadn't had a fever since.

Everything about the procession was beautiful, but Ryan shifted his weight and focused his attention at the back of the tent once again. *Come on, Kari, girl. Walk down the aisle. Show me that I'm not dreaming.*

When the music changed, the guests stood and faced the back of the tent. The traditional wedding march played as Kari and her father entered. For several seconds, the two of them stood frozen in place while Kari looked for Ryan.

Their eyes met then, and Ryan's jaw dropped ever so slightly. She was the most beautiful woman he'd ever seen. He'd loved her nearly all his life. *God, thank you . . . thank you.*

Kari and her father began their walk, but never once did Ryan break eye contact with her. His heart pounded against his chest, making his tux and tails tremble. He folded his hands in front of him and grinned at the woman who was about to become his wife.

When they reached Ryan, Pastor Mark looked at Kari's father and nodded. "Who gives this woman to be married?"

"Her mother and I do." John Baxter stepped forward, briefly lifted Kari's veil, and kissed her on the cheek. Then he took her hand and placed it in Ryan's.

When John was seated next to his wife, Pastor Mark took a deep breath and began. "Sometimes, in the course of the job, a pastor has the privilege of marrying two people who have something special, something other people long for." He paused and looked at the wedding guests. "Kari Baxter Jacobs and Ryan Taylor are people like that."

He talked about their childhoods, how they had been friends as kids, and how God had brought them together through sometimes difficult circumstances. "But our God is a God of second chances and mended dreams." Pastor Mark smiled. "That's why Kari and Ryan are standing before you today."

He shared with the guests the fact that the couple had received premarital training, and that in every way possible, they'd attempted to put God first in their relationship. "What happens when two people make that decision?" A light chuckle came from the man. "God becomes a part of that union from the moment they say 'I do.' "

Ryan glanced at Kari and they exchanged a private smile.

Pastor Mark mentioned that Kari and Ryan had written their own vows but also how that hadn't surprised him. "These aren't new words, friends. The vows you're about to hear express feelings that have grown between these two since they were in high school."

Ryan went first. He was no longer nervous as he took Kari's hands and spoke straight to her heart. "Kari, you are my heart's song, the one I long for and live for, the only one I could ever share my soul with." He gave her fingers a gentle squeeze. "I want to share with you everything about the future. The joys and sorrows, the happy times and the hard ones."

His voice grew thicker . . . filled with the feelings he wanted to get across to her. "Kari, I promise to be true to you, to pick you up when you fall, and to celebrate with you when life gives us reason to smile. I promise to be a godly father to Jessie and whatever other children the Lord might bless us with."

The lump in his throat grew a notch. "Will you take my ring and my name and all my tomorrows, and will you stay by my side for always?"

Tears glistened in her eyes, but her smile told him she could hardly wait to say yes.

He was almost finished. "Marry me, Kari girl; share my life with me, from now until death parts us."

She ran her thumbs over the side of his hand and bit her lip. "Yes." The look on her face blocked out everything else in the tent. "I will."

It was Kari's turn, and she'd worried that in the excitement of the moment, she might forget her vows. But after hearing Ryan's words, she was mesmerized, drawn into the spell of what was happening between them. Suddenly everything she wanted to tell him was right there in her heart.

She searched his face, his eyes, and for the briefest instant she was sixteen again, opening the door and seeing Ryan on her doorstep, a dozen red roses in his hands. "Happy Birthday, Kari . . . go out with me tonight?"

The memory was gone as quickly as it had come.

Pastor Mark turned to her and smiled. "Kari, you may speak your vows to Ryan now."

Kari looked deep into Ryan's eyes. "Ryan Taylor, I've loved you since the first day I met you, even when it seemed that my love for you might only be as friends. You captured my heart when we were barely more than kids, and since then you've always owned a piece of it."

Ryan bit his lip and gave her a lopsided grin. His eyes stayed on hers as she continued.

"I never dreamed back then that God would give us today, that he would lead us to a place where we could stand here before our friends and family, before God, and promise each other a lifetime. But here we are." Kari's voice cracked and she blinked back tears. "So now, before God and our guests, I promise to love you and honor you, cherish you and care for you all the days of my life. When the journey we're about to take leads us to the mountaintops and when it leaves us in the valleys, I will be by your side."

A single tear fell on her cheek, and before she could do anything about it, he released her hand and caught it on his thumb. She gave a quiet sniff. "You were my first love, Ryan Taylor, and here, now, I promise you will be my last. For by marrying you, we will forever be one, and that piece of my heart that has always been yours, will finally be here—" she touched her fingertips to her chest—"right where it belongs."

Kari saw in Ryan's eyes the fullness of the moment, the love and joy and amazement they both felt now that this day had arrived.

Pastor Mark gave them a few seconds to collect themselves. Then he stepped forward and turned first to Ryan. "Do you have the ring?"

"Yes." Ryan turned to Luke, his best man, and Luke handed it to him.

Pastor Mark asked Ryan to repeat after him as he was putting the ring on Kari's finger. "With this ring, I thee wed."

"With this ring—" Ryan's eyes danced as he looked from the band of white gold and tiny diamonds into the deepest part of her soul—"I thee wed." He slipped the ring onto her finger and looked to Pastor Mark.

"Okay, Kari, it's your turn." The pastor smiled. "Do you have the ring?"

"I do." She turned behind her to Ashley, her maid of honor. Ashley pressed it into her hand, and Kari focused once more on the pastor.

"Repeat after me." He paused and a smile played on his lips. "With this ring, I thee wed."

Kari took Ryan's left hand and slipped the ring partially onto his finger. "With this ring—" she moved the ring over his knuckle to the place where it would stay forever—"I thee wed."

As she said the words, there, in front of more than a hundred people, Kari felt the strangest sensation deep within her, and in that instant she understood where the feeling came from.

The piece of her heart she'd been missing for so long was back.

🌿

Kari and Ryan were about to be announced as husband and wife when something near the back of the tent caught Ashley's attention.

By then, the flaps had been pinned open so the Baxters' yard was clearly visible through the entryway. Ashley studied the spot, and something shadowy seemed to hover near the right side. But the longer she looked at it, the more it seemed to be her imagination.

The wind, probably. She shifted her attention back to Kari and Ryan. The wedding was beautiful so far, the ceremony like something from a storybook. How fitting, after the love the two of them had shared and the rocky journey that had led them from that first backyard barbecue to this moment.

One of Kari's friends came up from the side of the tented area and sang a Steven Curtis Chapman song, while Kari and Ryan lit a unity candle. The words fit Kari and Ryan perfectly, declaring a type of love that would be there for the other person, no matter what.

Ashley's throat tightened. That was the type of love she would have had with Landon had things worked out differently.

She shrugged off the thought. She couldn't give in to her sorrow. Not here, not at Kari's wedding. Next week she had an appointment to meet with her doctor. Her father had done extensive research and learned that because of the university, Bloomington was as good a place as any to receive treatment for HIV. She'd scheduled a blood test for Cole also. Just in case.

Everything weighed like a steamroller on her shoulders, but there was no point thinking about it now. Other than Luke, her siblings still didn't know, and neither did her mother. Ashley had begged her dad to keep quiet about her situation, at least until she could figure out a plan.

Tonight, one last time, she wanted to be only Ashley. Not Ashley with HIV. She would laugh at the wedding toast, and dance with Cole, and marvel in the love that surrounded her. Because time was a thief, and after next week there was no telling when she might have a night like this again.

Ashley cleared her mind. The song was over, and Kari and Ryan were beaming at each other.

"And so—" Pastor Mark took a few steps back and directed his attention toward the guests—"by the power vested in me, I now pronounce you husband and wife." He paused and smiled at Ryan. "You may kiss the bride."

Like a scene from a movie, Ryan moved a step closer to Kari and lifted her veil. For a moment, time seemed to stand still as the two of them looked at each other. Ashley smiled right along with them as Ryan leaned closer and gave Kari a gentle, tender kiss, a kiss beyond passionate.

The guests broke into applause, and Pastor Mark waited until quiet fell over the group once more. "It is my great privilege to introduce to you Mr. and Mrs. Ryan Taylor."

The crowd was on its feet, and Ashley glanced at her parents. Their eyes shone with unshed tears, and Ashley did a quick scan of the rest of the guests. It was obvious everyone felt the same way about Kari and Ryan—that they simply belonged together.

Every single person was smiling.

Kari and Ryan led the way down the aisle toward the tent exit. Ashley and Luke were next. She looked at her brother and they both grinned.

"You're gorgeous, big sister." Luke linked his arm through hers.

"Thanks." Her voice was soft, meant for his ears alone. He complimented her often lately, as though he sensed the heaviness in her heart and wanted to do whatever he could to help relieve it. Especially since he was moving to New York City in a week to be with Reagan and the baby.

They walked arm in arm down the aisle, out the exit, and into the next tent, where they set up a receiving line along one side of the reception area.

One at a time the guests filed past first Erin and Sam, then Peter and Brooke, Ashley and Luke, and lastly, Kari and Ryan. Their parents were seated at one of the round tables near the front of the tent, next to Ryan's mother, and a few other close friends.

Ashley had thought she would find this part of the wedding annoying, telling a stream of people hello again and again. But now that the moment had come, she was enjoying herself. The line was filled with cousins she hadn't seen in years, former teachers and school friends, neighbors from the old house, the one that had been down the street from the Taylor family, and several of her father's colleagues.

Each person's face carried with it a memory, the ways they'd shared in the Baxters' lives. And as such, the receiving line was almost like a living scrapbook of happy moments. Moments Ashley would need to hang on to in days to come.

The last of the guests were making their way past the wedding party when Ashley realized a hush had fallen over her siblings. She felt Luke stiffen beside her. At that same instant she glanced down the line and saw her.

Reagan Decker.

She was dressed in a tan-colored long skirt and a white blouse, her hair in a loose ponytail. And in her arms was Luke's son, Tommy.

"Reagan . . ." Luke's eyes grew wide as he went to her. With gentle fingers he took hold of her elbow and leaned close enough to brush his lips against her cheek. When he pulled back he nuzzled his face against Tommy's and kissed his forehead. He searched her eyes. "What . . . how did you . . . ?"

Her cheeks looked flushed, and Ashley noticed something else. Reagan's hands were trembling.

Ashley remembered the isolation and fear of her first hours home from Paris. *God, let her feel loved. Please.* She stepped forward and put her arms around Reagan and Luke and the baby. "Welcome, Reagan. I'm glad you came."

"Thanks." Reagan's face filled with gratitude, and her voice fell a notch. "And thanks for telling him, Ashley."

"I thought you might be mad." Ashley hadn't spoken to Reagan since, but things seemed fine between them, and she was glad.

Sam and Erin drew closer, as did Brooke and Peter, and at that moment, Kari and Ryan saw what was happening. In a rush they followed Ashley's lead and took part in the group hug. When they each pulled back a bit, the love that was directed at Reagan and Luke and Tommy was enough to move Reagan to tears.

"He's beautiful, Reagan."

"It means so much that you came."

"Can I hold him . . . please?"

Everyone was talking at once. Ashley took a step back so her siblings could see Luke's son. She'd already had a chance to hold him. The commotion they were making alerted her parents, and Ashley watched as first her mother, then her father stood from the table and headed toward the wedding party, which was now fully surrounding Reagan and Luke and Tommy.

Her mother took hold of her father's hand and the two of them stopped, frozen in place. Ashley could see by their expressions that only now did they fully realize what had happened. That Reagan had brought Luke's son to the wedding so they could be with the rest of his family.

Where they belonged.

Slowly, her parents made their way into the circle, and her mother drew Reagan close in what was a long, rocking embrace. They were both crying when they separated, and her mother reached out her hands toward little Tommy. "May I?"

"Yes." Reagan sniffed and wiped her cheeks with the back of her hand. "That's why I came."

Their mother took the baby and cradled him close for a long while, then passed him to their father.

Ashley felt tears in her eyes again and wished for the tenth time that day that she had an easel or a sketchpad. Anything that would help her capture the moments playing out before her. She could read her mother's face as easily as ever. Enamored of this little miniature Luke and yet desperately sad that in a week, Luke and his son and fiancée would be gone—maybe forever.

Other than visits, her parents would not get to watch Tommy grow up the way they'd watched Cole. But then, at least Tommy would have Luke.

Fatigue swept Ashley, and she pulled away from the group. She scanned the crowd and saw Cole with Maddie and Hayley at the table where her parents had been sitting. Ashley made her way across the tented area to the beverage cart and took a glass of water. Then she found a quiet place near the back of the tent, at a table no one had yet claimed.

The day had been so wonderful, and now this. Reagan . . . here with Tommy. It was more than Ashley could've imagined. Telling Luke had been the right thing to do. And what better time than now for Reagan to bring the baby to Bloomington, with everyone gathered for such a happy occasion.

Ashley lifted her glass and took a sip of water when she sensed something move at her side. Before she had time to look up she heard his voice.

"You have the most beautiful hair."

Slowly, as though in a trance, she set the glass back on the table and turned toward the sound. As she did, her heart stopped. "Landon . . ."

"Really—" he locked eyes with her and touched his fingers to one of her curls—"has anyone ever told you that? You just have the most beautiful hair."

Her heart melted, and she was in his arms before common

sense could stop her. With the rest of her family and the wedding guests distracted at the other end of the tent, she and Landon held on to each other until Ashley caught her breath.

"You're here." She leaned back and studied him, taking in the black slacks and white button-down shirt, the tie that held a hundred shades of blue. The sight of him made her heart do a double beat, the way it had in dozens of dreams since she'd left New York City. But this wasn't a dream, because she could feel him in her arms, smell his cologne and the familiar scent of his shampoo.

He held her eyes and gave her a weary smile. "I told you I would."

"Landon . . . why? I thought we decided—"

"*You* decided. *I* told you I'd be back."

As wonderful as he felt close to her, as much as she wanted nothing more than to never let him go, she knew better. The test results were still the same. "I can't offer you anything; don't you see that? You deserve someone different. Someone healthy . . . with a future."

"Oh, but Ashley—" he wove his fingers through her hair and seemed to search the deepest parts of her soul—"you're forgetting something."

"What?" She closed her eyes and leaned into his touch, mesmerized by his presence, the nearness of him. "What am I forgetting?"

"You're forgetting how unfair that would be."

She opened her eyes. What was he saying? And why had he come, when this next good-bye would only be more painful than the last? The lump in her throat made talking all but impossible, but somehow she found her voice. "Unfair?"

"Yes." He was still looking at her, still searching her eyes with that focused, captivating intensity. "Unfair for me to find someone else . . . when for the rest of time I will never love anyone the way I love you."

There.

He'd said the thing she'd wondered about since the moment she'd watched him step onto the hotel elevator that awful night. No matter that she might get sick, no matter that marriage and forever might not be in their future, he loved her. It was as simple as that. He loved her, and nothing was ever going to change his mind.

"Really?" She searched his face. "Really, Landon?"

He brushed his knuckles against her cheekbone, along the line of her jaw. "Yes."

She looked for some sort of crack, a fear or a doubt that might be lodged somewhere in his heart.

There was none.

The truth sent wildly varying emotions racing through her. She was terrified at what his determination could cost him, what he could be missing by choosing her over someone healthy. But at the same time she was desperately relieved, as though a dying part of her had suddenly and swiftly come back to life.

A dozen questions demanded her attention, but one was louder than the rest. "How, Landon? How do we do this?"

He took her hands in his. "We start by holding on. To each other. To this moment. To every day God gives us." His eyes grew damp, but a smile played on the corners of his lips.

"Then what?" Her words were a choked whisper, tainted with all the joy and torment welling within her.

In the distance, Cole's voice rose loud above the mingling guests. "Landon!" They watched as he jumped up from the table and headed toward them at a full run. "You came back!"

Ashley glanced at her family and saw that they had turned her way now, smiling and nodding to each other, surprised and clearly happy to see them together. Sam and Erin waved, and Kari and Ryan began moving closer, probably intent on welcoming Landon to the party.

She looked at Landon, desperate for him to finish what he'd been trying to tell her. Even if they found a way to hold on, how could they move ahead from here? "What, Landon . . . what then?"

He brought his face close to hers so she could hear him even above the nearing shouts of joy from Cole.

His clear, calm words told Ashley he'd thought them out long before coming here. "We never let go, Ash. No matter where tomorrow takes us, we just never let go."

As long as she lived, Ashley was certain those words would continue to play in her head: *"We never let go, Ash. We just never let go."*

It was true, wasn't it? No one knew the future. And wherever the next day or even the next hour took them, if they never let go of each other, of God, they might never have to. They could face her future together, taking every step with God, begging him for a miracle.

If they kept holding on, it could happen.

"Landon!" Cole reached them and jumped into Landon's arms. "I'm so glad you're here." His little-boy vest rode up and gathered near his chest as he wrapped his arms around Landon's neck.

Ashley watched them, memorizing the picture they made, these two she loved more than any others in the world. And in that instant Ashley knew Landon had to be right. Because after being with him now, after knowing that he had returned to her and loved her despite her frightening future, one thing was certain.

She could never again let him go.

MORE ABOUT THE BAXTER FAMILY!

Please turn this page for a bonus excerpt from

R E J O I C E

the fourth book in the

REDEMPTION SERIES

by Karen Kingsbury with Gary Smalley

From

R E J O I C E

by Karen Kingsbury with Gary Smalley

CHAPTER ONE

THE SWIM PARTY seemed like a great idea, the perfect ending to a perfect summer.

Brooke Baxter West's partner at the pediatric office had a daughter Maddie's age, and to celebrate her birthday, the family had decided to invite ten kids and their parents over for an afternoon in their backyard pool.

For two weeks Maddie and Hayley had been looking forward to it, seeking out Brooke every day and tugging on her arm. "Mommy, when's the swimming party again?"

But two days before the big event, one of the other doctors in the office received word from the West Coast that his aging grandmother had only days to live. Before he caught an emergency flight to California, he asked Brooke if she'd take his on-call duty for the weekend.

"You're my last hope," he'd told her. "My family needs me."

Brooke hated being on-call when she was spending an afternoon with her girls. But other than the swim party, the weekend was open, and she could take the pager with her. The chances of getting a call on a Saturday afternoon were fairly slim.

Now the big day was here, and Brooke was having doubts. She should've called around, found someone else to take the on-call duty. Her kids needed her at the party, and if she was called away, she'd miss out on the last hurrah of the summer.

Brooke slipped on a pair of shorts over her swimsuit. She was raising the zipper when she heard Peter's voice ring through the house from downstairs.

"Let's go, girls." Frustration rang in his voice. "The party starts in ten minutes."

Brooke grabbed her bag—the one with the life jackets and sunscreen—and rolled her eyes. What was wrong with him, anyway? He was constantly grouchy; the two of them hadn't had a normal conversation in weeks. Their home was so tense that even little Hayley had noticed it.

"Is Daddy mad at you, Mommy?" she'd asked earlier that week.

Brooke had mumbled something about Daddy being tired, and that yes, they should pray for him. But in all truth, she was sick of Peter's attitude. He treated her like she was incompetent and irritating. The same way he'd treated her ever since Maddie's diagnosis.

Didn't he get it? Maddie was better now; no fevers for more than two months.

Brooke ran into Hayley and Maddie in the hallway and grinned at them. "I'm wearing my swimsuit!"

"Goodie, Mommy." Maddie jumped up and down and reached for Hayley's hand. "We can play tea party on the steps."

They joined Peter downstairs and rode in relative silence to the house across town where Brooke's partner, Aletha, and her husband, DeWayne, lived. On the way up the steps, Hayley took hold of her hand and squeezed it three times. The sign Brooke used with the girls to say, "I love you."

At three years old, Hayley was still small enough to carry, so Brooke swept her into her arms as they headed down the walk toward the front door. The love from her youngest daughter was the perfect remedy for Peter's coolness.

"You're a sweet girl, Hayley; do you know that?" Brooke shifted her pool bag to her shoulder.

"You, too, Mommy." Hayley rubbed her tiny nose against Brooke's. "You're a sweet girl, too. Know why?"

"Why?" Brooke and Hayley trailed behind Peter and Maddie, but Brooke didn't mind. She loved moments like this with her girls.

"Because—" Hayley tilted her head, her pale blonde hair falling like silk around her little face—"I love you, that's why."

The door opened and Aletha smiled at them from the front step. "Hi. The party's out back."

Peter pulled out a smile, the one he wielded whenever they were in public. Brooke wanted to take him aside and ask him why he couldn't smile that way at her, but she never had the chance.

At that moment her pager went off.

She unclipped it from her waistband and stared at the small message window. *Urgent*, it read. The hospital's main number followed the word.

Peter looked over her shoulder. "What is it?"

"A hospital call." She couldn't hide the disappointment in her voice. "Maybe it's nothing."

A group of children ran into the foyer and surrounded Hayley and Maddie. Brooke ducked into the nearest bedroom and pulled her cell phone from her purse. "Dr. Brooke West here. Someone paged me."

The nurse on the other end rattled off the information. One of the patients from their office had been admitted with a staph infection. It looked serious. They wanted a pediatrician from the office in to consult. Immediately.

"I'm on my way." Brooke hung up the phone and returned to the foyer.

Peter caught her look and raised his eyebrows. "Well?"

"I have to go." She did a quiet huff. This was the part of doctoring that she hated. The part that interfered with family life. "I'll be back as quickly as I can."

Maddie ran up to her. "Natasha wants us to swim, Mommy. Can we, please? Can we right now?"

"Well, baby—" she looked up and saw Hayley standing a foot away, waiting for her answer—"don't you want to wait till Mommy comes back?"

"We can swim later, too. Please, Mommy? Can we?"

Natasha ran up then and hugged Maddie. Their families had been friends for years, and Maddie and Natasha were best buddies. "Please, can we swim?" Natasha linked arms with Maddie, and they smiled their best smiles.

Brooke could feel the fight leaving her. So she'd miss out on some of the fun. She'd be back in time to swim with them, wouldn't she? "Okay, but let me talk to Daddy first."

Peter had moved into the living room, where he and DeWayne were seated side by side, their eyes glued to the television. The play-offs were on, and Aletha had warned that having the party during a game could mean the loss of one or more of the men.

Brooke crossed the room and positioned herself in front of her husband. "I have to go, but the girls want to swim." The bag in her hands was bulky, and she set it on the floor between them. "Here're the sunscreen and life jackets. The girls need both before they can go out back."

"Right." Peter leaned sideways so he could see the TV. "I got it, honey."

The term of endearment was for DeWayne's benefit, Brooke was sure, and she didn't appreciate the way he looked past her to the game. "Peter, I'm serious. Don't let them outside without wearing sunscreen and a life jacket. Neither of them is pool safe."

He shot her a look, one that said she was embarrassing him. Then he yelled out, "Hayley . . . Maddie, come here."

The girls scampered into the room and came up close to Peter. "Yes, Daddy." Hayley spoke first. "Can we swim?"

"Not yet." Peter looked once more at Brooke and then unzipped the bag. Quickly and with little finesse, he lathered sunscreen into his hand and then tossed the bottle to Brooke. "Do Hayley."

She needed to leave, but this was more important. Moving as fast as she could, she squeezed the lotion into her hand and positioned herself in front of their youngest daughter. "Here, sweetie. We don't want a sunburn, right?"

"Right, Mommy."

Brooke rubbed the sunscreen over Hayley's arms and legs, her back and neck area, and finally her face. She finished the job just as Peter finished with Maddie. Then Peter tossed her the smaller life jacket. This time he said nothing, and that was fine with Brooke.

These days, the less he said the better.

She took the blue-and-aqua life jacket and carefully slipped first one of Hayley's arms, then the other, through the holes. Next she latched the buckles down the front and attached a strap that ran from the back of the vest, between her legs, to the front.

Brooke had researched life jackets, and this style was the safest.

When Maddie's vest was on, Peter gave Brooke one last glare. Again because of DeWayne seated beside him, he kept his tone light, almost friendly. "There you go. See you later."

Brooke said nothing. Instead she turned and bid the girls a quick good-bye. She found Aletha and promised to be back as soon as possible. A minute later she was in the car, doing a U-turn toward the hospital. With every mile she felt the distance between herself and her daughters, certain that they were playing in the pool by now, and knowing she was missing out.

It took all her effort to convince herself that the party would still be in full swing when she returned, and that she and Maddie and Hayley would have their tea party on the steps of the pool.

Then—other than her relationship with Peter—everything about the day would work out just like it was supposed to.

Peter was grateful the play-offs were on.

Because as much as he liked DeWayne and Aletha, the last thing he wanted to do was spend Saturday with a bunch of doctors. Swimming wasn't his thing, and this game would be easily one of the most exciting ever. Besides, most of the guests were bound to be Brooke's friends, people he barely knew. The prospect of catching a game with DeWayne was what swayed him to come.

Especially after Brooke took the on-call assignment.

What had she been thinking? Of course she'd get called on a Saturday afternoon. That was when kids needed doctors most of all. Soccer injuries, illnesses that had brewed all week at school. Insect bites. Weekends were notoriously busy for pediatricians.

The fact that she'd let the other doctor talk her into taking his on-call was further proof that she wasn't capable. Not nearly as capable as he'd originally thought her to be. Back when they'd met in med school, her confidence and competence had been part of what attracted him to her. But after the situation with Maddie—when she'd insisted that their daughter didn't need a specialist—Peter had seen his wife in a new light.

One that was far from flattering.

An hour passed, and the sound of children came from the other room.

"Okay," he heard Aletha tell them. "Dry off, and we'll have cake."

It was the seventh inning, and his team was down by one. Peter hoped they could keep the cake thing quiet—at least until the commercial. Not that he didn't like birthdays, but he'd had one of the longest weeks in his life. He'd gone without sleep for two days, and now he was spending his Saturday at a five-year-old's birthday party.

At that instant—with the tying run on third and a home-run hitter at the plate—Maddie and Hayley skipped up to him. Their life jackets made a trail of dripping water, and they were shivering cold. "Daddy, can you take off our jackets?"

He glanced at them and then back at the TV. "Just a minute, girls. Daddy wants to see this."

The pitch was good. The batter cut and connected, but the ball flew over the catcher and into the stands. Another foul tip.

Peter looked at his daughters again. "Okay, now what?"

"We're dripping, Daddy." Maddie took a step forward. "Can you take off our jackets, please?"

"Sure, pumpkin." He unsnapped the buckles on both vests and helped the girls remove them. "Take them to Natasha's mommy and ask her to hang them near the bathtub."

The next pitch was a perfect strike, making the count full.

Hayley stepped up. "Daddy, when's Mommy coming back?"

"Soon, baby." He leaned around her and watched the man at bat belt one out of the park. The moment it was gone, he and DeWayne stood up and slapped their hands in a high five. "That's my boys."

"Bigger than life." DeWayne gave a few nods and sat back down. "On their way, baby. On their way."

"Daddy—" Hayley tilted her head—"I love you."

Peter eased himself back to his seat. He didn't take his eyes from the game. "Love you, too."

She was already out of the room when he yelled back over his shoulder. "Don't go outside again without those life jackets."

He focused on the screen. The go-ahead run was on third with just one out. If they won this game they'd take a three-two lead in this series of games.

The game was over, the win in the books, and Peter was thirty minutes into a discussion on the merits of switch-hitting and relief pitching when he heard Maddie calling him from the other room.

"Daddy! Daddy, quick! Help!"

Peter held up his hand to DeWayne and raised his voice. "In here, baby."

Maddie tore around the corner. Her hair was dry and her eyes round. "Daddy, I can't find Hayley."

He was on his feet, his heart suddenly in his throat. "What do you mean, honey?" Fear dug its talons into his back, his neck. It was all he could do to keep from sprinting toward the backyard. "You were supposed to be having cake."

"We did. Then we 'cided to go swimming, Daddy." Maddie's mouth hung open. "But Hayley said she wanted to be first. Now I can't find—"

Peter didn't wait for Maddie to finish. He took off for the patio door, not so much because of what Maddie had said, but because of the thing she was holding in her hands. The thing Peter had only that instant recognized.

Hayley's life jacket.

A WORD FROM KAREN KINGSBURY

 M OST OF YOU have read *Redemption* and *Remember*, the first two books in the Redemption Series, so you know how the series got its start. But in case you're new with us, here's how it happened. When Gary Smalley contacted me about writing fiction based on his relational teachings, I was thrilled. When he said, "Think series," I went blank.

For weeks I prayed about the series, asking God to show me a group of plots that would best exemplify the kind of love taught and talked about by Gary Smalley and the staff at the Smalley Relationship Center.

Ideas would come, but they seemed too small for something as big and life-changing as the dream Gary and I had come to share. Then one day on a flight home from Colorado Springs, God gave me the Redemption Series—titles, plots, characters, themes, story lines. All of it poured onto my notebook while goose bumps flashed up and down my spine.

The basic heart and direction of the series remain true to that early vision. However, as the Baxter family has come to life, their problems have changed and adapted to fit their personalities, and certainly to fit the landscape of events happening around them.

Our initial view of Ashley, for instance, didn't include her turning up HIV positive. But much of what we intend to do with the Redemption Series is illustrate the consequences of relational choices. And for Ashley, this is one very realistic consequence to her time in Paris.

We had no idea that the attacks on America would change our world on September 11, 2001, and those of you who read *Remember* know how those events changed the direction of the Redemption Series and the lives of the characters. The same way those events in some way changed all of us.

Luke Baxter was, from the beginning, the good son. But we discovered something about Luke in the first book of the series—his goodness was untested, his faith shallow and superficial. After September 11, he led the way in determining the strange turns his life would take. Really, as the writer, I merely followed along trying to keep up and allowing God to use him to teach the lessons you've seen come to life in *Return*.

Think about Luke back in the beginning of this series. Cocksure, judgmental, certain that his charmed life was the direct result of his good living. Ah, but how quickly such a fragile faith collapses when trials come. Sometimes such a one goes through years—decades—of pain before returning to the skeletal remains of a faith forgotten.

You may know someone like that. A friend or brother. A lost son or daughter. If so, I pray that you've seen a glimpse of God's faithfulness between the lines of *Return*. Yes, Elizabeth Baxter was right. God is the Hound of Heaven . . . always pursuing, seeking, anxious to restore, desperate to redeem.

In some ways Luke's story illustrates the theme of the series—redemption. God wants to redeem all of us—whether we've strayed from a phony faith or never believed in the first place. Remember Jesus? He was the one who told the story about the lost sheep, how a shepherd might have a hundred sheep, but if one strays he'd leave the ninety-nine to find it.

Wasn't that John Baxter's heart?

No matter that Maddie was well or Ashley was selling her paintings in New York City, his thoughts were with his son. Funny thing, we didn't intend for *Return* to be a modern-day look at the prodigal son story, but that's what it became. And it's where many of you are now.

Either running away from the Hound of Heaven, or praying for someone who is.

At the same time, *Return* showed us that we cannot fully come back to the people we love without first returning to the God who paid for our redemption.

Along another plotline, *Return* allowed you to see Kari and Ryan marry, promising to live their lives for God first and each other, second. A few of you were frustrated after reading *Remember,* disappointed to see that Kari and Ryan hadn't married in that book. But grief comes at a cost. Time is needed to heal the wounds of loss, and a rushed commitment—no matter how wonderful—is not usually the answer.

Kari and Ryan heeded God's leading in their walk with him and each other—and as a result their wedding was longer coming than some would've liked. I hope that by now you've agreed that their big day was worth the wait.

I was talking to my 14-year-old daughter, Kelsey, the other day, and she expressed some of the impatience we all feel at times. For Kelsey it was impatience over braces and boys and knowing that her season for love and relationships is far down the road yet. Our discussion gave me the chance to give Kelsey a word picture.

Imagine the last wedding banquet or dinner party you attended. Often before the food is set out, the staff places garnishes of endive lettuce along the white-linen-covered serving tables. How silly would it be to arrive at the banquet and find yourself so impatient for the meal that you settle for the garnish?

Wilted lettuce or a banquet?

Doesn't seem like a contest, does it? But sometimes in our rush for what we want, we're willing to settle for the garnish instead of God's best. In *Return*, we saw Kari waiting and how wonderful it was, how rewarding for her and Ryan to know that they handled everything about their relationship the way God wanted them to handle it.

Again, normally I don't leave my readers wondering what will happen to my characters. And though *Return* offers some answers, clearly it also raises many questions. Questions about Ashley and Landon, and if you read the first chapter of *Rejoice* . . . questions about Brooke's family.

What will become of Ashley and her precarious health? Will

she find a way to stay with Landon, or will she feel compelled to release him? And what about the dear people at Sunset Hills Adult Care Home? Will Ashley stay with them, and if so, will Irvel continue her downhill slide into poorer health?

Brooke and Peter are struggling—that much is clear. But why, and how will their fledgling faith be affected if they're visited by tragedy? How will John and Elizabeth play a role in the next season of the lives of their children?

And most of all, how will God continue to work redemption in the lives of this single Indiana family?

As much as I'd like to answer those questions, I cannot. God is still working the story, making it breathe and grow and change with the characters in a way that he directs. The stories that will come in Book 4 (*Rejoice*) and book 5 (*Reunion*) are written across the tablet of my heart, but not yet on the printed page. As soon as they are available, we'll get them out to you.

In the meantime, I pray that you see the bigger picture in the Redemption Series. That God waits for you with open arms—every morning, every night—wanting you to return to him, return to your first love with Jesus Christ. It might be that you never left him, but still he waits for all of us, wanting us to draw nearer.

My prayer is that the Redemption Series helps you see Christ at work in a way you perhaps have never seen before.

If you are one who doesn't understand about redemption and God's plan of salvation for mankind, please contact a local Bible-believing church and ask one of the leaders to lay it out for you. I believe that if you're in this situation, you read this book for a reason. You might think you picked it up at a store or borrowed it from a friend or a library. But the truth is God wanted you to read it so he could speak something very important to your soul. The truth that he loves you and has a place for you in his family.

On a personal note, know that my family is doing well. Our children are still between the Ds. No one dating, driving, or in diapers. But nothing stays the same and by the time you're reading *Reunion*, Kelsey will be begging us for driver's training. Life has a way of constantly throwing lessons at us, and with God at our side, the learning is a joyous adventure.

Kelsey and 11-year-old Tyler are involved in Christian Youth Theater, a growing company of talented directors and coordinators who provide top-notch theatrical productions in a Christian environment. CYT just came to our area, and we are blessed beyond words that our artistic children have a Christian outlet where their talents can be used for God and the community. The youngest boys, Sean, Josh, EJ, and Austin, are all still tearing up the basketball court and soccer field. Donald loves coaching them, and the thrill of parenting continues.

We covet your prayers and encouragement. As always, I'd love to hear from you. Contact me at my Web site: **www.KarenKingsbury.com**, or by writing me at my email address: rtnbykk@aol.com.

Blessings to you and yours . . . in his light and love,
Karen Kingsbury

A WORD FROM GARY SMALLEY

 The goal of the Redemption Series is to give you an unforgettable story with a minute or two of relational advice at the back of each book. *Return*—like the two books before it—touches on some of the most practical relational areas of all, areas many of you are dealing with even now.

The issue of honoring those you love by returning to them is one that applies to both healthy and unhealthy relationships. With healthy relationships, returning is a daily event. Let's take a closer look.

RETURNING AND THE HEALTHY RELATIONSHIP

The Bible warns us of the importance of returning to our first love—Jesus Christ. Any of us who have tried to live the Christian life know what this means. Returning to our God is as constant and necessary as breathing in and out. We have a sin nature, an innate ability to stray from the Lord. But if we recognize our need to return to God and if we do so on a daily basis, we will continue to move ahead in our relationship with him.

The same principle can be applied to our relationships with each other. Many things strain at the ties that bind us to our loved ones. Busyness, misunderstandings, distance—both physical and emotional—missed opportunities, and a host of situations specific to each of us.

Say, for example, you have a parent or parents who live far away. Your life is busy and so is theirs. Over time, busyness becomes silence, and silence can become strained. With a mentality of constantly returning to that relationship, you might make a determination to call your parent or parents once a week or once every other week. By doing this you express honor and love and a decision to not let time cut the ties.

Without making that conscious decision to keep returning to that person, your relationship will at best be mediocre, and will always carry the potential to become unhealthy. Let's look at a few ways we can continually return to those we love.

1. Schedule occasional date time.
   - Realize that this will be different if the date is with a daughter or a mother or a spouse.
   - If you are prone to letting time slip by, make sure to mark this on a calendar or Palm Pilot. (Call Sue this afternoon to catch up.)
2. Use together time to remind the person you love why you love him or her.
   - Laugh and reminisce about days gone by.
   - Find creative ways to do a checkup on whether the memories you're making are as memorable as those you once made.
3. List the reasons why this person is important to you.
   - Set aside time to jot down the reasons you love this person. Be specific.
   - Share this list with the person at one of your regular meeting times, either by phone or in person. This will feel like a shower of love to the person you care about, and will go a long way to making him or her feel that sense of returning that is so crucial in any relationship.

RETURNING AND THE BROKEN RELATIONSHIP

As much as God wants us to keep returning to the importance of our relationships, he has another relational truth that's crucial not only to our dealings with one another, but also to our dealings with Christ.

Numerous stories are told through Scripture showing the importance of mending broken ties between us and the people we love. One of my favorites is the story of the man who is told not to leave his offering at the altar for God until he makes amends with his brother first.

Many of you reading this will find yourself relating to the Baxter family, grieving the loss of one of your own, one who has left the fold and ventured out on his own away from his family, his faith, and his future dreams. For you I pray an ocean of faith, rivers of patience, and a constant rain of God's grace until the day of that loved one's return.

Others of you have perhaps done the wandering. You've walked away from a relationship for one reason or another. Maybe you've justified it, written that person off as being too controlling or overbearing, too negative or too judgmental. In the process you've done what millions of people have done through the ages—you've cut ties with someone you love. God knows that this type of cutting wounds not only the one you've walked away from, but you as well. The kind of cut that won't heal unless you do the one thing God wants you to do: return.

Here are some ways you can return to someone you've left behind:

1. Write a letter.
   - Often times what can't be said face-to-face or even in a phone conversation, can be expressed with the written word. Writing a letter gives you a chance to edit yourself, read over what you've written, and make sure it's exactly what you want to say. Also, any words of love expressed in a letter will jump out at someone you've cut out of your life. Once you've written it, don't let anything stop you. Send it . . . send it now.
2. Make a phone call.
   - One young man I worked with had been cut off from his parents for three years. The reason? His parents didn't agree with his career choice. In a move of independence and defiance, he moved to another state, stuck with his career choice, and went about life. After reading *Redemption* (the first book in the Redemption series), this young man prayed, grabbed the telephone receiver, and held his breath. Then he dialed a series of

numbers he hadn't dialed for three years. Next he did this:

3. Apologize.
   - Nothing mends ties faster than an apology. It is the Superglue of relationships, followed up by the next most important words.

4. Say, "I love you."
   - When the young man from the example above made his life-changing phone call, he apologized first. Then he told his parents the truth. Life's too short to keep silent about love. "I love you, Mom and Dad. I love you." What happened next is perfect proof of why we must return to those we've walked away from. His parents wept. They apologized and expressed their love. A week later his father got on an airplane, flew to his home, and spent three days learning to appreciate this young man's career choice.

With those simple thoughts in mind, answer the following study questions and take stock of your own relationships. Until next time, know that we pray for each of you and believe that God will continue to use this series to make a life-changing impact on your relationships.

For more information about how the concepts in the Redemption Series can save or improve your relationships, contact us at:

The Smalley Relationship Center
1482 Lakeshore Drive
Branson, MO 65616

Phone: 800-84TODAY (848-6329)
Fax: 417-336-3515
E-mail: family@smalleyonline.com
Web site: www.smalleyonline.com

Discussion Questions

Use these questions for individual reflection or for discussion with a book club or other small group. They will help you not only understand some of the issues in *Return* but also integrate some of the book's messages into your own relationships.

1. What caused Luke to leave his family?
2. How did fear play a part in his departure?
3. How did pride play a part?
4. What was his father's reaction to Luke's departure?
5. Recall the scene when John Baxter was at his son's apartment, confronting him about his girlfriend. How could you identify with John's feelings?
6. How did you identify with Luke's feelings?
7. What did John say to Luke before he left? Do you think he meant the things he said? Why or why not?
8. Have you ever had a time when you left someone you loved?
9. Why did you leave?
10. What emotions played a part in your leaving? How did you feel after you left?
11. If you have now returned to that person, how did you go about returning?
12. Did that person you left express words of unconditional love the way John did to Luke? If not, what did that person say to you?
13. Did someone you love ever leave you? Why?
14. What emotions did you feel when that person left? What did you do about those feelings?
15. Did that person return to you? If so, why? What were your feelings when he or she returned?
16. Luke's mother told him about the Hound of Heaven. Explain who that term refers to, and how God worked that way in Luke's life throughout this story.

17. How did God work that way in Landon's life?
18. How did God work that way in Reagan's life?
19. How have you seen the Hound of Heaven working in your life or the life of someone you love?
20. Besides the situation with Luke, what other aspects of this story dealt with returning to people you love?
21. Give three definitions of *return* as it applies to relationships.
22. Which most relates to your life? Explain.
23. Identify one person who either needs to return to you, or whom you need to return to. Make a plan to carry out that return sometime soon.
24. Identify a relationship that is suffering from busyness, time, or distance. Make a plan to return to that person on a regular basis as a way of honoring him or her.
25. List three things you have learned about relationships by reading *Return*.

Also in the Redemption Series . . .

R E D E M P T I O N

R E M E M B E R

R E T U R N

R E J O I C E

R E U N I O N

Other Relationship Books by Gary Smalley

Food and Love
One Flame
Love Is a Decision (with John Trent)
Bound by Honor (with Greg Smalley)
Joy That Lasts (with Al Janssen)
Love That Lasts Forever
The Language of Love (with John Trent)
The Blessing (with John Trent)
The Two Sides of Love (with John Trent)

Other Emotionally Gripping Fiction Titles by Karen Kingsbury

Where Yesterday Lives • *Waiting for Morning*
A Moment of Weakness • *When Joy Came to Stay*
A Time to Dance • *On Every Side*
Halfway to Forever • *A Time to Embrace*
Gideon's Gift—A Christmas Novella

The REDEMPTION

Series by Karen Kingsbury and Gary Smalley

Novelist Karen Kingsbury and relationship expert Gary Smalley team up to bring you the **Redemption Series**, which explores the relationship principles Gary has been teaching for more than thirty years and applies them to one family in particular—the Baxters. In the crucible of their tragedies and triumphs, the Baxter family learns about commitment, forgiveness, faith, and the redeeming hand of God.

Check out the first two novels in the **Redemption Series** today!

Redemption is a story of love at all costs. Kari Baxter Jacob's husband is having an affair with one of his students. Stunned, Kari returns home to the Baxter family to sort things out. But when an old flame shows up, Kari is more confused than ever. How can Kari forgive her husband for the hurt he has caused? And what about her own revived feelings for Ryan, a man she knows she should avoid? Only as she turns to God can Kari find healing and redemption.

Remember follows Ashley Baxter on a journey from tragedy to healing. Ashley has locked up her heart, convinced that no one—including God—could love her. Then comes the nightmare of September 11, which forever changes the lives of the Baxter family, leading them to make decisions that are both heartbreaking and hope-filled.

Visit us at movingfiction.net

Check out the latest information on your

favorite fiction authors and upcoming new

books! While you're there, don't forget to

register to receive *Page Turner's Journal*, our

e-newsletter that will keep you up to date

on all of Tyndale's Moving Fiction.

MOVING FICTION ... *leading by example*